RAGNAR'S CLAW

SUDDENLY THE STINK that hit his nostrils suggested something that was not even remotely human. The figure emerging from the smoke reinforced this impression. It was larger than a man and it moved much, much faster. Four huge arms, tipped with monstrous rending claws, swivelled from its shoulders. Row upon row of hideous fangs gleamed in its mouth. A horny shell of armour encased its body. It loped along on clawed and padded feet. Its manner suggested the scuttling of some enormous insect.

'Genestealer!' Ragnar yelled, taking a bead on the thing with his bolt pistol and squeezing the trigger. Quick as he was, the thing was quicker. It jinked to one side and his shells passed over its head. Ragnar had never seen anything move so swiftly. The fear he had felt earlier returned like a wave of ice running through him and, for one horrible vital moment, he froze. The thing came straight at him and it was on him before he could react. Its weight crashed into him, bowling him over with irresistible force.

He knew that his split-second of hesitation was going to cost him his life.

D1210101

A WARHAMMER 40,000 NOVEL

Space Wolf

RAGNAR'S CLAW

By William King

A BLACK LIBRARY PUBLICATION

Games Workshop Publishing
Willow Road, Lenton,
Nottingham, NG7 2WS, UK

First US edition, October 2000

10 9 8 7 6 5 4 3 2

Disitributed by Simon & Schuster
1230 Avenue of the Americas
New York, NY 10020

Cover illustration by John Gravato

ISBN 0-7434-1155-2

Set in ITC Giovanni

Printed and bound in Great Britain by
Omnia Books Ltd, Glasgow, UK

See the Black Library on the Internet at
http://www.blacklibrary.co.uk

Find out more about Games Workshop
and the world of Warhammer 40,000 at
http://www.games-workshop.com

PROLOGUE

As the shell seared past, Ragnar threw himself flat behind the low pile of rubble, trying to make himself as small a target as possible. That had been close, too close. The shot had almost parted his hair. Only his lightning-quick reflexes and the microsecond's warning provided by his superhuman senses had got him out of the way. If he had ducked half a heartbeat later, his head would have been an exploding fountain of gore and bone. Ragnar had seen it happen too often to have any doubts as to what his own fate would have been.

Now, however, was not the time to brood on might-have-beens. Now was the time for action, the time to teach the infidel cultists trying to slay him the penalty for attacking one of the Emperor's chosen Space Marines. He raised his head slightly, lifting it just above the parapet of rubble, his superhuman senses taking in the entire scene. Everything imprinted itself in his mind in one split second, then he ducked down once more before his enemies could fire.

He sorted through all the impressions he had picked up; not just the sights but also the sounds, the smells and the less tangible cues from the mixture of senses in his altered brain. He recalled the ruined city, stretching as far as the eye could see.

The enormous blackened stumps of the smashed skyscrapers, the burned out wreckage of ground-cars and tanks which filled the street. The infernal blaze of the fuel pumping station that had been hit by a missile and which had now burned on for days, sending huge tongues of flame leaping into the darkening sky. He remembered the crimson and purple clouds contaminated by chemicals from the mighty industrial plants which had once provided this city with wealth and importance to the Imperium.

He recalled the earthshaking roar of distant artillery as Basilisk tanks shelled the rebel positions, and the stutter of small arms fire in the near distance. He could hear the guttural shouts of rebel officers ordering their unruly troops into new defensive positions and the faint scrape of ceramite boot on stone, inaudible to normal human ears, that told him his own troops were close by. He even recognised the footfalls as belonging to young Brother Reinhardt. He made a mental note to remind himself, after this engagement was through, to have a word with the Blood Claw. He was supposed to be moving stealthily. Not even his leader should have been able to pick out his position by the noise he was making.

Of course, Ragnar had other ways of spotting his troops. The wind carried their distinctive scent to his sensitive nostrils even over a gap of fifty paces. He could pick their clean, cold aroma out from all of the tangled mess of background stinks – the rotten-egg taint of industrial pollution, and the even subtler, sicker taint, which marked the Chaos-touched presence of heretics.

Bones of Russ, how he hated that foul stench! He had never got used to it, though it had assailed his nostrils on countless occasions for over a century. There was something deeply offensive to him in the very odour of those who had forsworn their souls to Chaos, a thing that made the hairs on the back of his neck rise, and filled his heart with a red desire to kill and rend. Not even the fact that he suspected that this was a deliberate product of the process of alteration that had turned him into a Space Marine, could alter the basic, primal nature of his hatred. The unquenchable anger affected him as instinctively as the urge to seek its prey drives a wolf. An apt analogy, thought Ragnar, for he was a human wolf, and the Chaos-worshipping scum were his rightful prey, fit subjects for the Emperor's vengeance, delivered by he and his fellows, humanity's superhuman protectors. They had turned their backs on humanity and offered themselves up to the gods of darkness in return for power, or more likely the promise of power. Ragnar knew that it was a false promise. The only reward most of those deluded fools would receive would be the stigmata of mutation, and a degeneration of mind and spirit until their souls matched their twisted bodies. It would be a mercy to kill them before that happened, although most of them would never appreciate the natural justice of such an end.

Here, amongst these blasted ruins, the stink seemed worse, even, than before, for along with the taint of Chaos was the stench of sickness, of some foul pestilence that had infected the heretics, and the people of Hesperida alike. It was a sour, unclean reek that made his throat constrict. It brought back too many old memories, ones he had thought long buried. He pushed them to the back of his mind; now was not the time to lose himself in reverie.

These reflections had taken less than five heartbeats perhaps. In the midst of battle, Ragnar's mind worked at a speed far beyond the merely human. He realised he had only been keeping himself occupied until his troops were massed in position for the final assault. He focussed his mind back on the problem at hand, selectively editing the memory of the scene he had just witnessed, using his superhuman abilities with a skill born of long decades of practice.

Using ancient meditation techniques taught to him in the fortress-monastery of his order, he focussed upon the impression of the one part of the battlefield that was currently important to him: the rebel position directly ahead. He consciously selected all the crucial details. The walls of sandbags hastily thrown into position to plug the gaps in the building walls. The heavy bolter team ensconced in the twisted wreckage of a tank just in front of the building. The edge of a peaked cap which marked the presence of a rebel officer glaring out of the barred windows on the remains of the second floor. All was more or less as he had expected it to be when he had surveyed the enemy stronghold earlier. There had been no important changes in the heretics' disposition. His basic plan remained sound.

It would simply be a matter of hitting them at their weakest point, blasting the sandbags out of the way and then scouring the building of every last Chaos-worshipping wretch. Nothing too difficult, he thought – even though his force was outnumbered at least five to one. Such numbers did not really matter, Ragnar knew. In battles such as this, the quality of the troops counted for far more than the quantity. His men were Space Marines, Adeptus Astartes, hardened warriors drawn from a world of fierce fighters, put through the toughest testing regime ever devised, then subjected to a process of genetic re-engineering which had transformed them into supermen, many times faster, stronger and tougher than mere mortals. They were armed with the best weapons and equipment the Imperium could provide. They lived lives of monastic discipline; when they were not fighting in the Emperor's service, they trained to fight. They were the best troops the millions of worlds the Imperium of Mankind could produce.

And their opponents? Scum, pure and simple. They were conscripts, pressed into the service of a rogue planetary governor; men so lacking in faith that they had forsworn their oaths of allegiance to the Emperor, and given themselves body and soul to the dark powers of Chaos. Of course, they had some military training, and they were not without a certain desperate bravery, but there was no way they could withstand an assault by the Space Wolves.

Ragnar knew the rest of his force was in position. He sensed that the Blood Claws, ferocious young assault troops, were in cover in a shell crater not too far from him. Within moments Brother Hrothgar's Long Fangs would open fire and that would be the signal for the assault to commence. Ragnar smiled wolfishly, lips curling to reveal the huge canines that were the genetic marker of his Chapter. The coming few minutes were always the times he loved the most, when combat was up close and personal, and a man could take the measure of his foes, hand to hand.

A flickering vapour trail was all the warning he needed that Brother Hrothgar had opened fire. The enemy heavy weapon vanished in a sun-bright explosion as the missile launcher did its work. The staccato roar of bolters filled Ragnar's ears as the remainder of his men opened up on the enemy position. They were throwing down a curtain of fire in the way that only Space Marines could, shooting with a speed and precision unknown to lesser warriors. Ragnar risked another glance up and saw huge chunks of masonry being shattered to stone chips by the torrent of bolter shells. He could hear the screams of the enemy wounded and dying, smell the blood and the sour stink of spilled guts. The enemy were well and truly suppressed, pinned down by the unexpected hail of shells, unable or unwilling to stick their heads over the parapet and risk having them blown off. Ragnar knew that this would not last for long, that soon they would regain their courage and return fire – or at least, they would if they were given the chance. Ragnar was not about to allow them that.

Now was the moment to attack.

THE SPACE WOLF sprang lightly to his feet, the servomotors of his centuries-old power armour whining inaudibly to all but his own razor-keen senses. He leapt towards the enemy position, confident that his own highly trained troops would recognise him and hold their fire. He knew that the pack of Blood Claws, twenty strong, was forming a flying wedge behind him. They were directed at the pile of sandbags in the breached wall, the weakest part of the enemy line. In another moment, the Wolves had ceased firing at that area and concentrated their shells on the defences surrounding and overlooking it. For a few brief moments, Ragnar and his assault troops had a clear run up to their objective, a safe corridor through the rain of fire.

One of the enemy officers, wearing the peaked cap and long greatcoat of a lieutenant, dared to stick his head above the parapet, obviously wondering why bolter shells had ceased to impact on his part of the line. A look of surprise and fear flickered across his face as he saw the oncoming wave of Space Marines. Ragnar gave credit where credit was due: the heretic did not remain frozen for long. After an instant of hesitation he turned his head and began screaming instructions to his troops.

It was a mistake. Without breaking stride Ragnar raised his bolt pistol and put a shell through the man's head. It exploded like a melon hit with a sledgehammer, a puddle of brains and blood filling the peaked cap as it fell from his head. Shouts of confusion echoed from behind the wall of sandbags, then a few heretics, braver and perhaps more experienced than the rest, stuck their heads up in order to take shots at their attackers. But a wave of withering fire from the Wolves behind Ragnar scythed through them, sending their corpses tumbling back amongst their comrades.

With a single mighty bound, Ragnar cleared the wall of sandbags and dropped into the rebel position. It was dark but his altered eyes adapted instantly and he took in his new surroundings in a glance. All around were the enemy, clad in the crumpled and filthy uniforms they had once worn so proudly as part of the Imperial levies, but their insignia had been ripped off and hastily replaced with the evil symbol of the Ruinous Powers, eight arrows radiating outwards from a single watchful eye. The stink of disease was strong, more powerful even than the reek of unwashed bodies and death. All of the heretics looked emaciated and unclean. Some showed the signs of something far, far worse. Most of the men looked superficially human, only slight bulges and blisters indicating where they were about to change. A few, however, were more twisted and warped, corrupted by the evil power they served.

One mutant close to Ragnar had scaly skin and clutched its lasrifle with fingers that resembled small tentacles; his eyes extended on long, slug-like stalks. A second heretic was huge: chest barrel-like, his arms as thick as a normal man's thighs, his fingers ending in long cruel talons. His face was pockmarked with craters of glowing, greenish fungus, which wept an oddly luminescent pus as he opened his mouth to shout a warning.

Ragnar thumbed the brass ignition switch on his chainsword and the mighty weapon leapt to life, shuddering in his hands as the potent microengine in the hilt brought the rotating blades up to speed. Without thinking, he snapped off a couple of shots, sending the taloned giant straight to hell with a hole in his guts big enough to put a fist through. The force of the second shot blasted Slugeyes backward three yards into the wall. Ragnar snarled in satisfaction, then ducked as two of the rebels regained their wits enough to fire at him. The glittering trails of laser fire passed over his head. Screams sounded behind him as the beams seared the flesh of other heretics who had been attempting to sneak up on him.

He threw himself forward, bringing his chainsword around in a long sweep, beheading one mutant and hacking the arm off a second, before burying the duralloy blades deep within the chest of a third. With one swift kick, the Wolf dashed the corpse from his blade and raced on, heading for the chamber's exit. Triumphant howls and despairing cries from behind told him that his fellows, the Blood Claws, had arrived and had already begun the bloody work of butchering their foes.

Ragnar raced into the corridor. The head of a heretic officer poked round a door. 'What is going on?' he shouted, in oddly accented Imperial Gothic.

The man's face was pale and he looked ill. His body had the lean look of one who had suffered a long sickness; his eyes burned with a feverish light. He obviously had not recognised Ragnar for what he was. Ragnar took his head from his shoulders with a sideways cut of his blade. Blood fountained, splashing the ceiling with red. Ragnar heard screams as the corpse tumbled backwards into the room beyond. Swiftly he holstered his pistol and tapped the hilt of the microgrenade dispenser on his belt. The small oval disk of a frag grenade dropped into his gauntleted fingers. He pushed the timer three times to set the detonator to go off in three seconds, then lobbed the grenade into the room. He doubted that the terrified men within even realised what was happening until, a few heartbeats later, they were torn apart by the force of the explosion.

Ragnar poked his head around the doorway and surveyed the mangled corpses. Amid all the ruin one man still moved, frantically trying to bring his lasrifle to bear on the Wolf, his breath coming from his ruined chest in horrible gurgles. Before the wounded cultist could draw a bead on him, Ragnar whipped his bolt pistol from its holster and put him out of his misery with one swift, precise shot, before he could even offer a prayer for aid from his Dark Gods.

The Space Wolf paused for a moment to listen. All around he could hear the sounds of combat and death spreading through the building, like ripples in a pool after a heavy stone has been dropped into it. He knew that all through the building his warriors were passing like a cleansing flame, scouring out the dark taint of heresy. Nothing could resist their relentless onslaught.

His nostrils caught the stink of burning flesh and opened wounds, of blood and spent bolter charges, of bone marrow and brain tissue. The convection currents in the air brought him other subtler scents: the faint pheromone traces of fear and anger, the distinctive scent of his battle-brothers, the foul

taint of Chaos-contaminated flesh and once again the sour
tang of some strange disease. He knew without being told that
victory was within their grasp.

The scent of Brother Olaf reached him, approaching fast
from the rear. Olaf was the youngest of the Blood Claws and
the least stable. Of them all, he had come closest to devolving
into a Wulfen during his transformation into a Space Wolf, and
he shared with those cursed men-beasts a terrible rage and an
unslakeable thirst for combat. Ragnar knew that with time, the
young man would settle down and make his peace with the
beast within him. All Space Wolves did eventually – assuming
they survived all of their initiation.

Ragnar risked a glance back over his shoulder and saw that
the beast was almost in control of young Olaf as the young
warrior charged up behind him. His eyes were wide, the pupils
dilated; froth foamed from his lips and spittle drooled from his
mouth. His neck muscles writhed like great cables as he
howled his fury and bloodlust like a challenge. At this
moment, he was definitely out of control. The spirit of the Wolf
was in him.

Ragnar stepped aside to let him pass and the Blood Claw
raced past down the corridor towards another wave of heretics
drawn by the sounds of battle. Ragnar followed in his wake,
content for the moment to observe, to intervene only if the
youngling got himself into more trouble than he could handle.

Not that it looked likely. Olaf's bolt pistol spat death at the
leading heretics and moments later he sprang across the
corpses of his targets to wreak havoc on the survivors with his
blade. Cutting and stabbing relentlessly, he drove the heretics
back down the corridor. It was only as he passed an open doorway that the trap was sprung on him.

A huge arm emerged and a fist the size of a shield closed
around Brother Olaf's head. Almost at once Ragnar caught the
scent of ogryn, one of the giant abhumans who were sometimes attached to the Imperial levies, mutants suffered to live
by the Imperium because of their toughness, loyalty and
strength. Unfortunately they were also very stupid and would
follow their officers into heresy without the slightest thought of
the consequences. Now one of them had Brother Olaf in a grip
strong enough to crush even the reinforced bone structure of a
Space Marine skull by merely clenching its fingers.

Ragnar was not about to give it the chance. He sprang forward and with a mighty cut severed the huge boil-covered hand at the wrist. It dropped to the floor and for a moment the fingers flexed in nervous reaction so that it seemed to scuttle like a huge spider. A bellow of rage and pain rumbled from behind the door. Ragnar took a step forward and peered within. A massive face glared down at him, mouth distended in shock and anger. Even the ogryn's features showed traces of disease. Enormous blisters filled with pus marred its cheeks and neck. It sounded very unhealthy, air rasping through lungs filled with phlegm. Even so, it showed no sign of weakness, only an unrelenting urge to maim and slay.

Ragnar raised his pistol and sent a bullet through one of the ogryn's eyes. Still it did not fall, but reached out for him with its remaining good hand. Was the creature simply too stupid to die, Ragnar wondered, or was some dark sorcery at work here?

Not that he cared. Pushing Olaf out of the way of the creature's blow, the Wolf dived to one side himself. The ogryn brought its fist down as if swatting a fly. Even off balance, Ragnar had the co-ordination to lash out with his chainsword. It bit off two of the monster's fingers and embedded itself in the palm of the beast's hand. Like a child recoiling from a scalding stove the ogryn sharply withdrew its hand with a hiss.

Ragnar held onto the hilt of his chainsword and was lifted clear of the ground. He felt himself start to fall as the teeth of the chainsword ceased to find traction. Yet for a moment he had another clear shot at the monster, so he put a bullet through its other eye, convinced that blinding it at least would give him all the advantage he would need in the coming fight. It was more than enough. This time the bullet passed clean through the abhuman's thick skull and blew its few brains over the wall of the chamber. The massive corpse toppled like a falling oak. Ragnar landed on his feet and glanced around to see that Brother Olaf had continued down the corridor, leaving a trail of death and destruction in his wake. Under the circumstances, Ragnar deemed it advisable to follow.

OLAF HAD MADE his way to a wide hall. The ceiling was half blown away and broken ceramic tiles strewed the floor. Exposed pipes erupted from the floor and electric cables writhed like snakes from the remnants of the walls. The heretics here milled around in confusion, unable to decide whether to advance or flee the building. The indecision cost them their lives. Olaf charged right into the middle of them, lashing out left and right with his blade, killing with every stroke. His howling battle cry echoed around the furthest reaches of the hall, like the call of some avenging spirit. Ragnar was but two strides behind him and, if anything, was even more lethal. He fought with an easy grace and precision, not a movement wasted, not a blow going astray, smiting around him like a warrior god sprung to life from ancient legends. Before they even had time to realise it, half the heretics were dead. The others turned to flee but Ragnar pumped bolter shells into their backs before they could reach the exit, unwilling to stain his blade with the blood of such cowards.

Olaf glared around him, a blood-maddened wolf seeking new prey. None was visible but that did not matter. He threw back his head, nostrils flaring as he sniffed the air for the scent of heretics. He seemed to catch something, for he cocked his head to one side and listened for a moment – before striding for a metal door set at the rear of the chamber.

Before the Blood Claw could reach it, the door was thrown open and a man emerged. He was tall and cadaverous, his skin pale as parchment and his eyes glowing with a sickly green internal light visible in the gloom of the chamber. He wore the uniform of an officer of the planetary levies but he was obviously something more than that, more than that and worse. Around him buzzed a huge cloud of flies. They crawled over his flesh and covered the upper part of his skull like a helmet. As they writhed and buzzed, patches of leprous white flesh became visible beneath them. It was a sight somehow more obscene than the insects themselves. The man's face was lean and almost fleshless. His cheeks had sunk, and his lips had drawn back to reveal teeth and gums marred by massive white abscesses. The man's appearance reminded Ragnar of a skull, but the living flesh that still clung to this skull made it far more horrific than the bones of the dead.

The stink of disease was so strong that Ragnar knew at once that here was the source of the contagion which had infected the heretics in this building. Ragnar fought down a shudder, for he recognised the presence of evil magic. This one was a powerful sorcerer, no doubt sworn to the Chaos power known as Nurgle, the Lord of Pestilence.

Olaf did not care. He raced towards the newcomer as if he were just an ordinary trooper. The sorcerer grinned, exposing rotten teeth, then made a sweeping gesture with his hand. A nimbus of dark power boiled around his taloned fingers, becoming a ball of glowing green fire as he finished the gesture. The ball of tainted energy swept outwards towards Olaf, emitting a buzzing like the flies, catching him on the chest. For a moment nothing happened, then a yellowish glow limned Olaf's form, spreading around his body until it encased him. Then a cold fire seemed to consume him. There was no heat, no stench of burning, no sign of anything at work except potent magic. His armour bubbled and blistered and began to run like liquid, taking the flesh below with it. For a moment, Ragnar had a glimpse of the reddish augmented muscles of a Space Marine. Then these too were consumed, rotting to black pus, flowing to the ground like water and evaporating away. In another instant only Olaf's skeleton, so like and yet so unlike that of an ordinary man, remained. Ragnar had a clear view of the heavy bones, the reinforced joints, the unnaturally thick skull, and the mighty fangs... then that too decayed, leaving only a swiftly fading, glowing outline hanging in the air. Olaf was gone as if he had never been. The glow that had surrounded him coalesced into a ball of fire once more.

The sorcerer's insane, gurgling laughter filled the hall with evil glee. He coughed in a long wracking spasm that bent him almost double, then spat on the floor. The huge gobbet of green slime that dripped from his mouth bubbled and evaporated on the floor. He smiled at Ragnar as if they were old friends and, in a voice that seemed to consist of the buzzing of thousands of insects, said, 'Lord Botchulaz sends his greetings.'

At the mention of that name, Ragnar almost froze, reminded of horrors long past and griefs so ancient that he thought he had forgotten them. Words of defiance froze on his lips as images of evil and despair flashed through his brain.

The magician made another gesture with his hand and there was no time now for anything but action. With eye-blurring speed, the ball of corrupting flame sailed through the air towards the Space Wolf. Having seen what the thing could do, Ragnar had no intention of letting it touch him. He dived forward beneath it, sensing the evil power of the thing as it passed over his head. He aimed a shot at the Chaos-worshipping sorcerer with his bolter. The man raised his other hand in a warding gesture and the shell was deflected to one side.

By Russ, this was a powerful one, Ragnar thought, greatly gifted by the powers of Chaos.

Ragnar felt the surge of energy at his back which told him the ball of flame was searing up behind him. He sprang to the left, the servos in his power armour straining, and it blazed past him, leaving a flickering trail in its wake. The sorcerer made another gesture and the thing he had created looped towards Ragnar once more, blazing round and down in a deadly arc. This time Ragnar leapt upwards and over it. He felt the power of its presence once more as it passed below him. As he leapt, the Wolf loosed another shot but once more the heretic warded it away with a gesture.

Nothing for it, thought Ragnar, but to settle this up close and personal, the old fashioned way. He dived forward, sensing the ball of fire moving in pursuit, and hit the ground rolling. He tumbled all the way to the mage's feet and lashed out with his chainsword at his foe's legs. The mage tried the warding gesture once more but he was too slow. Even as he did so Ragnar changed the point of impact of his blow and took the man's arm off at the elbow. Black blood flowed thickly from the stump like molasses and instantly began to congeal around the wound. Another gift of the Dark Powers, Ragnar guessed. He smiled nastily and stabbed again. His ancient blade embedded itself in his foe's guts and hung there, blades screeching as it tore the fiend apart.

Ragnar sprang suddenly to his left and the ball of flame missed him and impacted on the mage. Instead of reducing him to nothingness, it was absorbed into his body without causing him any apparent harm. Russ take me, Ragnar thought, but it had been worth a try.

He reached forward once more and pulled his blade free, making sure to turn it in the wound for maximum damage. With a hideous slurping sound the whining chainsword came free, dragging ropes of tangled intestine with it. The sorcerer showed no sign of any pain. A look of discomfort passed over his face as he began the gesture that would summon the fireball again. This time Ragnar severed the man's head from his shoulders. Even as it fell, the Wolf struck the skull again, searing it in two with his chainsword. The sorcerer's body fell to the ground as though pole-axed.

Ragnar looked at it for a moment, as if half expecting it to stir, but nothing happened. The combat was over. He looked around with some satisfaction but could not see any more targets. All around him the sounds of combat were dying away. It seemed like his men were achieving their objectives. Trying to forget what the magician had said, Ragnar turned and raced back the way he had come. It was like running through a slaughterhouse. Blood and gore decorated the walls. He sniffed the air, taking in all the scents, and knew with certainty that only Space Wolves were left alive in the building. It came as no surprise to him when the signal crackled over the comm-net.

+Objective secured.+

NIGHT GATHERED. The old yellow moons glared down through the contaminated clouds. Ragnar stood on the roof of the battered factory and glanced out into the night, braided hair flapping in the cold breeze. Over there the war still raged as other units of Imperial troops struggled to contain the heretics. A flower of fire blossomed where a shell exploded. A few moments later there was a crack like thunder. Ragnar was aware of the vibration of the distant explosion passing through the structure beneath his feet.

Down below, the Blood Claws celebrated. They gathered around a blazing fire and roared chants drawn from the epics of their people. They told of their deeds and the deeds of their ancestors. Some of them shouted out what they had done today, the number of heretics they had killed and the way they had killed them. He smiled at the innocence of their boasting. They were so proud of themselves and what they had done, filled with the simple pride of men who were being blooded, on their first campaign; feeling, for the first time, the thrill of war as it was waged between the stars.

He knew that their boasting was as much to relieve tension as to impress their peers. All of them knew how many of their number had died today. All of them had taken part in the funeral rites which Ragnar had led. Now their task was done, they were coming to terms with the fact that they were still alive, that men, evil men, had tried to kill them, and that they had endured. Ragnar could well remember the shock and the thrill of that realisation himself. There were times when it seemed like only yesterday that he had fought in his own first off-world campaign.

Everything had seemed simpler then somehow, before his rise to command, before the long series of adventures and wars which had seen him rise faster and further than any Space Wolf had ever done before. There were occasions when he wondered whether it was worth it, when he envied the Blood Claws their innocence. They did not yet know what it was like to feel the responsibility for another Space Wolf's death. All through the long evening, as the reports came in and the factory complex was secured, Ragnar had replayed the battle in his mind, wondering if there had been some way to do it differently, some tactic that would have prevented Olaf and the others from dying. But if there was he could not see it. This was war, and in wars men died, even Space Marines. Perhaps Russ and the Emperor could have done better than he, perhaps another commander could have, but there was nothing now he could do about it. What was done, was done. He simply had to accept that and put it behind him. Tomorrow the war would continue. Tomorrow a new battle would be fought.

Still, at that moment, he longed to return to a simpler time, to the time when it had all seemed easy. But he reminded himself: it had only seemed easy. Even in his youth there had been losses, and horrors and intrigues. He let his mind drift back to the events he had been trying to suppress since his encounter with the sorcerer.

He gazed out into the night, remembering.

CHAPTER ONE

ALONG WITH his fellow battle-brothers, Ragnar stood at the entrance to the landing bay, his weapons holstered, his newly acquired Blood Claw insignia displayed proudly on his shoulder-pad. They were all waiting for Inquisitor Sternberg to descend from his ship.

The Space Wolf took another deep breath and tried to calm himself. He knew that the monstrous vessel before him was only a shuttle, not even one of the huge craft that plied the unthinkable distances between the stars, but even so the sheer scale of the thing was enough to take your breath away. It seemed as large as the village in which he had grown up, a great wedge of ancient ceramite and duralloy, pitted by meteor trails and seared by weapon impacts. In a strange way, it was beautiful. Gargoyles clutched the fins and the Imperial eagle had been embossed on its side with a craftsmanship that no jewel-smith from his own people could have hoped to rival. He studied the crystalline portholes in its side, looking to see if anyone glanced out at them.

His mouth felt strangely dry. He was about to experience something he would have considered an impossibility but a few short months ago. He was about to encounter strangers from another world. He told himself that he would not gawk and stare, but the thought was still an astonishing one. A season ago, when he had still lived in the Thunderfist village, he had believed that the universe was a great sea dotted with endless islands and girded about by a mighty serpent. Since the time he had been selected to join the Space Wolves, he had learned differently, so differently. He now knew that his homeworld, Fenris, was a sphere floating in the endless immensity of space, orbiting a star that he had once thought was the Eye of Russ. He knew now that it was but one star amid millions which made up the galaxy and the Imperium of Mankind, and that, somehow, mighty ships moved between these worlds. Moreover, he had learned that each world was different, and that many were homes to different nations and peoples. In this they were like the islands in the Worldsea of Fenris, for there too the islands were homes to clans, each with different customs and beliefs. The other worlds were like that and there was scope for far greater differences between the inhabitants of planets than of the islands of Fenris. Some, he had been taught, were homes to foul mutants, others to alien races inimical to mankind. Some worlds were entirely sheathed in metal and inhabited by teeming billions pressed cheek to jowl. Others were empty wastes of ice and snow on which dwelled fur-clad nomads. Some were deserts of fire, yet more airless barrens where life survived only in ancient cavern cities. His mind could only begin to comprehend the merest fraction of all the endless possibilities they represented.

As he had tried to do so many times recently, Ragnar pushed such thoughts from his mind and tried to concentrate on the task at hand – but it was difficult. He wondered what the passengers on this ship would be like. Would they have green skins or two heads? There was no way of knowing until they emerged. He wanted to look around him to see what his brother Blood Claws were doing or thinking, but he did not. They were an honour guard for these new arrivals, and they were meant to show discipline and restraint. It would not do to go staring about him like some youngling.

He could just picture the expressions on the faces of those around him though. Sven's ugly broken-nosed face would be looking hungrily as if the strangers might be carrying something good to eat, all the while trying to restrain a grin from twisting his features. Ragnar's old rival and former blood-enemy Strybjorn would have an expression of angry contempt locked on his dour, brutal face. Lean Nils would be fighting to keep a smile from erupting on his lips as he wrestled with his urge to toss insults at Sven. All of the others would be fighting with their own impulses. It was not easy for them. They were all Blood Claws, newly initiated, and their heads and hearts were still filled with the wild animalistic urges that were a side-effect of their transformation into Space Wolves.

Pretty much all of the Chapter currently resident in the Fang was here awaiting the new arrivals. They had been drawn from their lairs and meditation cells all over the great armoured mountain to be here and welcome this inquisitor. Only mighty Logan Grimnar, the Great Wolf himself, legendary leader of all the Wolves, and his household were not present. Grimnar waited in his lair for the inquisitor to come and see him, as was fitting. Nevertheless, Ragnar thought this Inquisitor Sternberg must be a mighty man indeed to warrant such a welcome to the Fang. There must be over a hundred Space Wolves here, plus over a thousand retainers. Few strangers were ever welcomed to the home of the Wolves and few indeed were greeted with such ceremony – or so Sergeant Hakon had told him. His former instructor had returned from the mountains some weeks back to take charge of the Blood Claws after the death of Sergeant Hengist. If he concentrated, Ragnar could catch the veteran Wolf's scent, and it immediately brought to his mind's eye a picture of the sergeant's massive frame and lean, leathery face.

Ragnar found himself considering the rumours he had heard about Sternberg. Some of the thralls had claimed that he had fought alongside the Space Wolves on several occasions, once even saving the life of the Great Wolf himself. Others claimed that he came all the way from the ancient homeworld of Terra, sacred home of the beloved God-Emperor himself, bringing news of an important mission for the Chapter. Still others claimed that he was here to spy on the Space Wolves for the distant masters of the Imperium, hoping to find the taint of heresy in the Chapter and so be allowed to order its dissolution.

Ragnar doubted the last. He knew, as only an initiate could know, how utterly loyal the Wolves were to their duty. They would all of them, Ragnar included, have died to the last man rather than betray humanity to the darkness. There was no way they ever could be found wanting.

He fought back a sudden shiver as a dark memory intruded. Ragnar knew that not even Fenris was free of the taint of Chaos. Mere months ago he and his fellow Blood Claws had uncovered a nest of heresy in the mountains to the north of the Fang; a nest so deep and so filled with foul enemies that all the Wolves present on the planet had been massed to deal with it. He pushed the grim thoughts aside. He knew that it was all too possible that the inquisitor would be accompanied by one who could pluck such thoughts from one's mind – and what had happened during that encounter with the renegade Marines of the Thousand Sons was no one's business but the Chapter's.

As if in direct response to his ill-considered thoughts, the great door in the side of the shuttle hissed and opened. A boarding ramp extruded itself from the spacecraft's side and rattled down to the plascrete floor of the hangar. Ragnar drew a breath and turned his face into a frozen mask as the first of the strangers came into view. Disappointment warred with relief in Ragnar's mind. The stranger was surprisingly normal but impressive nonetheless. He was a tall man, almost as tall as a veteran Space Wolf, and almost as broad too. His body was encased in dark ceramite armour which left only his grizzled grey-haired head visible. A pair of well-used weapons were holstered at his hip, a long pistol of unusual design and a chainsword. A great red cape fluttered in the breeze caused by the induction fans which pumped air into the chamber. The cape's wide cowl was thrown back to reveal the man's head, but Ragnar guessed that was not always the case. He glanced around him; his gaze appeared to take in every last detail of the scene quickly and smoothly. The man smiled easily, showing white teeth in a face tanned dark as well-seasoned witchwood. He paused only for a heartbeat and then strode down the ramp. It flexed slightly beneath his weight. Ragnar guessed that the armour was a lot heavier than it looked, and was, like his own, animated in part by servomotors.

As the newcomer began his descent others emerged from the ship behind him – and at the sight of the first Ragnar's breath hissed from his chest. She was quite possibly the most beautiful woman he had ever seen, certainly the most striking. She was tall and willowy with dark brown skin, her black hair cropped short to her head. Indefinable symbols had been tat-tooed or scarred on her forehead. Her armour was similar to that of the man before her, as was her cape – but not quite as ornate, and with far fewer symbols and badges embedded in it. Ragnar was guessing, but he felt fairly certain that this indicated she was of lesser rank than the man he assumed was Inquisitor Sternberg. It was certainly the way of things among the Space Wolves, where men proudly wore the campaign badges and honour studs they had earned in battle for all to see. His ultra-keen eyes made out the name engraved in curled Imperial Gothic on her chest plate: *Karah Isaan*.

After these first two, the rest of the strangers were a disap-pointment. There were many in the uniforms of warriors, perhaps a bodyguard, most likely the ranking officers of the inquisitor's entourage come to consult with the Great Wolf. Ragnar knew that Imperial inquisitors often travelled with what was in effect a small personal army ready to do their bid-ding and cleanse heresy upon their orders. That they might be here to protect him from the Wolves was such a ludicrous con-cept it took a few heartbeats to insinuate itself into Ragnar's brain. He dismissed the idea as laughable. The Wolves would not attack their guest – and in the almost inconceivable event that they decided to, mere mortals could not stand against them.

After the warriors came men and women cowled in the dark blue robes of scribes. Each carried a leather-bound libram chained to a thick leather belt at their waist. Ragnar was unsure whether these were books of lore or for making new records. He decided that he would ask one of them, if he ever got the chance.

As they paced down the ramp, Ragnar caught their strange off-world scent for the first time, and suddenly he was filled with a nagging sensation of unease, a premonition of doom. The beast within him stirred and he felt an urge to rend and tear at these newcomers, to strike them down as if they were his sworn enemies. He had never felt anything quite like it before. As if sensing it, the female inquisitor glanced around her, and caught his eye. Gazing across at her hooded brown eyes Ragnar felt suddenly calm. His sense of unease diminished, but did not vanish entirely. He tried to push it to one side. These were trusted allies, he told himself – yet a need to be wary remained.

As the first inquisitor reached the plascrete floor of the hangar, Jarek Bluetooth, the Great Wolf's chief bondsman and steward, walked forward to greet him. He reached out and clasped arms, hands gripping at the elbow in the traditional Fenrisian greeting. Sternberg did not seem at all surprised by this. He smiled again and, once the clasp was ended, bowed from the waist in an elaborate and courtly fashion. As one, all the folk of his retinue, newly alighted behind him, did likewise.

'In the name of Logan Grimnar, Great Wolf and Chieftain, I bid you welcome!' Jarek said proudly. He spoke in the Gothic tongue of the Imperium, which made his rough voice sound even harsher.

'I thank the Great Wolf for his welcome, and request an audience with him at his leisure.' Compared to Jarek, the inquisitor's voice was smooth and pleasant, yet it held steely undercurrents. Quite plainly this was a man used to getting his own way. Unsurprising really, Ragnar knew, considering the man was authorised to investigate all manner of heresies in the Emperor's name. Only the Space Marine Chapters considered themselves beyond the remit of His Divine Inquisition, for they were bound by laws and traditions which predated the Imperium itself. Ragnar's teachers had been quite specific on this point. The Space Marines were an independent force within the great swathe of humanity and proud of this fact. Indeed, they had been one of the major contributors to its founding and as such were granted many privileges. They were loyal only to the Emperor himself, not to his minions in the Ecclesiarchy.

There was something about Sternberg's tone that whispered a warning to Ragnar. It was not that he could detect any falseness in it, for he could not. It was just something about it that made his hackles rise. He was surprised that none of his fellow Wolves shared his unease, but he sensed that their scents had not changed. He appeared to be the only one who felt the way he did. Perhaps it was a flaw in him, something left over from his recent transformation into a Space Wolf. He knew he was still sometimes given to visions and hallucinations as well as fits of anger and hate. His elders told him these would fade in time as he became accustomed to the change. Perhaps that was the problem here.

'The Great Wolf will be pleased to grant his old comrade an audience immediately,' Jarek replied formally and fell into step beside the inquisitor. Sternberg and his retinue made their way through the double line of Space Wolves assembled to greet them. As they passed the last of the honour guard, the Space Wolves themselves formed up in ranks behind them and, marching proudly, escorted them to the lair of Logan Grimnar.

A HUGE PAVILION had been erected within the Great Wolf's hall. It was made from the finest grey silk and one side of it was open to face the doors through which Sternberg and his escort entered. The inside was illuminated by floating glowglobes hovering just below the tent's ceiling. Two ever-burning braziers flickered and crackled close to each edge of the entrance. Each gave off the smell of the incense used in the sacred rituals of the Imperium. Ragnar recognised this particular scent: silver-root. It was said to be a powerful ward against evil influences.

In all his time within the Fang, this was the first time Ragnar had been permitted to enter the Great Wolf's lair. There had never really been any need for him to go beyond the training areas, the cells in which the novice Space Marines dwelt and the communal areas shared by all the Great Companies. One day soon, Ragnar knew, his pack of Blood Claws would be assigned to their own Great Company and become part of the greater command structure of the Chapter but for the moment they were in a sort of limbo, waiting to see which company would need replacements either for casualties or for those Blood Claws who had been promoted to the Grey Hunters.

The Great Wolf's lair was huge, taking up one complete level of the Fang. The trek there had not been long, though. A series of grav-tubes had carried the whole party through the maze of the ancient fortress, but if the newcomers had felt any of the wonder that Ragnar had once felt on first seeing the inside of the mountain fastness, they kept it well hidden. He guessed that in their travels they must have seen many imposing sights. Part of him longed to share in that experience, to travel off-world, to see new things and go to new places. He knew that some day he would do just that, yet as far as he was concerned the day could not come quickly enough. Still, some part of him also feared that day; he was not entirely sure why. He suspected that some part of being human was always to have some fear of any new experience.

The Great Wolf awaited them, bedecked in splendour. He was a massive man, a truly mighty warrior to Ragnar's eyes. His chest was larger than an ale barrel and his arms were like tree trunks. A huge grey beard tumbled down his chest like a waterfall. A mane of grey hair erupted from his head and fell down past his shoulders. His eyes, ancient and unknowable, were like chips of ice. His face looked like it had been carved from granite and the scars on his cheeks looked more like the product of decades of erosion than the result of wounds. They reminded Ragnar of ravines driven into the hard stone of mountains. Around Grimnar's shoulders was thrown a great wolfskin cloak which some claimed dated from the time of Russ and was said to be impervious to heat, cold and flame. The head of the wolf rested on Grimnar's head like a crown. Dangling from a cord around his neck was the Amulet of Russ, a simple-looking device, crudely made to resemble the head of a wolf from some unknown metal. It was said to be the repository of great power for its wearer. It was a talisman that was supposed to protect against all manner of evil sorcery and shield its owner from all evil influences.

Dozens of battle honours had been worked onto the Great Wolf's armour, for Grimnar had served in hundreds of campaigns over the past seven hundred Imperial Standard years. That thought itself was almost enough to make Ragnar's mind reel. It was ten times the life span of the oldest mortal man on Fenris, yet Logan Grimnar showed no signs of weakness. Instead he gave off an aura of boundless health, strength and energy. He was the most regal man Ragnar had ever seen. He seemed born to command, a chieftain worthy of the greatest of warriors, commanding limitless obedience from those who fought for him. And so it should be, Ragnar thought, for this was the man who led a Chapter of the Emperor's finest.

Logan Grimnar sat stern and commanding upon the Wolf Throne. It appeared to be made of ancient stone, carved with runes that looked almost as old as time and seemed to have been cut there by wind and rain. The throne had been made to hold a man even larger than Grimnar. It dated from the time of Russ and it was possible that the great Primarch himself had once sat in it. The back of the seat was carved to resemble a great snarling wolf's head looming over the sitter. Each arm of the throne was its paws. The strangest thing about the throne was that it did not rest on the floor, instead it floated about a hand's breadth above it, and it turned as the Great Wolf wished, seemingly guided by his will. Ragnar could not help but notice that the Great Wolf's armoured form similarly did not touch the stone of the throne, but instead seemed to float just shy of its surface. He now knew a little about the ancient magic of suspensor systems and he guessed that one of them was in use. At the very least it would surely make sitting on the hard stone more bearable, although Ragnar suspected that it had another use. On the back of the throne fluttered two vast banners: one bore the two rampant wolves that were the insignia of Grimnar, the other the snarling wolf's head that was the symbol of the Chapter. They fluttered and rippled, though there was not the slightest hint of a breeze to move them.

Within the shadows of the pavilion, flanking Grimnar's mighty throne, stood the folk of his lair, the Wolf Priests resplendent in their wolf-hide cloaks and wearing their aura of age and command. Ragnar recognised Ranek, the eldest of them all, who had inducted the young Blood Claw into the Chapter all those months ago. With them also were the metal-clad Iron Priests, their helmets moulded to represent wolf's heads. And there were even several Rune Priests, long bearded, carrying huge wooden staffs carved with mystical runic symbols. All of these men had about them an aura of age and wisdom that was palpable. All of them were veterans of a hundred campaigns.

Ragnar wondered if Inquisitor Sternberg was conscious of the honour being done him by this assemblage of all the notables of the Chapter. It seemed so, for the man raised his hand and all his retainers halted, leaving him to advance alone towards the throne of the Great Wolf. Once he stood before Grimnar, he dropped to one knee and bowed his head like a man swearing fealty to his jarl. Grimnar slid forward and dropped from his throne, before laying one massive hand on the inquisitor's shoulders.

Ragnar watched closely as the two met and was surprised by something he caught from the corner of his eye. Brother Ranek, too, was looking at the inquisitor. Ragnar saw a flicker of quickly concealed suspicion pass across the man's ancient gnarled face and vanish. Ranek turned slightly; he had noticed Ragnar's gaze. Their eyes met and he was sure the Wolf Priest could guess what he was thinking. After a moment, Ranek looked away.

'We meet again, Ivan Sternberg,' the Great Wolf said, his voice like two great granite boulders rubbing together. 'It has been a long time.'

'Too long, Logan Grimnar. It does me good to see you looking so hale and hearty.'

'I thank you, Ivan Sternberg. You too look well. As well as the day you stopped those orks stabbing me in the back.'

'It was an honour to be of service to one of the Imperium's greatest warriors, praise His name. I thank the Eternal Throne I was simply in the right place at the right time.'

'Nonetheless, you took a wound for me, and I owe you a debt of honour. I told you that day you had but to name the boon and if it was in my power to grant it, I would.'

Ragnar fought down the urge to take a deep breath. It was a measure of the trust that the Great Wolf placed in this man that he would make such a statement. It was the sort of pledge that might be redeemed with the very life or honour of Logan Grimnar, and through him, his entire Chapter. The fact that it had been made told Ragnar that the Great Wolf considered both things safe in Sternberg's keeping. Surely this made his own suspicions unworthy and invalid. If the Great Wolf trusted this man, who was Ragnar to doubt him?

He made a mental note to ask one of the Rune Priests about the inquisitor when the chance arose. He was sure there was an epic tale concealed within the Great Wolf's simple words.

'I do have a request to make of you, and I would consider your granting it a repayment of any debt you may feel you have incurred with me.'

'Name it.'

The beautiful woman behind Sternberg coughed loudly. The inquisitor turned to face her.

'Do you think this is wise, Inquisitor Sternberg?' the woman asked without preamble. Her voice was calm and clear. Ragnar found it enthralling. Sternberg turned to gesture at the woman.

'May I present my apprentice, Karah Isaan?' he said smoothly. Somehow he managed by his manner to convey the impression that she had spoken with his blessing, rather than interrupted a private conversation between him and the Great Wolf.

Grimnar nodded civilly to her. 'What do you mean, Karah Isaan?'

'I mean this matter concerns the security of the Imperium.'

Grimnar's booming laughter echoed around the chamber. 'We are quite used to dealing with such matters in the Fang!'

If the young woman was daunted she gave no sign. 'I am sure you are, Great Wolf.' Her face twisted slightly as she hesitated on pronouncing the title. It dawned on Ragnar that she would have far preferred to be using something more formal. She was quite obviously unsure of how to deal with the legendary leader of the Space Wolves. 'It is just there are many others here who might... overhear... our discussions.'

'If you do not trust any of your people, send them away!' Grimnar boomed.

The woman's face flushed a little. She tilted her head back and opened her mouth to speak. It seemed to Ragnar that she thought the Great Wolf was being wilfully obtuse. 'That is not...'

'I know what you meant,' Grimnar said, and this time his voice was glacier-cold and full of authority, the voice of a chieftain dealing with an ambassador who had made an impertinent request. 'Whatever you have to say, you can say in front of any of my warriors. You can trust them as you would trust me. It is your Inquisition which keeps secrets, even from itself, not my Chapter.'

Ragnar was a little shocked that the female inquisitor seemed to be suggesting the possibility that anyone in the Fang might be disloyal, even a traitor. He could see that the same thought had occurred to others. Some hands flexed as if their owners might be considering reaching for their blades and calling her out to fight for the honour of the Chapter. A gruff glare from the Great Wolf stilled all such activity. The woman did not quail in front of Grimnar, but she did flinch slightly and a look of surprise froze on her face. It dawned on Ragnar that as a member of the Inquisition she was probably more used to making people fearful than to quaking herself. It took her but moments to recover.

'I apologise if I have given offence. I was unsure of your customs here.'

Ragnar considered another of the Great Wolf's statements. Was it possible that other servants of the Imperium withheld information from each other? That seemed like sheer foolishness to Ragnar. A warrior needed all the information available to make decisions, or so he had been taught. It seemed clear that the woman thought differently. She had been quite prepared to tell something to Grimnar alone without his followers hearing it – as if Lord Grimnar would not tell them if he deemed it needful for them to know.

'Forgive Karah,' Sternberg said. 'She is young and she has but recently become apprenticed to me. She does not yet know how to deal with Space Marines.'

'In truth, Ivan Sternberg, few folk do,' Grimnar shrugged good-humouredly. 'But you have yet to name this boon you require of me.'

Sternberg paused for a moment, considering. Despite his smooth words, he appeared to be thinking about what Karah had said. Ragnar could smell his momentary indecision. He was sure every Space Wolf present could. He wondered if the inquisitor himself was aware of this. Perhaps he was, for he reached his decision quickly.

'My homeworld of Aerius has been smitten by a deadly plague. Millions are dying even as I speak.'

Ragnar could not see what the Space Wolves could possibly do about this. They were warriors, not healers. If Grimnar thought the same he kept it well hidden, merely nodding attentively as Sternberg spoke.

'Our healers were baffled. All the remedies tried by our apothecaries failed. It seemed a cure for the plague was beyond all of our alchemical lore. It appeared to the rulers of Aerius that perhaps the plague itself might be a product of dark sorcery or some ancient curse, so the governor's astropath requested my aid. I returned to my homeworld as soon as my duties allowed, for Aerius is a mighty industrial world, and keystone to the Imperium's control of its sector. By the Emperor's grace, I arrived before too much time had passed.'

Sternberg paused as if gathering his thoughts once more. Ragnar could tell that the man was something of an orator, and that the real reason he paused was to give his words time to sink into the minds of the audience. At the mention of 'sorcery' and an 'ancient curse' a perceptible thrill had run through the chamber.

'There had indeed been many strange portents. A great comet had appeared in the skies of Aerius, the baleful star of legend, which appears only once in every two millennia, and whose appearance always presages doom. Showers of falling stars descended on the world at the moment of its appearance. Strangest of all, an eerie glow surrounded the great Black Pyramid.'

A look of recognition had appeared now on the face of Grimnar and some of his advisors. 'There was a battle there once…' the Great Wolf murmured.

'Aye,' Sternberg said. 'One in which your Chapter took part, alongside the armies of the Imperium against the alien eldar. Near two millennia ago.'

'The Balestar blazed down on that battlefield too,' Grimnar added. 'What is the significance of this?'

'That battle did indeed take place under the light of the balestar, and there was at the same time an outbreak of plague on Aerius, though not as virulent as that which afflicts the world now. It ended when the battle was won, which many took to be a sign of the Emperor's favour.'

'Go on.'

'When I reached Aerius much of the world had already been quarantined. There seemed to be nothing I or any of my advisors could do. Over the comm-net we could see pictures of the terrible effects of the plague. I decided to consult the Oracle of Chaeron, who resides in her ancient citadel on the surface of that dark moon.'

'I have heard of this oracle,' the Great Wolf said. 'A most holy woman, blessed by the Emperor. What did she have to say?'

'Her words were enigmatic, as always. In her temple chambers she told me: *The Balestar lights the sky once more, and the Unclean One's way to freedom. His ancient prison walls are near undermined and his pestilence is loosed upon the world.*'

'Enigmatic indeed.'

'Aye, Great Wolf. I asked her if the Unclean One might be bound once more…'

'And what did she say?' Grimnar asked eagerly.

'Her reply seemed equally unhelpful: *The eldar key, now three, must be made one again. To make the prison hold once more, it must be taken to the Black Pyramid's central chamber.*'

'One part of that riddle seems clear, at least,' said Logan Grimnar. 'She refers to the Black Pyramid, under the shadow of which that great battle was fought.'

'Aye, and that is less helpful still. For the pyramid has never been opened. Many have tried, using all the techniques known to the Imperium and never once have its walls been breached. Whatever sorcery its creators used is proof against all humanity's efforts.'

'Russ once said: *An undaunted spirit will find a path, though it leads through a forest of blades.*' Sternberg smiled.

'The Inquisition teaches its members that every question is an answer in hiding, every problem a solution in disguise.'

'Did you find your answer then, Ivan Sternberg?'

'I believe so. I fasted for three days and meditated upon the oracle's answer. I prayed to the Emperor for guidance.'

'Were you answered?'

'I believe so, for it came to me that perhaps I had misunderstood the oracle's words, for her voice is soft and her speech slurred with age. It seemed possible to me that she meant eldar key, not elder key.'

The Great Wolf exchanged a significant glance with Ranek and the other Wolf Priests. 'That would fit with our saga of the battle.'

Sternberg's smile widened and his manner became excited.

'Your Chapter, I am given to understand, has in its possession an artefact known as the Talisman of Lykos. It is a crystal, many-faceted, reddish in colour. It was taken in battle with the eldar two millennia ago after the battle on Aerius. It is a fragment of a greater whole, a talisman of great power, used by the eldar Farseers and destroyed during the final conflict.'

Grimnar cocked his head to one side and smiled coldly. His eyes were fixed on Ranek, the Rune Priest.

Ranek held his chieftain's gaze easily as he said, 'That is so, Great Wolf. Though I would give much to know how this outsider knows what lies in our Hall of Battles.'

'It is not a secret,' Sternberg said. 'Your Chapter are not the only people who keep records. The Inquisition, too, has extensive archives, and there was an inquisitor present when that trophy was taken. He recorded that it was given over to the safekeeping of the Space Wolves. I wanted to know more before I troubled you with a vaguely worded prophecy, Logan Grimnar, so I went immediately to Abramsas and consulted with the archivists of my Order. One part was given to the Wolves. One part was given into the keeping of the Imperial Guard Commander, Byran Powys, and one part was given to Inquisitor Darke. All of them had fought in the battle on Aerius.'

'What happened to the others?' Grimnar asked.

'Powys and his men returned to Galt. There is no record of what became of his part of the talisman. Inquisitor Darke and his starship, the *Epiphany*, were seen to make a warp jump into the outer systems, but never arrived at their destination. The only part of the Farseer's artefact whose whereabouts are certain is the part you hold.'

'Why do you think it is significant?' Ranek asked sharply.

'The eldar are an enigmatic people and not given to explaining themselves, but before he died, the Farseer referred to the arcane thing he carried as a "key".'

'And you have come to Fenris on the strength of this?' enquired Ranek. If the Great Wolf felt any annoyance at the way Ranek was interrupting the discussion he did not show it. Then again, Ragnar thought, it was the duty of his councillors to ask questions and to give advice.

'We both know, Brother Ranek, that the fate of entire worlds has been decided by things that seem less significant. Who am I to doubt the oracle's words? All I can do is pray that my interpretation of them is correct, and that I may save the people of Aerius.'

Sternberg paused a moment, then added: 'The oracle's words have been confirmed by seers of my own Order and by my own consultations with the Imperial Tarot.'

'The Tarot is notoriously ambiguous,' pronounced the chief Rune Priest, Aldrek. He ran one bony, claw-like hand through his long white beard. The metal raven on his shoulder cawed ominously.

'Just so, but my readings have been remarkably uniform, and at every consultation the same combination of cards has occurred. The Eye of Horus in combination with the Great Hoste, the Shattered World above the Emperor's Throne reversed. The Galactic Lens reversed.'

Once again there was an ominous silence from those gathered around the Great Wolf as they pondered the meaning of the inquisitor's words.

'That is a very bad combination of cards,' Aldrek said. 'It signifies great danger for the Imperium: the gathering of the powers of Chaos, the death of worlds.'

'I know this,' Sternberg said plainly. 'Which is why I am here.'

The ancient warriors around Grimnar exchanged glances. Ragnar wished he knew what they were thinking. Eventually Aldrek spoke.

'This is a very grave matter, Great Wolf. I ask permission to withdraw with my brothers and consult the runes.'

Grimnar nodded his assent and the Rune Priests withdrew towards their own chambers without further ceremony, their footsteps echoing off through the vast lair. Ragnar wondered what was going on. He knew almost nothing about the Imperial Tarot but it was obvious that his superiors were treating the inquisitor's words with the greatest concern. He felt it incumbent on himself to pay close attention to what passed here. Perhaps it was not the inquisitor who had caused his sense of foreboding earlier, but the knowledge he carried.

'We must await the deliberations of our Rune Priests,' Grimnar said. A look of disappointment must have passed across Sternberg's face, for the Great Wolf added, 'Only a fool ignores the wisdom of his advisors, Ivan Sternberg, and no Great Wolf can afford to be that.'

Sternberg nodded. 'Of course. I understand. I also believe that the runes will confirm what I have said.'

'I never for a moment doubt it, Ivan Sternberg. Still, while we wait we must eat. A feast of welcome has been prepared. And such a feast: I have not looked upon its like in a hundred years.'

'Then it must be a sumptuous banquet indeed, old friend, for I remember you and your companions as being the greatest trenchermen I have ever set eyes upon,' the inquisitor grinned.

'Let us go to table. Descriptions are all very well, but you cannot eat words.'

THE GREAT HALL was lit by a massive fire. Giant flambeaux, treated with some chemical process to make them burn brightly and for many hours, blazed in brackets set on the vast stone walls. Servants hurried about, carrying great platters which groaned under the weight of venison and boar and bread and cheese. Serving maidens brought great tankards filled with ale. Grimnar, Sternberg and his retinue all sat at one

large table, toasting each other between mouthfuls of food.
Ragnar and his companions sat at the Blood Claw table and
exchanged glances. It was obvious to Ragnar that his comrades
were all as baffled by the speeches of the inquisitor and the
Great Wolf as he was, but he could see that they were all just as
curious too. It had all sounded significant and ominous and
hinted at mighty deeds to come – deeds in which they themselves might play some part. Ragnar breathed an earnest prayer
to Russ that it would be so.

The young Wolf tore a hunk of breast from the chicken on
the table before him and stuffed it into his mouth, washing it
down with a swig of ale. The foam bubbled in his mouth. From
the corner of his eye he caught sight of the female inquisitor
staring at him and he coughed in surprise, sending a mouthful
of ale spraying over Sven.

'As always, you have some difficulty holding your bloody
drink, Thunderfist,' Sven growled at him. 'Perhaps you should
stick to milk. Everyone knows you prefer it.'

'The day I cannot drink you under the table is the day I will
do so,' said Ragnar immediately, casting his eye back in the
direction of the inquisitor. He was disappointed to note that
her gaze was fixed upon Sternberg and the Great Wolf once
more. However he saw that the Wolf Priest Ranek was now gazing at him significantly, and he looked away hurriedly.

'That sounds like a bet,' Sven said. 'Pity I can't bloody take
you up on it! I would not want to force you to forswear ale for
the rest of your life. That would be a punishment worse than
death.'

'Are you afraid?' asked Ragnar.

'Only for you. I will accept your bet but only if the forfeit is
that the loser must drink only milk for the next week. Wouldn't
want you to go the way of Torvald.'

Ragnar considered that that sounded fair. It meant that neither of them would be honour-bound not to touch ale for the
rest of their lives, a forfeit which would have been torment to
any Space Wolf. In the whole history of the Chapter only one
man had ever had to pay that ultimate price, Torvald the Mild,
and it was said that he had gone mad. Ragnar reached for the
jack to begin drinking but, before their match could begin, the
doorway to the Great Hall was flung open. The Rune Priests
had returned and their faces were grim.

They marched straight up to the main table and as their presence was noted, silence filled the chamber. All eyes focussed on them respectfully. Logan Grimnar cocked his head to one side. 'You have consulted the runes, brothers.'

It was not a question.

'We have consulted them, Great Wolf, casting them in the prescribed manner, as our forebears have done these past ten thousand years.'

'What did they reveal?'

'The future is cloudy and grim, Great Wolf.'

Nothing new there, Ragnar thought. Few prophets would ever get a reputation for folly by saying such words.

'But we believe we must grant Inquisitor Sternberg all the aid we can. It appears the menace of the Dark Enemy looms and it can only be forestalled by the use of this talisman which has been spoken of. That much is clear to us.'

Logan Grimnar considered these words for a moment. 'Then it pleases me to grant your boon, Ivan Sternberg,' the Great Wolf said, addressing the inquisitor. 'It appears that in doing so I may perform service for the Imperium and for my brethren.'

Inquisitor Sternberg nodded his appreciation. 'I thank you, Great Wolf.'

Ranek leaned forward and whispered something in the Great Wolf's ear. Logan Grimnar nodded and turned – and for some reason his piercing gaze fell on Ragnar for a moment. After three heartbeats, Grimnar's gaze swung back around and he nodded to Ranek. As the hubbub of the meal returned around him and he directed his attention to the meal once more, Ragnar thought nothing of it – but a few minutes later Ranek was at his shoulder.

'Brother Ragnar, I wish to speak with you,' the Wolf Priest commanded. 'Come to my chamber now.'

'Looks like you've weaselled out of the bet,' Sven said.

'There will be others,' Ragnar muttered, wondering what could be so important as to drag him and the Wolf Priest away from the feast.

CHAPTER TWO

'THIS IS AN important task, Brother Ragnar,' Ranek said emphatically.

Ragnar, standing at ease before the Wolf Priest, gazed around the chamber for a moment. It was not one of the larger rooms used by the Wolf Priests for meetings. It was not a sacred place at all, just a room in the Great Wolf's lair assigned for their use. No, more than that, Ragnar suddenly realised – it was a chamber assigned to Ranek. He could smell the old man's scent, which was as potent here as the scent of a wolf in its lair. All the other scent traces were faint by comparison. He looked at it with new eyes, looking for some insight into the personality of the old man.

'I believe you,' Ragnar said, 'but why are you giving it to me? Surely there are others who can perform it better. Why should I be the one to deal with these outsiders?'

Ranek, settled upon a stone seat before him, ran one grizzled hand through his long white beard. His keen blue eyes bored into Ragnar's. Ragnar forced himself to meet the old man's gaze despite the discomfort. 'You don't want to do this, do you, laddie?'

Ragnar scratched his head. It had been some time since the priest had called him that. It brought back memories of his very first meeting with the old man, what seemed a lifetime ago, when he had still been a barbarian living on an island lost amid Fenris's world-girdling oceans. 'No, sir. I do not.'

'Why not?'

It was a good question but Ragnar was not exactly certain of his answer. He really did not want to show the newcomers around the Fang, although he was actually quite curious about them, keen to know more about them. Why was he so reluctant to spend time with them? 'I would rather be training with my battle-brothers,' he managed.

'That's understandable, but you will still have plenty of time to do that.' Ragnar could tell from his scent that Ranek did not really believe him.

Ragnar shrugged and continued to study the Wolf Priest's room. It was no larger than a meditation cell, and it was spartanly furnished. There was a huge slab of granite which was used as a table, and the carved block of stone which the old man used as a chair. Thick furs were cast over it to pad the rock. Doubtless the Wolf Priest had hunted down the beasts himself. On the desktop sat a glowglobe, one of the eternally burning lights of the ancients. It was set into the skull of some suspiciously humanoid alien monster. Beside this puzzling artefact lay rolls of parchment and one of the feather-tipped stylos used by the Space Wolves when they had to write. Ranek followed Ragnar's gaze and understood.

'An ork,' he said, glancing at the skull. 'The greenskin was the first off-worlder I ever killed. I took its skull as a trophy. I was going to use it as a drinking cup.'

Ragnar looked at the old man fascinated. He had never heard this tale before. He wondered at the age of the skull. Given Ranek's age it must have been taken from its original owner centuries ago.

'Not a good idea. Wrong shape, really; the beer drains away through the eye sockets.' It took Ragnar a few moments to realise that the old man was making a joke. The priest bared his large fangs in a grimace that Ragnar knew was meant to be a smile. It vanished as quickly as it came. 'You haven't answered my question.'

Ragnar looked at him. 'I think I have.'

Ranek shook his head. 'You have spoken truth as far as it goes but you are not telling me all that you think.'

Ragnar smiled at the Wolf Priest this time. Ranek was too difficult to deceive. He might lack the thought-reading powers of the Wolf Priests but his disconcerting cold eyes could see into a man's heart with equal ease. Ragnar decided he would air his doubts. That was the way of his people.

'I have no real answer, lord. There is just something about these strangers that makes me uneasy. I don't quite know why but I sense a wrongness about all of this. I am not sure the Great Wolf should have granted them permission to come here. I do not think he should let them examine our trophies.' Even as he dared say them, a part of him wondered whether he should voice these doubts. Who was he, a mere Blood Claw, to question the judgement of the Great Wolf? On the other hand, it was the enshrined right of every Fenrisian warrior to speak his mind, and the Space Wolves were nothing if they were not Fenrisian warriors.

To his surprise, Ranek was standing straighter. His scent told Ragnar that the old priest was paying closer attention to him.

'You have doubts about the strangers?' Ranek asked.

'I know not, not for sure. Maybe about their mission. About something. There is something here that makes me uneasy.'

Ranek nodded, almost to himself. 'I agree with you.'

Ragnar was not surprised. He could sense something of the old man's moods from his scent. Reading scents was part of being one of the pack. It was what let the Space Wolves act with a co-ordination and precision that few other humans could match.

'Unfortunately the Great Wolf does not see eye-to-eye with me on this.'

Ragnar raised an eyebrow and altered his stance uneasily. Such dissension in the upper ranks was rare. No, he corrected himself; he did not know that. It appeared rare. Perhaps it was always there and he just did not have the opportunity to see it. He was a Blood Claw and in training, and he rarely mixed with the Chapter's mighty rulers. There were few opportunities to. They were out in the field for so much of the time; in comparison, he as yet had not gone much further than the Fang.

'Logan Grimnar trusts Inquisitor Sternberg. The inquisitor saved his life long ago and there is a debt of honour there.'

'Are you saying you do not trust him?' Ragnar dared. It was a bold question for a Blood Claw to ask someone as senior as the Wolf Priest but somehow Ragnar knew he would get an honest answer. Ranek smiled, but there was no warmth in the man's lined face.

'I trust him well enough,' he said. 'I have no doubt of his loyalty to the Emperor. There is no taint to him or to any of his retinue… but he is not one of us. He is not one of the pack and there are mysteries within the Fang that are only for us of the pack to know.'

Ragnar thought he knew what the Wolf Priest meant. There was a bond between those who had been initiated into the Wolves, who had passed through the Gate of Morkai and bore the geneseed of Russ within their bodies. It was something that no one else could share. These off-worlders were outsiders and more. They were not of the pack. They did not share the sense of place and group identity that every one the Chapter members did. Then another part of what the Wolf Priest had said to him sank in and he almost laughed.

'I am only a Blood Claw,' Ragnar said. 'I know very little of any mysteries.'

Ranek smiled back at him. 'Then you cannot give them away, can you?'

This time Ragnar did laugh, suddenly appreciating the old Wolf Priest's cunning. It was true: he could not reveal what he did not know. On the other hand, those who had progressed further into the Chapter would know more of the ancient mysteries, certainly – but was it really so likely that they would give them away to strangers? He voiced his question aloud.

'All too possible,' Ranek said. 'Inquisitors are good at ferreting out secrets. They cannot help it. It is their great yet unenviable task in life. I would go as far as to say that it is their life. It would take a warrior of great cunning to converse with them and be able to keep secrets.' His tone changed again and became utterly serious. 'And I have my doubts about what is going on here. I do not know why it should be, but I feel the same as you do. My instincts tell me that there is something dangerous afoot, something that threatens the Chapter. Ragnar, I want you to show these strangers about, and I want you to keep a real eye on them. Furthermore, I want you to come and tell me everything you see. You are quick and your senses are keen. This is why I have chosen you for the task.'

'Do you want me to report directly to you, lord?'

'Yes.'

'And nobody else? Not even the Great Wolf?'

'Only if he asks that you do so.'

'I will do as you command,' Ragnar said uneasily. He wondered what was really going on here. He sensed dissension within the high command, cross-currents in the sea of Chapter politics that he could only guess at. Perhaps the Wolf Priest was acting on instructions from the Great Wolf; perhaps he simply wanted Ragnar to believe that he was acting on his own initiative. Why that might be the case, Ragnar could not guess. Such speculations made his head spin, so he suppressed them. It was always easiest to stick with the simplest line of reasoning until that was proven wrong. Besides, in a way he was glad he had been chosen for the task. He was curious about the strangers… particularly the woman.

'Good,' Ranek said. 'Be open with them. Show them around. Tell them what you know.'

'And tell you what they ask about?'

Ranek nodded and gave a wide, fang-filled smile. Ragnar wondered what he was letting himself in for.

THE GREAT WOODEN door swung back and Ragnar ventured warily into the chambers assigned to the inquisitor and his retinue. Already they had changed their surroundings. The air smelled different, full of the cloying scent of incense and odd, subtle off-world perfumes. From deeper inside the chambers came the sound of voices chanting. A litany was being recited in Imperial Gothic, the standard language of the Imperium and all its liturgy. Somewhere the praises of the Emperor were being recited, over and over. The ancient words echoed around the hallway.

Heavy crimson brocade drapes had been hung up to cover the bare stone of the walls. Ragnar wondered how the fitting could have been made so quickly, until he saw that each section of cloth hung from a suspensor globe floating on its own antigravity field. He ran his fingers over the cloth. It was thick and soft, of far finer weave than anything produced on Fenris. Each vast rectangular section was trimmed with gold and precious stones, and emblazoned with the symbol of the Inquisition. Before him two enormous braziers burned – and between them stood two black-robed men. Huge cowls hid their faces. Bolt pistols were held in their hands. The left-hand sentry extended his open hand in a gesture that told Ragnar he was to stop.

'What is your business here?' the right hand sentry asked, almost as if they were not in the depths of the Fang. As if Ragnar had no right whatsoever to be there.

'I am Ragnar of the Space Wolves. I have been sent to act as Inquisitor Sternberg's guide to the Fang.'

The sentry spoke into a small brass device on a leather strap at his wrist. The words were framed in a language which Ragnar did not recognise, though that was hardly surprising; there were millions of tongues in the Imperium, and he spoke only the language of Fenris and Imperial Gothic, which had been drummed into his brain by the tutelary engines of the Fang. The Wolf waited, studying the strangers closely, annoyed by their arrogance but determined not to show it. He breathed in their scent. It was human but held many faint alien taints. It was the scent of men who had grown up eating different foods, breathing different air, under a different sky from the one under which he had been born.

'You may proceed, Ragnar of the Space Wolves,' the sentry said. The pair turned on their heels to leave an opening between them for him to pass through. It was performed with a discipline and a precision that Ragnar found almost amusing. Part of his education had concerned the military training of other Imperial units. He knew that they were addicted to marching and moving in formation and all manner of shows of discipline that the Space Wolves rarely indulged in and considered pointless ostentation. Of course, he had been led to believe, they in turn thought the Space Wolves barbaric. To each his own, Ragnar thought, moving forward.

One of the sentries fell in behind him, Ragnar not sure whether this was to show him the way or to escort him as if he were a prisoner. Two more dark-cowled guards had already emerged from the inner chamber, as if produced by a machine to take over their place, and they took over chaperoning duties. He could see how some visitors to an inquisitor might be intimidated by such behaviour. He might have been himself, had they not been in the heart of the Fang. Besides, he seriously doubted that these two warriors, well trained as they might be, could even slow him down when it came to a real battle. He was, after all, a Space Marine.

They arrived at the inner chamber and Ragnar saw that it had been partitioned off like the first with many drapes. It was like being in a huge multi-sectioned tent. It gave each person in the retinue some privacy; moreover, from a military standpoint, it altered the lay of the land, and might confuse any intruder for a few moments. Ragnar almost laughed at the thought. As if that could possibly stop the Wolves right in the middle of their own lair. He shook his head realising that he was being naïve. This arrangement was simply a standard procedure for these people, not some special set-up for here in the Fang. Perhaps in other places, on other planets, it would serve its purpose admirably. He decided to withhold judgement.

He was led by the two guards through a winding maze of cloth corridors. It did not trouble him. He could find his way through the labyrinth from memory if need be and, even if that had not been the case, it would be a simple matter to follow his own scent trail back to the exit. He realised that the layout was another clue about these off-worlders. They thought in terms of mazes and puzzles, of deception and trickery. Their thinking was most likely equally convoluted and circuitous.

As they proceeded through the structure, Ragnar noted the activities around him. In some of the curtained chambers, men meditated. In others scribes scratched away with stylos on the parchment pages of huge librams. Ahead of him, he could hear the clash of blade on blade. It sounded as if two people were engaging in combat practice.

The three of them stepped through an entrance where the hangings had been folded back and Ragnar could see that he had been correct. The salt smell of sweat and the hard acrid stink of aggression struck his nose with an almost physical assault. He twitched his nostrils and watched carefully. Inquisitors Sternberg and Isaan were sparring with each other on a padded combat mat. They were using a style he had never seen before, long cloaks held in one fist, knives in the other. They were using the cloaks as weapons, flicking them at each other to obscure vision, using them like nets to try and entangle the other. Ragnar watched in fascination.

They were both very skilled. Sternberg was larger and had the longer reach, but the woman was quicker and somehow she seemed able to anticipate the man's movements better. Sternberg faked a slash and stabbed forward, but she was no longer before him. Her cloak lashed out to entangle his legs. Looking at the way it moved Ragnar could tell it was weighted, designed to be used as a weapon. That too told him something about these people. They thought to conceal weapons even within innocuous items of clothing. He imagined that the weights sewn into those hems, whipped forward at the end of a cloak, might be able to knock a normal man out, perhaps even break his head, though he doubted they would have any effect on the reinforced skull of a Space Marine.

Sternberg leapt upward, letting the cloak pass beneath him but that was a mistake, Ragnar could tell. Taking even one foot off the ground usually was in close combat. It put a man off balance. Leaping into the air was worse. You had no purchase on anything. Isaan proceeded to demonstrate this admirably. Her straightened arm slammed into Sternberg's chest, sending him tumbling backwards. His fingers opened and the cloak tumbled to the floor. Ragnar thought him bested for a moment, but then realised that the truth was otherwise. As he hit the ground he rolled over, feet passing over his head, but even as he did so his newly freed arm slammed into the ground and his whole body rotated, bringing his feet into position to kick the legs from underneath the woman. She tumbled backwards onto the mat, and the man moved forward with a turn of speed he had not previously demonstrated, to end with his knife at her throat.

'Yield,' he said smoothly.

'I yield,' she panted. 'Good move, the last. I had thought you a little slow today.'

Ragnar studied them again, looking at Inquisitor Sternberg with new respect. He had obviously planned out the whole thing, lured his colleague into his trap and then swiftly implemented it. He had used his mind as a weapon as well as the knife and it was difficult to tell which was keener. Ragnar slapped his open hand against his breastplate in warrior's applause. Sternberg turned at the sound, and bowed to him with a smile.

Ragnar took a moment to study the inquisitor. Close up, the man looked as hard as a Wolf Priest. His hair was so grey it was

almost white but other than that he looked youthful. His skin
was tanned and his teeth were white and even. His eyes were
grey, calm and watchful. His smile was pleasant, even friendly,
but that friendliness never quite seemed to reach his eyes.

'Greetings, my friend,' Sternberg said evenly, despite his
recent exertions. 'What brings you here?'

'I have been sent to be your guide and to answer any questions you may have about the Fang.'

'And about what I came here to find?'

'I know nothing about such things – but I can take you to
those who may do.'

'Good,' the inquisitor said. 'I am most keen to start. Lives are
at stake and we do not have any time to waste.'

'Then let us seek out the archivists,' Ragnar said.

MATTERS WERE NOT going well, Ragnar thought. On the surface
the inquisitors seemed relaxed and charming but Ragnar could
tell by their scents that they were angry and frustrated. His nose
never lied about such things. No Space Wolf would be fooled
by their appearance, and the archivist, too, was a Space Wolf.
He, in turn, seemed to be responding to the visitors' suppressed
impatience with an anger of his own.

To distract himself from the swirl of emotions, Ragnar
gazed around this section of the Hall of Battles. One corner of
the vast chamber was filled by flickering viewscreens and the
huge brass and iron chassis of the ancient cogitation engine.
The air smelled of ozone and machine oil. The hiss of pistons
and the hum of capacitors reached his ears. In the walls were
countless niches filled with smooth stone tablets. Ragnar
knew that these were runestones, and that in some way
known only to the Iron Priests they stored great volumes of
information that the machine could read. The stones were a
near-indestructible repository of lore from throughout the
Space Wolves' history.

'It will take some time to find out what you require,' Archivist
Tal said testily. He was an elderly Wolf Priest, even older-look-
ing than Ranek but far less burly. Age seemed to have pruned
every fragment of spare flesh from his frame. His beard was
long and straggly. His one good eye was sunk deep its socket.
The green-tinged camera lens of a bionic device glittered in
place of its twin. Ragnar could see the inquisitor's face reflected

in its polished glass. When the archivist raised one hand the nails were so long they looked like talons.

'How much longer?' Sternberg asked him. His voice was calm, well-modulated. Had Ragnar not been reading the man's scent he would have detected no trace of impatience in it.

The archivist shrugged and the raven hopped from his shoulder and began to scrabble along the desk, before it flexed its wings and took off. Ragnar watched the bird go. For a moment it looked like a scrap of shadow under the vast cavern roof, then it disappeared into the gloom. This part of the Hall of Battles was not well lit and it smelled fusty with age. 'Who can say? I will notify young Ragnar when I come across the rune-stones pertaining to what you require. In the meantime it would be best if you returned to your chambers. Your presence here is merely a distraction.'

'The Great Wolf said that these people were to be given all the co-operation they required,' Ragnar said. He did not feel quite as calm as he sounded. The archivist was notoriously crotchety.

'It is not for you to remind me what the Great Wolf said, young Ragnar. My memory is quite good enough for that. I am the Keeper of Records. I can recall what he told me only yesterday. I am just saying that things would go quicker if I did not have people here asking me fool's questions and goading me with fool's statements.'

'I can see that,' Ragnar said tetchily.

'And I don't need any of your lip either, youngling. I am not so old that I can't administer a sound thrashing to any beardless cub that cheeks me.'

Ragnar looked at the old man sullenly. He seemed serious but it was hard to tell. The archivist was known to have a strange sense of humour. Age had made him somewhat eccentric; senile, some claimed. Ragnar breathed in the man's scent. There was some resentment there. Judging by his stance and his tone it was not directed at Ragnar but at the off-worlders. It seemed that the archivist, too, was reluctant to give up the secrets of the Space Wolves to people he did not know.

'Can you not at least give me some idea of how long?' Ragnar asked, now using the native tongue of Fenris, a speech that doubled as the secret battle language of the Space Wolves. He saw the archivist's good eye flicker once in the direction of Sternberg. His own gaze followed.

'As long as it takes,' said Tal. Ragnar caught what he was looking at too. No flicker of understanding passed over Sternberg's face. Presumably the inquisitor did not know their language, then. For some reason Ragnar found himself hoping that was the case.

'There are millions of runestones, Blood Claw, and the indexes are not necessarily all that reliable. Such procedures take time. You would do well to learn patience, as would your off-world companions.'

'I will bear that in mind,' Ragnar said sourly. 'I hope all of the people on Aerius who are dying learn patience too. The fate of a world hangs in the balance here.'

The archivist snorted. 'When you reach my age, youngling, you will realise that the fate of a world always hangs in the balance somewhere.'

'How much longer is this going to take?' Inquisitor Isaan asked, glancing around the Hall of Battles with impatience. She did not sound happy. Things were obviously not going quite as well as she had imagined.

'As long as it takes,' Ragnar said. He followed her gaze, oddly glad that Sternberg had not accompanied them, allowing him to be alone with the woman. Sternberg had shown far less interest in the wonders of the Hall than she and waited with the archivist.

The great statue of Oberik Kelman, 23rd Great Wolf of the Chapter, glared down angrily at the pair of them. Kelman had been a famously temperamental man, given to terrifying rages when frustrated. Just at the moment Ragnar thought he knew how the Wolf must have felt. He was struggling to keep his temper in the face of the inquisitor's impatience. It was not that he blamed her. He too would have liked to have seen quicker progress but he also felt that she blamed him, and her constant questioning of him would not make things happen any quicker.

'And how long precisely will that be?' Karah Isaan glared at him with cat-like green eyes. She was almost as tall as he was, brown skinned, with a pert nose and wide lips. Her hair was lustrous black. She was quite the most exotic woman he had ever seen, but right at this moment there was nothing remotely attractive about her.

'I can see why you are an inquisitor,' Ragnar replied. 'You do not easily abandon a line of questioning.'

'And once again you are avoiding giving me an answer.'

'The answer is plain, lady: I don't know. I am not an archivist. I am only here to be your guide.'

'And to be our watchdog.'

Ragnar looked at her, startled that she would suggest such a thing. In that tone of voice it was close to being an insult. 'Those are words I would call you out for, if–'

'If I were a man?'

Ragnar almost smiled. That was exactly what he had been going to say. The womenfolk of the islands did not fight, and he had no idea how to deal with a woman who behaved as if she were the equal of any warrior. Instead of speaking he merely grunted assent.

'I would not let that stop you,' she said. 'I have been trained to fight. All of my calling are.'

'I am sure. But it would be a most terrible breach of hospitality. We do not slay our guests.'

'You are very certain you could slay me.'

'Yes.' A simple statement of fact. 'I am a Space Marine.'

Another simple statement of fact. He was one of the mightiest warriors humanity could produce, enhanced in a hundred different ways, taught to kill in every way, bloodied in combat against the vile forces of Chaos. There was no way any normal mortal could stand in combat against him.

She smiled at him, showing small perfect teeth. It was a cold smile, with nothing friendly in it. She moved her hand. Ragnar sensed a gathering of energies, but was unsure of what was happening.

Then he tried to move and his limbs would not respond.

A psyker, he realised. She was a psyker, one of those witches gifted with extraordinary mental powers, one of which was now quite obviously the ability to paralyse any target she wished.

Ragnar suddenly felt very foolish... and very angry. He exerted his strength, willing his limbs to respond. Her arrogant smile grew wider and colder as she watched him struggle. This just served to make him angrier still. Somewhere in the dim depths of his mind, the beast that had been part of him since he became a Space Wolf began to snarl with frustrated rage. It did not like being caged, even if the cage was his own body.

Perhaps this was the threat he had sensed when the strangers had first appeared. Psykers were notoriously prone to possession by the daemons of Chaos. Perhaps even now one of them had wormed its way into the very heart of the Fang.

'Space Wolf, I could kill you now and there is nothing you could do about it,' she said calmly.

CHAPTER THREE

RAGNAR COULD ALMOST smell the woman gloating – and he was livid. He could not sense any other alteration in her scent. She did not appear to be tainted by Chaos. Perhaps, after all, she was simply doing all this to prove a point. Beads of sweat stood out on his brow as he forced his numb limbs to move. Time seemed to slow to glacial time as he urged his body to reject her hold on him.

One of his fingers quivered slightly and a look of utter shock appeared on her face, as if she had never seen anyone break her hold before, no matter how slightly. He smelled her sudden loss of confidence, and a faint flicker in the power as that affected her control. Suddenly, somehow, he could move. It was like being encased in molasses but at least his limbs were his own once more. He seemed to be moving with incredible slowness, but at least he was moving.

She let out a faint shriek. His hand was round her throat, almost before he had thought of it. With his superhuman strength all he had to do was close his fingers and her windpipe would be crushed.

'And now I could kill you,' he hissed. 'And there is nothing you could do about it.' He opened his hand and stepped back.

'But that would be neither honourable nor hospitable.'

They stood for a moment, glaring at each other. Both of them were breathing hard. He realised that the use of her powers must be as draining to her as hours of heavy exercise was to him. He himself was exhausted from resisting them as he had not been after a two hundred mile forced march.

'You are very strong-willed,' she said eventually, and he was not sure whether it was admiration, fear or dislike he smelled – perhaps some combination of them all.

'Apparently,' he said.

'And there is something else within you. I sensed it, as I wove the web.'

'Is that what you call it?'

'I saw something like a wolf: large, dark, fierce.'

'It was something woken when I joined the Chapter,' he said, not sure whether he should be discussing this with anyone from outside the Space Wolves. 'A Wolf Spirit.'

'No. It's part of your own spirit. Something that separates you from normal people.'

'It was bound to me.'

'I suppose that is one way of looking at it. Albeit a primitive way.'

'Now you are being insulting again.'

She smiled and this time there was some warmth in the smile. 'I do not mean to be. It is just that when you are a psyker you become very aware of things. One is that the way people see the world is the way the world is – for them. That doesn't mean that it is the way the world really is in an absolute sense.'

That was a concept of some sophistication but Ragnar thought he could see what she meant. He knew his own view of the world had changed radically since he had joined the Wolves. Once he had seen the world very differently, with the eyes of a Fenrisian barbarian. Now he looked at it with the altered eyes of a Space Marine. Perhaps it was possible that some day he would learn something that would supersede his current view of the world. It had happened once; he had to admit to the possibility that it might happen again. On the other hand, he did not want to follow this line of thought too closely. Down such paths lay heresy, not a fate any Space Marine wished to consider. 'Perhaps you are right. But do you know what the world is like, in an absolute sense?'

'You still have not answered my question,' she said. This time she sounded marginally friendlier and her smile held more warmth.

'If one method of questioning fails, you try another,' Ragnar said.

'And you find another means of evasion.'

'Truly I do not want to. I am not an archivist. I know there are many millions of runestones kept here in these Halls. Not all of them are catalogued by the Thinking Engines. Some records exist only in runescript inscribed on the tablets of stone themselves. Others are held only in the sagas memorised by the Wolf Priests.'

'There are gaps in the records of your auto-librams.'

Ragnar was not familiar with the term, but it sounded like she was referring to the Thinking Engines. He nodded thoughtfully.

'It is the same with us,' she continued. 'The machines are old, dating from the Dark Age of Technology, and their systems have been reconsecrated many times by the tech-priests of the Adeptus Mechanicus. Each time that happens, information is lost. There are flaws in the copying process. And, of course, much information is recorded under the individual seal of a specific inquisitor – and sometimes those seals are lost when the inquisitor dies and no one can then access his records.'

Ragnar looked at her. This was the most forthcoming he had ever seen any member of Sternberg's retinue. Something in her scent told him to be careful. Perhaps this was a trick the inquisitors used, confiding a little information to make the person they were talking to do the same. Not that it mattered very much, he thought. There was nothing here to hide – as far as he knew.

'And of course, some records are destroyed.'

Ragnar glanced at her in astonishment. 'Deliberately?'

'Yes.'

'Why?'

'Because the knowledge in them is deemed too dangerous for anyone to possess – because it might lead to heretical thought or heretical deed or because it pertains to certain things that were not meant to be known.'

'Who decides that?'

'The Masters of our Order. Sometimes individual inquisitors. Over the millennia the definition of what constitutes heresy has changed. Yesterday's blasphemy is today's orthodoxy. Surely it is the same with you?'

Ragnar just looked at her, mouth open with disbelief. He did not think that this was the way the Space Wolves looked at things at all! He could tell by the way that she tilted her head, and by the alteration of her scent, that even his lack of reply was considered an answer. He had told her something and it was being filed away in her memory for future use. To fill the silence, he said, 'We do not believe that is the case. We hold with the old ways from the time of Russ. The truths do not change.'

He stopped, realising even as he spoke that the silence had been another inquisitor's trick designed to make him talk. So simple, but so effective. He stopped again.

'You might think that is the case but I'm sure if you looked closely at the history of your Chapter you would see that it's not true.' A hint of challenge was in her voice. He wanted to respond instantly, to contradict her, but he could see that was what she wanted, another trick. He was starting to understand the game. Well, he could play it too. 'Do you always interrogate people?'

She smiled and lowered her gaze, then shook her head. Her laughter was quiet and self-mocking. 'You are good at this,' she said. 'I see why they gave you to us.'

Clever people often saw subtlety where there was none, Ragnar thought to himself – and then wondered if that was really the case. Was Ranek being subtler than he had imagined by doing this? Was that the reason he had been chosen for this task? Was Ragnar's presence some sort of elaborate trick, designed to make the inquisitors think one thing, while another happened? Or was it he, Ragnar, who was now being overly subtle? It was enough to make his head spin.

'Yes,' Inquisitor Isaan said. 'I always interrogate people. It is what I was trained to do. Trained all of my life the way you are taught to fight and kill. Trained in such a way that interrogating people is part of my thought pattern and habits. Trained in a way that makes it automatic and unstoppable.'

'You sound a little bitter.'

'Maybe I am. A little.'

And maybe you're not, Ragnar thought. Maybe this, too, is just another pose to win the confidence of the people you are talking to. He began to see how being with the inquisitor was starting to infect his own thoughts. He was starting to think with a subtlety and deviousness that was not normal for him.

'I am not sure I would like to live in your world,' he said eventually.

'Someone has to. Someone has to find the Emperor's enemies just as someone has to slay the Emperor's foes.'

'There is truth in what you say.'

'Always, if you look for it. That, too, is part of being an inquisitor.'

'You would know more about that than me,' he said with decision. Then another thought occurred to him. 'You are a psyker. Why do you not simply lift the knowledge you need from other people's minds?'

She smiled again, this time coldly, as if this was a subject she did not care to discuss. 'Some psykers have that gift, but not I, my talents run in... other directions. Even for those with the gift it is not that simple. A strong-willed individual can resist them. More subtle ones can mask their thoughts or even send false thoughts. And there are other risks...'

'Risks?'

'Yes. Those who enter the minds of heretics often become heretics in turn. Their very thoughts are a contagion.'

'There are more ways of entering the minds of heretics than by simply reading their thoughts. I would have thought that trying to understand them could lead you down the same path. At least, so we are taught.'

'There is wisdom in that,' the inquisitor said. Silence fell between them for a long moment.

They walked back to the part of the hall where Inquisitor Sternberg waited for the archivist to do his work.

Ragnar could tell by the way the man was standing that he had not yet got what he came here for. Perhaps it was time to try a distraction, he thought.

And he believed he knew just the thing.

'AND WHERE ARE we going?' asked Inquisitor Sternberg.

Ragnar could hear the beating of the man's heart, strong and regular. He shook his head and the noise disappeared into the background, became one with the hum of the grav-pod as it flashed upward through the elevator shaft towards their destination.

Questions, always questions, thought Ragnar. It was all these people ever seemed to think about.

'You shall see in a moment.'

'This one is not an easy one to get answers from,' Karah Isaan said. Her hand flickered in an intricate gesture. Some sort of secret sign language, obviously, like the one the Space Wolves themselves used in certain circumstances.

Sternberg shook his grizzled grey head and his smile widened. 'That's something of a compliment coming from an inquisitor,' he said.

Ragnar sensed the change in his scent and studied the man closely. It was an attempt at humour, even friendliness. He was watchful. He felt he was getting the measure of these people now. Even friendliness was a weapon to them, just one weapon in their arsenal, one of the many techniques they used to get information from people. Ragnar did not know why this made him wary. He had nothing to hide. They were on the same side. Both were soldiers in the service of the Emperor of Mankind. Yet there was something about them that made him want to keep his guard up, a sense of duplicity, of hidden motives cunningly concealed, that was alien to his culture and to his experience. Perhaps it was simply part of their exoticness, but he did not particularly like it. And perhaps it was this deeper sense of threat that still tugged at his brain. He did not know why he felt it, but it was there.

He tried to push that thought aside. Perhaps it was the nature of their work. Inquisitors were the investigating agents of the Imperium, trained to detect threats to the security of the human realms, hidden and unhidden. They lived in a world of concealment and secrecy, of duplicity and darkness. Living in that sort of world must have some effect on them, help turn them into what they are.

'Why will you not answer?' Sternberg asked. He smiled as he said it. This was all part of the game for him.

'I think you will realise why when we get there.'

'It's some sort of surprise, then,' Karah suggested.

'It is difficult to conceal anything from two such clever inquisitors as you,' Ragnar said with just a trace of irony.

'Humour? From a Space Marine? Who would have expected that?' said Sternberg. There was a trace of irony in his voice too, Ragnar noted.

At that moment the gravpod stopped. The light within flickered from red to green. A soft chiming note sounded and the door swished softly open. They walked forward into a massive chamber, part of a natural cavern in the flank of the Fang, one side of which had been walled off with translucent crystal. The only illumination came from the inside of the grav-pod and the cold light of the stars visible through the armourglass of the window. The sky was black. The moon was visible.

'Is it a projection?' Karah asked. 'It is daytime, yet the sky is as dark as night.'

'I think I understand,' Sternberg said softly, 'and I think I know why our young friend did not tell us where we were going.'

He stepped forward into the room and the other inquisitor followed. As they advanced towards the edge of the room, Ragnar was rewarded with their gasps of wonder and the change in their scents that told him they were genuinely astonished. In a way it was gratifying to think that he could still show two such far-travelled and cynical souls something that would excite their sense of wonder. It also meant that he felt some kinship with them, for there was something special about this place which always astounded him too, no matter how many times he came here – and he had come here often since he had become a Blood Claw and authorised to enter certain of the restricted areas of the Fang.

He joined them at the window, and looked down upon the world. Quite literally, the whole horizon was filled by the curved mass of Fenris. It shimmered against the cold darkness of space. This part of the mountain, high up near the peak, projected right above the atmosphere, and gave a view over a vast swathe of the polar continent of Asaheim. Below him he could see the swirling of clouds, the lesser mountains, the glaciers and the lakes as if laid out on a slightly arched map. The slopes of the mountain tumbled away beneath them to vanish into a sea of clouds far below.

'I have often heard it said that the Fang is one of the true wonders of the Imperium,' Sternberg said in a voice hushed and full of awe. 'And now I understand why.'

'It is truly beautiful,' said his female companion. From their scents Ragnar could tell they were both sincere.

'Thank you for showing us this place, Ragnar,' Sternberg said. 'For as long as I live I will remember this moment.'

Ragnar felt his smile vanish suddenly. He did not doubt that what the inquisitor said was true. It was also that he felt that nothing the inquisitor saw would ever go unrecollected. Ragnar suspected that they were trained to remember everything the way he was trained to fight.

Memory, too, was one of their tools, he thought. No – one of their weapons. He could see he was going to have some difficulty trusting these people.

THE CLEAR, bell-like tone sounded in Ragnar's ear. He came instantly awake, moving from strange dreams of off-world conflict to the dim shadowy light of his cubicle instantly. Responding to his movement the glowglobes brightened. He reached for his comm-net earpiece, which lay on the hewn slab of rock beside the pallet on which he slept. He pushed it into place then pressed the subvocaliser into position on his throat.

'Ragnar. What do you want?'

'I have found the thing your off-world friends were looking for.' The archivist's voice sounded high and cracked, even over the fuzzy tones of the comm-net.

'I will notify them at once,' Ragnar said.

'You do that.'

THE AIR STANK of ozone and machine oil. The sound of great pistons made the air vibrate. Huge arcs of Universal Fire leapt from massive conduction coil to massive conduction coil. A nimbus of light surrounded the great Thinking Engine. Iron Priests bellowed chants designed to propitiate the ancient spirits trapped within the machine and bind its power to their purpose. One of them tapped something on a keyboard so old that most of the ceramite keys had been replaced with others carved from black basalt or whale tusk ivory. A junior Iron Priest slapped cooling unguents onto the machine from a ceremonial urn. Ragnar guessed that if the Engine grew too warm, the spirits within would grow angry and seek to escape – but that was only a guess, he really knew very little about the mysteries of the Machine Spirits. He was glad to leave the whole ritual in the capable hands of the Iron Priests, Emperor watch over them.

One of them fed a smooth black runestone into a brass orifice in the machine. The lights grew brighter, the scents more intense.

Suddenly there was a sound like a small bolter starting to fire and from a slot in the side of the machine a long scroll of parchment began to unroll. Ragnar could see that runic characters covered the page. Ragnar hoped that the archivist was correct. He risked a look at the small slab of black marble which had been dropped into a restraining slot on the machine's side. Even as he watched, the runes along its top, which had previously been invisible, lit up, shedding a light that reminded Ragnar of molten steel. All they spelled out was a cryptic mass of numbers and letters.

The scroll unwound for an age. Ragnar looked over at Sternberg and Isaan and smelled their impatience. The man in particular seemed almost feverish. There was a gleam in his eye which made Ragnar think of someone whose weird had come upon him. Or perhaps of someone who was approaching a long cherished goal. Beads of sweat were visible on his forehead. The woman hid her impatience better but Ragnar could see she was tense. She pressed her palms together and closed her eyes. Her lips moved slightly and Ragnar knew she was muttering the words of a prayer or meditation exercise. He did not understand the words but the tone was unmistakable.

Eventually the scroll stopped unwinding and the Iron Priest stepped solemnly forward. Making a gesture of benediction in the direction of the engine of the Ancients, he tore the paper loose, rolled it up gently and handed it to the archivist. He, in turn, unrolled it on the metal-shod desktop, studied it closely and then stamped it with the seal he kept at his belt.

The old archivist nodded once, cackled loudly, rolled it up again and handed it to Ragnar. 'This is what you are looking for,' he said. Before Ragnar could reply, he turned and walked away. Ragnar handed the scroll to Inquisitor Sternberg. The man unrolled the scroll, looked at it, smiled sickly and handed it back to Ragnar. The Wolf was suddenly aware that the metal masks of the Iron Priests were all watching him. He was uncomfortably aware of their scrutiny. He gently unrolled the scroll and studied it. The words had all been burned onto the page in some peculiar fashion but they all seemed perfectly clear to him – then in a flash realisation came. The scroll was written in Fenrisian runescript, which the inquisitors could not read.

'Would you like me to translate this for you?' Ragnar asked. Sternberg nodded. 'It might take some time. The language is archaic and poetical. Some of the terms look a little obscure.'

'By all means take whatever time you deem necessary,' the inquisitor said coldly. 'We have plenty of it.'

Ragnar could hear the sarcasm in his voice and smelled his anger and his impatience. He knew he had better get to work quickly. Every second of delay might mean thousands of lives lost to the plague.

RAGNAR SAT cross-legged in his cell and ciphered out the words. The story had all his attention now. It was a record of a campaign fought against the alien eldar some two thousand years before, written by the long dead Space Wolf, Brother Jorgmund. Ragnar was struck by the fact that of all the great inventions with which the Emperor had gifted humanity, writing was perhaps the most important and the most under-rated. By using it he was communing with a man dead for nearly two millennia, hearing his words, grasping his thoughts. It was a minor miracle to which he had never before given thought.

He proceeded with the translation, surprised at how well he handled the process. The tutelary engines had done the work of burning Imperial Gothic into his brain well. Only rarely did he struggle to find exactly matching words and phrases as he turned the words from Fenrisian into the tongue of the Imperium.

The tale of the campaign was long and involved. For reasons known only to themselves, the eldar had attacked the Imperial world of Aerius. Brother Jorgmund thought it was typical of these treacherous alien humanoids that they struck without warning, dropping from space in their oddly constructed ships, brutally massacring Imperial soldiery and then ringing around the great Black Pyramid with their forces while their sorcerer leader, Farseer Kaorelle, worked his sinister magic. It was during a particularly ill-omened time. The balestar glittered in the sky and plague ravaged the world.

The Space Wolves had responded to the call for a crusade to push the eldar from the surface of a world that rightfully belonged to humanity. They had descended with chainsword and boltgun to cleanse their foul presence from the world. The fighting had been particularly bitter around the Pyramid where the eldar sorcerer had used his most potent magic. According to Jorgmund, the Rune Priests claimed that the Black Pyramid was some sort of nexus of strange mystical forces. He also noted a local legend that it had been built by the eldar back in the mists of time.

After several battles in which the defenders of humanity gained the upper hand, the sinister aliens refused to reveal their purpose. Instead they proceeded with their arcane rituals. What might have happened had they been allowed to complete them, only the Emperor upon the Golden Throne might have been able to foresee. Instead, at the climax of their ritual, the Space Wolves aided by elements of the Inquisition and the Imperial Guard, had managed to break through their defensive perimeter, overwhelm the Farseer's guards and seize the instruments with which the aliens were manipulating vast flows of psychic power.

As they died, the vile alien scum had shrieked that the Space Wolves were making a terrible mistake and that their folly would be the undoing of all the races of the galaxy. Ignoring the villainous lies of the eldar magi, the Space Wolves had taken possession of the alien talisman central to the magical ritual. Fortunately during the great conflict it had been broken into three separate parts, and whatever powers it possessed had become dormant. The Space Wolves had taken one of the segments of the broken artefact. The others had been taken by an inquisitor and the Imperial Guard regiment from Galt as trophies of another great Imperial victory.

Examination of the fragment of the ancient alien talisman by the Chapter's rune priests had revealed that the artefact possessed sorcerous powers of a great and unknown sort. The process of examination would continue at some future date; in the meantime, other duties called the Chapter, and so the talisman was entombed in the Vaults of Victory to await further examination. That was the last reference Ragnar could find to it.

He leafed hastily through the rest of the scroll but it dealt with another campaign against orcs in the Segmentum Obscura. There were no further references to the Talisman of

Lykos. He finished the translation and marked the parchment with his personal rune. It was time to take this information to Sternberg. So far everything the inquisitor said had been confirmed by the records.

Ragnar could not see how finding the talisman might help the people of Aerius, but he realised that this was more the inquisitor's field than his. He was a warrior, not an adept at dealing with sorcery.

ONCE MORE Ragnar found himself in the Great Wolf's chambers. Beside him stood Henrik Sternberg and Karah Isaan. The two inquisitors looked calm and relaxed, but Ragnar could smell their nervousness. He did not blame them. The Great Wolf was a presence to make the bravest quail.

'We have found the information we sought, Logan Grimnar,' Inquisitor Sternberg said.

'I am glad we could aid you,' the Great Wolf replied.

'I have a second boon to ask.'

'And what would that be?'

'I wish to see this ancient talisman, to ascertain it is the thing we seek.'

The Great Wolf raised an eyebrow. He leaned forward in his chair. 'I suspected that might be the case. I have already commanded the Rune Priests to open the Vault for you. I see no reason why we should delay your quest any further.'

'I thank you, Great Wolf,' Sternberg said with a small bow of his head.

RAGNAR WATCHED the small group from the edge of the chamber. No one had commanded him to attend the ceremony but then again, no one had told him not to. He had been ordered to accompany the inquisitors whenever they went abroad in the Fang, and as far as he was concerned, that was his duty until his orders were countermanded. So he had every reason to be there. Besides, he was curious.

They were deep below the Fang in a place which had obviously not been visited for hundreds of years. The chamber was perhaps a hundred strides across, the ceiling as high as five men. The walls were roughly hewn from the stone, so roughly hewn in fact that Ragnar suspected that the chamber might once have been a cave. The air smelled fusty. The only scent aside from their own belonged to the automated drones which performed maintenance in the area. Ragnar recalled the approach to this place, along miles of corridor. Every ten paces or so, huge armoured blast doors, marked with the seals of ancient warriors, had lined the way. The Rune Priests had led them unerringly to this one place, and with a wave of their hands and a muttered incantation had broken the seal and opened the door.

Inside they had found a chamber with an even heavier blast door. It was obvious that whatever was held within this chamber was to be well-protected – or well-sealed, Ragnar had thought.

Now the Rune Priests were chanting once more, while two of them turned the huge windlass that opened the second door. The inquisitors and the Great Wolf watched them in silence, their scents and their body language communicating an attitude of reverence. Nearby, the Great Wolf's honour guard of warriors stood at the ready. Ragnar could tell from their scents that they were almost as curious as he was, although their postures communicated nothing but an echo of their lord's reverence, and a readiness to spring into action in a heartbeat, even here in the deepest and most secure part of the Fang.

Ragnar was glad of this. For as the huge bulkhead creaked open, an eerie glow leaked through the ever-widening gap and fell upon the people in the chamber. Shadows danced away, as if seeking shelter in the darkest corner of the room. When the light fell on him, Ragnar thought he felt his skin tingle for a moment. The hairs on the back of his neck stood on end. A palpable sense of barely contained power filled the air.

Looking through the opening, Ragnar could see into a smaller chamber, just as irregularly walled as this one. In that chamber was a dais; on that dais was a plinth; on top of that plinth was a crystalline case. From within that case came the eerie glow. Even as he watched, the shimmering faded. Either his eyes were adapting to the light or the power which had caused the glow was fading somewhat. As it did so, the source of the glow became obvious. It was a gem, about the size of a hen's egg but multifaceted, cut by a jewelsmith of incredible skill. The others strode into the room. Drawn by the sight of the thing, Ragnar followed. No one objected.

They moved closer to the crystal case, Ragnar as close behind them as he dared. Everyone seemed so distracted by the sight of the talisman that they had forgotten all about his presence.

This close, his keen eyes could see that the jewel was set in an intricate frame of gold. The frame was marked with odd eldar runes which Ragnar could not decipher. It was attached to a chain of some silvery substance he had never seen before. It was obviously intended to hang around someone's neck. Probably one of those alien sorcerer priests he had heard of. Part of the frame was broken and he could see, too, that the gem it contained had roughly shattered edges on two sides. Where the talisman had broken apart, Ragnar realised.

It was not the talisman's appearance that was the most striking thing about it. It was the aura of power that surrounded it. No one looking upon it, or standing in the same chamber with it, could possibly doubt that this was an object of vast significance. Ragnar knew he was no psyker but he could feel the energies pulsing and seething within the thing. Unbidden, a vision of an alien mage, inhumanly tall with an oddly elongated physique, clad in ornate ritual garb, sprang into Ragnar's mind. The talisman glittered on his throat.

Ragnar heard Inquisitor Isaan gasp. She looked pale and a little frightened. Ragnar knew she was a psyker and most likely much more sensitive to the emanations of the thing than he was. He wondered, if it was having this strong an effect on him, what it must be doing to her.

Without being bidden to do so, Inquisitor Sternberg reached out and slid open the crystal case. He reached in and lifted the talisman by its chain. His face wore a look of reverence. With visible reluctance he handed it to Karah.

She took it by the chain, and as it passed to her, the glow returned. She stopped for a moment, frozen, then shook her head. She seemed a little dazed but she passed her hand near the crystal and nodded.

'Is it the amulet we seek?' Sternberg asked her quietly.

'Yes. Of that, there can be no doubt. It is a thing of power. Its aura is very strong and many of the impressions are confused. But I can tell you one thing.'

'What?'

'In order to use it, we need to possess all of the parts. There are strong psychic connections between this object and its kin.

I believe I could use it to locate the others. Given time. And possession of this one.'

She and her fellow inquisitor turned as one to regard the Great Wolf. Ragnar knew exactly what they were going to ask.

RANEK THE WOLF Priest strode up and down the chamber, pacing back and forth like a caged beast. 'I do not like this at all,' he was saying.

'I can see that,' said Ragnar. 'But the Great Wolf has already given his permission.'

'And that is that, eh? The outworlders come here, ask for one of our ancient treasures, an artefact of monstrous power, hidden from elder days, and Logan Grimnar just says "yes".'

'It is not that bad,' Ragnar said. He did not like arguing with the Wolf Priest but he felt compelled to defend the Great Wolf's decision. And not just because one of its consequences elated him. 'They are our allies in the service of the Emperor. They are proven and worthy warriors, and fell foes of the enemies of the Imperium.'

Ranek's lips quirked a little cynically, Ragnar thought. 'And besides, you get to go with them, off-world, as one of the talisman's guardians, don't you, young Ragnar?'

'I am one of the honour guard,' Ragnar admitted.

'Well, at least Grimnar has put Sergeant Hakon in command,' Ranek said sourly.

Ragnar was not so sure he liked the sound of that. His memories of Sergeant Hakon, the former instructor at Russvik, were not exactly fond ones. Hakon was a hard man, sometimes cruel. Still, thought Ragnar, he was an able warrior and a good commander. Ragnar did not have to like him to respect him. He was not going to let anything spoil this day for him. He was filled with excitement at the imminent prospect of going off-world, of venturing out beyond his home system on one of the great ships which plied the endless lanes between the stars.

CHAPTER FOUR

RAGNAR ALMOST LAUGHED aloud as he watched the great shield of the world drop below the horizon, remembering the way he had arrived at the Fang, what seemed half a lifetime ago. Once more he was strapped into the couch of a Thunderhawk gunship. Once more he was passing beyond the atmosphere of his homeworld. Once more he was watching the planet fall away beneath him.

Only this time it was different. This time he was not on a short hop designed to put him down somewhere else on the planet's surface. This time he was heading out into the depths of space, to where the inquisitors' ship waited in orbit. This time, he was going to leave his homeworld behind and go somewhere unimaginably distant from Fenris. Furthermore, it was possible, he had to admit, that he would never return. That knowledge made his departure all the more poignant.

He looked down onto the surface of his home planet with an emotion he had never really felt before, a feeling somewhere between love and longing almost. He watched clouds scud over the vast ocean and glimpsed islands through the gaps in the vapour. He recognised some of them in outline from the maps and globes he had studied in the Fang. He knew that he would not be able to pick out his home island, the place where he had grown up, fallen in love and finally fallen in battle, only to be resurrected into the ranks of the Space Wolves. It was simply too small.

It occurred to him that quite soon he might feel the same way about Fenris. It was only one world but there were millions of such worlds in the Imperium, separated by thousands of light years of distance. He had heard it said that if a man could visit one new world in the galaxy every day of his life, he would not have visited a thousandth of the inhabited worlds by the time he died.

For a moment a sense of his own smallness in the vast scheme of things filled Ragnar. He closed his eyes and breathed a silent prayer both to the Emperor and to Russ to watch over him and his companions, then smiled. Cold comfort there. Both were chill distant gods, remote from man, their duties performed on a scale that gave them little time to watch over tiny specks like him. They gave men courage and strength and cunning at birth, then expected them to forge their own destinies.

The moment of weakness and loneliness passed, to be replaced by a feeling of excitement about the approaching journey. He could scent that his brothers from the Blood Claw pack shared both his excitement and his unease. He could taste both in the slightly metallic air. He was reassured by the presence of so many recognisable scents. He was proud that he was one of the five who had been chosen to accompany Sergeant Hakon and guard the ancient talisman. And he had to admit that if he had chosen his companions himself, these would have been the ones he would have picked. It was reassuring to have his pack-brothers around him, to feel part of something larger than himself. He was glad of the presence of even those brothers he did not like as people – and in that moment, was certain that they felt the same way about him.

He opened his eyes again and glanced around the darkened compartment of the Thunderhawk, able to distinguish his comrades even in the subdued light of the dimmed glow-globes. Seated next to him was Sven, muttering and cursing to himself, and grumbling about his hunger. His coarse features were twisted into a snarl, his stubby fingers locked together as if in prayer. He grunted and belched, then looked over at

Ragnar and winked. 'Silent but bloody deadly,' he muttered, and then Ragnar noticed he'd farted. The stink was awful for a moment in that enclosed space. Such was the keenness of Ragnar's senses that he could distinguish the varying scents of what Sven had had for breakfast that morning.

'Fish gruel and black bread,' Ragnar said, without meaning to.

'Always a good base for a gas attack,' Sven muttered cheerfully. A bright gleam entered his eye. All of the Blood Claws were having some difficulty adjusting to the awakening of the Wolf Spirit within them. In Sven it took the form of this constant talking to himself and mumbling.

'I don't think the engines need any more thrust,' Nils murmured from the seat behind. 'We're going quite fast enough. I swear, though, that Sven rose two finger's breadths out of his seat.'

'You're just jealous,' muttered Sven. 'You can't match my awesome power.'

'It's Sven's secret weapon when we have to fight aliens,' Ragnar said, knowing this was all so childish, but unable to stop joining in with their banter. 'He's going to gas them to death.'

'Better make sure he doesn't do for us first,' said Nils. 'I know our implants are supposed to let us adapt to poisons but that was beyond a joke. My head is still swimming.'

'In the name of Russ, be quiet,' dark-haired Lars murmured from the other side of him. 'Can you children never be serious? I can barely meditate for all your chatter.'

'Yes, your holiness,' Sven said and farted again to let Lars know what he thought of his complaint. In truth, all of the young Blood Claws were becoming a little tired of Lars and his constant carping. In him the Wolf Spirits seemed to have fostered an excessive humourless devotion to the religious aspects of their calling. If any Space Wolf could be called ascetic, it would be Lars. Rumour had it that he was going to be tested again for nascent psychic powers by the Rune Priests. He had been having dreams recently and visions which some thought might be prophetic – but which Sven and Nils put down to too much meditation and fasting.

'He did. He took off. I saw him,' Nils insisted, smirking. 'And I swear I felt the ship accelerate.'

'That wasn't funny the first time,' Strybjorn growled suddenly down the line at them. Ragnar flinched a little at the sound of his old rival and enemy's deep, powerful voice. He still did not like Strybjorn, even though he had saved the fellow's life on their last mission, and his instincts almost rebelled at the thought of having a deadly rival alongside him. Still, of all the men in the Blood Claw pack, these were the ones he knew best. He had trained with them, fought with them, messed with them, and they were as close to him now as his flesh and blood kin once had been.

He glanced along the row of shaven heads, each with the one long strip of hair across the skull that was the mark of the Blood Claw, down the vaulted chamber, towards the front of the craft. He could not say that the people up there were his kin. Right at the front of the craft, close to the command deck, Inquisitors Sternberg and Isaan were strapped into old leather gravity chairs. Between them was the lead-lined casket containing the fragment of the Talisman of Lykos. They had decided to accompany it in the Thunderhawk rather than return to their ship with their own people.

Beside them sat the head of the honour guard, Sergeant Hakon. His scarred face was an impassive mask. His back was rigid. He looked ready to fight at any time. As if feeling Ragnar's gaze, he glanced backward at where the Blood Claw and his companions sat. One look from those harsh grey eyes was enough to cow them all into silence. All of them remembered him well from Russvik and few indeed, even the irrepressible Sven, were willing to risk his displeasure.

Ragnar closed his eyes and began the first of many meditation exercises to clear his mind. Around him he sensed the others doing the same.

THE FIRST GLIMPSE of the inquisitors' spaceship was a disappointment. Ragnar opened his eyes when he felt the Thunderhawk begin to decelerate and a mild discomfort in his inner ear told him that the craft was engaged in some sort of manoeuvre. He glanced through the thick, scratched plexiglass of the porthole and noticed that there was a tiny sliver of metal gleaming in the distance, barely visible even to his keen eyes in the blackness of space. As he peered, it began to swell in his field of vision, growing rapidly as they approached it.

Ragnar began to appreciate that in space distances were deceptive. There were no landmarks to give scale to what you were seeing. As the inquisitors' ship began to grow, and kept on growing and growing in his sight, he suddenly realised how big it really was. Gasps from around him told him the others did too.

The thing was a flying mountain, a huge wedge of steel and ceramite which dwarfed the Thunderhawk the way a whale might dwarf a minnow. As they neared it, the Space Wolf could see that it bristled with enormous weapons. Huge turrets and emplacements bulged in its side. The Imperial eagle painted on its meteor-pitted flanks was almost a thousand strides across. Beneath it, in Imperial Gothic script, were painted the words *Light of Truth*. Ragnar guessed it was the ship's name. Ragnar had never seen any work of man which gave the impression of enormous power that this starship did. It made his heart beat faster to think that this was the work of mere humans, and under his breath he muttered a short benediction to the Emperor of Mankind.

Smaller spacecraft hovered around the behemoth, coming and going like the shoals of small fish that surrounded an orca. Ragnar watched amazed as their running lights flickered past in the darkness like so many swiftly falling shooting stars. He saw the others lean forward to look in amazement too – all, that is, except the two inquisitors and Sergeant Hakon, who looked as bored and unexcited as people who had witnessed such wonders a million times. Their scents told Ragnar that was true; they had.

Slowly the Thunderhawk rotated around its axis and the great starship slid smoothly from view to be replaced by the vast field of stars once more. A warning bell tolled to announce their imminent arrival at their destination. The sensation of weight returned. Ragnar felt as if a great powerful hand were pushing him into his seat as they decelerated.

Below them the sides of the starship became visible again, a plain of metal and ceramite from which rose turrets and pipes and gratings. Warning lights winked as they rotated so they were landing flat onto the surface of the spacecraft. Jets of gas erupted from funnels and became floating crystals of ice in the chill of space. Ragnar remembered from his basic training that it was cold enough out there to freeze an unprotected man in mere seconds. It was something he had never really considered until that moment, and he was suddenly glad of the ancient armour which covered his body.

The Thunderhawk was on its final approach now, and momentarily it went dark as they raced down through a huge metal cave in the side of the ship. Ragnar was thrown forward and held in place only by the restraining straps as the ship came to rest. The vibration passing through the Thunderhawk told him that somewhere a huge airtight doorway was sliding into place. Looking through the thick porthole, he could see vapour rising like mist all around them and patches of rime congealing on the gunship's side. Air was being pumped into the landing bay and freezing on contact with the ship's sides which were much colder at that moment than the ice floes of Fenris.

Another bell sounded, telling them it was all clear and safe to disembark without protection. The airlock door swished open and for the first time Ragnar caught the strange sterile scent of the interior of a starship. He caught the tang of thousands of alien aromas, things he could not quite place, mixed with the scent of machine oil, technical unguents and cleansing incense. He heard the clamour of voices, the whirr of unseen machinery and the constant drone of recyclers which pumped air around the ship while cleaning and purifying it. He realised that he was now living in a totally separate, self-contained world, floating free in space, made ready to go anywhere the inquisitors commanded.

He suddenly felt very far from home indeed.

SOLDIERS GREETED THEM as they exited the ship. They were clad in black uniforms similar to those worn by the Imperial Guard but marked with the sigil of the Inquisition. Ragnar knew that these were Guardsmen seconded to the inquisitors' service for the duration of his mission. Even though they were drawn up in tightly disciplined ranks, they did not impress him. He had a young Space Marine's natural contempt for lesser warriors, untempered yet by the experience of fighting alongside them. It was not the men or their leaders who drew Ragnar's attention but the towering figure that stood at their head, waiting to greet Sternberg and Isaan.

He was a large man, even bigger than Sergeant Hakon, who was huge even by the standards of Space Marines. He was dressed in a uniform of inquisitorial black which fitted him as tightly as a glove. Black leather gauntlets gleamed on his hands. High leather boots encased his powerful calves. His head was bare and shaved hairless. His nose was beak-like, almost aquiline. His lips were thin and cruel. Black eyes dominated the gaunt fanatical face. He glanced at the Space Marines with respect but no fear.

'Inquisitor Sternberg. It is good to have you back. You too, Inquisitor Isaan.' His voice was booming and powerful and there was a coldness to it that might have chilled Ragnar had he been anything but a Space Marine. It was the voice of a man used to command, and Ragnar could tell from its authority that it had boomed out over a thousand battlefields.

The man's left hand was gone, no doubt left on some distant battlefield, replaced by a mechanical metal claw. A bolt pistol and a chainsword hung from a broad leather belt at his waist. Three honour studs similar to those worn by elite Space Marines were driven into his shaven head beside the sign of the Inquisition which had been tattooed there. Obviously, Ragnar thought, this was a man who took his duties and his loyalties seriously.

'It is good to be back, Commander Gul,' Sternberg said, as he and Isaan returned Gul's salute, right fists hitting their chests just above the heart. 'May I present Sergeant Hakon and his pack of Blood Claws? They are our guests on board the *Light of Truth* and the honour guard of a very special cargo.'

'Your mission was a success then, my lord inquisitor?' Gul asked. White teeth flashed, and the tan of the man's skin made them look even whiter. Ragnar caught the man's scent. There was keenness and excitement there – and something else, some disturbing undertone which he could not quite put his finger on. That in itself was disturbing, for as a Space Wolf he had learned to trust the perceptions of his senses implicitly. Despite himself, his earlier foreboding about the inquisitors returned redoubled. He wondered whether he should share them with the others. Perhaps when they were alone.

'We have what we came to find, and are on the trail of the other things we seek.'

'I pray to the Emperor that that will be soon,' Gul said. 'We must find the answer before the plague devours our home-world.'

'I share your prayers, commander,' Sternberg said.

Gul seemed to have as much of a personal stake in this as either of the inquisitors. That was not necessarily surprising if he was the commander of the inquisitors' bodyguard, for Aerius was their homeworld. Still, the man's scent had cancelled something of the earlier favourable impression the man had made. Ragnar decided that he did not entirely trust Commander Gul.

Nor were the glances his troops threw the Blood Claws altogether reassuring either. Ragnar sensed hostility there – not that it troubled him much. It could simply be jealousy of an elite unit or it might be resentment that the Blood Claws were there to perform a duty they thought should rightfully be theirs. Ragnar knew that only time would tell which.

'I will have your men shown to their quarters, Sergeant Hakon.' There was respect and courtesy in the tone Gul used towards the Space Wolf. Hakon nodded and stooped to pick up the heavy casket containing the talisman one-handed.

'My orders were not to let this out of my sight,' he said, looking directly at Inquisitor Sternberg.

'Of course, my friend,' the inquisitor said soothingly. Ragnar shivered. They were on the Inquisition's ship now, surrounded by their troops. They numbered but six, while Sternberg's minions were thousand strong. Space Marines or no, Ragnar doubted that they could stand against all of them. Regardless of whether Hakon held the talisman or not, it was at this moment safely in the inquisitors' possession whenever he wanted it.

'THEY DO ALL right for themselves, these bloody inquisitors, don't they?' Sven murmured disrespectfully, sticking his head around the doorway of Ragnar's chamber. Ragnar sensed that he was not as displeased as he sounded. Glancing about their new quarters, neither was he. Compared to their cells back in the Fang, these chambers were positively luxurious. Not that he had much to measure them against, but Ragnar suspected that compared to almost anything, they were luxurious.

This room was huge, forty strides by twenty strides with a high ceiling, and each Space Wolf had been given his own chamber just like it. The floors were of gleaming inlaid marble, covered in thick rugs of exotic weave. The drapes upon the panelled walls were as plush as the carpets. The chairs were of soft padded leather, the furnishings of fine wood and bone ivory. There was a televisor screen built into a mirror which stood on an intricately carved stand. Paintings of alien landscapes hung around the walls. The only clue to the fact they were on a spacecraft was the porthole in the middle of one wall, through which stars were visible against the infinite blackness of space.

'It's palatial,' agreed Ragnar, glancing around warily. 'One of the nicest dungeon cells ever built, I would say.'

Sven exchanged looks with him. Ragnar could tell that his fellow Blood Claw shared his feelings about the place. He had seen the way Sven studied the layout when he came in. The only visible entrance to each chamber was the one leading into the central communal eating hall. There were only two exits from there: one at the north end, one at the south. It was easily defensible but it would be just as easy to pen them in. In fact the huge blast doors which gave access to the hall looked like they could be welded shut. Not that it would be needed, Ragnar thought. He doubted that any of the weaponry the Blood Claws currently carried could force them if they were simply locked and barred. Those armoured doors must be a span thick.

'Might not be wise to say such things too loud,' Nils said quietly, coming through the doorway. He glanced around and whistled. 'I see you have a window. Walls have ears. Remember this is an Inquisition ship.'

'What do you mean by that?' Ragnar asked, although he could already guess.

'Sergeant Hakon said these quarters were the ones used by important guests–'

'That's bloody us, all right,' Sven said.

'And important prisoners,' finished Nils. Ragnar caught on at once. He could see how useful it might be for the Inquisition to be able to overhear what went on in these chambers. Most people would be too wary to speak openly in them of course, but you never knew…

'Of course, we're honoured guests,' he said. 'And we've nothing to hide.'

'That's bloody right,' said Sven. He banged his chest and belched.

'Of course, to understand us they'd have to be able to speak Fenrisian.'

'Hakon says some of the ancient Engines can translate any language.'

'I wonder why old Hakon was telling you all this,' Sven said.

Ragnar knew already. Hakon, too, was wary of what might happen here, and wanted them to be on guard.

'THIS ISN'T A ship, it's a damn city,' muttered Sven, glaring around him moodily. Ragnar grinned sourly. Sven had done nothing but complain since Sergeant Hakon had sent them out to get a feel for the starship. Both of them understood that what the sergeant was really saying was: find out the lay of the land.

Ragnar knew what Sven meant as well. They had wandered through seemingly endless metal corridors and chambers for hours and he had lost count of the number of people he had seen. The crew of this vessel must be numbered in the thousands, he thought. The large open plaza they stood in now was full of men toiling away on huge arcane engines. It smelled of machine oil and recycled air and the stink of stale sweat. Ragnar was reminded of the town of the Iron Masters back on Fenris, but this was on a far vaster scale. Looking at some of the men, he saw that they were chained to their machines. He glanced around, located a man in the ornate uniform of a ship's officer and strode over to ask him why.

The officer was a tall man, his hair dark beneath his peaked cap but his face unnaturally pale. He looked like he had spent a lifetime cloistered in the dim, unnaturally lit confines of the great starship. As he spoke his face was grim. 'Indentured. Pressed into service. Dirtside scum, sir, most of them. Criminals sentenced to work ship. Minor traitors who are repaying their debt to the Imperium for their crime. Most of them will serve for twenty-five standard years. If they live that long. It's a hard life. There are accidents.'

Ragnar considered the man's words as he glanced at the thin starved wretches, their legs chained and manacled to the machines they serviced. A lifetime unable to move more than two strides from the same place. If it were him he would most likely go mad, he thought. Or try to escape.

The officer seemed to read his thoughts. 'It makes mutiny difficult too. It's difficult to communicate with anybody save those who work on their own machine. And if they get uppity they don't get their portion of food until they calm down. Don't spare any sympathy for them, sir. They're criminals and they deserve what they get.'

Ragnar wasn't sure any man deserved this, but he held his peace. 'And once they have served their sentence they are free to leave the ship?'

'No, sir. They are free to move around it,' the man replied with a grin. 'Provided they obey the rules and do what they are told. Most of these men are here for life. This is a prison as well as a starship.'

'There must be a lot of desperate men aboard then.'

'They soon learn to serve the Emperor with a will. They know what will happen if they don't.'

Ragnar waited expectantly to be told why. He wasn't disappointed.

'They can be lashed or chained or subjected to some of the experimental questioning engines the inquisitors keep up front. If they are incorrigible they go for a walk.'

'A walk?' Ragnar asked, puzzled.

'Through the airlock. Without a suit.'

Ragnar was not sure he liked the relish with which the officer said these things, nor the way the man studied him, as if searching for a particular reaction to his hard words. Without further comment, he walked away and Sven followed. But the officer's words stayed with him. This ship was a prison. It was designed so that there could be no escape. Not even for Space Marines.

RAGNAR AND SVEN continued their wanderings through the great ship. It seemed almost as vast as the Fang, an endless warren of metal corridors, snaking pipes, ventilators, toiling machinery and men. Ragnar's earlier fears that they might be prisoners had proven groundless. No one interfered with their movements. No one had forbidden them to go anywhere. As far as he could tell, and he had exerted his very keen senses to the fullest to find out, no one was even following them. They were not watched and they were free to go wherever they wanted. Of course, it was likely the inquisitors had other means of locating them, if they wished, and there was no way off the ship now that the Thunderhawk had departed – unless they took the drastic step of seizing one of the shuttles. But then again, could any of them fly one?

Sternberg had claimed there was a teleporter on his ship. If that was true, it was a sign of the regard the inquisitor was held in. Such devices were as rare and precious as they were temperamental. Only the Terminator companies of the Space Marine Chapters used them, and then only during missions of utmost urgency and importance. The mystical ancient devices allowed small groups and cargoes to be shifted between themselves and other areas without crossing intervening space, or so the knowledge placed inside Ragnar's head told him. Maybe the device could be a way off this vessel, if the time came for it to be needed. If you knew the rituals to invoke its power. If they could find the chamber in which it rested. If... Ragnar found himself wondering why he was spending so much time planning an escape. Was he really so uneasy? He could not answer but his instincts told him he was right to be concerned.

Ragnar pushed the thought aside. Why was he thinking like this anyway? The Inquisition was not his enemy. Its members served the Emperor the same as he did. They had the trust of the Great Wolf. They were honourable people. Perhaps he was just nervous about being trapped on this ship, about going on this immense journey, far from the Fang and his world. In many ways the ship reminded him of the Fang. But the Fang was anchored to the good solid rock of Fenris. This ship was anchored to nothing; it floated in the airless void of space. If certain important systems failed, they would all die. His armour could recycle oxygen and waste-products for him, keep him alive for weeks if need be, but it could not do so indefinitely, and from where they were there was no way to swim home. They were very far out on a dangerous sea, with no land in sight.

The area through which he and Sven were striding was virtually empty. The lights were few and far between. It was a cavernous vault, a storage bay of sorts. Huge crates bearing the twin-headed eagle seal of the Imperium were stacked almost to the ceiling. Huge roaches scuttled up their sides into the shadows. Cunning-looking rats watched them from dark corners. Ragnar could smell their excrement and their foul, musty odour. He was not fond of rats.

In the distance he could hear men moving. These were not prisoners. They could come and go as they pleased. Either they were freedmen, or officers, or maybe they were some of the real crew, trained starfarers rather than indentured prisoners of the Inquisition. Ragnar and Sven strode through the aisles. He could hear the men coming closer. They appeared to be on convergent courses. Ragnar wasn't too bothered by that. He would be interested to meet more starsailors and talk to them. He wanted to understand all about this ship: the way it worked, the way its crew was organised, everything. Perhaps when he found the time, he would talk to the inquisitors about it. If they would talk to him now. This was, after all, their ship. They had duties here that might be too important to neglect.

The Space Wolves emerged into an area more brightly lit than the rest of the bay. Men worked here on massive scaffolds, transporting the crates like ants bearing rocks. These must be rations, Ragnar thought, or maybe machine parts or something else, he added. He became suddenly aware that he had no idea what they might be. The workings of the ship were indeed a mystery to him.

Close by, on ground level, were a number of men. They worked a winch that lowered a small platform down the scaffold, bringing crates to the floor. Another group of rough-looking men supervised the work. As the two Space Wolves came into view, one of the men looked up. Ragnar sensed the tension in him. The man was ready to do violence. A near imperceptible change in Sven's stance told him the other Blood Claw had detected it as well. Despite his knowledge Ragnar forced himself to look relaxed even though he was ready to spring at a heartbeat's warning.

'What have we here?' asked the man. He was wearing a uniform that marked him as part of the ship's main crew. He carried no sidearm or any obvious weapon, but the heavy crowbar he held in his hand would be an adequate substitute, Ragnar thought. 'Some of the Emperor's chosen. Sacred Space Marines, eh?'

The tone was scornful but Ragnar sensed fear in the man too. It intensified when he used the words 'Space Marines'. It seemed the reputation of the Emperor's finest preceded them.

'Greetings. We are proud to be members of the Space Wolves,' Ragnar said smoothly, in Gothic. He sensed other members of the group were getting ready for a fight now. He was not quite sure why, but their hostility was obvious. And all of these men had crowbars in their hands.

'And don't you bloody well forget it,' Sven added truculently.

Inwardly Ragnar winced. Tact and diplomacy were not skills in which Sven excelled. His tone made the men around them more hostile. What by Russ was going on here?

'Cocky pups, aren't you?' said the crew leader. 'Maybe we should knock some of that cockiness out of you.'

'You're welcome to bloody well try,' Sven said, not at all bothered by the fact that they were outnumbered almost ten to one. Ragnar knew he had reason for his confidence. These were normal men armed with crowbars. He and Sven were Space Marines, and they carried bolt pistols.

'Big words for a man armed with pistol,' sneered the officer.

'I wouldn't need it to deal with a cockroach like you,' Sven said. 'Nor your dozen girlfriends neither. Ragnar, if you would step aside for a moment, I'll teach these thralls a lesson.'

Arithmetic was not a skill that Sven had much time for either, Ragnar noted. Still he had to admire Sven's style. The number of their enemies in no way daunted him.

'Arrogant whelp!' another starsailor sneered. This one was a burly, brutal man. A white scar ran the length of his tanned face. Ragnar had enough experience of wounds to know a knife scar when he saw one. Ragnar felt a sudden surge of anger in himself, the beast struggling to free. Why were these men trying so hard to provoke them? They surely must know they had no chance in combat.

Perhaps because he was concentrating so hard on the sneering sailors, Ragnar almost missed the major threat until it was too late. Only the whoosh of air and a shadow growing on the ground near him gave him the slightest of warnings. It was enough. Even as he dived to one side, pulling Sven with him, he glanced up and saw the falling crate. Two starsailors had pushed it down on them from the pile above. The anger within Ragnar turned to fury. These men must be punished. The crate smashed into the floor. Splintered wood flew everywhere and silvery cans of meat ration tumbled out onto the floor.

Seeing that their ambush had failed the rest of the men advanced, brandishing their crowbars or vicious curved billhooks; they were intended to handle cargo but their sharp points looked as if they might pierce ceramite.

Idiots! Ragnar thought. Well, they would soon learn their lesson.

He surged forward, not even drawing his pistol. No need to waste precious bolter shells on these scum. He lashed out with his right fist at Scarface. The impact of the blow, driven by Ragnar's mighty augmented muscles and the servomotors of his armour, mashed the man's nose flat. The thug flew backwards as if hit by a battering ram. His falling body slammed into the men behind him and sent them tumbling. Ragnar reached forward, picked up one of the fallen men and effortlessly hoisted him clean above his head. The man's feeble struggles availed him nothing against the Space Wolf's awesome physical power. Ragnar tossed him headlong at a pair of his companions, bowling them over. Sven dived past Ragnar into the ruck, striking left and right with his armoured fists. With every blow he downed another man. It was like watching a whirlwind tear through a field of barley; the sailors had no chance whatsoever. Sven was moving so fast Ragnar doubted that anybody else could even follow his motions. Only his own razor keen senses allowed him to see anything other than a blur.

Bones cracked. Blood flowed. Men fell. Ragnar glanced up and around him, to see that more of the starsailors had grabbed the chains of the lift and, showing more bravery than common sense, were dropping into the fray. Ragnar snarled, showing his fangs, and let out a long ululating howl of battle lust. The sound of it so unmanned one of the dropping starsailors that he let go of the chain and dropped to the ground. From the way he flopped, like a newly landed fish, Ragnar could tell that his back was probably broken. His shrieks spoke of awful agony.

To Ragnar's surprise, his anguish did not cause his companions to reconsider their folly and flee, but seemed to spur them on to attack with redoubled fury. Ragnar ducked the swing of a crowbar, then plucked it out of its wielder's hands, like a man taking a stick from a child. For a moment he considered using it as a weapon against his assailant, but then tossed it contemptuously aside. It buried itself in the thick wooden side of a crate and stayed there quivering.

The man kicked at Ragnar. His foot connected with Ragnar's armoured side with a crunch of breaking bone. The man's mouth dropped open and he screamed in pain. Ragnar's punch silenced him. The thug fell to the ground, blood and broken teeth dribbling from his ruined mouth. Ragnar glanced around him and noticed with some satisfaction that Sven had all but finished off the rest of their attackers. He had the uniformed leader by the throat and held him easily at arm's length, one-handed. The ringleader's feet dangled half a stride above the floor.

Ragnar heard the last of the men from above drop to the ground behind him, and turned to face the new threat. He saw there were only five of them and dived into their midst, howling his war cry. His outstretched hands closed around the arms of two of his attackers. He closed his fingers and felt fragile human bones break. A kick with his right foot propelled another man ten strides and sent him smashing into a wooden crate. The man landed badly and then tumbled to the ground.

The remaining two, seeing the way the fight was going, turned to run. Ragnar was not about to let that happen. He sprang forward and grabbed them by the necks and then knocked their heads together. The two men dropped at his feet, unconscious. Ragnar turned to look back at Sven. He had dropped the stunned body of the ringleader at his feet. The Wolf gave Ragnar a sour look.

'Not much bloody fight in this lot, was there?'

'I haven't even got a scratch on my armour.'

'Well, they messed up mine!'

'How?'

'By bloody well bleeding on it, Russ damn them! I'll have to give it a good clean now.'

'TWO MEN DEAD! Fourteen men hospitalised. Five of them critically and four more temporarily unable to work because of their injuries. What do you have to say for yourselves?' Commander Gul demanded in a tone that brooked no excuses.

'I thought we had killed more. We must be getting soft,' Sven said disdainfully, looking around the commander's spartan rest chamber as if admiring the decor. He did not care for Gul's tone, that much was obvious. 'We will next time if they try and ambush us again.'

'You say they attacked you?'

'Are you implying that we are somehow mistaken?' Ragnar shot back. 'They insulted us, then some of their companions tried to drop a crate of canned meat on our heads.'

Gul had seen the site of the battle for himself. He seemed a little mollified, and unclenched his fists. 'Some of the crew are a little testy, it is true. The different work squads don't like each other, let alone any strangers on the ship. There might be more of these attacks. Perhaps in future it might be better if you remained in your chambers unless summoned.'

And was that, Ragnar thought, the whole point of this little exercise? His suspicions of this ship and its crew returned redoubled.

CHAPTER FIVE

RAGNAR WATCHED uncomfortably. As part of the talisman's honour guard, he was bound by chains of duty to be present at this moment, but he wished it were not the case. Sorcery, even sorcery performed in the service of the Imperium, made him more than uncomfortable. He didn't need to look around to tell that his battle-brothers felt the same way. Their scents told him all he needed to know about their concern.

The chamber was deep in the hidden heart of the *Light of Truth*. All around them were thick steel bulkheads. The doors had been sealed, the lights dimmed. The heady smell of narcotic incense filled the air and made Ragnar's mind swim until his body adjusted to the presence of the drug. The floor was bare metal; in the centre was a double circle inscribed in sanctified inks and salts. Between the outer and the inner rings were various symbols sacred to the Emperor and the Inquisition. A series of lines radiated out from the exact centre of the circle. Ragnar did not know why, but he knew that somehow the direction in which they pointed was significant. At the end of each line was a blazing copper brazier, the source of the incense.

And at the exact point where the lines converged, Inquisitor Karah Isaan sat cross-legged on the cold steel floor. She was naked save for the talisman, which dangled from her neck. Ragnar could see the whitened scars that marked her dark brown skin. Badges of honour from old combats, he expected. The woman breathed deeply and rhythmically. She was gathering her powers for an attempt to psychometrically locate the next part of the amulet they sought. Ragnar had heard Sternberg and Hakon discuss this earlier. Apparently there was some sort of psychic link between all the different segments of the broken talisman, and these could be used to divine their exact position in relation to each other. Ragnar was not quite sure how this worked, but then psykers and their arts were a total mystery to him.

Around the circle stood the Blood Claws, all five of them, together with Sergeant Hakon and Inquisitor Sternberg. All of them watched, grim-faced, as Isaan continued her ritual. Ragnar sensed Sternberg's excitement. The hunt was on again. They were about to take another step forward towards saving his world from the plague.

Inquisitor Isaan started to chant in Imperial Gothic, the elevated language of ancient psyker litanies rolling from her tongue. The rhythm of the words lent them power, made her voice seem deeper and more resonant, as if something else was speaking through the woman's mouth. Regrettably that was all too possible, Ragnar knew. Psykers were notoriously prone to daemonic possession, which was why most of them were soul-bonded to the Emperor, or fed to him as sustenance in his Golden Throne. Ragnar guessed that, like the Space Marine Chapters, the Inquisition had its methods of screening and protecting its psykers. He only hoped they were as effective as those used by the Fang's rune priests.

He guessed that protection was the reason for the circle and those sacred symbols. They were designed to protect the psyker from unwholesome external influences as the ritual progressed. Ragnar gave his attention back to his own prayers. The inquisitor had instructed them all to pray silently as the ritual progressed so that no malign influences might be attracted by their thoughts. Ragnar wasn't sure what she meant by that but he was determined not to take any chances. He prayed fervently to Russ and the Emperor to watch over them, and guide the psyker in her task.

Suddenly the hairs on the back of Ragnar's neck rose, and it felt like the temperature had dropped a degree or two. His mouth opened in an involuntary snarl. He sensed the presence of something. Strange energies crackled in the air around them, unseen and yet undeniably present. There was a smell like burnt metal. He opened his eyes once more and gazed at Karah Isaan. At first he doubted his eyes: was there the faintest trace of a halo of light surrounding her head? Maybe. No, definitely. As he watched, prayers forgotten, it grew brighter, until it was a shimmering circle of amber light which grew stronger as he watched, became brighter and brighter until it eclipsed the dim lighting of the room and made the female inquisitor the focus of every gaze.

Her short-cropped hair rippled slowly, as if caught by a breeze, although there was not the slightest breath of wind within the sealed chamber. When she opened her eyes, Ragnar could see the unnatural light within them. Her pupils and iris glowed like two tiny suns, as if they were part of a binary system within her head that provided the illumination for the halo. Slowly she raised her thin brown hands until the talisman was cupped between them. It, too, began to glow, the light of her halo catching on the thousands of facets of the gem, becoming split into millions of points, refracting all around the room. Ragnar could see the beams of light playing over the faces of his comrades. Some of them landed on his own chest like the eerie red dots of a targeting laser. The thought made him shiver slightly and give his attention back to his prayers.

The chanting continued. Ragnar watched in fascination. From the woman's mouth a mist had started to emerge, a writhing vapour which shimmered and glittered and swirled around her – and then began to take on concrete shapes, like images projected by a holosphere. Ragnar saw a world gleam against the cold depths of space. He saw the blue of oceans, the white of clouds and the green of jungles.

Even as he watched, the bizarre scene projected in the air changed. It was as if they were dropping from space onto the surface of the world. One continent leapt into view. They dropped closer towards an endless sea of green. The dizzying speed of descent slowed. Ragnar saw huge towering trees, and brightly coloured flowers almost as large. Huge insects. Strange beasts. A monstrous stone temple, ancient, shaped like a stepped pyramid, covered in strange eroded carvings of humanoid faces. Creepers and lichens swelled into view. Ragnar shivered, sensing some sort of inimical presence in the air. He wondered about daemons and prayed more fervently. The temperature in the room was dropping very rapidly now and the stink of burning, mingled with the incense, was foul.

The point of view descended, passing like a ghost through the walls of the pyramid and into a hidden chamber at its core. On an altar tended by emerald-robed priests lay an amulet twin to the one that glittered on Karah Isaan's neck – save that the gem was green and seemed slightly smaller. This was what they sought, Ragnar knew.

The chill in the air of the chamber deepened. Ragnar's breath came out as a stream of mist. Droplets of moisture seemed to condense then freeze on his armour. He was a Space Marine and his armour was designed to let him survive in far more extreme temperatures, but still he felt the difference. The sense of an evil presence deepened and the picture changed again, swirling, condensing, until it formed a single huge, green-skinned head. Malevolent yellow eyes glared out at everyone in the room. Huge tusks protruded from the thing's leathery lips. A massive scar ran from the forehead across the left eye, down across the mouth and ended on the right side of its chin. It looked as if it had been crudely stitched together with rough twine, and the twine left in place. As Ragnar watched, the thing opened its mouth and bellowed in rage. The echo of that distant roar seemed to ring in his own head. It was spoken in a language other than his own, but still he understood the meaning.

Come here, and you will all die! Every last one of you!

The vision vanished. There was a shriek of pain. A gust of wind which came from nowhere blew out all the braziers and the lights flickered. For a moment the room was plunged into a blackness as deep as death.

INQUISITOR ISAAN shivered. She was wrapped in Sternberg's cloak now but it was still cold in the metal chamber. A sense of that brutal alien presence lingered all around them, making Ragnar's fingers seek the butt of his pistol.

'That was an ork,' Sven muttered. Ragnar nodded slowly. He remembered the descriptions of the things, and the images which had been pumped into his brain by the tutelary engines back in the Fang. They were a warrior race, savage, brutal and wicked, utterly without redeeming features. They fought endlessly to conquer and enslave any world they came to.

Sternberg stared at Karah Isaan meaningfully, a fanatical glint in his eyes. 'Your vision quest was successful?'

The woman shivered and nodded. 'Yes.'

'Names! Places!'

Sternberg sounded like a man possessed, Ragnar thought.

'Galt,' she said simply.

'Then that was the Temple of Xikar?'

'Yes.'

'So the talisman ended up there.'

The woman looked very weak and pale. Using her strange powers had obviously drained her. She looked direly in need of rest and yet her colleague showed no sympathy. He touched the communication amulet on his throat. 'Helmsman! Lay a course for the Galt system. I want to get there with all possible speed.'

Moments later, in answer to his command, a deep siren sounded and the lights flickered in an alert pattern. In the distance Ragnar could hear feet pounding down the corridors, as starsailors raced to prepare the ship for the jump into the warp.

'Best return to your chambers,' Sternberg said to the Wolves. 'No leap into the Immaterium is a pleasant experience.'

RAGNAR LAY ON the old leather of the acceleration couch in his chamber. A starsailor had entered earlier and showed him how to strap himself in. He had been surprised to find that the chairs doubled up as acceleration couches. A touch of a hidden button and they folded outwards and backwards, extruding restraining straps which looked thick enough to hold a bull mastodon. The harness was controlled by a quick release button similar to the ones on the restrainer straps in a Thunderhawk. The Blood Claw wondered why they could be necessary. The huge starship had seemed utterly stable the whole time he had been on it. The starsailor had been insistent though. He claimed that everyone not performing vital duties absolutely requiring freedom of movement would be doing the same. The tenseness of the man's body, together with the undertones of dread and anticipation in the man's scent, convinced Ragnar. This man claimed to be a veteran of a thousand warp jumps, yet still he was afraid.

'Never gets any easier, sir,' he had said, just before he left the room. Now bells clanged throughout the ship and warning sirens blared. The lights flickered from normal to red, then back again. There was no doubt about what was going to happen next.

A final long siren wail blared. Over the intercom, a deep voice boomed: 'Thirty seconds to jump. May we be blessed in His sight.'

Ragnar felt a sick feeling of anticipation in the pit of his stomach, and just for a moment wished that all of the pack had been assembled in one chamber. He knew there would be something reassuring in their mere presence. Might as well wish to be back on Fenris right now, he thought sarcastically. It's not going to happen.

His double heartbeat accelerated. He began to sweat. With an effort of will and the words of a Litany of Calming, using the control of his nervous system granted to him as a Space Marine he brought his heartbeats back to normal, and stopped the sweating. Immediately he began to feel the panic subside into mere unease.

'Twenty seconds to jump. Watch and guide our path.'

Still he felt anticipation. He had never made a warp jump before, although all his training had told him it would be a very strange experience. The ship would be passing out of this space-time continuum and into another place where matter did not exist and time flowed strangely. In some ways it would be like a submersible going under water. It would become lost to the sight of all tracking devices which operated in the normal universe, until it emerged in real space again. Of course, this might not happen. It was all down to the skill of the ship's Navigator, who would set his course by the mighty beacon of the Astronomican on distant Terra, and would try to find a path for the starship through the treacherous currents of warp space.

The warp itself was a turbulent medium, unstable, as full of ebbs and flows as a mighty ocean. It was said to be haunted by daemons and ghosts and the hulks of the thousands of ships, some of them human, which had been lost in it since time immemorial. It was a shifting, ill-understood realm which filled even those who travelled through it with superstitious dread. All manner of tales were told about the warp. Of star-sailors who travelled through it convinced that only days had passed and who later emerged to find centuries had gone by in real time and that all who knew them were dead and gone. It had happened even to the Space Wolves. Ships had been deemed lost for hundreds of years and then their crews had returned to the Fang, unheralded and unexpected, to rejoin their comrades. And other, stranger fates had befallen travellers as well. Sometimes crews would travel out and return what seemed days later to their comrades; only when they emerged from their ships, they had grown old and senile and some had died of ageing. Their crews felt like they had been lost for decades in the warp, and showed all the effects of having been so. Sometimes entire crews went insane the moment they slipped into the Immaterium. No one knew why. And some-times, most ominously of all, ships, even entire fleets vanished, never to be seen or heard from again. It was all down to luck, the favour of the Emperor and the skill of the Navigator.

'Ten seconds to jump. May He return us safely.'

Ragnar wondered if anything would go wrong this time. He hoped not but it was always a possibility. All he could do was strive to keep calm, and pray to the Emperor and to beloved Leman Russ for succour, cold comfort though that might be. The worst thing, he thought, was the helplessness. He was a Space Wolf, trained for battle, schooled to face a thousand per-ils in the line of duty. Right now there was no way he could control the outcome, or indeed have any effect on it. He could not take his bolter in his hand and slay a visible foe. He could not take cover and retreat from the danger. All he could do was wait, and try to endure the knowledge that his fate was in the hands of other men. He tried telling himself that the Navigators had been as hard-schooled in their trade as he was in his, but it did not help. At the end of the day he was a Space Marine, a man of action, and this sort of waiting came hard to him.

Still, he remembered the words of Ranek during one of the many sermons the Wolf Priest had preached during his induc-tion to the Space Wolves: When there is nothing to do but wait, then wait is all you can do. He knew he must simply let go of his worry; it was counter-productive, could not affect the out-come one way or another. That was what he strove to do now.

'Five seconds to jump.'

Whatever was going to happen was going to have to happen soon, Ragnar thought. In the distance he could hear the howling of the engines as their power emission began to reach a peak.

'Four.' Was that a faint halo of light beginning to appear around all the furnishings? The howling rose and lowered in pitch until it became a noise like thunder and a whine like a plummeting Thunderhawk.

'Three.' Yes. The halo was there and getting brighter. Distant thunder rattled the metal walls. The ship was vibrating; it quivered as if with eagerness, anticipation. It reminded the Space Wolf of a wardog being readied to hunt.

'Two.' The whole ship was shaking violently. Would it break apart in the warp?

'One.' The whole of the vast starship seemed to spring forward, like a hound that had been straining against a leash and was now released. There was a huge thunderclap of sound, and the ship rang as if it had been hit with a titanic hammer. Ragnar wondered how it could endure the stress, then thought of all the gigantic bulkheads and reinforcing struts he had seen on his earlier wanderings. Had those been as much to resist the strains of the warp jumps as to protect the ship in battle, he wondered?

The ship shuddered hugely. Ragnar could hear the metal creak, like the masts of a ship in a storm. It felt as if massive forces were being brought to bear on the ship, now puny in comparison to the typhoon in which it seemed caught. With his enhanced senses Ragnar could feel the tension in the juddering vibrations of the couch beneath him. Was the *Light of Truth* about to shatter like a dragonship dashed against a reef?

The Blood Claw felt a surge of nervous fear in the pit of his stomach and fought to control it. What was that shrieking sound? It sounded like the wailing of lost souls. And that ominous scraping? Was it the claws of daemons dragging themselves along the hull? The stories he had heard came back to him. He had a half-horrified, half-fascinated desire to look out of the porthole but it had been sealed with massive metal shutters in the run up to the jump. It was said that looking out into the warp was a sure way to madness. Yet he felt the tug of morbid curiosity.

Could it really be the souls of lost starsailors he was hearing? Or the call of daemon lovers to the curious and unwary? Were these things really penetrating the shields and baffles which protected the ship,` or were they simply products of his own morbid imagination? Part of him was curious and part of him hoped he would never find out.

The ship seemed to have settled now. It shuddered and shivered occasionally but it was less unsettling than the movement of a ship on the sea and Ragnar was well accustomed to that. After a moment's hesitation, he hit the release mechanism on the restraining straps and rose to his feet. His keen ears picked up the sharp metallic ringing of the other Space Wolves doing the same.

Ragnar emerged from his chamber into the central hall. Sven strode into the room almost simultaneously. He looked at Ragnar and grinned.

'Well, we're bloody well away now,' he said and laughed aloud.

'Aye! That we are.'

A curious anti-climactic feeling had settled on Ragnar. They had made the jump. They were in warp space and speeding to their destination. All they had to do now was get out again.

GALT.

Ragnar called up details of the system from the ship's mnemonic banks. The information flashed onto the old televisor, a mixture of pictures and Imperial runes. Not an enormous amount of detail, but that was to be expected. It was consulting only the Index of the Compendio Mundae, which contained only the most basic of details. More could be summoned on request, providing the information was not in some way under a ban or interdiction.

Ragnar's eyes flickered quickly over the screen. Sun: yellow and terrestrial type. Six planets. One inhabited, known as Galt Three. Two moons. A warm world. Closer to its sun than Fenris, and on a regular helical orbit, not elliptical as his own home world was. Three large continents. Three-quarters ocean. Some large island chains. Most of the human population was confined to the largest continent, where most of the landmass was covered in tropical rainforest. Several large cities. Lots of logging and agriculture. Most common export to the

Imperium was the buds of the red lotus used as the basis of many Imperial alchemical products. Also many pre-Imperial ruins – temples, cities, roadways. These indicated the presence of a primitive human culture which had survived the collapse at the end of the Dark Age of Technology. Naturally the cults had been expunged when the people of Galt were welcomed back into the fold of the Imperium. Many of their sacred places had become monasteries and seminaries used by the Ecclesiarchy.

The Temple of Xikar was one such place, an enormous complex set in the jungle which had become home to the monastic sect known as the Brothers of Perpetual Bliss. The sect had been investigated for the contamination of heresy on several occasions, but the inquisitors detailed to the task felt that its deviation from the broad thread of Imperial scripture fell within acceptable and tolerable norms. The inquisitorial jargon made Ragnar's head swim but he deduced that what it really meant was that the Inquisition had decided not to cleanse the Brotherhood with fire and the sword.

And now one of those temples was found to contain part of the Talisman of Lykos. Ragnar wondered how it had got there.

'I AM GLAD you are all here. A problem has arisen, I am afraid,' Inquisitor Sternberg said. He glanced around the vast command deck. His keen eyes seemed to rest on every Space Wolf in turn, measure him, and then move on. Once his steely gaze had moved on, Ragnar risked a glance around the room. All of the Space Wolves were present, along with the two inquisitors, the ranking officers of the *Light of Truth* and the commanders of the inquisitor's bodyguard.

'And what might that be?' Sergeant Hakon asked, with an edge in his voice. The rest of the pack strained forward, keen to hear. They could all sense something in the inquisitor's manner and in his scent. Ragnar thought it was a mixture of anger and frustration.

Sternberg turned and gestured to his military commander. His cloak flowed smoothly with the gesture. 'Gul?' he said.

Commander Gul strode forward into the centre of the room. Overhead the stars beamed in through the crystal roof of the chamber. Ragnar thought it was good to see them again, although he was a little thrown by the strange new constellations which were visible. He was glad the ship had emerged safely from the warp.

'We emerged into normal space about six hours ago. Since then our astropaths have been picking up various messages from the surface of Galt Three.'

'Messages?' asked Hakon.

'Appeals for help. Military communications. A general alert signal appealing for aid against the invasion.'

Invasion, Ragnar thought? Who would be foolish enough to invade an Imperial system? Then he smiled at his own naïvety. There were plenty that would do it. Alien races, even rebel Imperial governors. Such things had happened before.

'I instructed our astropaths to make contact with their counterparts on Galt Three and the following details have emerged. About six months ago standard Imperial time, a hulk emerged from warp space. It drifted within three standard units of Galt Three and as it did so it unleashed a host of smaller craft, thousands of them.

'Must have been quite a large hulk then,' ventured Sven with a smirk.

'Obviously,' Gul said, as if Sven were an idiot. Which, right at that moment, Ragnar decided, was how he sounded. Hulks could be almost any size. They were huge agglomerations of dead ships which for any one of a dozen reasons came together to form immense space-going craft, often larger than many cities. They drifted in and out of the warp seemingly without reason. Most were uninhabited, but some were homes to various lifeforms. These could be as innocuous as prospectors looking for ancient secrets among the wrecked ships or as threatening as broods of the dreaded genestealers. They could show up at any time, in any system, drifting randomly on the currents of the warp.

'These ships were the spearhead of the ork invasion.'

'Orks!' various people muttered at once.

Ragnar thought about the face they had summoned up during Karah's ritual. That had most definitely been an ork. The Space Wolves looked pleased. Here were foes worthy of the name. The orks may be brutal and barbaric but they were mighty warriors, and fearless. Gul looked over at Mozak, the Chief Astropath.

'Yes, undoubtedly orks.' Mozak was an old man with a quavering voice and milky white, blind-seeming eyes. He was frail and he leaned on a staff almost as tall as he was. Occasionally Ragnar had come across him tapping his way along the corridors of the ship. He had always nodded to Ragnar, as aware of his presence as any sighted man. His psychic powers must in some way be a substitute for his eyes, Ragnar knew. 'There have always been some present on the surface of Galt Three, lurking deep in the jungles. They have never formed much of a threat to the Imperial population. Occasional raids, burnings and lootings, that sort of thing.'

'But their presence may have attracted the orks from the hulk?' Hakon asked.

'Perhaps – or perhaps the two facts are unconnected. We shall never know. What we do know is that it is common for orks to suddenly mass huge formations of troops and go on the rampage. These are in some ways like Imperial Crusades. The ork hordes gather troops and manpower as they go until either the leader dies, his savage ambition is slaked, or they are stopped by external forces such as military intervention or a natural disaster. While these crusades are under way ork morale is high and the sheer momentum and scale can make them irresistible.'

'What has this to do with our quest?' asked Hakon.

'Galt Three appears to be right in the middle of one of these ork rampages,' Sternberg cut in. 'The orks landed and began arming the local ork population which, it turns out, was a lot larger than anybody thought, and are now scything across the planet, smashing any resistance as they go. In short, Galt Three is now a warzone.'

'Worse than that,' the Chief Astropath added. 'It appears that one of the major centres of ork military effort is Xikar.'

'Where the temple is,' Gul added unnecessarily.

'That's going to make getting our hands on the talisman a little difficult, isn't it?' Hakon said.

'You could say that,' said Sternberg with an odd crinkle of his lips which Ragnar realised was meant to be a smile.

'Is it possible to drop down into the temple and quickly retrieve the talisman fragment?' Ragnar dared to ask. All eyes turned on him but to his relief he saw that no one seemed to think he had spoken out of turn. 'A lightning raid?'

'Anything's possible,' Gul said. 'The question is whether you can succeed.'

'We'll never know unless we try,' Sternberg added.

'According to the Imperial authorities on Galt, there are tens of thousands of orks down there, perhaps hundreds of thousands. Intelligence is vague. Compared to those numbers all the troops we have on this ship are merely a drop in the ocean.'

'No one's suggesting we try and destroy the entire ork army,' said Gul. 'We need only find the talisman and then get it out.'

Ragnar was a little shocked by the callousness of this. After all, Galt was an Imperial world and they were the Emperor's warriors. Weren't they supposed to help defend the human worlds against just such a menace as these orks represented? He said as much out loud.

Inquisitor Sternberg regarded him coldly for a moment before speaking: 'Our current mission takes precedence over any military intervention we might make. There are simply not enough of us to make much of a difference anyway. Galt Three is a lightly populated world, unimportant in the grand scheme of things. Aerius is a vitally important Imperial installation. Its loss would be a disaster.'

'Nonetheless,' Ragnar felt compelled to say, 'are not the people of Galt as entitled to Imperial protection as the people of Aerius?'

'Your devotion to humanity does you credit, young Ragnar,' Sternberg smoothed. 'But you must leave it to your superiors to look at the bigger picture. I am in charge of this mission and I must make the decisions here.'

Ragnar looked at Sergeant Hakon for support but to his surprise sensed that the older Space Wolf was behind the inquisitor on this. Sternberg could see it too.

'Good. As I see it, a large scale operation would simply draw attention to our presence. What we need is a small, crack unit to teleport dirtside, infiltrate the Temple of Xikar and, Emperor willing, seize the talisman.'

It took Ragnar only seconds to realise just who on the ship who would be perfect for the job.

RAGNAR GLANCED around at the ornate inner sanctum of the teleportation chamber. It was an intimidating place even for a Space Wolf. Everyone who was to be subject to the ritual stood inside a circle of silver inscribed on the floor. Each circle was linked to the others by lines of metal inlaid in the floor. All were inscribed with ancient runes. A mighty double circle enclosed the whole area, and he guessed that the symbols inscribed there were warding signs, designed to contain the energies which would soon be unleashed, and protect the transportees from the daemons of the warp. Robed and cowled tech-priests moved between lecterns set on a great balcony halfway up the chamber wall. Monstrous engines surrounded by the witchfire halos that marked the presence of the Universal Fire loomed above and around them.

Ragnar heard the master tech-priest begin his plainsong chant. He and his acolytes moved their hands over their altars in ritual gestures, throwing the mighty tripswitches in the sanctified order laid down by their hallowed, time-tested rituals. As they did so, the smell of ozone began to fill the air, mingling with the scent of machine oil and technical incense. Witchfire flickered along the lines joining the circles and illuminated the circles and the runes. The lights in the chamber dimmed till only the glow of the teleporter and the power machines provided any illumination. The air shimmered around in the space between the lines of the great circle of containment.

Ragnar's mouth felt dry and the hair on the back of his neck prickled. He knew that teleporters were not entirely reliable, that sometimes those who were supposed to be transported simply vanished and never reappeared. No one knew what happened to them. He prayed to the Emperor that he and his companions would arrive safely but could not concentrate on his devotions. The ship rocked. The floor vibrated beneath his feet.

He knew they were performing a dangerous manoeuvre. Bringing the *Light of Truth* close enough to the world to teleport them to the surface meant bringing it close enough for the enemy fleet to engage them. Ragnar was unsure how long even the powerful Inquisition ship could hold out against a whole ork fleet – hopefully long enough.

He was excited at the prospect of imminent action – but also filled with resentment at the cavalier way in which his pleas to aid the population of Galt had been rejected. Ragnar could tell that all the other Blood Claws felt only the excitement, and for this he did not blame them. After all, this was to be their first teleport and their first step onto the surface of an alien world. It was their very first off-world mission and they were going to face their first alien foes. In a sense it was everything they had ever trained for; it was what their lives were about.

He could see the others only as shadowy outlines. There was Hakon. There was the squat shapes of Sven and Strybjorn and Nils and the other Blood Claws. Inquisitor Sternberg was present. So was Karah Isaan, the talisman around her neck as it had been since the ritual. If the Space Wolves went into battle, it went too. Ragnar gave her a slight smile and was surprised when it was returned. He was surprised and a little flattered to note that none of the Inquisition troops were coming. Only the two inquisitors themselves were considered sufficiently well trained and competent to keep up with the Space Wolves, and the Space Marines were deemed to be the entire bodyguard they would need. Ragnar felt that was probably true. If he and his comrades could not keep Sternberg and Isaan alive, he doubted that the presence of twenty or so normal human warriors would make much difference.

He gave his weapons and armour one final check, automatically murmuring the words of the Litany against Corrosion, and invoking Russ's blessing on each bolter shell. Such things were important.

A bright light flashed. There was a brief feeling of dislocation. Ragnar felt as if he was being turned inside out, flung around violently, stretched and crushed all at once. His skin tingled as if it were being pricked by millions of tiny needles. His brain felt afire. There was a brilliant flash of light, and a darkness deeper than any he had ever known.

It was too late now, he knew, to do anything but pray.

CHAPTER SIX

THE PRESSURE GREW and grew. The wolf spirit stirred within him, responding to the unfamiliar stresses being placed on his body. He bared his teeth and fought down the urge to let loose a long howl. They wanted to arrive silently.

Suddenly the pressure stopped. There was a hard bump and he was thrown forward almost to his knees. The breeze was hot and humid on his face and carried a host of unfamiliar scents. Ragnar smelled decaying vegetation, the perfumes of narcotic flowers, the scent of alien animals. It was a heady mix and he felt a strange exhilaration flood through his veins. They were down, and safely too. They were on the surface of a new world.

Ragnar opened his eyes and glanced around. They were in a clearing, near the temple. Everything looked verdant and lush, a riot of greens and yellows. Vast trees surrounded them. A cacophony of birdsong and insect chittering filled his ears. His glance told him that all the others were present and ready for action. He was particularly pleased to see Inquisitor Sternberg, since he carried the beacon, a small cube of brass and coiled wires which would allow the *Light of Truth* to locate them and teleport them back on board. At this moment it was their only way off-world.

Hakon made a chopping gesture at his throat indicating they should all be silent, and then made the hand sign for dispersal. The Blood Claws began to move across the soil of this new world. Ragnar fell in behind Sven. He felt oddly light, and knew that the gravity of Galt Three was less than that of Fenris – not by much, but enough to be disorienting until his body made the adjustment. Matching Sven's wide strides, he jogged away from the drop point towards the undergrowth, moving to establish a defensive perimeter on the edge of the jungle.

He could hear his comrades moving to take up their positions, every Space Wolf deploying as they had been taught to. Moments later Sergeant Hakon, Sternberg and Isaan followed. Ragnar didn't bother to turn and look. He simply knew from the sounds and the scents that it happened. His task currently was to keep an eye on the jungle and make sure they were not surprised.

It was just as well he did not have to rely on his vision, he thought. Mere strides from the clearing's edge the jungle became severely dense. Huge trees loomed overhead, and massive plants, flowers and bushes choked the spaces between them. Creepers and vines descended from the branches. Dust motes flickered in the beams of light that penetrated the thick canopy of leaves overhead. A blood-sucking insect landed on Ragnar's face. His sensitive skin detected its bite. He resisted the urge to slap it. His body could compensate for any allergic reaction. He knew his internal glands were already beginning to secrete chemicals into his sweat which would repel the insect's fellows in future.

He concentrated as he had been taught, listening for any sound of enemy troops, casting around for the scent of unfamiliar humanoids. He could detect no threat. He could hear only the sounds of small animals moving through the undergrowth and the buzz of insect wings. It appeared that their arrival had gone unobserved. So far, so good, the Wolf thought.

Sergeant Hakon dropped down alongside him. He paused to study the dim green readout of the inertial locator on his wrist and then gestured for Ragnar and his team to take point and move off in the direction of the temple. Unbidden, Sven set off first, with Ragnar and the others following close behind in narrow formation.

Cautiously but purposefully the Wolves began to advance through the jungle. Ragnar gently parted the foliage ahead of him, bolter held ready to meet any threat. Suddenly he felt more alive than he had since the day he and his fellow Blood Claws had entered the foul Chaos lair beneath the mountains. This was what it meant to be truly alive, he thought.

He glanced down at the locator on his wrist, now keyed to Sergeant Hakon's own device. The clearing was about two thousand strides west of the temple. Not far over open terrain, but difficult to tell how long it might take in this jungle. He was glad now that he and the other Blood Claws had put in such long hours in the jungle caverns beneath the Fang. Such simulated environments couldn't quite prepare you for the real thing but they helped a little. One of the major differences he realised was the noise. In the Fang they had used recorded sound but that had been flat and unnatural compared to the cacophony which enveloped them now.

Overhead bright birds cawed and sang. Fat, gaudily coloured insects buzzed. The leaves of palm trees rustled together. To his left came the sound of something big smashing down from overhead. He glanced up and caught sight of a huge nut dropping from the branches of one of the trees. Just after it hit the ground there came the sounds of a struggle: small animals fighting over it. Must be edible, at least to them, Ragnar thought briefly. Probably to him too. He was a Space Marine. His stomach had been altered to allow him to consume almost anything that any creature in the galaxy might find edible.

He breathed deeply, relying more on his nose and his ears for advance warning of any trouble. The only humans he could smell were the inquisitors and his battle-brethren. Back in the Fang he had been exposed to the musky scent of orks by the tutelary engines. Right at this moment he could detect nothing like it. There were animals, warm-blooded ones, around him. He could smell fur and droppings.

Somewhere off to the right he could hear running water. Something slurped around his foot. The ground was becoming a little soft. They were on the edge of a swamp, doubtless fed by the stream he had sensed. He looked up ahead. Sven was already thigh deep in mud. It slurped around his legs as he advanced. It did not seem to be slowing him down all that much, but Ragnar was not sure that it was not a mistake to continue right now. If they were attacked, the mud would slow them down and make swift movement difficult. On the other hand, it was probable that no one would expect them to advance directly through a bog either.

Doubtless Sven had considered this before deciding to push on. Ragnar decided not to order him to halt and skirt the swamp just yet. It was the first real command decision he had taken in some time, and he was not sure it was the right one. Still, there was no point in second-guessing yourself once a decision was made. All he could do was stay alert and try to be aware of any change of circumstances that might make him alter it.

As they progressed, the swamp grew deeper. The ground around Sven was starting to take on the consistency of soup, more fluid than solid. Ragnar could feel small splashes of moisture on his face, caused by his own movements. He glanced down briefly and saw that muck was clinging to the carapace of his armour. He grinned wryly – another cleaning job later. Providing he was still alive.

Suddenly he felt tense. He was not quite sure why. A heart-beat later, his unease communicated itself to the rest of the pack. Sven stopped, cast his head back and sniffed the air. All the rest of the Space Wolves had stopped moving too. Ragnar breathed deeply.

Yes! There was a slight taint to the air, a musky scent close to, but not quite like, that of the ork stench they had been exposed to in training, but that was only to be expected. Not all orks smelled exactly the same, just as not all humans did. It was close enough though. He saw Sven nod involuntarily a moment later. Although his nostrils were not quite as keen as Ragnar's he had caught it too. Ragnar tried to guess their distance. There was a slight breeze and the wind was blowing towards them. That made it difficult to tell exactly. All he could really tell now was that there were orks in the vicinity, or had been recently. There was nothing for it now but to push on, but far more cautiously than before.

Sven had reached the far side of the boggy ground. The surface was down to his knees again, leaving a brownish residue on the thigh guards of his ancient armour. An insect bit Ragnar's face again. Once more he resisted the urge to slap it. Sven reached solid ground. Sure of the surface now, he crouched down and then threw himself flat and began to wriggle forward like a snake. Closing behind him, Ragnar did the same. The smell of ork was getting stronger.

He checked the locator on his wrist: two hundred strides to the temple. A leaf brushed his face and tickled it. He fought down the urge to sneeze, sniffed the air, stuck out his tongue and tasted the pollen-like substance that had landed on it. Fungal spores, he guessed. From somewhere at the back of his mind came the knowledge, placed there by the engines in the Fang, that orks cultivated certain types of fungus as food and the basis of crude fermented drinks. Was this another sign of their presence? Ragnar guessed he would know soon enough. Another scent struck his nostrils. Burning. No, not burning: burnt stuff. Wood. Vegetation. *Flesh.*

Through a gap in the foliage ahead, he caught sight of the temple. A huge clearing had been gouged out of the canopy above. The smell of burnt wood was intense. Ragnar realised that it was the sign that a battle had been fought here, with weapons that had caused the jungle to burn; quite a difficult feat, given the amount of moisture in the air. The temple itself was huge, a massive stone ziggurat, weathered grey by wind and rain and by the roots of plants which had embedded themselves in the cracks and then grown. Curtains of creepers crawled down the centuries-old sides. The thing seemed truly ancient, rooted in a time and place beyond memory, when men worshipped other, more primitive gods. It was a heathen monument, an imitation mountain, built by men who wanted to attract the attention of some primordial deity. It was, in its crude and brutal way, impressive.

Very cautiously indeed, Ragnar gestured for his companions to stay down, then he moved forward. The stench of ork was even stronger here. It had a leathery, sweaty quality, sharp and feral, musky and strong. From far ahead Ragnar heard an unusual sound which stood out against the constant background hum and chatter of the jungle. It sounded at first like grunting but then Ragnar realised that it had a pattern: it was speech of a sort. The voice was deep, deeper than any human's. Ragnar imagined that it came from the chest of something larger than any man.

Until now he had maintained comms silence, even though the pack was on a sealed and scrambled net. He did not want any signal pulse giving away their position. It was just possible, even though their communicators were set to the lowest possible emission, designed not to project at over a hundred strides, that someone nearby with the appropriate equipment could detect the signal if they were looking for it.

Now it seemed more urgent to prevent the two inquisitors blundering into the enemy. He did not doubt that any of the Space Wolves present would detect the orks before they saw them, but he was not sure of the normal humans at all.

+Ragnar+ he subvocalised. +Have made contact with the enemy. Be still until further notice.+

He needed no acknowledgement. He knew that he would be obeyed. That was the way the pack trained to fight. At the moment, he and his team were at the point. His battle-brothers trusted him to take the appropriate action. He would not fail them.

Ragnar writhed further forward, making as little noise as he could. Suddenly he was at the edge of the jungle, looking across the clearing towards the Temple of Xikar. He could see now that his initial impression had been false. The ziggurat he had seen was but one of many, and far from the largest. Xikar was a huge complex of monuments. All of them just as old, and just as impressive, as the first. It held his attention only for a moment, until his eyes flickered to the source of the grunting voice.

He knew at once that his hearing had not misled him. The speaker was indeed an ork, and it was far larger than a normal man, larger even than a Space Wolf. Its chest was as round as a barrel and its arms were thicker than most men's legs. Its skin was an oily green in colour. Huge tusks jutted upwards from a massive jaw. The skull was ape-like, the bestial yellowish eyes set in deep cavernous sockets. It was humanoid but its legs were oddly short and its arms incredibly long compared to a man's. The whole impression was of ape-like power and savagery, an impression only partially belied by the array of equipment that festooned its powerful body.

A jacket of thick armour encased its upper torso, leaving its leathery green arms bare. A huge bolt pistol was clutched in one gnarled hand, and a chainsaw-bladed axe a normal man would have struggled to lift was held negligently in the other. A barbaric helm that would have been more at home on some primitive tribesman sat on its head. High boots of scuffed leather protected its legs from the grasping brush.

The creature was not alone. It was talking to someone, or something, but Ragnar could not see who. It addressed its grunting remarks through a cavernous doorway set in the side of the ziggurat. A high pitched chittering voice responded from inside. Ragnar sniffed the air, for the first time becoming aware of a different scent. One more acrid, and sharper than that of the ork, and far fainter. It was the scent of something ork-like and yet not an ork. He paused for a moment, frozen into absolute immobility, and waited to see what would emerge.

He did not have too long to wait. A small head poked around the doorway, cautious and wary. It belonged to another green-skinned creature less than half the size of the ork, but obviously in some way related to it. It had the same greenish skin and yellowish eyes, but where the ork's features reflected a brutal strength and self-confidence, this creature's were sharp, sly and cunning. Its movements were cringing and Ragnar noticed that it did its best to keep out of reach of the ork.

A gretchin, he thought, recognising the creature from his lessons back in the Fang.

It, too, had very long arms in proportion to its size, but where the ork's fingers were stubby and powerful, this one's were long and clever and dextrous. A cowl projected from the leather jacket which covered its torso and partially obscured its head. An autorifle was slung over the gretchin's back. The weapon was huge compared to the gretchin and Ragnar was surprised the little alien had the strength to lift it. In the gretchin's hands was clutched a stone box. The creature obviously strained to lift it and seemed concerned to hold on to it. The ork was watching closely, as more gretchins emerged from the opening. These held their autorifles in their hands and pointed them at something, all the while chittering triumphantly. As Ragnar watched they emerged into the light, followed by a battered-looking human in green robes. The man's head was shaved. On his forehead was a tattoo of the Imperial eagle surmounted on a stylised ziggurat. This was one of the monks from the temple, Ragnar realised. And he was plainly a captive of the brutish aliens.

Ragnar wondered what this signified. Were orks already in possession of the temple? If so, why were there not more of

them? If there was an ork army present, the whole place should
have reeked of it. Instead he could catch only the scent of these
raiders.

From the distance there suddenly came the sound of random
sporadic shooting. Ragnar briefly wondered if his Blood Claw
had been detected but the sound was coming from too far
away, on the other side of the ruins. It was answered by bursts
of fire and the sounds of ork bellowing from other areas.

What was going on, he wondered?

The answer came swiftly. The ork aimed his gun into the air
and let out a long wild whoop. It was a display of mindless
enthusiasm, of delight in noise for the sake of noise, of shooting for the sake of shooting. A senseless waste of ammunition,
Ragnar thought, but then the ork went quiet again. An expression of brooding menace passed across its face. The sullen
atmosphere of violence suddenly fell on the small group at the
edge of the temple.

As he watched, the gretchin began to caper around their prisoner, until the ork bellowed an order and cuffed the nearest
creature on the ear. Instantly the gretchin calmed down, seeming petrified with fear of their huge master. The ork advanced
on the human prisoner. A swift open-handed slap sent the
wretch reeling to the ground. Blood flowed from his nostrils
and he choked out a couple of teeth. Ragnar gathered a new
respect for the gretchin. They were tougher than they looked if
they could take such a cuffing from an ork.

'Slave!' the ork bellowed in very bad Gothic. 'You slave!'

The monk rolled on to his knees and began to intone a
prayer to the Emperor. A boot from the ork sent him sprawling
into the dirt again, muddying his tattered robe. Ragnar could
smell the man's sweat and fear, but still he rose and started to
pray once more, asking the Emperor to deliver him.

Ragnar wondered if this were a sign, whether the Emperor
had guided him to this place at this time for a specific purpose? That was a dangerous assumption, Ragnar thought.
What if they attempted to free the monk and instead gave
away their presence here to the ork forces? This was supposed
to be a swift and daring mission, and perhaps this would put
it at risk. On the other hand, they had come for the fragment
of the sacred talisman, and perhaps the monk could guide
them swiftly to it. Surely he would have knowledge of where it

lay within this huge complex. That would make his rescue worth the risk – provided they could pull it off. And provided the ork didn't kill them or alert its kindred. Ragnar came to a swift decision: do it.

He glanced behind him to where Sven lay. He looked at the ork and ran his finger across his windpipe in the universal gesture for slitting throats. Sven nodded his acknowledgement with a keen smile. With the knowledge of imminent action, Ragnar's mind cleared. Almost as one, he and Sven rose to a crouch. A mere twenty strides separated them from the ork. The greenskin had its back to them, menacing the prisoner once more. The gretchins' attentions were all on the human's torment, except for the one who had opened the stone box and was tipping its contents onto the ground, an expression of pained concentration on its face, its greenish tongue protruding through its teeth.

The key to the success of this was in quick decisive action before any of the alien scum could respond.

Ragnar charged forward, determined to wait to the last second before activating his chainsword so as not to give away the element of surprise. If possible he was determined to fire no shots. No sense in giving away their location unless they had to.

Ten strides. Ragnar's loping pace covered the ground quickly. So far not one of the enemy had noticed them; their attention was riveted to their sport. Ragnar showed his fangs in a feral snarl. He sensed Sven loping along a few paces behind him. Instinct told him that Sven would take care of the gretchin while he despatched the ork. That suited Ragnar just fine.

Five strides. The greenskin with the open chest looked up from the pile of ceremonial regalia it had turned out onto the ground. It must have caught sight of them from its peripheral vision. Its eyes went wide in startled surprise. Ragnar hoped that it would stay frozen in inactivity for just a few moments longer.

Four strides. Three. The gretchin opened its mouth to scream a warning to its fellows. As it did so, Ragnar thumbed the activation rune of his chainsword, offering a silent prayer to Russ as he did so. The blades roared to life. As Ragnar took his penultimate stride he was already starting his swing.

For a creature so large, the ork responded with surprising quickness. Its head swivelled on its shoulders to look back in the direction of the noise, then its whole body pivoted to face the new threat, its chain-axe starting to rise in a parry. But it was already too late. Ragnar brought his chainsword down like a thunderbolt from the heavens. It cleaved right through the ork's neck just above the neck guard of its armour and separated the head from its body in one flickering stroke. As if unaware that it was already dead, the ork's torso kept moving. The axe continued to rise before flying upward from the ork's nerveless hand. Fingers clutched around the trigger of its bolter in a final futile response to death, the crude weapon sending a flurry of shells into the ground. Each impact raised a small fountain of dirt around its feet. Blood flew from the severed neck. The helmeted head rolled to the ground and glared at Ragnar with undiminished hatred. The eyes still moved, following his flickering motion.

Sven, meanwhile, had ignored the gretchin with the treasure chest and piled into those around the prisoner. They were much slower than their ork master and just as equally doomed. Sven took the head off the first with one sweep of his blade, buried the chainsword to the hilt in the chest of the second and sent the third tumbling to the ground with a brutal blow from the butt of his bolt pistol. It rose to its feet trying to swing its autorifle to bear. The gretchin with the chest meanwhile let out a long panicked shriek and turned to flee. Ragnar wasted no mercy on it, impaling it on his chainsword from behind. The force of his blow lifted the small body right off the ground for a few moments until the rotating blades chopped it in two and the partially bisected corpse flopped to the ground, watering the earth with its foul greenish-yellow blood.

Ragnar glanced around quickly to see Sven finish off the last gretchin. It raised its autorifle in a futile effort to parry the chainsword which was even now heading for it. Sparks flew as the blades bit into crude gunmetal, then the autorifle parted into two sections and Sven's chainsword crunched into the gretchin, killing it instantly. A swift glance around and a sniff of the air told Ragnar there were no more threats in the immediate vicinity. He strode over to the praying monk, who looked up at last as he noticed the Space Wolf's shadow pass over him. A look of surprise and fear passed over the man's face as he saw the unexpected apparition of a bloodstained Space Marine looming over him.

'On your feet, brother!' Ragnar ordered him. 'The Emperor has answered your prayers and delivered you.'

The monk fainted dead away.

Ragnar glanced around, checking all was safe. The light of life had finally faded from the dead ork's head. The brief, brutal struggle was over.

'GET UP, MAN,' Ragnar insisted impatiently. He tapped the monk as softly on the face as he could. The slap of his ceramite gauntlets on flesh still sounded harsh but right now they had no time to be gentle. Ragnar looked around in exasperation as the monk remained comatose. They stood in the chamber from which the prisoner had been taken by the gretchin. Sergeant Hakon, the two inquisitors and Sven were also present. The other Blood Claws had taken up their positions, forming a defensive perimeter around the area. The greenskin corpses had already been dragged out of sight into the woods.

'Stand aside,' said Inquisitor Isaan, brushing past Ragnar and standing over the recumbent monk. She passed her hand over the unconscious man's face. Ragnar felt a prickling at the back of his neck which told him that she was bringing her hidden powers to bear. The monk's eyelashes flickered. He groaned, then sat bolt upright.

'Who are you?' he asked in a cracked voice. Both his tone and his scent told Ragnar that he was very frightened.

'Do not be alarmed,' Isaan said as levelly as she could. 'You are safe. I am Inquisitor Isaan, on the Emperor's service. This is Inquisitor Sternberg. These men are Space Wolves of the Astartes. We are on a mission vital to the security of the Imperium. Who are you?'

'I… I am Brother Tethys, a scribe… of the Order of Perpetual Bliss. I thank you for saving me from those horrors. They would have killed me or made me a slave but for your intervention.'

'Is that what happened to your brethren here?' Isaan asked in a sympathetic voice. The monk nodded. His thin ascetic face looked on the verge of tears. He held one gaunt, bony hand up in front of his face. Ragnar could see that it was shaking.

'Were your brethren taken?'

'Most of them. Taken or killed when the temple fell. We tried to fight but there were just too many of them. When the orks burst through the perimeter walls, some of us fled into the hidden passages, hoping to save our scrolls and treasures and perhaps carry on the fight in secret.'

'How many of you?'

'I do not know that. Not many. I saw several hundred of the brethren rounded up and marched off by the ork scum. I watched from one of the spyholes in the Great Temple. They were loaded into some manner of huge landcrawler and taken south. Probably going to the siege of Galt Prime City.'

'How many orks are left in the ruins?'

'Not that many. The ones here seem to have been left behind by accident. Maybe they were drunk or lost when their comrades left. Who can really tell with such brutes?'

'How did they come to capture you?'

The monk shrugged. 'I left hiding to try to steal some food from the granaries. Hopeless really: the orks had already taken it. They must have caught sight of me as I returned to this chamber, followed me. Why is this important to you?'

'I am trying to get a picture of what happened here – and, to tell the truth, what sort of witness you are.'

'I am loyal to the Emperor. I did my duty with my brothers,' Tethys insisted angrily.

Ragnar was not entirely sure this was the case. Something in the man's scent suggested both shame and the fact that he was not telling the whole truth. Isaan's voice was gentle and reassuring. 'I am sure you were. Who could blame you if you fled when the orks overran the walls? There were so many of them and they were so savage. There were many of them, weren't there?'

'Thousands upon thousands. A numberless horde. A sea of howling green faces. We killed so many of them but they just kept coming and coming. And they had huge war machines armed with terrible weapons. Where did they come from? I would not have believed there were so many orks on the planet. Or that they could be so well-armed.'

'They came from beyond the heavens. But do not worry. The Emperor will punish them for their misdeeds. The Imperium always triumphs in the end. Now tell me, Brother Tethys, why did the orks attack here?'

'Who can tell why such brutes do anything? They were drunk with bloodlust and the desire to kill.'

'Yet they took prisoners – slaves, you said.'

'Only once the battle was long over and they calmed down. Once they were inside the temple grounds, things were terrible. They swarmed everywhere, killing and looting all as they went. Then their leaders seemed to re-establish some sort of control and they went to the sanctum, and pillaged the ancient treasures. Perhaps that is what they sought – our sacred relics.'

'Sacred relics?'

'There are many such here: the bones of holy men, devices of great sanctity created in ancient days – an amulet worn by the Emperor himself, it is said, broken in some ancient battle. One day it will be repaired and used to resurrect the Emperor.' Ragnar saw the inquisitors stiffen like hounds which had caught a scent.

'What did this amulet look like? Like this one?' She gestured to the fragment of the talisman hanging around her neck. 'Have you seen it?'

'It is a holy thing,' Tethys said, suddenly circumspect. 'I should not talk of it to strangers.'

'We are servants of the Emperor, trusted ones. It is our duty to preserve such relics from the claws of those who would defile them. It is your sacred duty to help us do this.' She made another pass with her hand. Once more Ragnar felt psychic power flow. Tethys stiffened a little and then seemed to relax. 'Yes. I understand that now,' he said in a colourless voice. 'I must do my duty to the Emperor most high.'

'Tell us about the amulet.'

'It is a device of silvered metal on a chain of true silver. Within it is set a green jewel of a thousand facets. It looks on one side as if it had been broken from a larger gem. That side is jagged, not smooth and polished. The high abbot wears it on the night of the Blood Moon when performing the rite of ultimate-'

'It sounds like what we're bloody well looking for,' Sven said impatiently.

Inquisitor Isaan swung her head around and silenced him with a poisonous glare of her dark brown eyes. The meaning was clear: *Do not interrupt.* She glanced back at the monk, who had opened his mouth to speak once more.

'If you seek the amulet it is too late. The orks have taken it. I saw it around the throat of their leader. I am not surprised. Our visionaries claim it is an object of great power.'

Isaan looked at Sternberg, then at the rest of them. Her face related all that needed to be said.

CHAPTER SEVEN

'THERE CAN BE no turning back,' Inquisitor Sternberg said grimly. 'We must recover the Talisman of Lykos from those ork brutes.'

Ragnar and the other Blood Claws stared at him. Ragnar could tell his battle-brothers shared his momentary sense of disbelief.

'The thing is gone, man!' Sergeant Hakon said. 'An ork army has taken it.'

'Then we shall retrieve it!' Sternberg said in a voice that permitted no opposition.

'And how precisely will we find it?' Hakon demanded. 'These jungles are swarming with orks. There are ork forces all over the continent. How can we find a single ork amidst them?'

'How did we locate the talisman in the first place?' Sternberg countered.

'I can use my… gifts,' Karah Isaan suggested. 'The link between the two fragments still exists – the closer they are the stronger the link gets. Now I can sense the general direction. As we get closer I will be able to pinpoint it exactly.'

'Could we not teleport back to the ship, perform the ritual once more, and teleport back down?' Ragnar suggested.

'The *Light of Truth* has been driven out of teleport range by ork warcraft,' Sternberg said. 'It is moving out to rendezvous with the approaching Imperial relief fleet. It will return with the task force in one standard week.'

'You hope,' Hakon said.

'With the Emperor's blessing, it will be so.'

'Well if we're stuck down here for a bloody week anyway...' Sven started. A stern look from the sergeant silenced him.

'And what will we do when we find the bearer of the talisman? This is no ordinary ork. It is a warlord. He will be in the middle of the horde and well protected.'

'Are you not Space Marines? Is this not the sort of mission you were trained for?' Sternberg said.

A silence came over the small group. It was broken by the distant sounds of the remaining orks letting off their weapons. Everyone present looked at each other warily. Ragnar considered the inquisitor's words. He was certain that if there was a way, they could find it. After all they were Space Marines, the Imperium's elite warriors. He was just not sure there was a way to do what the inquisitor wanted in the time they had available.

'You are proposing we locate this ork, steal into its camp, snatch the artefact, and then escape?' Hakon summarised. His tone was one of heavy sarcasm, but from the way he tilted his head, Ragnar could see he was giving the matter serious consideration. The Blood Claw could understand that. If the deed could be done, it would be a mighty feat of arms, worthy of a saga hero. In fact, Ragnar was thinking, perhaps this would be the way into the sagas for all of them. Their names would ring down the millennia in the annals of the Chapter. If they survived. And if they succeeded. He had to admit they sounded like very large 'ifs'.

'Precisely,' Sternberg was saying. 'That is, if you think you and your warriors can perform this mission. If you can't, you can wait in the jungle and Inquisitor Isaan and I will proceed alone.'

Hakon laughed softly. There was no way he was going to allow that. It would not redound to the Chapter's credit, for its warriors to withdraw and abandon two servants of the Emperor on such an important mission. On the other hand, that mission might well prove to be suicidal. Ragnar understood the sergeant's dilemma. 'I would not allow that,' Hakon said finally.

'You cannot stop me. I am not one of your Chapter. You cannot command me to do anything,' Inquisitor Sternberg said, his face set.

The sergeant shook his head slowly. Space Wolves were not famous for their respect of any authority save their own leaders, and that they gave grudgingly to men who had earned it. A leader who made foolish decisions did not remain one long, rarely became one in the first place.

Ragnar wondered whether Hakon was going to make all of this crystal clear to the inquisitors or whether he would find another, more diplomatic path. The sergeant gestured at the amulet which Isaan wore. 'I am responsible for the safety of the talisman,' he said smoothly. 'I will not allow you to proceed if your actions endanger it.'

The two men glared at each other, and for a brief moment Ragnar felt that they might come to blows. He watched with interest. He had no doubts as to who would win under those circumstances.

Karah Isaan, witnessing the mounting tension, looked from one to the other and back. 'There is no need for this. We are not enemies here. We all wish to serve the Imperium.' She gazed meaningfully at Sternberg. 'Perhaps the sergeant has a point. Perhaps recovering the talisman is not possible.'

'And perhaps it is. We should at least endeavour to find out,' Sternberg insisted.

Ragnar could see the sergeant nod. He could tell Hakon was considering the inquisitor's words. He wondered whether Isaan was using any of her mind tricks on him. He did not think so. There was no sense of any power flowing here and he was sure he would notice. Unless, of course, he told himself, the power was being used to ensure that he did not. He pushed the thought aside; he doubted whether that was even possible.

'Are there any alternatives?' he heard himself start to say. 'Could we not wait for the fleet to arrive and then bring down a strike force from orbit?'

'Time is of the essence,' Sternberg said with a shake of his head. 'Who knows how long it will take the fleet to fight its way into position to allow our forces to make planetfall?'

'If nothing else, we can be advance scouts for the invasion,' said Hakon. Ragnar could tell he was starting to warm to the plan.

'Perhaps we should see where the other talisman is,' Isaan suggested.

'I think we can all agree on that,' said Sternberg.

His companion reached up to touch the amulet, where it dangled from her neck. 'I will do so at once.'

INQUISITOR ISAAN emerged from the chamber in which she had performed her ritual. Ragnar did not need her scent to tell him she was troubled. Her face wore a frown and her dark eyes were slitted in thought.

'What is it?' he asked. The others were silent, waiting for her answer.

'Something strange is happening,' she said. 'I could sense it through the link. I think the ork chieftain is starting to use the talisman's powers. He has found some way of tapping into them.'

'What does that mean?' Hakon asked.

'I do not know exactly what yet,' she said. 'But I doubt that it can mean anything else but trouble.'

Somehow Ragnar was not surprised to hear this. 'Where now?'

'The orks are south of here, along the river. I saw a city under siege.'

'Galt Prime,' Brother Tethys spoke up. 'Our capital.'

From the distance came a sound like thunder. Ragnar wondered what it was. He turned his face to the sky and soon worked it out. Three long exhaust contrails slashed across the blue like a swipe from the claws of a giant cat. Even as Ragnar watched he noticed the dots that were the source of the vapour. They grew in his field of vision until he could see that they were stubby winged, crudely fabricated aircraft.

'Get down,' he yelled. And threw himself flat.

Karah did the same. The ork warplanes passed directly over the temple complex. They were flying low, looking for something.

'I think we should get as far from here as we can before the orks start looking for us,' said Karah.

Ragnar could see she was scared. He did not blame her. He too wondered if it was a coincidence that the ork craft had appeared so soon after she had made her psychic link with the ork warlord. Perhaps if she could sense him, he could sense her. It was not a reassuring thought.

BRINGING A RELUCTANT Brother Tethys with them, they ventured into the maze of tunnels within the walls of the huge stone pyramids. It was quiet and cool and the walls blocked off all sounds from outside. Ragnar wondered how safe this was, and then realised it didn't matter much. If the orks were looking for them, it was most likely safer than being in the jungle. Ork troops would be out there right now, trying to pick up a trail.

Brother Tethys held one of the ancients' ever-burning glow-globes in his hand. The light made the pinkish fingers of his flesh seem translucent. It was an illusion Ragnar had seen before but nonetheless a potent one. All around him he was aware of the smell of death. He noticed that the walls were full of alcoves and in each alcove lay a desiccated corpse. This was obviously some sort of burial place. Beneath each alcove was carved the name of a monk, in Imperial runes, to make them sacred but there was no air of holiness about this place, no smell of sanctity. It was a boneyard, pure and simple, and they were heading ever deeper into the middle of it.

'The temples are huge,' Tethys said. 'They have been sinking underground for years. The pyramids you have seen on the surface are only part of much larger structures beneath the grounds. They go down a long way. We could hide here for months and never be found.'

'Not much food down here…' Sven muttered only half-seriously.

'There's always this salted meat,' Nils said, gesturing towards the corpses. Hearing the sharp intakes of breath from the inquisitors and the diminutive monk, he added hastily, 'I was joking.'

'We'll have less of your humour, Brother Nils,' Sergeant Hakon said.

'How are we going to get to the fragment of the talisman?' Ragnar asked, to break the tension.

'These tunnels lead to the river; the river leads to the city of Galt Prime. We can take a boat down there towards the ork lines.'

'Then what?' Ragnar asked. He knew it was a question that had been on all the Blood Claws' minds.

'Then we'll see,' said Sergeant Hakon.

'And how are we going to get down the river?' asked Sven. 'I don't fancy swimming.'

'Once we're out of the temple complex we'll build a raft and head downstream. According to Brother Tethys the current's strong, so it shouldn't be too much work.'

'What if those warplanes come back?' asked Nils.

'We'll spear that orka when we see it,' Hakon said, then lapsed once more into silence.

THE RIVER WAS broad and brown, and it stank. It reeked of rotting vegetation and algae and wastes pumped into it from the temple complex. Ragnar wondered how much longer that would happen. He doubted that the orks would maintain the machinery there. From what he had seen they had already begun the business of dismantling it all and incorporating it into their crude engines of destruction. As a race they seemed inveterate scavengers and tinkerers. Still there was no doubting that their primitive-looking devices worked. Those warplanes had been effective enough.

Cloying mud sucked at his boots as they struggled along an overgrown pathway between the trees away from the tunnel that had emerged in the riverbank. Once they were sufficiently far away from Xikar to feel safe they would begin the construction of their raft and start the perilous journey downstream. Ragnar felt eyes upon him and looked over to see Inquisitor Isaan was watching him thoughtfully.

'Don't worry,' he said to her. 'We'll make it through safely.'

'I don't doubt it,' she replied. 'The Emperor is watching over us.'

She didn't sound or smell as certain as her words implied, Ragnar thought. But she managed a smile and strode softly forward into the gathering gloom.

THE RAFTS WERE hefty enough to be stable, made from tree trunks cut down with chainswords and lashed together with constricting vine. The Wolves had made two of them, together with punting poles from the bamboo reeds that grew all along the jungle edge. Not that they were needed, Ragnar had seen: the current was strong enough to carry them at a speed well beyond that even a Space Marine could march at through the dense jungle.

The expedition had split into two groups, one for each raft. On the leading raft were Inquisitor Sternberg, Sergeant Hakon, Strybjorn and Lars. On the second raft were Ragnar, Karah Isaan, Sven, Nils and Brother Tethys. Nils stood at the back of their raft, guiding it with the long bamboo pole. Lars was doing the same on the other raft.

Even the threat of ork air patrols had receded. In many places the jungle was so overgrown and entangled that the huge multi-trunked banyan trees grew right over the river, blocking out all but a few blinding rays of sunlight. It was like sailing down a tunnel beneath the trees. It was as Brother Tethys had said. There were few of the greenskins left in the temple complex and they seemed to be savage and purposeless, mere flotsam left behind when the tide that was the great ork horde had moved on.

The jungle was alive with life. Large, shaggy ape-like creatures crashed through the canopy overhead. Massive panther-sized beasts, mottled and six-limbed, lurked on the branches and studied them with enormous unblinking eyes. Now and again Ragnar caught sight of an enormous serpent-shape slithering through the branches. It must have been thirty strides long at least with a body thicker than an ale barrel. He wasn't too troubled. There was no beast in this jungle he couldn't handle. In his experience few natural living things were impervious to chainsword blades and bolter shells.

He shook his head and told himself that such overconfidence was dangerous. What if he was attacked by surprise? Or while asleep? What if some creature was strong enough to crunch through his armour? He knew it was unlikely. His Space Wolf senses were such that they would alert him to almost any threat even while asleep. And ceramite would prove impervious to any natural fang or claw.

Don't be so certain, a part of him told himself. You don't know that. Men have died in far less dangerous places than this by thinking the way you do. After all, he was a stranger here. What did he really know of this world? Some of the plants and animals were similar to those on Fenris, that was all.

In a way this was hardly surprising. Most of their ancestors had probably come from distant Terra all of those tens of thousands of years ago during the first great human Diaspora, when Man had set out to colonise the galaxy and remake it in his own image. They were the descendants of those old creatures and plants, reshaped to fit their new homeworlds.

Around the next great bend, huge, dusty brown reptiles basked along the riverbank, presumably some species of dragon. Their immense jaws looked as if they could down a man in one gulp – even one armoured in ceramite. Ragnar kept his hand near the holster of his bolt pistol as one of the creatures slithered down the muddy bank and into the water. For such a large creature it moved with surprising stealth, the splash it made when it entered the water would have been barely audible to any man save one with the enhanced hearing of a Space Wolf. The creature very much resembled a log as it floated down the river towards them. Ragnar could see that the colours of its leathery hide could almost have been designed to mimic old or rotting wood. He wondered how many innocent river fishermen had been deceived by that, how many animals that had come to the river to drink or cross the waters. Well, he was not fooled, and he could tell by the scent of his companions that they were not either.

He looked at Sven and the inquisitor, who had already drawn their weapons. Nils held the pole one-handed and waited to see what the creature was intending to do. By the tension in his body Ragnar could tell he was ready to draw his pistol at a moment's notice and open fire. A swift glance told him that the folk on the other raft had perceived the threat as well, and were ready to help. It seemed apparent that the monster would reach Ragnar's raft first – and it was coming on quickly. Brother Tethys had finally noticed what was going on, and was unshouldering the autorifle.

'Riverdragon!' he almost shrieked as if everyone else were unaware of the threat. Ragnar laid a hand reassuringly on his shoulder.

'Don't worry, we've seen it,' he said. 'Use the bolt pistol. It fires explosive shells. More effective against a creature this size.'

If Tethys heard a word Ragnar said, he gave no sign of it. He reeked of panic. No, of terror. 'Those things are dreadful, the scourge of the river. They pull you under and keep you there till you drown.'

Ragnar wondered if that was a less pleasant death than being torn apart by those huge fangs and then gobbled up. He shook his head. He doubted that there were any pleasant deaths. The creature swam closer. Ragnar could see that its tiny-seeming legs, out of proportion to that huge body, were working beneath the water, and occasionally the thing propelled itself forward with a swish of its huge tail. He was beginning to get a sense of quite how large it was, probably twice as long as this whole raft. He was aware of the tiny, intelligent-seeming eyes gazing at him from either side of the beast's snout. It was a chilling sight, and sent cold fingers of fear running up and down his spine.

'By Russ, it's bloody huge!' Sven said. 'Wonder what it tastes like. I'm getting fed up with tree bark and cockroaches.'

'I've speared bigger orkas,' Ragnar said, levelling his bolter and aiming it directly at the riverdragon's eye.

'Orkas don't have teeth like that,' Sven said.

The riverdragon had opened its mouth and suddenly row upon row of yellowing tusk-like teeth, each as long as a dagger, became visible. Its features distorted and its eyes narrowed, making it hard to aim for them.

'It's like you, Sven,' Nils said out of the corner of his mouth, drawing his bolt pistol and getting ready to shoot, never taking his eyes off the beast for a second.

'What do you damn well mean by that?'

'It opens its mouth and its head disappears.'

'Ha bloody ha! Another crack like that and you'll be joining it for a swim.'

Ragnar heard further splashes from the riverbank and knew that more of the huge reptiles were dropping into the water. Suddenly the situation had become very threatening indeed, and he reckoned that his earlier confidence might have been a little misplaced. All the creature had to do was rear out of the water and it could smash the raft to flinders. He was reminded of the battle he had fought with the seadragon back on Fenris, what seemed half a lifetime and half the galaxy away.

'Shut up and shoot!' he said and opened fire. The roar of bolt pistols filled his ears as the Blood Claws joined in. Rocket contrails blazed towards the beast. Its flesh erupted where the shells bit into its leathery hide. The creature emitted a long, hissing screech but kept on coming. Ragnar wondered if the creature felt any pain or whether they had simply angered it. Looking at those jaws and the massive ropes of muscle on either side of them, he wasn't so sure now that his armour could survive being bitten by them. He certainly had no great desire to find out.

The beast kept swimming on through the hail of fire. The Space Wolves on the other ship had joined in now. Huge chunks of flesh were being blown out of the beast, and Ragnar was sure he could see the white of bone amidst the pale pink meat. Still the creature showed no sign of dying.

Ragnar pulled the trigger again and again, hoping in vain to put a shell through the beast's eye and blow out its brain. But its head was thrashing from side to side and it was difficult to aim precisely. The Wolf pulled the trigger rapidly, sending bolter shell after bolter shell hurtling towards the beast. Its leathery skin was torn and shredded, but to Ragnar's awe the massive skull endured the pounding. What was the beast made of?

He kept firing but risked a glance towards the riverbank. Three more of the huge beasts were coming ever closer, making no attempt at stealth. Their tails churned the water as they swept swiftly towards the fray. Ragnar wondered whether they were drawn to the commotion or by the smell of blood. He cursed under his breath. If one of the creatures was proving so hard to kill, he did not relish a conflict with four of them.

'It's too dumb to die!' Nils shouted above the bolter blasts.

'Just like you then!' Sven snapped back.

The creature was less than twenty strides away and closing fast. Ragnar's mind raced. Perhaps a change of tactic was called for. 'Inquisitor! Can you use your powers on it?'

'I don't know if it has a mind to affect,' Isaan called back.

'Don't say it, Nils,' shouted Sven. Then suddenly the beast was gone. A huge wave of water rippled towards them as it dived below the surface. For a moment only the massive tail was visible and then it, too, had vanished.

'Did we get it?' Ragnar shouted.

'Say what?' asked Nils in a tone of innocent confusion.

'I don't think so!' bellowed Sven, looking all around them.

'I don't like this at all,' said Nils.

Ragnar risked a glance towards the other beasts. They were less than a hundred strides away. Too close for comfort, Ragnar thought.

'Watch out!' Sergeant Hakon bellowed.

What does he mean, Ragnar thought – and then felt the whole raft lurch upwards. He frantically tried to regain his balance as he tumbled towards the water. It occurred to him in that moment, exactly what had happened. The cunning beast had erupted from the water underneath them, lifting the whole raft into the air. Ragnar watched the jungle wheel about below him and then he shut his mouth as the murky water engulfed him.

Desperately he fought to hold on to his bolt pistol. It was a terrible disgrace for a Space Marine to lose his weapon. The strangeness of that thought under the circumstances hit him. The water was a maelstrom of churning waves and bubbles. It was dark but nearby he could see the enormous shape of the riverdragon whirling to face them. When seen from the surface, the beast looked clumsy but once you were in the water with it, it suddenly seemed unbelievably sinuous, swift and agile. He glanced around and saw the others were also in the water, limbs fluttering as they tried to head towards the surface.

He holstered his pistol and struck upwards himself. Keep calm, he told himself and prayed for the others to do the same. He knew that many brave seamen on Fenris had died in situations like this simply by making stupid mistakes. Sometimes in panic they swam downwards instead of up, pushing themselves ever deeper below the waters from which they were trying to escape. Ragnar wondered just how deep the river was here, then decided now was not the time to try and find out. His head broke the water. He saw some of the others bobbing to the surface near him.

He sensed the nearness of the riverdragon and felt a moment's dread as he imagined those huge jaws opening up below him, and then taking him down in one gulp.

'Look out!' he heard Sergeant Hakon shouting again.

He glanced around and saw that the wounded beast had broken the surface and was coming towards him. Its jaws were open wide. It was like looking down a long, pink, tooth-filled tunnel. Ragnar could not remember ever seeing anything quite so fearsome. The oily, reptilian smell of the beast filled his nostrils, along with the scent of its blood, and the rotten meat trapped between its teeth and the flesh decomposing deep within its corrupt bowels. It seemed to him that, at any moment, he too might become just another bit of butchered meat in the creature's stomach. He wondered for an instant whether his life was really over. Then, deep within his own brain, the beast that was part of him awoke, and responded to the threat with instinctive cunning. What the monster could do, he could do.

As it bore down upon him, he waited until the last second, until the jaws were almost closing upon him, then took a lungful of air and dived, kicking strongly. The riverdragon passed overhead, seeming as large as the hull of a great dragonship. Incongruously, in that moment, Ragnar's memory had a flashback to the times when as a lad he had dived from his father's ship and swum beneath it, purely out of bravado and to prove that he could do it to his watching friends.

He saw the great clawed paws thrashing the water, and the supple curve of the huge creature's spine as it turned to try to catch him. Was it his imagination or did the thing actually seem slower? As it swam, it was leaving behind it a wake of oily black blood. Ragnar could taste it in the water. Perhaps all those bolter shells were taking effect after all. Watching the thing spin around, though, it seemed unlikely to save him. The huge jaws gaped once more as the beast came for him again. He kicked out, trying to evade it, but the river was the creature's native habitat, not his own, and in its turgid waters it was far more agile than he, especially enclosed in his power armour.

He felt the jaws close around him. He felt the pressure on his chest plate as the teeth started to clamp down. The riverdragon gave a swift flick of its head, like a dog with a rat in its mouth. If Ragnar had been an ordinary man, he knew his neck would have broken in that moment. But he was not a normal man, he was a Space Marine, and his body had been reconstructed to withstand far more stress than any normal human beings'. The whiplash threatened to drive the air from his lungs. Sparks flickered in his field of vision. He felt vertebrae grind as his neck muscles took the strain. Ragnar prayed to Russ and refused to black out. He fought to retain consciousness.

There was a sense of increased pressure. He realised that the beast was taking him down, trying to drown him as it would its normal prey. No, maybe not. It was swimming away from the rafts. Ragnar could see them on the surface, shimmering in a patch of sunlight. Perhaps it was carrying him to its lair, to feed its young. Perhaps it was doing something else entirely. He had no idea and no time to speculate. His armour had switched into oxygen recycling mode. He was in no danger of drowning for the time being. Systems designed to keep him alive in the depths of space would have no trouble doing so here. The major problem was that the jaws were still closing. He could hear the ceramite creaking, feel armoured plates grinding against each other. Prickles of pain from his sensory systems told him that at certain stress points there was a danger of the armour giving way. If that happened, other systems might fail, and then indeed he might drown.

Looking up he could see a new danger threatened. The other riverdragons were diving downwards, coming for him – or perhaps they were coming for their wounded brother. Could it be that the smell of blood was driving them into a frenzy and attracting them towards their prey, the way it did with sharks in the Worldsea of Fenris?

Ragnar could see that his supposition was right. The largest riverdragon was coming for his captor. Another two were circling around them, looking for an opening. Suddenly bubbles of air and billows of blood surrounded Ragnar as the two giants closed for battle. Out of the corner of his eye, Ragnar saw a massive claw sweep towards him. The force of the blow was immense. His head reeled with pain. Blackness filled his field of vision. Just as suddenly the pressure on his chest relented. His monstrous captor had let him go in order to use its own jaws to fight with.

Not that it would necessarily do him any good. One of the other beasts might scoop him up, just another tasty morsel. He fumbled with the utility belt on his waist, and felt his fingers close on the grenade he sought. Through the water he saw another beast coming at him, a nightmare vision of massive teeth and mighty jaws, tiny eyes glittering with ancient malice and hunger. Limbs working as if in slow motion in the water, he pushed the grenade into its mouth and kicked out, heading for the surface, wondering what would happen next.

For an instant, nothing occurred. He looked down at the riverdragon and saw it arching its back as it prepared to come up after him. Then its whole body seemed to inflate from within. Its stomach expanded, as if the creature had swallowed something much too big for it. Its jaws distended, and even here under the water Ragnar was aware of its roar of pain. Then the flesh of the creature's belly parted, and its innards blew out into the water. It had swallowed the grenade, and then it had been blow apart through its soft unarmoured innards. Even as he watched, the other riverdragons hurtled towards it, determined to get at this huge easy meal.

Ragnar's head broke surface. He saw that the others had managed to pull themselves onto the raft and were watching anxiously. They grinned in relief as they saw him swimming towards them. Ragnar flopped up onto the raft, water running from his dented armour. He turned his head and gazed back. The water churned and turned dark with blood. It was the only evidence he could see of the titanic struggle taking place in the gloomy depths, and it faded from view behind them, as the raft drifted around a bend in the river.

'Say that I'm mindless just like that bloody beast!' he heard Sven say, before lying back and shutting his eyes.

CHAPTER EIGHT

THE JUNGLE BEGAN to thin out. The river became wider and darker. Ragnar handled the pole easily, keeping the raft on the left bank under the outlying branches. Ahead of them were all the signs of war. Huge smoke clouds billowed darkly into the sky, reaching upwards like the stretching fingers of giants. Great tracts had been ripped from the nearby jungle by the movement of huge machines. Ork warplanes roared overhead, flashing across the sky to deliver their freight-loads of bombs. In the distance, he could make out their target: the massive walled city of Galt Prime.

It was a city on a scale that did not exist on Fenris. Skyscraper towers loomed over the massive plascrete walls, each as huge as one of the islands that erupted from the Worldsea. And there were other things, monstrous war engines, large as the huge buildings, that moved towards the human city. Ragnar knew these were gargants, mighty metal death machines built in the form of primitive effigies of the orks' dreadful deities. They bristled with massive weapons. From where he was, Ragnar could hear the frightful roar as they lobbed giant shells into the crumbling city walls. Ragnar knew that the illusion of war was untrue. The city had already surrendered. The orks were merely indulging their appetite for destruction.

'Russ take us! It looks like we arrived just in time to save the bloody city,' said Sven, his lips twisting in a bitter ironic smile. Ragnar glanced over at him.

'Do you want to do it yourself, or shall I give you a hand?'

'I'm feeling generous so I'll let you share in my glory. You can have a couple of verses in the Saga of Sven.'

'As ever, you are too generous.' Ragnar was suddenly glad that Sven was there. For all his childish jokes and nasty moods, he could think of no one better to have at his back if they really were going to infiltrate this ork army.

'The best thing about this is that we'll have the element of surprise,' he said with a smile. 'They'll never expect us to come out of the jungle and completely overwhelm them like this. Inquisitor Sternberg is a master tactician.'

'I almost feel sorry for those orks,' added Sven. 'Almost.'

Ragnar knew the humour covered a very real tension. For the past few days, as they had drifted downriver, they had come upon ever more evidence of the orks' savagery. They had passed riverside villages burned to the ground and seen huge areas of the rainforest burning. As far as he could tell there was no reason for it other than sheer wanton destructiveness. It had been arson on a huge scale, the product of a mindless rage that Ragnar could not understand. This was hardly surprising: orks did not think like humans. They were, after all, a very alien race.

In the skirmishes they had fought and the ambushes they had laid for the orks, he had come to respect their brute savagery and battlelust. They were fearless foes, hardy beyond belief. He had seen one continue to fight after its arm had been blown off by bolter shells. When it ran out of ammo it had actually picked up its own severed arm to use as a club. The creature had seemed almost impervious to pain.

At first Ragnar thought the small groups they had encountered were patrols but then he realised that no such strategy was at work. They were merely stragglers who had got separated from the main ork force, either through sheer negligence or out of a cunning desire to find fresh places to pillage. Either the orks had no concept of effective strategy or they were overconfident and felt they did not need it. If the latter was the case,

Ragnar could understand it. As far as he could see the human defenders of Galt had mounted little effective resistance.

And that, too, was hardly surprising. Most of them were not warriors. They were farmers and foresters and traders who had lived for too long under the great shield of the Imperium's influence. They had not expected such a savage invasion. And according to Inquisitor Sternberg, there must have been corruption too on a huge scale. The Imperial Governor was supposed to maintain a powerful standing army but they had found no sign of it. During their late night discussions around the campfire, Sternberg claimed that the money had most likely been misappropriated, used to swell the Governor's private treasure chest. He also claimed that if the man were still alive, the Imperium would extract such a vengeance on him that he would wish the orks had killed him. The thought of the Governor's folly and mismanagement drove the inquisitor into a quiet rage the like of which Ragnar had never seen before.

They had monitored the comm-net and listened in horror to reports from the human towns and fortresses as one by one they fell before the invaders' superior numbers and weaponry. It seemed as if the entire embattled human civilisation was going down into darkness. The only cheering news was that the Imperial relief force was preparing to make a counter-attack as soon as the spaceways above Galt were cleared by the human fleet. It appeared such a decisive victory was but days away, but it had left them with a dilemma. Should they await the coming of the Imperial battle force and hide in the jungle? Or should they press on with their original plan and seize the fragment of the talisman? Ragnar had heard the arguments for both cases and had been unable to make up his own mind. If they remained in the jungle there was always the chance they would be discovered by ork forces and slain. Further, there was the chance that the bearer of the talisman would slip away in the fighting or that the artefact itself might be destroyed. The inquisitors were not sure if this were possible but if there was even the slightest chance of it then they did not want to take the risk. On the other hand, what were their chances of working their way into the very heart of this huge invading army without being discovered? There were times when it seemed reckless to the point of folly.

Ragnar could not make up his own mind but the part of him that was Fenrisian inclined towards the second option. It would be a glorious feat and one that would live long in the sagas if they could pull it off. But it was a big 'if', and the quest for glory became mere folly if it involved throwing away your life to no purpose. It was one of the things his instructors had drummed into him again and again during his basic training. So it had gone, backwards and forwards in his mind, as they progressed downriver. In all that time it had seemed a slightly unreal exercise, as they quested through the jungle towards their goal. But now the journey was over, and the point of decision was almost reached, and suddenly it was no longer something to be thought about, but something they would have to act and risk their lives upon.

Ragnar did not envy Sergeant Hakon and the two inquisitors at that moment. He was glad the decision was not his. He tried to tell himself that it was not that he minded risking his own life, but he would not want the lives of his comrades and friends hanging on his choice. And for the most part he managed to believe himself, though sometimes he caught himself wondering whether he really did want to risk his own life to find this precious artefact for Sternberg. Was it really worth his life? Was it worth all of their lives? The answer was straightforward: if they could save the people of Aerius, yes. But that too was a big 'if'.

Now their journey was almost at an end. The days spent travelling downstream, fighting off riverdragons and the endless nights filled with biting insects were almost over. Ahead of them lay Galt Prime and the massive ork force. It was almost time for them to implement their plan. Ragnar wondered whether any of them would survive it.

It was all very well to sit around a blazing fire and talk about infiltrating the ork camp and seizing the talisman they sought. It was another thing entirely to actually do it. Now that he had seen evidence of the sheer size of the ork force with his own eyes, Ragnar wondered if it were even possible. Inquisitor Isaan was confident that this close she could sense the location of the ork leader and the talisman he held but Ragnar was not sure that this would do them any good. He was sure to be protected by thousands of ferocious warriors, too many for even Sven to overcome in his wildest fantasies.

They poled the raft towards land and scrambled up the river-bank, weapons held ready. Ragnar threw himself flat and gazed out into the jungle. It was time to abandon the rafts and continue on foot.

THEY MADE CAMP that evening in a burned out building, what had once been a warehouse in a suburb a mile or so outside the city's main defensive wall. The building was tumbled down and showed signs of having been fought over. Bullet holes pockmarked the walls. The roof was half blown away and the support girders had half collapsed so that you could, if you wished, run up them onto the unsafe roof. The place smelled of gun smoke and blood and fear. Old bones, some of them cracked for marrow, littered the floor. Ragnar wondered whether this had been done by the human defenders, orks or the wild animals that had come in from the jungle to scavenge. It was something he didn't really want to think about, but the thought kept entering his mind unbidden anyway.

Huge cockroaches scuttled away from their dimmed glow-globes. Vicious-looking jungle rats, as large as small dogs, watched them with glittering eyes from the gloom. Ragnar guessed that it would not take too much provocation for them to attack. They looked like ferocious creatures but that was hardly surprising: most of the beasts on this world were.

He glanced around at his companions, his enhanced vision able to pick out every detail of their faces even in the dim light. Inquisitor Sternberg looked gaunt and worried. A strange fanatical gleam glittered in his eyes. He had lost weight in the jungle. Unlike the Space Wolves, he had not been able to survive by eating bark and grubs and leaves. His normal human stomach had forced him to live on powdered field rations, and while these contained everything a man needed to live on, they were hardly substantial fare. He now had the look of an ascetic martyr, the type Ragnar had seen pictured on stained glass windows on the *Light of Truth*. It was as if all excess flesh were being stripped from his body by some wasting disease. Ragnar wondered if that might not be the case. All manner of odd illnesses could strike a man down in the jungle. He himself had suffered a fever for several hours while his body adapted. It was so much harder for an ordinary man, he knew.

Karah Isaan had also lost weight but it seemed only to enhance her loveliness, emphasising her huge eyes and high cheekbones. Ragnar guessed that her homeworld was much more like Galt than Sternberg's for she seemed to have adapted to the heat and the humidity much better than her male counterpart. The talisman glittered at Isaan's throat. Normally she kept it concealed beneath her armoured chest plate but at the moment she was staring into the jewel's depths as if contemplating some holy mystery. Ragnar thought he could sense the swirl of her strange powers in the air about him.

Brother Tethys looked tired and haggard. The long days in hiding and the trip through the jungle had taken it out of him. His nerves had not been helped by the fighting in the jungle or the sight of what the orks had done to his homeworld. Ragnar thought he understood a little. He could imagine how he would feel if the orks plundered Fenris.

Sergeant Hakon seemed to have become younger. With every day of travel, and every skirmish fought, years had fallen from him. It was obvious to Ragnar that the old wolf was glad to be in the field again, and not stuck in the training camps of Fenris. Ragnar could identify with this. Like all Fenrisians, and all Space Wolves, he held that the only good death for a man was on the battlefield surrounded by the bodies of his foes. But it was more than that, Ragnar could see. Sergeant Hakon was enjoying himself. He liked being here on this alien world, amid the ruin and the death, with the prospect of a life or death fight ahead of him. He had the happiness of a man who was doing work which he had trained to do all of his life. It showed. Even though his face was grim and his bearing calmly alert, his movements had taken on a new grace, and his voice a new tone. His scent too had altered to convey this. Ragnar was glad. At times like this, the fact that the pack had a relaxed and competent leader was deeply reassuring.

He could tell that the others felt the same way. They were new to all of this, and this was their first major test. All of them had been blooded against the powers of Chaos in the mountains of Asaheim but this was their first time off-world. Each of them knew that, assuming they survived, it would not be their last. The life of a Space Wolf consisted of moving from planet to planet, campaign to campaign, as the Imperium and the

Great Wolf deemed necessary. All of them were nervous and excited.

Sven's face looked brutal and sardonic by turns as he glanced at his companions. His coarse features and broken nose made him look sullen, like a chastised teenager, but the quirk of his lips and gleam in his eyes told of his underlying humour. He opened his mouth and belched loudly, causing the two inquisitors to stare at him.

Nils's pale features and ash blond hair and brows made him look as young as a boy. His nervous movements were quick and bird-like and his head turned constantly as he surveyed the surroundings and sniffed the air. No chance of him being caught unawares, Ragnar thought.

Ragnar found Strybjorn's features as unreadable and expressionless as always. He was a man of few words and no idle chatter. His was a monumental face that looked as if it had been hewn from granite; Sven looked like a choirboy in comparison. The eyes were set in deep sockets. Strybjorn caught Ragnar looking at him and stared back, eyes flinty and dark. Ragnar wondered whether he still felt any trace of their old animosity. Sometimes, Ragnar knew, he himself did. It had not been entirely lost, even though each had saved the other's life. The two of them would continue to avoid each other as best they could, as they had throughout this mission.

Meanwhile Lars had his fingers interlocked in prayer. His gaze was fixed in the mid-distance and Ragnar wondered exactly what he was seeing there. Another of his visions? Or was he merely contemplating the sights of the day. Of all his companions, Ragnar understood Lars the least. He knew that the youth had several times been taken away by the Rune Priests to be tested. Ragnar did not know what for. Was it possible that he would be selected to join their ranks, or was there some other purpose entirely to it?

Sergeant Hakon looked around at each of them in turn. Ragnar sensed that the veteran warrior was measuring them, trying to judge their commitment and hardihood. Ragnar wondered whether he should feel insulted. After all he had passed all the tests that were required to join the Space Wolves, and he had been blooded in combat against the forces of darkness. He had proven his worth to the Chapter. Swiftly he pushed such thoughts aside. He knew that all of life was a test, and it was one that could be failed at any time. He knew that even the bravest of warriors could lose courage and break, and it only had to happen once for it to prove fatal to the man and his companions.

Hakon seemed to guess the thoughts passing through Ragnar's mind, for he smiled at him coldly, then glanced at the inquisitors. He didn't speak. Sensing the sergeant's gaze on him, Sternberg looked up. For a long moment, Ragnar thought that he, too, was going to remain silent but after a heartbeat, he spoke. 'We have reached the outskirts of Galt Prime. We are approaching the heart of the ork army.'

'The talisman is near,' added Karah Isaan. Her voice was strange, hollow-sounding, like someone uttering a prophesy or speaking in a trance. 'As we get closer the link grows stronger. I can see it now. I can see the bearer. He is an ork of fearful power, and he is the vessel of something greater. In some way, he is the focus of this ork army. He binds it together. He speaks for their gods or so he believes, and in a way this belief is true.'

'If we kill him will the horde disperse?' Ragnar asked. His throat felt suddenly dry. In her own way the inquisitor too seemed to be the focus of powers greater than herself. It was not entirely a comforting thought.

'I know not. It is possible. But first we must kill him. I am not sure that will be easy. Or even possible.'

'Anyone can be killed,' Hakon said. 'With a powerful enough weapon.'

'This warlord is tapping into the powers of the talisman, as well as his gods. He will not die easily. I can sense his soul from here. It is strong and will not pass into the void without a mighty struggle.'

'We are leaping ahead of ourselves,' said Sternberg. 'First we must locate this ork and that means finding a path through his army. That also may prove impossible.'

'We are a small force,' said Hakon. 'Moving quietly and by night we can manage it. The city is in ruins. There is cover. If we are careful...'

'Might it not be better to wait until the Imperial forces counter-attack,' Brother Tethys ventured. Ragnar could smell the monk's fear. He did not blame him. This was not his mission. He had accompanied them down the river. He had acted as guide where he could. If plunging into the heart of an ork army was not to his liking, who could blame him?

'We do not know when that will happen,' said Sternberg. 'Of course the Imperium will triumph eventually but this may occur too late for our purposes. We must act independently.'

'Assuming you manage to sneak in and kill this ork, how will you escape?' asked Brother Tethys. A not unreasonable question, thought Ragnar. He had been wondering the same thing himself.

'That depends on the circumstances,' said Sternberg. 'Ideally we will be able to use the teleport beacon to get us back to the *Light of Truth*.'

'Ideally?' asked Ragnar.

'The signal may be blocked by power fields or the use of certain energy generators. Alternatively we may have to cause a distraction and slip away in the confusion till we can find a place where the teleporter can be used.'

'It will need to be a big distraction,' Brother Tethys said. Ragnar heard the sarcasm and the questioning note in his voice.

'If you do not wish to accompany us, you do not have to,' Sternberg said coldly. 'You may leave at any time.'

Brother Tethys stared at the inquisitor. 'No. I will not slip into the jungle. You say this ork is the focal point of the horde, the one responsible for the attack on my homeworld. If you are going to kill him. I want to be there. I want to help you. He has a lot to answer for.'

Ragnar heard the unmistakable sound of the hatred in his voice and caught its acrid scent. He saw the eyes of the pack were focussed on the monk. They all respected his courage but Ragnar was not sure having him with them was such a good idea. He decided that he had better voice his objections. 'I do not know if you are capable of what we are about, Brother Tethys,' he said. 'We have all been trained to perform this sort of mission. We can infiltrate silently and effectively. You cannot.'

This, too, was a fair point. Ragnar had observed Tethys in the jungle. The man was brave and he could fight, but he was no master of silent infiltration. Several times his blundering had almost given them away to ork patrols as they waited in ambush. To Ragnar's surprise the monk only smiled.

'Perhaps you are correct,' he said. 'But Galt Prime is my home city. I know my way around its streets. I know the people here.

I speak the language as only a native can. I grew up poor and I lived hard and I know places to hide, all the back alleys and the hidden routes. Do you?'

Ragnar shrugged. 'I was merely making an observation,' he said.

'And a fair one,' Sternberg said. 'But Brother Tethys is right. He has knowledge of the city that might prove invaluable to us. We shall move on tonight and he will accompany us.'

RAGNAR CLAMBERED up the huge tree and focussed on the city through his night goggles. The ruined buildings and the awesome gargants leapt into view as he adjusted the focus. From his point of view, high in the treetops atop the biggest hill they could find, he had a fine view of the monstrous ork force. He was impressed by its size but its apparent disorganisation left him contemptuous. It seemed little more than a seething sea of heavily armed greenskin warriors with little or no idea of tactics or strategy. He prayed to Russ and the Emperor to keep such thoughts from his mind. It never paid to underestimate your opposition. The orks were a race of formidable warriors with an instinctive understanding of war.

While they looked like rabble they were capable of operating with a cunning and speed and grasp of the military situation that would have done credit to many an Imperial general. It was as if, like a Space Wolf pack, they had some sort of unspoken understanding of each other's actions. Ragnar wondered how that could be, then decided it did not matter. The teaching machines had placed many examples of ork martial prowess in his brain, and just in case he needed another, one lay before his eyes. The orks had laid waste to a human world and taken a fortified human city held by an Imperial army. It did not matter if it was under equipped and incompetently led. If they were a mindless bandit rabble they could not have achieved this. No, he would force himself to respect the orks no matter how brutish and stupid they appeared to be.

He ran his eyes over the visible force. The orks had punched through the walls in many places and were obviously confident they could hold the place. Only a small rearguard had been left behind. A mass of trenches and fortifications, gun emplacements and refuelling dumps spoke of the earlier siege. They had encircled the city with earthworks, minefields and razor wire, Ragnar could tell, before bombing and shelling it into submission. He could see the massive holes in the defensive walls where ork artillery had reduced the bastions to rubble. He could see the camps where prisoners and slaves were now being kept preparatory to being shipped off-world to act as slave labour for their new masters. The whole thing superficially appeared disorganised but somehow it was effective. Just like the orks. Their methods might be crude and direct but they worked. There was a lesson there, Ragnar thought, if we want to learn it.

He continued to scan the walls, memorising the layouts so that he could draw a map of their approach for Sergeant Hakon and the inquisitors. He had been chosen because he had the keenest eyes, and he was not going to let them down. More than his own life depended on this.

He noted the areas that were lightly guarded. He noticed the seemingly empty approach corridors. Were there minefields there, he wondered? He heard the distant roaring of engines and asked himself whether he had been spotted. He focussed in the direction of the sound, and saw a number of dust clouds rising. As he watched, a cluster of crude ork buggies hurtled along one of the clearways. A fusillade of shots went off as their drivers and passengers fired their weapons into the air. Were they about to attack each other? Had they spotted some human attackers? What was going on?

Without warning, one of the buggies swerved and crashed into the side of another. The buggy that had been hit bounced then rolled, crashing into the crude shanties of the gretchin troops, tumbling through the campfires before bursting into flames. Two orks threw themselves clear mere moments before their vehicle exploded. They lay on their backs clutching their sides, and Ragnar wondered whether they had been wounded or suffered some internal injury – then it dawned on him that they were laughing. To them, the crash was just a bit of fun. When he realised this, the purpose of the rest of the orks became clear. They were racing, competing against each other in their vehicles, the way the Space Wolves raced against each other on foot back on Fenris. To Ragnar it seemed like madness but then he could not claim to understand the minds of these green-skinned alien invaders. Shaking his head he shinned back down the tree, and made his report to Sergeant Hakon.

Using a twig he inscribed a map in the soft earth, showing the important details of what he had seen.

Hakon and the inquisitors listened raptly and then began to map out the best approach route. They were committed to going in.

As RAGNAR WATCHED, he saw a bright flash light the sky. It looked as if a star had exploded. An eerie blaze of light flashed across a portion of the night and vanished.

'A ship had died,' muttered Sergeant Hakon, and Ragnar was suddenly aware that the light had indicated the probable death of thousands of men or orks. Up there in the sky and silence a battle of inconceivable fury was being fought, and the light had been the only indication.

The moons were clear and bright. Ragnar cursed. This would work against them. The Space Wolves, with their heightened senses, could function well in the minimum of light. The treacherous satellites would only make it easier for ork sentries to spot them. Not that the orks seemed particularly alert, Ragnar thought, racing to the cover of the next tree. Not that they had any reason to be. What threat could a few solitary humans, trying to get into the city, prove to be to this huge army? Ragnar guessed that any small groups of humans the orks encountered would most likely be trying to break out of the city, not into it.

By night the ork camp was bedlam. He could hear them bellowing what sounded like drinking songs. He could hear the constant crackle of small arms fire which he now realised was merely a sign of ork exuberance except when it was a prelude to a drunken shootout between crazed bull warriors. The air vibrated with the roar of engines. The acrid smell of engine fuel assailed his nostrils. There was a constant clangour of metal ringing on metal as ork mechanics worked on vehicles and weapons. They seemed to have an urge to constantly tinker, and could never leave anything alone.

He looked back over his shoulder, and gave the all-clear sign. Lars and Strybjorn raced forward, moving up beyond his position so that they could cover his next advance. After them came the inquisitors and Brother Tethys. The rest of the Space Wolves brought up the rear. They were almost at the edge of the jungle now.

Ragnar's last advance brought him to the very edge of the trees. Ahead of him lay the huge ork camp, a sea of campfires and shadow figures. Muzzle flare illuminated the night as weapons were fired in abandon by their uncaring owners. He could see huge flaming jets erupt from the exhausts of the vehicles. There was one such crude buggy parked nearby. It was close enough for him to make out the riveted plates of its chassis. He could see two of the massive bestial aliens lounging on it. One of them swigged from a bottle of what smelled like pure alcohol and then passed it to the other. It grunted and laughed then downed the bottle in one hefty swig before contemptuously tossing it over its shoulder into the jungle. Ragnar thought he was lucky it did not hit him, for it fell nearby.

This was no use. They would have to skirt around these two sots and find another approach. The area beyond them was clear for a couple of hundred strides and then there were some ruins, which he hoped would provide cover. As he watched one of the orks let out an enormous belch and slid off the hood of the buggy. It pulled itself to its feet and began to lumber quickly towards the jungle's edge, grunting something to its bestial companion. Ragnar froze on the spot, wondering whether they had spotted him. He did not think so. He could detect no change in the scent patterns that might have spelled out their alarm. On the other hand, he was not familiar with orks, so how could he tell?

He stayed frozen in place wondering what to do as the ork headed straight for his hiding place. It still gave no sign of knowing he was there, but perhaps it was merely a cunning ruse, a trick designed to lull him into letting the thing get within striking distance. What was he to do? If he reached for his weapons the ork might spot the movement, if it was not already aware of him. If he did nothing he would soon find himself face to face with a foe nearly half again his bulk.

The ork stopped right in front of him. It seemed impossible to Ragnar that it could not see him. He heard buttons pop and the sound of water flowing. Ork urine splashed his armour. The ork let out a satisfied grunt and then a fart. The stink was so bad that Ragnar flinched. His slight motion must have drawn the ork's attention, for it looked down at where he crouched. Its eyes went wide and it opened its mouth to bellow a warning.

Ragnar knew he had only a heartbeat in which to act. He sprang forward, like a wolf pouncing on its prey. He chopped forward with the edge of his hand, smashing the ork's windpipe. The greenskin fell to the ground, gurgling horribly, unable to breathe. Ragnar kicked it in the face with his boot, and raced on towards its drunken companion. The creature looked at him in a befuddled manner, unable to understand what was going on. Ragnar leapt on it, getting one arm around its thick neck, and twisting.

There was a hideous cracking sound as vertebrae snapped. Ragnar's enhanced muscles enabled him to break the creature's neck with one mighty wrench. The whole action had taken only a heartbeat. It was all over in seconds. Ragnar glanced around to see if any of the other orks had noticed what happened. In the darkness and noise it was unlikely. But he was taking no chances. His enhanced eyes allowed him to see further into the darkness than a normal mortal. He could detect no sign that he'd been noticed. He let out a long breath. All was well.

Glancing back over his shoulder, he could see that the others still waited at the jungle's edge. He gave the thumbs up sign to Sven and Strybjorn and looked around once more. Nearby was the crude vehicle that the orks had been working on.

A plan swiftly formed in his mind. In the darkness it was unlikely that any ork would recognise them for what they were. Perhaps they could commandeer this crude buggy and use it to drive through the city, disguised as orks. It was a long shot too, but it might just work.

'BLOODY GREAT PLAN,' Sven said ironically. He looked comical with a massive horned helmet on his head and a crudely made ork jerkin over his armour. In broad daylight it would have been impossible to mistake him for an ork but at night the stupid brutes might take his squat, wide-shouldered silhouette to belong to one of their number. Ragnar was dressed similarly. Karah was hunched down on the floor of the front of the vehicle between them. The rest of the Space Marines, Inquisitor Sternberg and Brother Tethys hunkered down in the back of the buggy. It was fortunate, Ragnar thought, that there was plenty of room in the huge car. It seemed to have been made to carry over a score of passengers.

The controls were easily mastered. There was a huge steering wheel, a massive pedal to go forward, another for the brake, and a monstrous lever that took most of Ragnar's strength to move which controlled the gears. There was only a series of crude lights on the dash, no gauges or meters or any complex readouts. The whole thing could have been driven by a child, Ragnar thought, albeit a most gigantic, misshapen ogre of a child.

A big red button on the dashboard started things up. The engine roared like a wounded dragon. The air reeked of crude fuel. Its acrid stench assaulted Ragnar's nostrils. Still, he thought, as the buggy lurched forward, there was something appealing about driving the thing. He constantly fought the urge to stamp down the pedal and go roaring through the streets. Suddenly, he understood exactly why the orks raced so much.

Riding in this juggernaut of hardened steel, it was an almost irresistible urge. Of course, he thought. The orks had designed their vehicles this way. Was this urge to go fast a product of riding in the buggy, or was it a simple expression of the ork desire for speed? Which came first, the chicken or the egg? Certainly, it touched something deep within him, and he was not even an ork.

THEY RACED TOWARDS the edge of the city, moving all but unnoticed through the massive camp which surrounded it. The vehicle leapt and shuddered at every small bump in the road, and yet Ragnar was surprisingly comfortable. The suspension was good, obviously intended to carry the machine safely over the roughest of terrain, and his seat was thickly padded with leather. Two red cubes dangled from a thong tied to the roll bar.

Ragnar guided the buggy through a wide hole blasted through the thick plascrete of the perimeter wall. The massive burned-out hulks of ancient skyscrapers loomed over them like drunken giants. The air felt colder and yet from somewhere off in the distance Ragnar could smell burning. Perhaps the orks were cooking, he thought. More likely they were using incendiaries.

The night was filled with screams and shrieks. Overhead, starshells burst and red contrails marked the passing of ork rocket planes.

* * *

'WHICH WAY?' he asked Karah Isaan.

'Keep going the way you're going,' she told him. 'I'll tell you when to turn.'

They moved on through a night that seemed more like a war.

'You look like a bloody fool, Ragnar,' said Sven. 'That helmet makes you look like an idiot!'

'Compared to you, Sven, I look like a hero from a saga,' Ragnar replied. 'But then you always look like an idiot.'

'Can you two stop bickering for a moment?' said the deep voice of Sergeant Hakon from the back of the car. Ragnar flinched. It was not like the sergeant to complain. It was a sign of the tension they all felt. Just at that moment, an ork war buggy roared up beside them. One of the massive greenskins bellowed something in his incomprehensible language. He accompanied his bestial roaring with threatening gestures.

For a moment panic threatened to overwhelm Ragnar. What was going on? Had they been detected? Were these sentries some form of patrol? Beside him, he felt Sven stiffen and reach for his weapon. Ragnar reached out with his left hand to grab Sven's wrist, immobilising his arm. Now was not the time to start shooting.

He crouched low behind the wheel, hoping that the orks would not see he was human. The orks continued to grunt and bellow and make obscene motions with their hands. They revved their engine and pointed into the air with their weapons. Shots spat upwards into the darkness. Ragnar shook his head in confusion. He did not understand what was going on.

The largest ork, the one behind the wheel, roared a stream of incomprehensible gibberish. Its red eyes bored challengingly into Ragnar's. Even from here, above the acrid smell of the exhaust and the near overwhelming odour of the engine fuel, he could smell the alcohol on its breath.

Was this some sort of warning or some sort of challenge? He wished he spoke their language. But it was a useless wish; he did not. It was obvious that the orks were becoming increasingly frustrated. Their bellowing grew louder, their gestures more frantic. They continued to fire their bolters. One of them made an obscene gesture and their vehicle roared forwards, pulling ahead of Ragnar's as if eager to be ahead of him, then dropped back again.

Suddenly, he understood: *they wanted to race!* They had been challenging him. He knew he had to make a quick decision. What was he to do? Should he race them or ignore the challenge? Which would stand out more? It seemed a common sport among the orks. Might they be insulted if he refused and start a fight? He did not know. It was possible, and the last thing he wanted was to draw attention to himself and his companions.

Instinctively, he put his foot to the floor. The orks in the other vehicle responded with a chorus of jeers and more obscene gestures. Now he felt insulted. He wanted to show these brutes who was best. No Space Wolf was going to be looked down on by a bunch of green-skinned morons!

Part of him realised how foolish he was being. But something compelled him to race on. The buildings flew past. The night was alive with screams and roars. He could see ork faces flash by in the gloom. Ahead of them, one of the orks stood poised on the rear of the buggy. He had dropped his trousers and waggled his buttocks at them. It was not an appealing sight.

'I'd like to put a bolter shell up his arse!' Sven grumbled.

Ragnar understood. The ork's crude humour was an insult. He pushed the gear lever forward. The engine roared in response. The buggy bounced over the rough roadway. The wind rushed past his face. Transparent membranes slammed into place over his eyeballs, to protect them from the wind. Their speed increased with every notch he pushed the lever forward. His heart beat faster with excitement. They were gaining on the orks.

Suddenly from behind them came more roaring. Ragnar risked a glance back over his shoulder. He could see there were more buggies joining in the race. What had he started?

There were several more of the crudely built racers. They were massive vehicles, barbarically painted, adorned with spikes, covered in blocky ork script. Grinning ork faces leered at him from behind their controls. He could see that there was no getting out of this now.

'Watch out!' he heard Sven shout. Swiftly Ragnar turned. Ahead of them, the road was blocked by the wreckage of a massive ork truck. Swiftly he wrenched the wheel to the right. Tyres squealed as the vehicle responded. Ragnar was thrown back in his seat by the sudden movement. He felt another bump as the buggy ran over something solid.

'That'll teach him to waggle his arse at us!' Sven roared. Ragnar realised that the ork must have fallen from his vehicle and then been crushed under their wheels. Looking behind them, he could see it starting to climb to its feet. It stood there for a moment, a foolish grin on its face, caught in the head-lights of the pursuing vehicles. Then, with a horrible squelching sound, it was hit by the leading buggy.

'And that's the end of that,' said Sven with an evil grin.

Ragnar wondered if that was case. The ork already survived falling from a moving buggy and being run over by Ragnar's own vehicle. It was perfectly possible that it could endure being struck by another. On the other hand, it seemed unlikely that anything could survive being run over by the succession of vehicles which pursued them. Then it was too late to wonder about such things. The crushed ork was already a long way behind them.

The road ahead came to a junction. More and more ork vehicles moved in from left and right with no apparent order. The race leader wove through them, causing several to come to a screeching halt. Sparks flew, metal ground against metal, as cars collided. Orks brandished their fists in the air, several reached for weapons.

'Whose bright idea was this?' asked Sven.

'It was their's,' Ragnar said, pointing at the orks ahead of them. He wrenched at the wheel, narrowly avoiding a collision with the vehicle in frnont of them. 'Keep your eyes peeled for a way out,' he told Sven. 'Look for a side street with nothing on it.'

'Some chance,' said Sven. 'This city is crawling with the green-skin scum.'

'Just do your best!'

'I always bloody do!' said Sven. From behind them came the sound of an appalling multi-car pile-up. Ragnar guessed that for many of the orks the race was over.

AHEAD OF HIM, he could see several orks making faces. The dis-tance was closing between the two vehicles. Ragnar was gaining on them – and up ahead of them, the road was clear. Seizing his opportunity, Ragnar pushed the gear lever forward to the last notch. The buggy surged forward. Elation filled Ragnar. He was going to catch them.

Ten yards separated them now. Ragnar could make out every detail of the vehicle ahead. He could see every rivet and bolt on the metal plating. He could even smell the orks themselves; the night breeze wafted their scent to his nostrils. He could never get to like such a stink.

'We're gaining on them,' said Sven.

'Nothing gets past you,' said Ragnar. He was leaning forward on the gear lever, even though it could go no further, and unconsciously he was willing the buggy to go faster, ever faster.

There was only five yards in it now. The orks stuck out long black tongues at their pursuers. They put their fingers in their ears and twisted their faces into obscene grimaces. One or two of them brandished weapons. Ragnar wondered if they were going to shoot, or if this was mere posturing. With this free hand he reached for his bolt pistol.

'Bloody hell!' Sven swore. 'Are they looking for a fight? If so, I'll damn well give them one.'

'You are always ready for a fight, Sven,' said Ragnar. All the same, he was glad Sven was there. If violence started, he could think of no one better to have at his side.

They were almost alongside the orks now. He wondered if the creatures would notice that they were human. Not that it mattered. He suspected they would be just as hostile to their own kind at this moment in time.

As they drew alongside the ork vehicle, the creature driving twisted the wheel. The buggy crashed into Ragnar's. Metal shrieked and sparks flew as the two vehicles collided. Once again, Ragnar was thrown around in his seat. It was all he could do to keep his hands on the wheel and their course steady. On the floor between them, Karah Isaan gave a yelp of alarm.

'Do something!' shrieked Sven. 'You've got the controls.'

Two could play at this game. Ragnar twisted the wheel and deliberately smashed into the ork buggy. There was a tolling like a huge bell as the two machines crashed together. Ragnar felt as if he could almost reach over and touch the ork beside the driver in the other buggy. Not that he would have wanted to. Suddenly, he noticed two red eyes were glaring into his. A look of surprise crossed the ork's face. He knew that it had spotted that he was not like his opponent!

Sven had obviously noticed this too. He raised his pistol and put a bolter shell right through the ork's eye. Its head exploded. The shell passed right through its skull and lodged itself in the throat of the ork driver. He slumped forward over the wheel. The buggy veered off to one side, hit a low wall, then flipped over completely. Its skidded along upside down, sparks flaring from the tortured metal of the roll bar. From inside came the shrieks, bellows, and grunting of the orks trapped within. The buggy hit a wall. A fireball erupted as it burst into flames. The explosion sent shards of shrapnel spraying everywhere.

Ragnar glanced back, hoping that there would be no survivors. He saw nothing crawling from the wreckage. Behind them, other ork buggies veered wildly to avoid the blazing wreck.

'That was close,' said Sven. 'I think they recognised us.'

'You don't say? And I thought they just didn't like us.'

Sven gave him a nasty smile, and glanced backwards. 'Plenty more where they came from,' he said. 'No shortage of orks around here.'

Ragnar was forced to agree. He took a deep breath, muttered a thankful prayer to the Emperor, and exhaled. He felt surprisingly calm all things considered. And there were lots of things to consider. He was driving an unfamiliar vehicle through a city he did not know, surrounded by deadly enemies. This would have given most men pause, he knew. Still, he reminded himself, he was a Space Marine, for whom such strange experiences were almost everyday occurrences.

He gave his attention back to driving. The roads hereabouts were clogged with rubble and the wreckage of burned out vehicles. He was suddenly glad for the sheer simplicity of the ork controls. He shuddered to think what would have happened if he'd been in control of an Imperial Rhino, for example.

Behind them, two more ork buggies had ploughed into the wreckage of the first. Fuel had caught fire and a wall of flame barred the street. One after another, more ork buggies plunged through the conflagration. Ragnar could see one trailing a tail of flickering fire that reminded him of a comet. He grinned at Sven. The chase was on again.

'I hope you have your weapons ready back there,' he said. 'You might have a chance to use them soon.'

'I hope so,' he heard Nils say in a quiet but determined voice.

Ragnar kept the throttle open and they raced on through the night.

IN THE DISTANCE Ragnar could hear the roar of engines and the stutter of small arms fire, but around here they seemed to have left the orks behind. He was glad of the respite. The concentration needed for driving at such speed had tired even him, although he had to admit that it was exciting.

At least the race had carried them in the right direction, towards their goal. They had hidden the vehicle in the ruins of a burned out garage. Now they lay sprawled about it. Ragnar could see from the flushed faces of his companions that they shared his exultation. They had been just as excited as he had. Or almost.

'What do we do now?' he asked Inquisitor Isaan.

'We wait here,' she said. 'We should all get some rest.'

'That's not very exciting,' said Sven.

'I should think you'd had enough excitement for one evening,' said Karah.

'Sven never gets enough excitement,' said Nils.

'Not with you lot around anyway,' said Sven.

'Are we getting any closer to the ork warlord?' asked Ragnar.

'Yes,' said Karah. 'I can sense his presence now. It's like a beacon in my mind.'

RAGNAR LOOKED AROUND. He did not feel tired. He doubted that any of the other Marines did either. But Sternberg, Isaan and Brother Tethys were only human, and they needed their rest.

Ragnar sat alone, staring off into the darkness. All around him he could sense the presence of his battle-brothers. The mere fact that they were there reassured him. It was part of the pack instinct that he shared with all Space Wolves. Just the very presence of his comrades calmed some inner part of him. Each of the Claw had gone their separate ways to think and to meditate. Ragnar enjoyed being alone as much as he enjoyed the presence of his friends, but it was good to know they had not gone far.

Overhead, unfamiliar stars blazed down. Ragnar looked up at them in wonder. How far was he from home? What great distance had he come? Would he ever see Fenris again? He did not know. And at this moment, he did not really care. He was happy just to be here, and to be alive. He was happy just to look on these unfamiliar sights.

He smiled as he looked on the ruins of the skyscrapers. Back home there was nothing like these. Their massive presence reminded him of mountains, but these were mountains that had been built by men. And then destroyed by orks, he reminded himself.

He breathed deeply, taking in all the unfamiliar scents. Even the air here smelled different. Of course there was the reek of ork machinery and the orks themselves. It was everywhere. But underneath it lay another unfamiliar tang: the smell of factories, of industrial pollution, of great furnaces, and of all the things they had once produced. It was amazing to think that humans had produced all these things.

He gazed out into the shadows, searching for movement, for the unfamiliar outline that would tell that a hidden enemy was sneaking up on them. He knew that he was much more likely to hear or smell any foe before he saw them, but nonetheless the force of old habit made him rely on his eyes. He had changed so much in a few short months. He'd almost come to take his enhanced senses for granted.

Ragnar closed his eyes. He listened carefully with the concentration that only a Space Wolf could manage. He could hear the breathing of the humans inside the garage. He could hear the soft, stealthy movements of his comrades. He could hear the distant sound of weapons being fired and the scuttling of small rodents among the ruins. But he could hear nothing remotely threatening.

He breathed deeply, testing the air for scent. Nearby, all he could sense was the familiar reassuring smell of his battle-brothers, and the humans who accompanied them. Further off, he smelled animals and birds and the smell of effluent from the broken sewers. Once again, no threats.

He turned his awareness inwards, communing with himself as he had been taught back at the Fang. It was like looking inside a vast unfamiliar cavern. The teaching machines had placed so much knowledge within him that he had not had time to assimilate it. It was as if he contained whole libraries that he had not read. He knew the whole history of the Chapter was there somewhere, along with all the technical schematics of his weapons and equipment, and endless reams of knowledge that he might never need but that his tutors had deemed useful.

He became aware of himself as a small spark of light in that huge dark realm. And somewhere out there he sensed another presence lurking, the presence of the beast, of his soul's shadow, of the monstrous thing that waited within him. It did not frighten him now as once it had. And yet he could not quite come to terms with it either. He knew it was there. He could sense it just as he sensed the presence of his comrades close by. It was a real thing, as real as the dirt beneath his feet, or the armour that encased his body.

Yet he knew it was wrong to think of it as a being separate from himself. It was part of him, just as he was part of it. Now, at this moment, he was in control. He was in charge. He was the master. And it seemed hard to believe that it could ever be any different. But he knew this was not the case. He knew that in moments of stress, the beast would come to the fore, would take control, would live inside his body, inside of him

There had been a time when he found it terrifying that he was not the sole master of his own body. Now it was a thought he'd become accustomed to, as he had become accustomed to so much else about being a Space Marine. He knew from the older warriors that in time he would make his peace with the beast, just as they had.

Right now, he simply wanted to feel its presence, to know that it was there if he needed it. It was like having another ally, invisible and yet present. He wondered if his battle-brothers felt the same way or if each of them thought of the beast differently. It was not something they talked about.

From within the garage, he detected a movement. He could tell by the difference in her scent that Karah Isaan was awakening. The hackles on the back of his neck rose as he sensed something else. She was using her powers.

It occurred to him that in her own way she was just as set apart from normal humans as he was. What must it be like to have such powers? It must change a person, Ragnar thought. And it must change the way other people look at you. He thought of his own reaction on the day he had met her. Had he reacted so badly because she was an inquisitor – or because she was a psyker? He did not know. He did know that her powers frightened him; they reminded him of sorcery, of the witchcraft spoken of in whispers back in his home village.

And what was she doing now? What she working some spell? Was it possible that a daemon would come to possess her? The knowledge buried deep in his brain told him that this was a possibility.

At this moment, there was nothing he could do about it. She was a comrade, and part of the mission. If she turned against them he would kill her. He hoped this would not become necessary.

His reverie was broken. Now he wanted action or he wanted to sleep, he did not want to be alone with his thoughts. What was it about this woman that disturbed his soul? Was it that she was a psyker? Or was it something different, something more primal.

He stared up at the distant star hours. Morning seemed a long way away.

THE SUN BLAZED down on the ruins of Galt. Ragnar studied the horizon looking for some sign of threat. By day, the pall of smoke hanging over the city was obvious. The thunder of huge weapons could be heard in the distance, as the orks continued their mad wanton destruction. It seemed nothing could satisfy their appetite for wrecking things. They would not be happy until they had reduced first the city, then the entire world to rubble. Contemplating such a foe was a frightening thing even to a Space Marine like Ragnar.

'Soon it will be night,' said Sven from nearby. 'Then we'll be able to get going again.'

'I'm looking forward to it,' Nils said, off to the other side of them. 'All this stalking around ruins is getting me down.'

'And I still haven't bloody well found anything good to eat,' said Sven. 'Caught a rat this morning, could barely wrestle the little bastard down my throat.'

'Just like you not to share it with the rest of this,' said Nils. 'I could have done with a nice bit of roasted meat.'

'It wasn't roasted. It was still alive.'

The rest of the Blood Claws looked at Sven appalled, unable to believe what he was saying.

'Be that as it may,' Sergeant Hakon said. They turned; he was striding carefully over the rubble towards them, Inquisitor

Isaan and Brother Tethys in his wake. 'Best make sure your weapons are ready. Tonight it looks like we're going to see some action.'

'I know where the warlord is,' Karah Isaan said. 'He's not too far from here. He's taken over a huge building overlooking the central square. I can see it clearly in my mind's eye.'

'Most likely the governor's mansion,' Brother Tethys said. 'It's the largest building in the central area and it would appeal to the ork mentality. The whole place is a fortress. How are we going to get in?'

'So we'll just drive up and ask them to let us through, shall we?' Sven said sarcastically.

'That's exactly what we will do,' Karah said.

IT WAS NIGHT and the moons beamed down. The death flares of exploding spaceships lit the dark sky. All around them the ork throng roistered, brawled and drank. Weapons were discharged. Broken bottles were thrust into ork faces while spectators laughed. Ragnar glanced around warily; his disguise seemed very thin.

They had lowered the canopy on the buggy so it obscured their faces. Once again he and Sven wore ork armour. Once again the others hid out of sight in the back of the buggy.

'This is the stupidest plan I've ever heard,' muttered Sven. 'How did I ever let you talk me into this?'

'I thought you liked it because it was stupid. It suits your mentality,' replied Ragnar. But privately, he agreed with Sven. He could not see how they were going to carry this off. It seemed only a matter of time before they were challenged by some sentry, or invited to take part in another race by drunken orks. Still, all he could do now was keep driving, and pray to the Emperor that things would turn out all right.

They were approaching the town square. Ahead of them he could see a huge statue of what he took to be the governor. It had collapsed like a fallen colossus and now lay sprawled amidst the rubble. Its huge head had come away from the torso, and stared sightlessly at the sky with its stone eyes. The building itself was the only one left standing on the outskirts of the square. It had once been an impressive Imperial structure. Huge gargoyles clutched the four corner towers. A monstrous Imperial eagle, now defaced, spread its shattered wings over the entrance. The floodlights that had once lit it lay smashed near the doorway.

Lights blazed in many of the windows and huge banners covered in crude ork signs hung from beneath many of them. Here and there, Ragnar could see ork faces leering through the windows. He could also see the muzzles of great guns. The place was indeed a fortress.

'How are we going to get in?' he asked.

'Keep driving. Go out of the square and round the back, to where the old servants' entrance used to be,' Brother Tethys said.

Ragnar did as he was told. He brought the buggy to a halt in a huge open space filled with wrecked vehicles. It was obvious a battle had been fought here. The cars had been smashed with heavy calibre bullets. Skeletons still lay between some of them where cleanup teams had failed to find them. Ragnar felt his heart race. The moment of truth was upon them. How were they going to get into the building?

He brought the buggy to a halt in an open space. The engine noise died. The stink of engine fuel subsided. He glanced around. There were many orks here too, camped out in lean-tos made from wreckage or in the wrecks themselves. Some of them huddled around bonfires, warming their hands and toasting food. They looked barbaric, monstrous figures from the dawn of time. They looked as savage as any Space Wolf and they were far more numerous.

'What now?' Ragnar asked.

'Watch!' said Karah. She made a gesture towards the nearest orks and Ragnar felt a surge of power emanating from her. He sensed the sudden wariness of his battle-brothers as they detected the same thing. The pack was uneasy, he could tell. The orks turned and looked towards them. Instinctively Ragnar's hand went for his bolt pistol but a word from Karah stopped him. Slowly, as if compelled against their will, the orks lumbered towards them. They looked a little confused. Karah said something to them in their own guttural tongue, and they nodded.

'Conceal your weapons,' she said, 'and put your hands in the air.'

'Like hell I will,' said Sven.

'By Russ, just do it!' Hakon hissed. 'I see the plan.'

So did Ragnar. She obviously had the orks under psychic control. They would pretend to be prisoners and simply march in. If it was this simple, why had she not done it earlier? His answer was swift in coming.

'And be quick about it!' she said. 'These are strong-willed brutes. I cannot hold them for more than a couple of minutes.'

'That is all it will take to get us inside,' said Sternberg approvingly.

Tension filled Ragnar as they approached the doorway – would the ork sentries notice anything amiss; would they be challenged? One mistake would be all it took to bring a city full of greenskins down upon them. He felt his heart rate accelerate as they came to the entrance. He breathed a prayer and brought it back under control. He reduced the flow of sweat on his face by conscious effort. Around him he sensed his brothers do the same. The strain was so palpable he wondered the orks didn't sense it.

The orks on guard were even more massive than usual. Huge tusks protruded from their lower lips. Their eyes glowed with feral savagery. In their massive paws they held the largest and crudest boltguns Ragnar had ever seen. Still, he thought, crude or no, one shot from them would end his life. They looked down at the orks accompanying Ragnar's party contemptuously and bellowed a challenge. It was so sudden, and so shocking, it was all Ragnar could do to keep from drawing his pistol and beginning to shoot.

Their guards bellowed something back. The noise was so loud it was almost deafening. It appeared ork was a language to be shouted at all times. He looked over at Karah. She was pale and sweating, and he wondered if any of the orks would notice the stress written all over her face. Ragnar hoped that they would assume she was just another frightened human.

Whatever their escort said did the trick. The two massive orks stepped aside and let them pass. They were inside the hall, making their way deep into the heart of the ork citadel.

CHAPTER NINE

THE INSIDE OF the building had been devastated by the orks, who had wrought havoc everywhere. In every place he looked, Ragnar could see smashed furniture, vandalised walls, gouged paintwork, and bullet holes. Here, once more, was evidence of the orks' appetite for destruction. They seemed to take pleasure in it. They just seemed to like breaking things.

On and on they ventured, deeper and deeper into the building – and the further they went, the paler and more tired-looking Inquisitor Isaan became. The orks were becoming more and more restless. Ragnar could smell their confusion and their anger. He could sense that they were coming out of the hypnotic trance into which she had put them. He tightened his grip on the butt of his bolt pistol. If trouble was coming, he was going to be ready for it.

Karah was breathing ever more heavily; sweat beaded her tattooed brow. She stumbled as she walked and her chest rose and fell as if she had been running hard. Sternberg and Hakon also seemed to realise was happening. They could see that she was losing control. Without a word, each of them took hold of one of her arms and helped her along.

The party came to a flight of stairs. Up they went, further and further into the building. There were fewer orks here, and more open space. Ragnar sensed that the crisis was coming soon. The orks were becoming angry. They stared around them in confusion. They looked like sleepers awakening from a dream, which in a way they were. Ragnar pushed open a door which led into a wrecked office.

Looking around, he saw that it was empty. This was good. He stepped inside and gestured for the others to follow. The entranced orks did so, but slowly and reluctantly.

Once inside he closed the door. All around him, he could tell by the way his battle-brothers stiffened, that they sensed what was coming – and that they were ready. Ragnar chopped across the throat of one of the orks. The hulking creature let out a long gurgling gasp and collapsed onto the floor. As one, Ragnar's comrades fell on the other orks. It was over in seconds.

'What are we going to do now?' Sven asked.

'I don't know,' Ragnar admitted. He noticed that Sergeant Hakon was glaring at him.

'Perhaps, in the future, you'll let us know what you are going to do in advance, Ragnar,' the sergeant said. The hair had risen on the back of the veteran's neck. He was like an old wolf being challenged for leadership of the pack by a younger one. Instinctively Ragnar bared his fangs in response. The two of them glared at each other, suddenly locked in confrontation, oblivious to anything else. Despite himself, Ragnar felt the beast rise within him. In that moment, he was ready to leap on the sergeant, to rend and tear.

And he knew that the sergeant felt the same way about him. But Sergeant Hakon was older and wiser and more used to dealing with the beast within himself. He took a deep breath, spread his hands wide in a gesture of peace, and Ragnar could see him relax visibly. Something in the sergeant's manner calmed him in turn. He felt the fury seep away from him like water running down a drain.

'I– I will do that,' Ragnar said at last.

'Remember that,' said Hakon.

'Now we're in,' Sternberg cut in, as if what had just happened was of no concern to him. 'The talisman must be close at hand.'

He looked over at Karah Isaan hopefully. The woman stared down at the floor, unaware that all eyes were upon. Slowly, like someone coming out of a trance or awakening from a deep sleep, she raised her head. She glanced around with dark, blind-seeming eyes. Ragnar sensed her intelligence return only slowly. It was as if her mind had been somewhere else a long way off. She sighed, and then spoke, 'It is here. It is close. The ork-thing that carries it is using its power.

'And he is terrible.'

Ragnar heard the fear in her voice and smelled the terror in her scent. For the first time, he wondered what it was they were really going to face.

Silence fell as they all considered their options. Ragnar realised that none of them had really believed that they would actually get this far. They were winging it, improvising a plan in face of new and unforeseeable circumstances. He considered the obstacles that still lay ahead of them. They were in a vast, unknown building packed full of orks. They were hugely out-numbered. They were facing a foe whose psychic powers frightened a powerful inquisitor. And a foe, moreover, who would probably be surrounded by heavily armed bodyguards.

Their only advantage lay in surprise, in the fact that no one knew they were here. They could strike quickly and unexpect-edly. But how were they going to get out again? Assuming, that was, that they got their hands on the talisman in the first place. He could tell from the confused scents that all his companions were thinking along the same lines.

'We can use the teleport to get out,' Sternberg said suddenly. 'But someone will have to go to the roof and place the beacon.'

'What if there is no ship within range?' asked Hakon.

'Then we'll just have to think of something else, won't we?' said the inquisitor. His voice was steely with determination.

'No, then we'll bloody well die,' said Sven.

'Everybody dies,' said the inquisitor.

'Yeah, sooner or later,' Sven snapped back. 'But personally I'd rather it was later.'

'We all would,' Karah muttered from the corner where she had slumped.

'Sven, Strybjorn, Nils: you're going to the roof with the bea-con,' Sergeant Hakon said decisively. 'Ragnar, you and Lars are coming with me and… our guests.'

'I protest,' Strybjorn sneered. Ragnar shot him a murderous glance. 'Why should Lars and… and Ragnar have all the glory?'

'Because that is the way it is,' Sergeant Hakon. 'Brother Tethys, you go with them!'

'Yes sir,' the diminutive monk said, almost leaping to obey.

'We should wait a while,' Inquisitor Isaan said. 'Once the orks are drunk and sleepy it will be easier to move around the building.'

'Logical enough,' said Sergeant Hakon. 'Strybjorn, take first watch. Everyone else, get some rest before the action starts.'

IT WAS THE middle of the night. They moved quietly through the long dark halls. All around him Ragnar could sense sleeping orks. He could hear their snores; he could smell the alcohol on their breath. The whole party moved with a near-inhuman stealth. Despite their bulky armour, the Space Wolves were all but inaudible even to Ragnar's keen ears, and he doubted that any but a Space Wolf like himself could have heard the inquisitors as they padded quietly along.

It was dark, but here and there he could see faint lights gleaming. These were places to be avoided, and they all took pains to skirt around them. Ragnar was deeply aware of Karah Isaan walking just ahead of him. He seemed unnaturally sensitive to her movements, but then again, he suspected that they all were. She was the only one of them who truly knew where they were going.

He could sense the deep, dark fear growing within her as they ventured ever further, approaching their goal. A moment later, ahead of them the Wolf sensed rather than heard ork voices. Almost as one the party ducked through a doorway into the concealment of a quiet room. Ragnar held his breath as a clutch of ork sentries marched past. An anxious few moments of held breaths ticked by before any of them dared breathe. They had not been detected.

After ten more heartbeats they re-emerged into the corridor. Proceeding on their way, they entered a more luxurious part of the building. Here tapestries still clung to the walls and statues, though smashed or ridden with bullet holes, still stood guard in alcoves. Judging by the opulence of the fittings, these had obviously been the governor's apartments.

Up ahead he could hear the sound of shouting in guttural ork voices. They were approaching the warlord's lair. He felt his heart start to race once more. A prayer to the Emperor restored control and his twin heartbeats to their normal speed.

He noticed that Karah was chanting softly to herself. Her eyes were half-closed and a dim yellow nimbus of light played erratically around her head. He wondered what she was doing. Was she seeking to attract the attention of the great ork sorcerer from her scryings? Was this her long-awaited treachery? By the Great Wolf, what was going on here?

His hand reached for the butt of his pistol, then he suddenly spun around. Four orks, presumably guards, were stood in a shadowy archway. The orks were looking directly at them all, yet they paid no attention. The brutal creatures looked at them as if it were an everyday occurrence to have a group of armed humans creeping discreetly in their midst. Slowly realisation dawned on the Blood Claw. The inquisitor was using her powers to fool the orks, to befuddle their wits. He had no idea what the orks were seeing. Perhaps they saw other orks or perhaps they saw nothing at all. It did not matter; whatever it was, they were effectively shielded from the orks' sight.

Once more he noticed the sweat beading Karah's brow, and how drawn and pale she looked. He realised that all this use of her – considerable, there was no doubt about it now – psychic powers was taking a terrible toll on her meagre resources. He wondered how she would fare when they actually met the ork warlord.

They were now only ten strides from the huge entrance which was so obviously their destination. Two immense ork warriors flanked the archway. They were quite possibly the hugest creatures Ragnar had ever seen. They were at least a head taller than he was. Their arms were each as thick as tree trunks. Their leathery fists were the size of most men's heads. The guns they clutched in their hands were crude constructions of folded steel and wood, but they had the calibre of cannons.

Ragnar flinched warily as the party approached them, but the guards did not seem to notice him or the others. Their red eyes stayed focussed on the middle distance. Just ahead of him, Karah weaved on her feet as if she were drunk. Ragnar reached out and steadied her with his free hand. He felt her shiver under his touch. Her skin, midnight dark in the dim light, felt clammy and cold and he could feel the bone-deep weariness in her.

As he supported her, he felt a disturbing tingling in his fingers. He was aware of the flow of power through her, and sensed the huge amount of energy pouring out of her. How were they going to get through the door, he wondered, without the orks noticing? He felt her shiver, a great rippling shudder, and in that moment one of the orks turned. The halo of light around the inquisitor's head was suddenly so bright it was dazzling. The ork turned and stepped through the archway and they simply followed.

THEY FOUND THEMSELVES in a chamber that was all but overwhelming in its barbaric splendour. It was as if all the loot in the city had been poured into this one place. Piles of jewelled trinkets and silver coins lay everywhere, mixed in with heaps of custom weapons and ammunition. It was all obvious portable wealth, selected for its brightness and ability to attract the eye, rather than any genuine aesthetic merit.

In the very centre of the room, a massive ork even larger than his brutal bodyguards lolled on what had once been the governor's throne. Its skin was a strange sickly yellowish-green in the half-light. Its eyes blazed with their own internal fire and a glow that could only be madness. Huge tusks jutted from its slobbering lower jaws. Around the huge creature hung a palpable aura of power that it wore like a cloak. And on its knees lay a glittering gemstone that Ragnar recognised instantly as the second part of the talisman. He sensed the immediate response from Sternberg and Isaan and he knew from their scents that his battle-brothers had recognised it too. Its pale, sickly fire echoed the one in the ork's eyes. He could sense that the creature was drawing power from it in some crude way.

As the humans entered the room something bizarre happened. Without warning, a bolt of pure psychic energy flared from each of the two parts of the talisman simultaneously. Each piece suddenly glowed a hundred times brighter, and a complex net of energy sprang up between them. Scattered by the facets of the two gems, their light sprayed around the vast room.

Karah Isaan let out a groan and slumped to her knees. Ragnar sensed a dominating presence which she struggled to fight before it could overcome her spirit. The ork looked up at them almost casually, definitely unafraid, unnervingly like a man who has just had unexpected but not unwelcome guests drop in on him. There was an utter confidence in its manner that was daunting. It looked at them and spoke, using heavily accented and yet comprehensible Gothic.

'Arummm… Greetings, mortals. I am Gurg, speaker for Two Gods. It good you brought Eye of Gork to me. It goes well with Eye of Mork.'

Ragnar glanced at the bestial ork in wonder. Was it possible that the warlord had known they were here all along and had allowed them to come this far? Or was this just some supremely skilful bluff? Or was the creature simply mad? Its appearance certainly suggested that all or any of these wild suppositions could be true – yet there was that palpable aura of daunting power about the thing. Mad or not, this was a being to be feared, of that Ragnar had no doubt whatsoever.

'Give it and I spare your lives. Done me great service bringing it. Saved big trip. Hur! Hur!'

It took Ragnar a moment to realise that the strange barking sound which filled the room was the ork's laughter. He did not think he had ever heard anything quite so cruel. It touched the beast within him, and set his hackles rising. A raging fury bubbled into his brain. The stink of ork suddenly made him want to tear and rend. It was the feeling he had when he confronted Sergeant Hakon, but intensified a hundred times.

All around him, he could sense the same savage, bestial rage trying to overwhelm his battle-brothers. He felt their anger and their urge to strike. Only the grizzled old sergeant maintained any semblance of control, but, like the restraint of a wolf pack leader, it was enough to leash his followers, at least until they saw what he was going to do.

'Give us the jewel,' Hakon said, 'and we will let you live. Deny us, and you will surely die.'

'Hundred thousand ork warriors, all around? You who die.'

'I don't see any warriors!' Hakon spat back. 'Except these two, and they look useless.'

Gurg raised his hand. Green fire burned suddenly in the depths of his eyes. Green and yellow energies swirled out from his piece of the talisman. The two orks who had guarded the entrance suddenly stood straighter and a new keenness came into their eyes. They looked around at the interlopers and growled with suppressed fury. Had Ragnar been anything else but a Space Marine he might have known fear at that moment. As it was, his hair bristled and he bared his fangs in a gesture of aggression that matched the orks' own. Next to him, however, Karah Isaan tumbled forward to lie face down on the floor. The interplay of energies seemed too much for her.

Gurg grunted something to his minions in orkish and they stepped smartly to either side of his throne, their weapons held at the ready. Suddenly Ragnar wondered just exactly what he and his brothers were doing? Had they all suddenly become so enthralled by the sight of the talisman that they had lost any semblance of common sense? They should have killed the orks when they had the chance and that would have left the warlord alone in their presence.

But hardly defenceless, Ragnar told himself. A creature like Gurg, even without the mystic power of the artefact he had stolen, would never be that. He held his bolt pistol tightly, determined to fire if the orks made the slightest threatening gesture, despite any restraint Sergeant Hakon might show. A slight undercurrent in the pack leader's scent told him that Hakon had sensed this, and did not disapprove. Not for the first time, Ragnar was glad of the near telepathic sensory link he shared with his battle-brothers. This wordless communication was a huge advantage in situations like this. As were the heightened senses which told him that even now other orks were coming closer to the chamber, and that the jaws of a trap were closing. Hakon seemed to sense it too.

'Give me the talisman,' he said, 'This is your last warning.'

'You come take it, wolf boy,' the ork warlord sneered.

'With pleasure,' Hakon shot back, a low growl rumbling deep within his chest. The sergeant moved quickly but, fast as he was, the ork was faster. Even as Hakon's pistol rose to fire, Gurg had stepped aside from his throne. Moving with incredible agility for one of such huge bulk, he bent to snatch up a power axe lying nearby as he moved and returned to his full height as, all the while, a stream of tracer fire from the sergeant's bolt pistol traced around his movements.

Suddenly and shockingly, Gurg simply stopped moving and raised his hands. He howled a chant to his brutish gods. A green aura sprang up all around him and suddenly the sergeant's bolter shells were halted in the air, frozen mere inches from the warleader's leathery green flesh. The talisman's glow grew ever brighter to Ragnar's eyes. He sensed the huge forces the ork was drawing on. Using such energy for these purposes, he thought to himself, was like using a chainsword to chop twigs. The power of the talisman was obviously intended to fulfil a greater purpose although what that purpose might be Ragnar had no idea.

An evil smile twisted the ork's lips and revealed his yellowish tusks. He gestured and the shells reversed themselves and went hurtling back towards the Space Wolves. Had it not been for their lightning quickness in throwing themselves flat, they might have been hit. But all of them had senses of superhuman keenness, and reflexes to match. As one they took evasive action and thankfully the bullets passed over them.

As he twisted to watch, Ragnar saw one of them ricochet off Sternberg's armour, and several others buried themselves in the wall. Then all hell broke loose as Gurg's bodyguards opened fire, and the Imperial warriors responded. Ragnar knew it would be a short battle. With so much firepower being deployed and so little cover available, it was bound to be. More than that, the Space Marines and their allies needed it to be for he sensed the presence of a horde of approaching orks. He rolled across the floor and snapped off a shot at one of the bodyguards. The bolter shell smashed through its heavy armour and embedded itself in the ork's flesh before exploding.

The ork was thrown back off its feet but, incredibly, started to rise again. Ragnar was amazed – he could see a massive hole in the creature's armour and internal organs gaping from its open chest, yet the ork was still moving, and not only that still fighting, it swung its weapon towards Ragnar. He dived to avoid the hail of bullets flashing from its blazing muzzle.

Ragnar did not flinch, even though he momentarily expected to be greeting his ancestors in Hell. Instead he kept moving, knowing he was not quick enough to avoid the storm of lead if the ork kept firing and yet determined to try. The shooting ceased. Ragnar glanced over to see that the ork's head had been smashed to pulp by a well-placed shot. He was not sure which of his comrades had saved him, but he was determined to thank them later… if there was a later. Right now that did not look so certain.

Gurg strode towards him, his skin seeming to repel bullets as Ragnar's armour might repel rain. He looked ultimately fierce and determined and the massive power axe roared like thunder in his hands. He took a mighty swipe at Ragnar and the Blood Claw was only just able to leap clear. By Russ, the creature was fast! Ragnar wondered whether it was naturally so quick or whether its speed had been augmented by the awesome power of the talisman. The ork was by far and away the most formidable close combat opponent Ragnar had ever faced. Almost as soon as the fight began, he knew he was hugely overmatched and he was fighting for his life – but he was determined not to give up without a fight. Leaping backwards and away from the warlord, he snatched up his chainsword and thumbed the ignition rune. The sacred weapon, though many centuries old, roared to life in his hand and he raised it to parry the ork's next blow.

Almost as soon as he had done so, he knew it was a mistake. Strong as the Wolf was, the ork was far, far stronger. Its power was unnatural, even for one so obviously big and strong, and Ragnar knew immediately that some supernatural agency was at work here. Sparks flickered as their two weapons came together, metal grinding against metal, serrated blades interlocking with serrated blades. A smell of ozone and hot steel filled Ragnar's nostrils. The ork launched another sledgehammer blow, and his blade was smashed from his grip and sent flying across the room. For a brief moment, Ragnar stood defenceless before the massive ork leader. Gurg smiled at him nastily and aimed another blow.

At that moment, Ragnar caught a flicker of something from the corner of his eye. Lars leapt past him and barrelled into Gurg at great speed. It was a diving tackle of the sort Ragnar had seen Fenrisian youths use in their brawls. It was a crude tactic but it certainly proved effective. The gigantic ork reeled backwards, momentarily off-balance. Ragnar threw himself into the fray, leaping forward and seizing Gurg's hefty wrist with both hands before he could bring his axe down on poor Lars.

The mighty ork warlord, buoyed up with power from the talisman, swatted him aside as if he were a fly. The force of the blow cracked the carapace of Ragnar's armour and sent him hurtling across the room to smash into the wall with sickening force. He lay near to his still whirring chainsword. If it had not been for the reinforced bone structure of his head, Ragnar felt his skull might have been crushed by the impact. As it was, stars flickered before his eyes and his vision seemed to pulse from black to grey and then back again. He tried to force himself upright but he was too dizzy and weak. Despite all of the alterations made to his body during his transformation into a Space Marine, none had prepared him for combat with such a foe as this.

Gurg laughed and raised the talisman into the air. Lars lay at his feet, struggling to rise, to bring his weapon to bear. Gurg brought down one enormous foot, knocking the Blood Claw flat again. Another stomp and there was a sickening crack as Lars's neck broke. The scent of one of his own pack going down ripped a howl of pain and fury from Ragnar's throat. He just had time to snatch up his chainsword before the beast took over completely. A red wave of berserker rage tore through his brain, drowning out all pain and all fear. In a furious desire to avenge his fallen comrade, Ragnar leapt to the attack once more, swinging his chainsword with superhuman speed and force.

Gurg raised his axe and blocked the blow, but this time Ragnar was ready for the move and twisted his blade free. He unleashed another blow, and then another. The warlord parried both but he was obviously taken aback by the fury of Ragnar's assault. The Wolf forced the beast back, one step, then another and another. From behind him Ragnar could hear the sounds of firing as the others tried to pin down the approaching orks with fire. The sane part of Ragnar's mind, now buried deep within the beast, knew this was a forlorn hope at best. There was no way they could succeed in keeping so many orks at bay. There were just too many of them.

He kept up his attack, lashing out again and again, heedless of anything now save his desire to kill the giant greenskin before him. But it was no use. It seemed now like the ork had got his measure. His parries became surer and swifter, and his counterblows came back at Ragnar like thunderbolts. For all his speed and power, it was all Ragnar could do to keep the ork at bay. Slowly, one step at a time, it drove him back over the ground they had covered, and then further back still. Ragnar knew that he was never going to survive the fight. It was only a matter of time now before he misjudged one of the ork's attacks, or stumbled and fell under the sheer punishing power of his blows. It was a forlorn hope that he could manage to stand against a foe so mighty.

Already his arms ached. His fingers felt as if they were about to be ripped from their sockets every time he parried. Sweat beaded his brow, and despite the awesome reserves of stamina and fortitude built into his re-engineered body, he was breathing in gasps. The air rasped in and out of his lungs. This had been a foolish venture, he decided, doomed from the start. Still, at least he would die in battle, as any true Fenrisian warrior should, though it galled him to fall with his task incomplete.

Suddenly Sergeant Hakon was there, standing beside him, lashing out at Gurg with his own blade. The ork laughed as if delighted to have another foe to slaughter, and switched his attack to Hakon. Ragnar knew that the veteran was a far more experienced combatant than he, but even so he could see that the sergeant could do little more at the moment than hold the ork back, and soon he would be unable to do even that. But at least he had bought Ragnar a brief respite in which to gather his wits and his strength before returning to the fray.

He breathed deeply, praying fervently to the Emperor and to Leman Russ for guidance and aid. As he did so, he became aware of the alteration of Karah's scent from somewhere behind him, as she reasserted her power. When he heard her mutter the chant of a spell in some alien language he did not recognise, Ragnar risked a glance at her.

She stood, long legs planted far apart, her dark eyes glazed and half-closed, like one of the orks she had put into a trance. Her fragment of the talisman glowed brightly in her hand. He could see lights swirling within it, like water in a whirlpool. Energy seemed to be flowing back into it, somehow drawn from the talisman in the ork's hands. A startled look of surprise and anxiety flicker across Gurg's inhuman face. His attack lost some of its potency. He looked as if suddenly he were fighting two simultaneous battles. One, on the psychic level with Karah, and another on the physical level with Ragnar and Hakon.

'Whatever you're doing, Karah, keep it up!' he shouted, then wished he hadn't. All he had succeeded in doing was drawing the ork's attention to the inquisitor. Gurg knew now that he would have to kill her in order to survive. Determined to redeem his mistake, Ragnar plunged forward to attack and keep the brute away from the woman. Hakon sensed his intention and redoubled his attack as well. The two of them rained down blow after blow on the ork. Once again the warlord was forced to take a step backwards.

Ragnar sensed the build-up of psychic power around him. Swirls of light flickered past him from the direction of the female inquisitor. They impacted on the talisman in Gurg's hand. As the tendrils became brighter, the glow of the talisman and the glow that surrounded the warlord dimmed. It seemed that Karah was sucking the power away from the ork. Gurg became weaker and slower. New hope filled Ragnar and he continued to rain down blows on the greenskin, praying that his psychic shield would fail before the rest of his bodyguard could break through his comrades' wall of gunfire and come to their master's aid.

The ork growled deeply and struck back. The sheer ferocity of his attack took Ragnar by surprise, and the blade of the power-axe bit through the shattered armour of his chest plate, sending a surge of pure agony searing through him. He fought to retain consciousness as his altered nervous system sought to damp down the overload of pain. Endorphins and opiates poured out of altered glands to help him ignore the pain.

He bit his lips, drawing blood, in the effort to avoid shrieking like a wounded beast. Instead, he lashed out with his chainsword, and was surprised when it passed through the green nimbus and bit deep into the ork's flesh. Muscle showed through the rent in the armour, but the warlord's blood was strangely reluctant to flow. Even as Ragnar watched the flesh began to knit together again with a sick slurping sound.

'By Russ! Are you a troll?' he shouted in alarmed Fenrisian. The ork did not even bother to answer, merely aiming another blow at him, which would have severed his head if it had connected. Its return swing bit deep into the stonework at Ragnar's feet sending chips of plascrete flying in all directions. Sergeant Hakon took the opportunity to send his blade into the ork's neck, severing tendons and veins. But once again, the skin and sinew began to knit almost as soon as the wound was inflicted.

'I have favour of Gork!' Gurg screamed. 'And you now die.'

'It's the power of the talisman!' he heard Karah shout. 'He's attuned himself to it and now it's healing him.'

Ragnar ducked another swing of the huge axe. The woman's words filled his thoughts. If the talisman was what made the ork invincible, then perhaps he should try and get it away from him. Almost at once he saw his opening. He lashed out at the warlord's hand, smashing his blade into the fingers which grasped the talisman. It seemed as if Gurg realised what he was doing and closed his hand in a determined effort not to drop the thing, but it was too late. His fingers were severed. The second fragment of the Talisman of Lykos fell to the floor and the green aura faded from around the huge ork's frame. The brute responded almost instantly, bending down to try and grasp the thing, but Ragnar back-heeled it away in the direction of Karah and aimed another blow at Gurg.

This time the ork jumped back and clear. The warlord took in his situation at a glance and realised that without the talisman's power he had no chance against the Space Marines. Acting quickly, he turned and raced back behind the throne. Ragnar heard a door open and then slam shut. Even as the Wolf raced to intercept the ork, he knew he was too late.

He lashed out at the plascrete door with his chainsword. The blade whined as it ricocheted off the rock-hard substance. Behind him he heard Karah Isaan's triumphant shout: 'I have it. We can go.'

'Ragnar, regroup! We don't have time for that. We must get to the roof!' Hakon shouted.

Mind reeling with frustration and disappointment, Ragnar turned back. He could see that the others were already making preparations to depart. Karah brandished the amulet in her hand. Hakon was hoisting Lars's corpse onto his shoulders. Seeing Ragnar's troubled glare, he said, 'We leave no bodies for the orks, boy. We must reclaim his geneseed for the Chapter.'

Using the body partially as a shield, he raced out into the corridor. Bolter shells tore into poor Lars's corpse as the sergeant moved steadily down the corridor, eliminating his enemies with well-placed shots. 'I just hope the others have got the teleport beacon set up,' he shouted.

So do I, thought Ragnar, racing up the flight of stairs. Otherwise all of this is for naught.

Behind them, he could sense the horde of orks at their heels. Ragnar ducked as another bolter shell almost hit his head. He turned and grabbed Karah as she toppled forward. Briefly, he wondered whether she was hit, but then he saw she was merely exhausted. The use of her powers had drained her almost completely. She held out both parts of the talisman to him.

'Take them,' she said. 'I can't go on and they must be taken away from here.'

'Don't be foolish,' he replied, bending down and lifting her as if she were a child. He draped her across his shoulders and raced on. To him she seemed to weigh almost nothing. She was not much of a burden. 'Just don't drop those things,' he said, 'It'll be hell going back for them.'

'I'll try to remember that,' said her ironic voice from just behind his head. Ragnar heard ork war cries behind him. It gave his feet wings as he pounded on up the stairs towards the roof.

SVEN AND THE others were waiting for them. They had taken up position near a great rusted metal air vent in the centre of the roof that provided them with some cover. Ragnar thanked Russ for their foresight. He suspected they were going to need all the cover they could get in the next few minutes.

They had already set up the emergency beacon. The brass coils were humming and an array of runes flashed in sequence on the display. Ragnar sincerely hoped it had been configured correctly, for it was their only chance of escape. Space Wolf or not, he did not think they would long survive an encounter with several thousand greenskin warriors.

Ragnar and the others hurried to join their comrades. He could tell from the dour look on Sven's face that there was something wrong.

'Trouble?' he heard Sergeant Hakon ask.

'Aye, trouble,' Sven replied. 'The beacon is scanning for a carrier signal but we can't find it. We don't even know if any of our ships are up there and in range.'

'It's possible that the orks have a low-intensity power field around the building. It could be disrupting the signal,' Inquisitor Sternberg suggested, running a hand through his grey hair. 'If we can find some uncovered frequencies there's a chance we can punch the signal through. Let me see the controls, lad.'

The Blood Claws around the beacon did not move. They had all stood and were all looking at Sergeant Hakon in silence. They had noticed the significance of the burden he carried, and knew from the scent that Lars was not simply wounded but dead. Their own scents carried their grief and their concern to Ragnar's nostrils. Sergeant Hakon grimaced at them, showing his teeth.

'He met his end like a true Space Wolf. I suggest you prepare yourselves to do the same. If Inquisitor Sternberg cannot fix this beacon, all of our souls will go to greet the Emperor within the hour. Now move aside and let the man do his work.'

The Blood Claws did as they were ordered and Sternberg swiftly knelt over the beacon and began to make adjustments to the controls. 'Do not stray more than ten paces from me,' he said as he worked. 'If the ship can get a lock on us, they'll respond to the distress signal immediately. Anyone out of the beacon range will be left behind and there's not much anyone will be able to do about it.'

Ragnar strode over and gently placed Karah Isaan on the ground next to her fellow inquisitor. He was taking no chances with her safety, or the safety of the talisman, he hastily assured himself. She gave him a wan smile of thanks and drew her pistol, ready to defend herself. Ragnar turned and joined his companions. The Wolves had fanned out to cover all points of the compass. They all kept themselves facing outwards, and as spread out as possible. Ragnar knew they were all thinking the same thing he was. Clumped together at close range like this, they would be easy prey for a single grenade.

He could hear wild howls coming closer. Even as he watched, the first of the pursuing orks emerged from the stairwell – to be cut down by a withering blast of fire from the Space Wolves. Fortunately only a few of them could get through at a time. As long as the ammunition held out, they could be kept at bay.

'Watch out!' he heard Sven shout, just as the acrid stink of ork hit his nostrils. 'They're coming up the outside of the building too.'

'Fire escape's still intact!' he heard Tethys shout. Ragnar had no real idea what he meant. In the village where he had grown up no building had been more than a single storey high, and the Fang was carved from the rock of mountains. Even as he whirled and snapped off a shot, it dawned on him that it was probably some way out of the building in case of emergencies, if the internal stairwells were blocked or the dropshafts weren't working. Right now that did not matter. What mattered was that it was providing the orks with another means of getting to them.

Shots from behind him told him that a few of the greenskins were managing to escape from the exposed stairwell. He turned and fired from the hip, blowing the head clean off one of the brutes. Its brains splattered over its companions but they merely bellowed louder and ran faster. The chatter of gunfire from off to the right told him that some of the orks had taken up position on the edge of the roof near the fire escape and were pouring hot lead onto the Space Wolves from their flanking position. It was not looking good, and it was getting worse.

From below, he could hear the sound of breaking glass and the roar of what sounded like mighty rocket engines. Suddenly, dozens of ork troops rose into view, massive jetpacks strapped onto their backs, huge boltguns held in their hands. Ragnar shot at one of them. His shell buried itself in one of the jet-packs. Sparks flew and the ork swung out of control, smashing first into one of his companions and then into another. It gave Ragnar a small sense of accomplishment but he knew he had barely slowed the inevitable. There was no way so few of them could hold the teeming greenskins at bay. Even now more and more orks were clambering over the dead bodies of their comrades in the stairwell and charging into view. Overhead he could see a few of the rocket packers preparing to hurl down stick grenades. It seemed that, like it or not, they were going to have to spread out and away from the beacon or be torn apart in a rain of explosive death.

Bolter shells blazed all around him, taking out part of the air vent. Shrapnel spanged off his armour. If they stayed here, then the sheer weight of enemy fire was going to kill them anyway. Ragnar took a deep breath, offered up a prayer to sacred Russ, and prepared himself for a desperate last stand. He also prayed that he would meet his end as well as Lars had.

Suddenly the orks stopped firing, as if at a single command. He wondered why until he saw the massive figure of Gurg step out of the stairwell onto the roof. All of the orks held their fire at a gesture from their chieftain. Such was the barbaric majesty of the warlord that the Blood Claws, too, stopped shooting.

Only Inquisitor Sternberg kept moving, tinkering frantically with the controls of the beacon.

'Good fight,' the ork warlord boomed. 'Over now. Surrender, give me back jewel. Maybe let you live.'

'Space Wolves don't surrender to greenskin scum like you,' said Sergeant Hakon and made to raise his pistol.

'Fair 'nuff,' said Gurg with a shrug. 'Your lives over.'

'No! Wait!' Ragnar shouted suddenly. 'What are your terms?'

All of his comrades' eyes were upon him. He thought he saw contempt written on their faces. Not that it mattered. He was not really afraid for his life; at least that was what he told himself. He just did not want them to fail in their mission, and for Lars to have fallen in vain. Right now the most important thing was to buy Sternberg time to fix the beacon, whatever it took. It was their one hope of getting away from here with the talisman. At all costs he had to keep the ork talking. He saw Hakon's nostrils flare, as if reading his scent, and comprehension dawned on the sergeant's face.

'One wolf-cub fears for life,' Gurg rumbled. There was a note of malicious enjoyment in his voice.

Good, thought Ragnar, every little helps.

'I will wring his neck myself,' Hakon said bleakly. Ragnar was not sure whether he meant it or was simply acting out his part in the little drama.

'Just give him to us, sergeant,' he heard Sven say viciously. 'We'll make him suffer.'

'What are your terms?' Ragnar asked once more.

'Put down guns. Give me jewels. That's it.'

'Do you guarantee our safety?'

'Guarantee you die if you don't!'

'At least we'll die fighting, then, and not be tortured and eaten by you ork cannibals.'

'If you want!' The warlord began to gesture to his warriors to attack. Ragnar's mouth went dry. He thought the game was up and that it was all over. A quick glance told him that Sternberg had not yet got the beacon to work.

'No! Wait a moment!' Ragnar shouted. 'Are you really so afraid of us?'

'What you mean?'

'Do you fear to face me in single combat?'

'First you offer surrender. Then you offer fight me! Make up your mind, boy. What is it?'

'Will you fight me one-on-one, or are you afraid?'

'No afraid. No stupid either. Why fight you? Have you killed like this!' The ork snapped his fingers.

'Then you are afraid!'

Gurg turned away, shaking his head in disgust, and barked a quick command to his followers. Ragnar did not have to speak ork to know he was saying: 'Kill them.'

Suddenly the orks were raising their guns to fire. From overhead a mass of stick grenades began to fall. Ragnar knew there was no escape, no way out. His last desperate gamble had failed and that it was all too possible that his comrades would take the belief that he was a fool and a coward with them to the grave.

He tried to snap off a shot at Gurg, determined at least to try to kill the warlord, but a seething sea of green faces surged between them. Bolter shells blazed all around him. The sound of thunder filled his ears. Something hit him. Pain tore through him. A blinding flash filled his sight. There was a sensation of coldness, of being torn apart. Eventually it was over.

SLOWLY RAGNAR'S vision cleared. He looked around. The orks were gone. The air smelled different but he almost instantly recognised in what way. It smelled like the inside of the *Light of Truth*. Then it came to him that it could only mean one thing – that the beacon had worked, and that the teleport had reached down like the hand of the Emperor to sweep them to safety.

He glanced around at his companions to see the same look of shocked surprise on all of their faces. They were all just as amazed as he was to see that they were still alive. Ragnar felt his lips twist into a feral smile. Exultation filled his heart. They had done it. They had walked right into the heart of the ork stronghold, and escaped again, taking the talisman with them. They had succeeded in the first part of their mission.

The others were all staring at him. He wondered if they still thought he was a coward who would betray them, or whether they had realised that it had all been a ruse to buy them the time they needed. They looked worried and pale, and he wondered what was wrong. He opened his mouth to speak but no words would come out. He felt oddly weak, uncertain and dizzy. There was a strange buzzing sound in his ears.

Then he noticed the blood flowing from his side and face, and was aware of the searing pain flowing through him. He had been hit, he knew, whether by an ork shell or something else. He raised his hand to his face and felt a great open wound. He felt organs leaking through his sides and looked down to see something long and rope-like protruding from his stomach. He reached down and felt his own innards starting to tumble out. Perhaps he had not been so lucky after all, he thought, and tumbled forward into darkness.

CHAPTER TEN

RAGNAR'S EYES snapped open. He felt numb. Part of his body felt frozen. For a moment he was disoriented. He had no idea quite where or who he was. It seemed that he might be in the cold hell of his people after all. Perhaps he really had died with the rest of the Thunderfists when the Grimskulls attacked their village, and all of the other stuff, about going to the Fang and becoming a Space Wolf, was just a hallucination of his dying mind, a trick played by evil spirits. He stared at the unfamiliar metal ceiling and tried to tell himself that it wasn't true. Sweat beaded his brow, and he could feel his heart racing.

He was alive, he told himself. He was not dead. He was not

Like a message of confirmation sent by Russ, Karah Isaan's beautiful brown face came into view above him. He felt more than relief at seeing it. He felt a surge of something else, something he could not quite put his finger on, something he had not felt since Ana had been lost, something that really should have been impossible for him to feel as a Space Marine. He pushed the confused thought aside. He was alive. He was not trapped in some strange pre-death dream. At least he hoped not. It was a nightmare that he had often had since becoming a Space Wolf and it sometimes gave his life a complete sense of unreality.

'Where… am I?' he forced himself to ask.

'The sanctum of the *Light of Truth*,' she replied, reaching down to touch his brow with her long, cool fingers. 'You were very close to death, for a long time.'

'How long?'

'Weeks. We have made another warp jump into a new system while you lay in the healing sarcophagus.'

'What happened?'

'Don't you remember?'

'Not much.'

'You saved us. You kept Gurg talking just long enough for Inquisitor Sternberg to fix the beacon. It was quick thinking. He will want to thank you himself for it.'

'I meant: how did I come to be here? Was I wounded?'

'In several places. We had to dig bolter shells out of your chest and your head.'

'Was it serious? Will there be long-term damage? Will I be able to walk and fight again?'

'One question at a time, eh? I am supposed to be the inquisitor here.'

'Was that a joke?' he asked, confused.

'Yes, it was. And in answer to your questions, you will heal just fine. You Marines are made very tough, and your body will heal anything that does not kill it, or so our chirurgeon assures me. Says he has never seen anything like it – that the Ancients must have been miracle workers to make such a thing possible.'

'I have no idea what he means by that.'

'Nor I really. The chirurgeons have their own mysteries.'

He could tell by her scent that she was not telling the truth but decided it was not his business just now to pry into whatever forbidden knowledge she might possess. After all, there were certainly mysteries about the Space Wolves that he could not reveal to her. 'Are all the others well?'

'Yes. A few minor wounds, nothing serious. Except… except for Lars, of course. They have already performed the funeral rites for him.'

'And I missed them.'

'Yes.'

Ragnar felt a strange stab of pain and loss. It was odd to feel such a sensation for someone he had really barely known. Lars had been one of the quiet ones, had kept himself to himself, and now he was gone and Ragnar would never have the chance to know him. It seemed like such a waste. He told himself that it was his sickness and weakness speaking. Lars had died in battle like a true Wolf, and no Space Marine could ask for more.

'He saved my life, you know.'

'I was there. I saw it. He was very brave. But then you all were.'

'He saved my life, but I could not save his.'

'Sometimes these things happen. You did save mine though. And I am grateful.'

'I saved the talisman,' he said, surprised himself by how coldly his voice came out. He was ashamed when he saw the tiny flicker of hurt, quickly concealed, flare in her eyes. He wondered why he had said that, and in such a way. Why did he feel threatened by the closeness that seemed to be developing between them?

'No. You saved my life, and I am grateful. You could have taken the talisman and moved on, but you didn't it. You came back for me.'

He forced a smile. 'Maybe.'

'You should get some rest. Sergeant Hakon says he wants to have you back in harness soon. The others have repaired your wargear.'

'That should please them,' he said ironically.

'I don't think so. Sven told me to tell you that he's a Space Marine, not a bloody armourer, and that next time you can fix your stuff yourself no matter what Sergeant bloody Hakon says.'

Ragnar laughed in spite of himself. Karah's mimicry of Sven's voice was amazingly good. She obviously had a gift for it. 'I don't think he meant it. He has a good heart hidden behind a harsh manner, that one.'

'I know that too. How goes the war on Galt?'

'Imperial forces are moving into the sector. It looks as if there will be a massive spacedrop some time soon. We picked up some odd comm-net reports from the planet's surface before we made the warp jump. It seems like the ork forces are starting to fall apart and fight with each other. It may be that Gurg is losing his power.'

'Do you think it's because he lost face when we escaped?'

An odd grimace passed across her face. 'Maybe. But I think it was more than that. I sensed something while we were down there. Gurg was more than just a strong warlord. He was a sort of psychic focus for all the orks. He meant more to them than a mere general. He was sort of their spiritual leader as well, in a very real sense.'

'So?'

'I think he lost that power when we took the amulet. I think we somehow diminished him.'

Ragnar did not really understand. This was psyker talk and he had no experience of this sort of thing to relate to. He found it confusing, but he could see one hole in her argument, much as he wanted to believe it, and heroic as it made their mission seem. 'But if what you're saying is true, he was their leader before ever he got the amulet.'

'Yes, there is that,' she admitted with a nod, 'but being a psyker is as much about having belief in yourself as it is about being touched with the power. If we undermined his confidence in his abilities by besting him, it may be that we somehow undid his power as well.' She shrugged. 'I don't know. It's just a theory.'

'Still, it means that we may have done some good for the people of Galt and for the Imperium, as well as for our quest.'

'Yes, it does.'

'Then that is a good thing,' he said simply and smiled. She smiled back and opened her mouth to speak, then shut it again. She reached out stroked his brow and suddenly upped and went. Ragnar listened as her footsteps crossed to the door, then heard it whoosh closed behind her. He tried to pull himself upright but it was too much of a struggle. He realised that he must truly have been close to death indeed, for he knew how tough his altered body had been made. Anything that had left him feeling this drained and taken all of its resources to heal must have been all but fatal.

Still, he was alive, that was the main thing. And he had helped his fellows succeed in their mission. That was something too. It left him with a quiet sensation of accomplishment and pride. His thoughts turned back to the girl. What was really going on there? He was still wondering when he drifted off back to sleep.

HE WOKE WHEN he sensed someone in the chamber with him. He came awake slowly for a Space Wolf and thus knew he was still hurt. He relaxed a little when he caught a familiar scent, and opened his eyes to a familiar face.

'Brother Tethys,' he said. 'How are you?'

'I'm sorry for disturbing your rest, Ragnar. I merely looked in to see how you were. But it's good that you are awake. Now I can thank you for saving us. I thought my life was over back there on the roof.'

'Everyone seems to want to thank me for that today,' Ragnar said. 'Inquisitor Isaan was just in and she said the same thing.'

'She can't have been, Ragnar. She has been locked up in her chamber for the past day fasting and purifying herself for the Ritual of Divination once more. I believe she came to see you two days ago.'

'I have been asleep for two days?'

'Yes. The chirurgeons say it was good for you. It gave your body time to heal itself.'

Ragnar considered this. It was not a reassuring thought that he had lain unconscious and helpless for over two days. He must really have been hurt badly. Like a daemon summoned by an ill-considered thought, his pains returned. He was suddenly aware of a bone-deep ache that permeated his entire body.

Brother Tethys must have seen him wince. 'Are you hurt?' he asked with concern. 'Shall I summon help?'

'It is nothing but a minor ache.'

'Your wounds did not look that way to me. I was surprised that any man could survive them. Yet they say that Space Marines are more than human, so perhaps I should not have been.'

Ragnar wished that people would not dwell on how badly hurt he had been. It was not a comforting thought. It made him think of Lars, who had taken a wound from which no recovery was possible. Or was it? Could they not have been able to take him back to the Fang? The Wolf Priests had overseen his resurrection once, surely they could do it again.

The knowledge that had been placed in his brain by the tutelary engines surfaced in his thoughts. He knew it was not so. Unless the resurrection procedures were accomplished immediately on the field of battle, the lack of oxygen would cause brain damage. Even if resurrected the dead warrior would be little more than a vegetable if he were not helped within minutes.

He tried to push these dark thoughts aside, but he could not do so entirely. He felt them lodging deep in his soul along with something else, something that he knew he did not want to consider. To distract himself he asked Brother Tethys, 'Are you coming with us? Don't you want to go back to Galt?'

'I want to go back very much but I don't have much choice. The inquisitor is not going to turn his ship around just to take one unimportant monk back to his homeworld. Oh well, I always wanted to see other worlds. I suppose this is my chance. It's not quite what I expected though.'

Ragnar smiled at the little man's cheerful acceptance of his fate. 'You'll get back eventually, I'm sure. The Emperor looks after his own.'

'I hope so. Certainly the way you arrived to save me from the orks leads me to believe this is so.'

Ragnar found himself wishing that he could share this belief – but he could not.

'I am tired now,' he said. 'I must sleep.'

'I understand,' Tethys said. He bowed from the waist and left him to his thoughts.

'THE SLEEPER HAS bloody well awoken,' said Sven, as Ragnar walked gingerly back into the stateroom. He still felt weak but he was far better than he had been two days before. He had fallen into a healing coma as his body repaired itself. Now he had some energy he was sick of lying in the hospital bay and had decided to visit his comrades. It was an odd feeling, moving around without most of his carapace armour. He had grown accustomed to it, and now he felt almost naked.

Sven looked up at him and grinned.

'Good to have you back in the land of the living. The others thought for a while that you might not make it – but I told them you would live just to be contrary and annoy me. See who was right.'

Sven's tone was joshing but Ragnar could scent the concern behind it and was grateful. 'The witch helped too, when she wasn't casting her spells to see where this mad journey would take us next.'

'She helped?' Ragnar was perplexed.

'She used her powers to help heal you. Must have cost her a lot too. She always looked pretty pale and drained afterwards although I suspect it was from the strain of looking at your ugly face for all that time. We can't all be as good-looking as me, I suppose.'

Sven was one of the ugliest men Ragnar had ever seen. 'Thank the Emperor for that,' he said.

'No need for bloody blasphemy!' Sven said.

'Anything else new?'

'Not really. Not that anyone is telling us Blood Claws anyway. Hakon has been closeted with the inquisitors and Gul, doubtless trying to come up with new ways of endangering our lives. The crew still treat us like we were corpse-eaters. I wish I knew what was bloody well going on there. Why do they hate us so much? We're supposed to be the Emperor's finest, after all.'

'Maybe that's why.'

'You mean they envy me my distinction as well as my astounding good looks.'

'No, I mean that many of those men were impressed into the Emperor's service. You can't expect them to look with favour on his representatives.'

'No. But I can make them look on us with fear, and I have. I've knocked a few heads together.'

'That will increase your popularity for sure,' Ragnar said. Sven grinned his cheerfully ugly grin.

'You know I think all this time spent closeted with psykers has affected you, Ragnar. I think you're going soft. I mean you were always soft in the head, but now…'

'Care to try that theory out?'

'I don't beat up sick fools.' Ragnar sensed some menace in Sven now despite his jovial tone. It was a pack thing. They were like wolf cubs playfully testing each other, but testing each other nonetheless. Remembering how proficient Sven had been during their unarmed combat training, he wasn't sure he felt up to fighting him, just yet. Not unless he did something sneaky.

'Give me a couple of days, then I'll make you the sick one. A fool you are already.'

'I must be to waste my time in company like yours.'

'Any ale around here?'

'Some. And lots of other stuff too. Nils says the inquisitor has the booze of a hundred worlds on this ship. And the vittles are pretty good too, after what we had in the jungle.'

'Then let's go get some.'

'Fair enough,' Sven agreed. 'I'm starving hungry.'

'So what's new?'

As THEY SAT down to eat in Sven's stateroom, Nils and Strybjorn entered. They looked at the piled table and sat down and began helping themselves without asking. Nils gave Ragnar an encouraging smile as he chewed. Strybjorn, however, looked as dour and surly as ever. Ragnar didn't mind; it was good to see them all well. But sitting there, Ragnar felt there was something missing – then realised with a cold sensation that it was Lars. The Wolf had always been quiet but he had been there. Now he was gone, and his absence was tangible. The others sensed the change in his mood and responded. He could tell that they had done some of their share of grieving but he had missed out on it, being unconscious at the time.

'To Lars,' Sven said suddenly, raising his goblet to the light. 'Wherever he bloody well is.'

'To Lars,' they all echoed, then fell silent once more.

'Where have you two been?' Sven asked, glancing over at Nils and Strybjorn.

'We've been on the bridge, talking to the crew,' Nils said between mouthfuls. 'It seems we're welcome there, at least, ever since we brought their precious inquisitors back. Gul wasn't happy but then he never is.'

'Why wasn't he happy?' Ragnar asked.

'I don't think he likes us,' Nils said.

'Nobody likes you,' said Sven. 'I would have thought you'd bloody well noticed that by now.'

'It's funny. They always tell me what a great lad I am. It's just my idiot friend Sven with the bulldog face they don't like.'

'Come on, don't mess around,' said Ragnar. 'What's really going on?'

'Well, we found out where we're going,' Strybjorn spoke up. His voice was deep and gloomy, and his manner of speaking was slow and considered. Ragnar could smell his current puzzlement. 'And?'

'And, it's very odd. That's all I can say.'

'Why?'

'Because we seem to be heading out into the middle of nowhere.'

'We're in space. Remember your training. There's a lot of nowhere out here.'

'But we're going particularly far out. To a place where there are no inhabited worlds. To a dead sun called Korealis.'

'What's there? I thought we were looking for the third part of the talisman.'

'We are. That's where the witch told the Navigators to go when she came out of her trance. They are obeying her.'

'Well, I guess we will find out what's going on soon enough,' Ragnar said.

'I did hear one other thing, just as we were leaving the bridge,' Nils offered. Strybjorn looked over at him with a sour expression. Obviously he had missed something.

'What was that?' Ragnar asked.

'Two words.'

'I'll give you two bloody words if you don't tell us quickly,' Sven said eagerly.

'Space hulk,' Nils said with a nasty smile. Silence fell on the chamber. Ragnar reached for more meat and stuffed it into his mouth while he considered his battle-brother's words. They were enough to place a chill in his heart.

In training they had run through simulations of boarding space hulks. It was one of the things a Space Marine could be expected to be called on to do in a long career of serving the Emperor. Assuming he survived the experience, of course. Space hulks were among the most deadly environments known to mankind. Ragnar let his thoughts drift back to what the tutelary engines had taught him about the things. It was not reassuring.

Space hulks were gigantic structures, agglomerations of many craft, of rubble and debris, which accumulated in the warp. No one quite knew how or why this happened, but everyone knew that it did. And there was something about the hulks that no one quite understood. They drifted in and out of warp space, seemingly at random, with neither rhyme nor reason to their movements. Sometimes they would disappear for centuries, only to reappear again somewhere far from the last place where they had been sighted.

Most were harmless enough, mere junk in fact; sometimes a threat to navigation, sometimes containing secrets that had been lost in the dark depths of time. But sometimes they were the home to other things: to orks, and genestealers and far worse creatures. Indeed sometimes they were taken over by such creatures and used to drift from world to world. Come to think of it, hadn't Gurg's horde arrived in the Galt system aboard one? Was there some sinister pattern here that he could not quite see? Hulks were the common denominator in this sorry saga so far. He mentioned this to the others, but they did not seem impressed.

'Orks use anything they can get their filthy claws on. You saw what they were like on Galt,' said Nils. 'They cannibalise hulks the way they cannibalise everything else. There's nothing more sinister about it.'

'So you say,' said Ragnar. 'But I'm inclined to suspect the sanity of any man who can tell me there is nothing sinister about a ghost ship that drifts for centuries between the stars.'

'They're not all like that,' said Sven.

'Enough are.'

'You may have a point,' said Sven. 'But I'll be damned if I can see it.'

'The same goes for me,' said Nils.

'Look, I don't know. It may just be coincidence. It may be something else.'

'How will we be able to tell?' Strybjorn asked grumpily.

'You'll all be able to tell soon enough, because you're all going aboard,' Sergeant Hakon said from the doorway. Ragnar was amazed that for all their razor keen senses, the sergeant constantly managed to sneak up and take them unawares. Then again he had had several centuries of practice, Ragnar thought. If anyone ought to be able to do it, it was he.

'When, sergeant?' Ragnar asked.

'Within the next six hours. I want your gear checked and all of you ready to go.'

'Does that include me, sergeant?' Ragnar asked, not sure which answer he wanted to hear.

'Well, you're up and about aren't you? And you can hold a gun, can't you?' the sergeant snapped.

Ragnar nodded, feeling the urge to challenge the veteran take a hold of him once more.

'Then I don't see what the problem is,' Hakon said, striding towards the door. 'Do you?'

'No, sergeant,' Ragnar said, abashed.

'And since your fellow Space Wolves have been good enough to repair your armour for you, while you slept, I see no good reason for you to parade around here without it, do you, Blood Claw?'

'No, sergeant.'

Hakon turned at the door. 'And Ragnar…'

'Yes, sergeant?'

'You did well back on Galt. Welcome back.'

'Thank you, sergeant.' Ragnar felt a little uplifted by Hakon's words. Even so little praise from the taciturn old Wolf was praise indeed. His words of thanks fell on empty air. Hakon had already turned and left.

'So Ragnar is the sergeant's favourite now, as well as the inquisitor girl's,' Nils mocked. 'What a crawler.'

'Well somebody has to be a hero around here,' Ragnar said. 'But don't worry, when the skalds get round to chanting the sagas I'm sure they'll mention the fact that I had three trusty comrades who polished and mended for me.'

'I can see it now,' said Nils. 'Ragnar's Saga! A stirring tale of a warrior who died when his neck broke under the strain of carrying his huge head.'

'Whose constant boasting so annoyed his trusty comrades that they murdered him in his sleep, more like,' Strybjorn said nastily.

'Who spent so much of his time lying around and snoring while his companions did all the bloody work, that they eventually booted him off their ship,' added Sven.

'It's nice to know I'm appreciated,' said Ragnar. 'Now if you don't mind, Sven, how about passing me some more of that ale.'

'Yes, my liege,' Sven smirked, handing it to him in such a way that most of it went over Ragnar.

'And how about some more food,' added Nils, tossing a hunk of cheese at him. Within seconds food and ale were flying everywhere, amidst gales of raucous laughter.

RAGNAR STOOD ON the bridge of the starship and gazed around in awe. The place was huge, the size of a chamber in the Fang. The ceiling was vaulted like that of an Imperial chapel, and a huge stained glass dome in the roof depicted scenes of inquisitors plying their trade, fighting monsters and heretics, scourging the unrighteous, breaking unbelievers on the autorack.

All around robed and cowled Initiates of the inquisitor's retinue performed their tasks. At long benches, numerists of the Machine God fed endless streams of data into their consoles. At a high central lectern the astrogators checked their calculations and made minute alterations to the ship's course. Figures more machine than man, communed directly with the ship's central data-core. The air smelled of the purification incense liberally distributed by censer-swinging initiates. Such things were done differently on the ships of the Space Wolves and by the uniformed officers of the Imperial Fleet, but this was an Inquisition ship, and it was run in the Inquisition manner.

It occurred to him, for the first time, just how vast and variegated the Imperium was. Each of the great departments of the Ecclesiarchy was a world unto itself, with its own rules, codes, and functions. They stood apart from each other as well as the mass of humanity they ruled in the Emperor's name. It was only the core of shared faith that bound them, and the million worlds of the faithful.

On a massive central holo-screen a three dimensional replica of the system they had entered had just appeared. It flickered into being in response to the chants of the initiates and the technical prayers they offered up, seeming to float in the air above all of their heads.

Ragnar could see half a dozen worlds each the size of a fist circling round a small, dark star. They moved at differing speeds in their orbits. A tiny pulse of blue light in the shape of an Imperial eagle indicated the position of the *Light of Truth*. A red skull showed their eventual destination.

'That is Korealis,' Inquisitor Sternberg said, his resonant voice filling the chamber and echoing away into the gloom beneath the vaults. 'It is a dead sun, burned out, but not collapsed. Its surface is a cold shell of dust. Somewhere in its depths, fires still flicker but not enough to give light and heat.

'It was mapped by the Great Surveys of the 30th millennium when they passed this way, and it was mostly forgotten. According to our records, there is some evidence of heretical pre-Imperial civilisation on the planetary surface of the fourth world, but the place was deemed too remote to merit cleansing, and no threat to the Imperium itself. Now and again there have been reports of prospectors passing this way, and at one time it harboured a colony of pirates. The pirate station was destroyed in a combined action between the Inquisition and the Blood Angels, in the 39th Millennium. There is little else to tell about the place of any interest.'

'What is it exactly we are looking for, inquisitor?' Sven asked. 'I take it we didn't come here just so you could give us a history lesson.'

Sternberg laughed. 'No. Indeed not, Master Blood Claw. Indeed not. Perhaps Inquisitor Isaan would be good enough to answer your question.'

Karah moved to her fellow inquisitor's side and looked down on them from the lectern. 'I have performed the Ritual of Divination once more, using the two pieces of the talisman we have so far acquired. It told me that this was the place to come but little else. I saw a space hulk in my vision, a thing vast and old that has drifted in the warp for many centuries – but that is all I have seen. There is something about the influence of this star, or perhaps about the hulk itself which clouds the seeing. In any case, I know that what we seek is on the hulk and all that remains is for us to go and get it.'

'Will there be any fighting,' Strybjorn said flatly.

'Who knows?' she replied with a shrug. 'Hulks are notorious for harbouring malefic denizens. Once we are in range of it, we will run all the standard sensor divinations for life forms, which will give us a clearer idea of any threats that may be lurking within the craft.'

'Who will be going in?' asked Ragnar.

'As if you don't already know the answer,' Sven muttered from his side.

'The Space Wolves will spearhead the assault, accompanied by Inquisitors Sternberg, Isaan, and their bodyguards, led by myself,' said Gul.

'Within visual contact distance,' one of the initiates interrupted loudly. 'Summoning image to view.'

The plainsong of the technical acolytes changed tone and a new picture shimmered into being. Ragnar shivered at the very sight of it. If it was possible for any space going vessel to look haunted and accursed, it was this one.

At first sight it did not even look like a ship, more like a graveyard of ships. It was a vast agglomeration of debris, united by some strange force around a central core. It looked like a vessel built of scraps of dead ships by some insane artisan. Ragnar could see now why orks were so attracted to hulks. There was something about the jury-rigged nature of these vessels that would appeal to their crazed technologies.

But, in the name of Russ, the thing was vast. As he watched it swell into view, Ragnar saw that each of the individual ships that made up one small component of the structure was as large as the *Light of Truth*. The hulk was bigger than most islands of the Worldsea on Fenris. There must be more miles of corridor in there than in the Fang. Finding the third part of the talisman was going to be quite a task.

'Coming into range of sensor divination, my lord inquisitor,' said the Chief Initiate.

'Begin the ritual invocations,' Sternberg replied calmly.

Ragnar could smell the man's tenseness even over the mildly hallucinogenic aroma of the incense. The chants changed tone once more and the chamber dimmed. Beneath the image of the space hulk odd technical runes began to appear. They shimmered and danced, and Ragnar was aware that they contained a goldmine of information for those who could read them; unfortunately he could not.

'Interesting,' he heard Sternberg murmur. 'Continue with the divination.'

As Ragnar watched, a shimmering glow settled on the image of the hulk. Small red and green dots drifted over its surface. Then without warning the whole image became distorted, shimmered and winked out of existence. A stillness descended on the bridge of the *Light of Truth*. Ragnar was not at all sure what had happened, but he could tell from the scents of those around him that it was not good.

'What happened?' he asked.

'Those lights we saw just before the image was nullified tell us that there are living creatures aboard the hulk,' Karah said quietly.

'And the fact that our sensor sweep was interfered with tells us that they don't like prying eyes,' Sternberg finished for her. 'Chief Initiate Vosper, what happened?'

The Chief Initiate studied the monitor on the bench before him. 'It appears our sweep triggered some sort of automatic shielding device, my lord inquisitor. It will take several hours to work out exactly what type. I suspect from the auguries that it was not a product of any human technological ritual, but rather something alien.'

'Could it be that we have triggered some sort of automatic system on the hulk that has nothing to do with those life-forms aboard?' Karah asked.

The initiate bowed his shaven head and steepled his fingers. 'Yes, Inquisitor Isaan. That is within the realms of possibility. Although it's probably wisest to assume some form of hostile intent for the moment.'

'My thoughts precisely,' Sternberg said.

Privately Ragnar agreed with him. All of the knowledge placed in his memory by the tutelary engines led him to believe that if a creature was alien, it was undoubtedly hostile. So far nothing he had encountered had caused him to doubt the wisdom of those teachings.

'Ready your weapons,' Inquisitor Sternberg said grimly, turning to regard them all. 'It looks like we'll be going in armed.'

THERE WAS A strange sense of acceleration as the shuttle fell away from the *Light of Truth*. Ragnar studied his companions. This time it was not just him and the other Space Wolves. There were over thirty armed men of the inquisitors' bodyguard. They were garbed like Imperial Guard but were wearing full face helmets and oxygen tanks to protect them against any decompression, lack of air or poison gas in the hulk.

It was chilly inside the shuttle and the air smelled of peculiar chemicals. The confined space within the small chamber made him feel just a little claustrophobic. Ragnar glanced over at his comrades. They all looked more relaxed than he felt, but he could smell the tension in the air. They checked their weapons with the concentration of men who knew their lives would soon depend on them. He himself felt oddly reluctant. He wondered why?

His hearts were beating faster and he was controlling the urge to sweat only with a massive effort of will. Something inside his stomach felt loose. He realised that he was actually afraid, and afraid in a way he had never been before. He actually feared for his life.

What was going on, he wondered, gazing over Sven's shoulder and out the porthole? The stars winked coldly back at him.

This was not like him. He had been nervous before a battle before, but he had never felt this sense of near paralysis.

He tried to work out where it had come from, and the answer was blindingly obvious. It came from being so severely wounded and from witnessing the death of Lars on Galt. Ever since he had been resurrected by the sorcerer-scientists of the Fang, he had possessed a sense of his own immortality that had amounted to a feeling of near-invincibility. He had been hurt before now, but never so badly. He realised that he had not believed that he could actually die. He had known it intellectually. That had been drummed into his head often enough during his training back on Fenris, but he had not actually believed it.

He was, after all, one of the Chosen. His fallen body had been lifted from among the dead by the Wolf Priests and they had brought him back to life. He had been one of the lucky ones, a favourite of the gods, and so had his comrades.

Yes, he had seen people die before, even Space Wolves, during the battle with Chaos Marines at the Temple of the Thousand Sons. But they had not been people he had known that well. He had shared a history with Lars; they had come through the time of choosing together, and trained and fought alongside each other. They were almost the same age.

The connection had been made in his own head, he realised, between Lars dying and his wounds. He had suffered a great deal of pain at that time which had driven home the lesson of mortality in a way that nothing else could. He knew now that even though he was a Space Marine, and one of the Emperor's chosen champions, there was no special dispensation for him. A bullet could still kill him. A chainsword could still cut him down. His life could be ended like anybody else's. For a warrior that should not have been a frightening thought, and yet he had to admit that it was for him.

And now a new fear was growing in his mind, that his courage would be tested and found wanting, and that he would disgrace himself. Was it possible that if they were attacked he might be paralysed with fear or even turn and flee? He hoped not, but it was a possibility. He prayed to Russ and tried to dismiss the thought, but it stayed on and niggled at the back of his mind. Had his offer of surrender back on Galt been, on some level, a genuine one? Had he merely been voicing what his spirit was really thinking, instead of trying to trick the ork warlord?

He was aware that Sergeant Hakon was looking at him thoughtfully – and somewhat disapprovingly too, it seemed – and he wondered if the old Wolf could somehow read his thoughts. Did his doubts show in his scent? Were all of his comrades only too aware of his weakness? He hoped not, but how could he be sure? That was the curse as well as the blessing of the Space Wolf's pack awareness.

He felt another set of eyes fall on him, and glanced over at Karah Isaan, sitting surrounded by her armoured and helmeted bodyguards. She, too, seemed to be picking up some of his conflicting feelings. But she just smiled at him reassuringly, and he felt something like warmth flooding into his mind. Unconsciously he fought against it. He wanted no one else privy to his secret thoughts. He did not want to have to rely on any external help, from her or anybody else. It would be a true weakness, and not just some phantom conjured up by his own dark thoughts.

Somewhere within him, the beast stirred. He felt a growl of rage begin deep in his throat. It was not afraid. It was angry and was desperate to confront any foe. He knew that it would relish bloody combat with any threat that presented itself. It was good to know that it was there, and could be counted on to aid him. That was help that he was prepared to take, from something that was part of him, bonded to his spirit.

Slowly his fears subsided to a manageable level, but he knew that they were still there, and might return in a moment of stress. He let out a long, slow breath, and offered up a fervent prayer to Russ.

CHAPTER ELEVEN

THERE WAS A deep metallic clang, like the mournful tolling of some vast unseen bell, and a sudden bone-shaking vibration, as the shuttle came to rest alongside the space hulk. Ragnar sensed the change in mood as the Blood Claws rose and followed Sergeant Hakon to the front of the ship. Already the auto-borer in the nose of their ship was at work, chopping through the ceramite of the hulk's hull and preparing a way for their entrance. Soon it would pierce the hulk's side and expand like a flower blossoming to allow a boarding tunnel to pass through.

Ragnar's chainsword and bolt pistol were ready in his hand. He doubted that there would be immediate trouble but you never knew, and Space Marines always went in as if combat were mere moments away. There was a hiss of air as the pressures equalised between the boarding tunnel and the hulk's interior. Ragnar immediately tested the scent of the place. He did not like what he caught. The air was stale and cold and fusty, and held the taint of many subtle poisons.

Whatever systems kept the air pure here were working imperfectly, he could tell. And there were other things, the trace scents of living beings of many different types. Some of them were so old as to be barely discernible. He doubted that in any other place they would have lasted so long but here, with constant but flawed recycling, who could really guess at their age?

Gravity within the hulk was less than he was used to. He felt light and constantly had to fight to control his movements and keep his balance to prevent himself from floating upward towards the ceiling.

Sven and Nils moved ahead, one moving left of the tunnel's entrance, the other moving right. It was their job to scan the corridor and make sure there were no nasty surprises. Ragnar waited for the signal and then moved clumsily to join Sven. Strybjorn strode off to partner Nils.

Ragnar did not know quite what to expect but what he saw was anti-climactic. He was looking down a long metal corridor. The floor was covered in a sort of corroded mesh of mottled steel. Ancient-looking glowglobes flickered feebly in the ceiling. There were hatches lining the corridor and not too far off he could see a ladder that descended from above to disappear into a hole in the floor. There were tattered remains of ancient posters glued to the wall, written in some old human script he could barely understand. Long masses of exposed cables ran the length of the corridor, as if some long-dead engineer had jury-rigged a power circuit along it.

Sensing movement from behind him, Ragnar knew that the inquisitor's bodyguards were starting to make progress along the tunnel. He made a quick check to see if there was anything Sven had missed, saw nothing and began to move off down the corridor to make room.

'Interesting place,' Sven whispered ironically. 'I'll bet there's even less good stuff to eat here than there was in the bloody jungle.'

'I'm sure if you look you'll find a nice fat mutated cockroach,' Ragnar hissed back. 'You always find them on ships like this. The ancients used to carry them to eat the flakes of dead skin their bodies constantly shed.'

'Thank you, oh sage one,' said Sven, 'I knew that. The tutelary engines put the same knowledge in my head as they did in yours.'

'Yes, but you need a brain to be able to use that knowledge. It just echoes around in all the empty space inside your skull.'

'Ha ha. You missed your true calling, Ragnar. You should have been a bloody jester.'

As they paced carefully along, they surveyed all of the shadows for threats. Despite their banter, Ragnar could tell that Sven was just as keyed up as he was. He knew that both their senses were stretched to the absolute edge. No enemy was going to take them by surprise.

Ragnar flared his nostrils and opened his mouth to catch any random scents. Nothing threatening. He kept moving to the junction where the ladder entered the corridor. 'Down or up?' he asked Sven.

'Up!'

Ragnar nodded. Sven would look up and cover the ceiling at the ladder. It was now Ragnar's task to see that nothing surprised them from below. As he approached he kept sniffing, and he fell silent. He was all too aware of the chatter of the guardsmen behind him, and the scent of their armour and weapons. He still caught no hint of a threat.

Standing at the edge of the metal ladder and looking down he saw that it descended a very long way, vanishing into darkness far below. In his gut the beast writhed and growled. It did not like the look of that long drop at all.

'Which way?' he called quietly into the comm-net.

'Down,' came Karah's clear precise voice. Sven was already moving in response. He holstered his chainsword so that he would have a hand free for the ladder. The bolt pistol was still held firmly in his right hand. He swung himself out and began to climb.

'How far?' he asked.

'Until I tell you to stop,' the female inquisitor replied.

'Fair enough.'

THEY WENT DOWN a long way. Ragnar felt as if he had been climbing for weeks. Even his reinforced muscles were aching and he felt sorry for the normal humans who accompanied them. They must really be in pain.

The climb had been interesting though. His tutors had taught him that geological and archaeological remains were found in layers, and this climb reminded him of that. As they descended, their surroundings grew more ancient, it seemed, as if the hulk had been built outward from some exceedingly old core. They passed through levels that had spoken to him of many different cultures and civilisations. He realised that they really were descending, not through one huge spacecraft, but through an accumulation of smaller vessels that had been built in many different places and times, and which, over the years, had been occupied by members of many different races.

Everywhere he saw evidence of the crude handiwork of orks. Here and there he saw crudely daubed graffiti which bore the chilling marks of Chaos. How many different types of people had lived and died here, he wondered? How long had it been since this place was first occupied? Were these traces from individual ships in the time before they had drifted in to become part of the hulk or were they evidence of occupants in the time since? Only whatever dark spirit presided over this hulk could tell him, and there was no way he could commune with it, and no way he would want to even if he could.

Behind him he could hear the nervous chatter of the guards, as they kept up a constant cross-talk on the comm-net. He could smell their deepening unease as they proceeded, an unease that was only increasing with tiredness and distance from their mothership. Ragnar did not blame them. He was beginning to wonder at the wisdom of this penetration into the space hulk. To get back by conventional means was a long trek over dangerous ground, and the teleport beacon was very unreliable, as he had already discovered. Their line of retreat was far from secure.

And yet what other options had they? If they wanted to reconstruct the Talisman of Lykos and save the world of Aerius from the dark plague then they simply had to push on and pray for the best. Sometimes the only way was the longest way. As a Space Marine he realised he should not be daunted by that fact.

Gnawing unease had settled on him like a cloak. He did not like this place. With its endless miles of corridors it seemed like a twisted parody of the Fang, but it lacked the comforting scent of the Space Wolves and their vassals, and the sense of long, continuous and benevolent occupancy. If the Fang had been abandoned by the Wolves thousands of years ago, then used by whoever had stumbled across it as a temporary lair, it might have looked like this.

He muttered a prayer and tried to push away these grim thoughts. The oppressive atmosphere of the place was getting to him. Or perhaps it was something else. Perhaps the malevolent presence he imagined was real, and was placing these shadowy fears in his mind. Perhaps…

Get a grip of yourself, he told himself. Concentrate on the foes which might actually be there. Don't people this place with imaginary enemies while real ones are capable of sneaking up on you.

So he pushed on into the darkness and the gloom, all too aware that somewhere out there something wicked was waiting. He could tell from his comrades' unease that they felt the same way.

TEN HOURS IN, they stopped to rest. The Space Wolves could have kept going easily but the inquisitors and their bodyguards needed to stop.

They set up camp in a huge hall. It had once been a pavilion of some sort. Overhead was a crystal dome through which the stars had once beamed down. Now overhead they could see only the great shadowy bulk of another part of the hulk. Sometimes odd lights could be seen shimmering in portholes, which only added to the haunted atmosphere of the hulk. It was not a reassuring thought that behind the crystal there was only hard vacuum and a hungry void waiting to devour any unprotected thing that fell into it.

The floor was a vast mosaic, but the picture had long since been eroded away into a blur of shapes and colours. Without wind and rain, Ragnar could only imagine that this had been done by the passage of countless feet or vehicles. Dotted around were huge empty pits that had once been fishponds or swimming pools. In the middle of some were islands on which stood fountains. Here and there statues depicting an alien race that he recognised as the eldar stood on plinths. It was oddly peaceful and oddly beautiful and for the first time since their arrival on the hulk he had a sense of security. Perhaps that was why they chose the place to rest.

The warriors slumped down where they stood, leaving their lasrifles close at hand. Inquisitor Sternberg and Gul passed among them, dividing them up into watches. Without speaking, at a gesture from Sergeant Hakon, the four Blood Claws took up positions covering the four corners of the chamber. Ragnar knew they would prove far more effective sentries than any mere human. Hakon himself went to consult with the inquisitors.

Ragnar took up his position near one of the statues, thinking that not only would this give him a closer look at its alien workmanship, but that he could use it for cover in case of an attack. This was not a bad defensive site. The sunken empty ornamental ponds and the fountains they contained could be used like earthworks if danger threatened. They could have done worse.

He took a deep breath and murmured a prayer to the Emperor, willing himself to relax. His muscles were aching more than they should be, and he was tired in a way he had never felt since being chosen. It seemed that his wounds and his subsequent illness had drained him more than he had imagined. Perhaps this was why his imagination was playing up. Perhaps he was simply tired and ill. Somehow he doubted it. There was something about the gloom and stillness of the space hulk that was simply evil. He knew this to be the case. Right at this moment, he felt as if they had walked into a troll's lair unarmed.

He looked up at the statue. It showed a tall, lean humanoid garbed in oddly elongated, curved armour. The figure carried a gun of some strangely beautiful alien design in one hand, and a banner in the other. The face was hidden by a mask that was as beautiful as it was functional. The whole thing was made from a substance that Ragnar did not recognise. It looked like polished stone but something about it suggested bone. When he touched it, he felt a slight tingling, not unpleasant yet odd enough to make him snatch his hand away.

Who were you, Ragnar wondered? Some hero of the eldar fallen in battle long ago? A god they worshipped? Or a vain chieftain who caused his image to be placed here for eternity? It was another riddle to which he would never know the answer. The universe was full of them, a place of mystery and horror, that no man could ever really understand.

He wondered about the people who had made the statue. Where were they now? How had their ship come to be part of this hulk? Had they been lost in the warp and drawn into it? Had they dwelt here as part of the hulk, or had the ship been abandoned long before? It was a thing to tease the imagination of a man and drive him mad with speculation.

He had heard the eldar dwelled on huge spaceships, craft-worlds they were called, and had long since abandoned all surface dwellings. He knew they were a decadent and sinister race who performed arcane rituals for their own unguessable purposes, and who interfered in the wars of mankind for no discernible purpose. And now they were seeking parts of an artefact that had once belonged to that eldritch race. Was the fact they had found this hall significant, an omen? Or was it simply chance, the only pattern here being the one imposed on events by his own mind? No, there had to be a connection. Had not the eldar built the Black Pyramid on Aerius? Had they not been there the last time plague had ravaged that world?

He caught a familiar scent approaching from behind. 'Hello, inquisitor,' he said without turning.

'Practising your psychic powers?' Karah Isaan smiled softly.

'No. I recognise your scent.'

'What is it like?' she said, curious.

'Unlike any other.'

'I am the only woman here.'

'No. It is not that. You smell differently. Like someone who was raised on a different world from these folk. Amid jungles and flowers and under a hot sun. I have never been there but I would guess that Aerius is cold like Fenris in winter, and gloomy, and smells of industry and metalwork.'

'You would make a very good seer, Ragnar, for you are correct in almost every respect. And you can tell all that by scent? Your nose must be very keen.'

'Keener than a true wolf's, or so they say.'

'It would be quite a gift for an inquisitor. For tracking and questioning and such.'

'It is a gift given only to the Space Wolves, a legacy of the geneseed of Russ.' Remembering Ranek's words about secrets back in the Fang, he wondered if he was telling her too much. She moved around in front of him. He was struck by her beauty. She was a lovely woman, if rather stern-looking. In her own way, with her dark skin, brown eyes and alien scent she was as exotic and unknowable as the eldar. He guessed that, in some way, he was probably the same to her.

'I wanted to speak to someone,' she ventured. 'This is a vile place and I have no desire to share that thought with our troops.'

'This is an evil place,' he agreed.

'Your nose tells you that?'

'My nose and my spirit… and my common sense. Were it not our duty to do so, we should not have come here.'

'But it was our duty. And our duty often takes us to places we would rather not be, to do things we would rather not do.'

'I am a Space Wolf,' he said. 'I live to fight. There is nothing I would rather do.'

'You lead a rather simple life then, Ragnar of the Space Wolves.'

'No. You lead a rather complicated one.'

'Perhaps… but I sense there is more to you than meets the eye, Ragnar, and that you are not quite as unafraid as you would have me believe.'

Her words brought back his dark thoughts from earlier and he looked away, embarrassed. They were his secret shame, one that he wanted no one to know. He certainly did not want this woman, with her disturbing beauty, to be aware of them. He said nothing and simply stared off into the distance.

'There is no shame in being afraid in a place of darkness like this, Ragnar. There would only be shame if your fear mastered you. And I am enough of a seer to know that will never happen.'

Her words and their tone were meant to reassure him, he knew, but he was not reassured. He wondered if he would ever regain the feeling of invulnerability, of immortality, that he had once enjoyed. She seemed to sense his dark mood and turned and walked away.

Ragnar watched her go, and then gave his attention back to his guard duties. If there are monsters out there, he thought, let them come. They will find me ready.

AFTER SIX HOURS of rest, they broke fast on ration tablets washed down with purified water, and then pushed on deeper into the hulk. Once again the nature of their surroundings changed. The glowglobes became less common, and in many places they had burned out altogether. The shadows became deeper. The guards turned on the beacons on their shoulder pads to give them more light. As yet Ragnar's altered eyes could still penetrate the gloom easily, but the increasing darkness had a dampening effect on his spirits.

Sometimes, up ahead of them now, he thought he could hear sinister scuttling movements, so faint as to be barely perceptible even to his superhumanly keen ears. He tried telling himself it was rats or some of the huge mutant cockroaches that were all too common in ships like this, but he could not. A quick glance at Sven told him that his fellow Blood Claw was thinking the same thing. He raised his hand and gave the signal for Be careful. From the change in the rhythm of their movement, he knew without looking back that the guards were paying attention.

'Wonder if it's edible,' Sven said. 'I hate bloody food tablets.'

'We'll know soon enough,' said Ragnar, catching the tension behind his friend's words.

'You know what I like about you, Ragnar? You always have a stupid answer to whatever I have to say.'

'You know what I like about you, Sven?'

'What?'

'Absolutely nothing.'

'Like I said before,' Sven snorted, 'you missed your calling. You should have been a court jester, not a Space Wolf.'

Ragnar smiled and clutched his weapons tighter. If there was trouble ahead, he was glad Sven was there. Any man who could trade such dumb insults when danger threatened was worth having around.

THEY MOVED ON through the depths of the great hulk. Ragnar felt as if it were coming alive all around him. He had a sense of ancient evil things waking from long dormancy. Even with his hyper-acute senses he could not quite put a finger on why. There were subtle changes in the scent patterns in the air. The almost subliminal hum of the life support systems had altered. Occasionally he felt vibrations pass through the hull beneath his feet as if some giant were moving or a vast piece of machinery had been activated.

He could tell by the tension of Sven's body and the subtle alterations of his stance and scent that his fellow Blood Claw felt it too. Sven held his weapons ready and glanced around as if he expected to be called upon to use them at any moment.

Karah Isaan's words about a new threat coming from the ship that followed them echoed through his mind. Was this sense of

something stirring connected with their own presence, tres-
passing on the ship, or were the two unrelated?

'At the next junction take the passage that slopes down,'
Karah's voice sounded loud and clear over the comm-net ear-
bead.

The tension was starting to drain him. He spoke into the
comm-net: 'Are we any closer to what we seek, or have we been
wandering around in circles?'

'Be patient, Ragnar; we're getting there,' Karah soothed.

'Thank Russ for that,' Sven muttered.

AS THEY PROGRESSED downwards, it became evident that machinery had been switched on. Huge compressors were at work,
great flexible accordion tubes expanding and contracting.
Mighty pistons pumped up and down. Huge clouds of steam
and smoke swirled out of cracked and defective piping.

'What in all the bloody cold hells of Frostheim is going on
here?' Sven asked.

'It looks like somebody activated all of this machinery,'
Ragnar replied.

'You don't bloody say,' said Sven. 'I mean – why?'

'It could have switched on automatically when we came in.
Some ancient devices do that.'

'Or, Ragnar? I hear an "or" in your voice.'

'Or maybe somebody switched it on to provide themselves
with cover. Noise, smoke, confusing smells. They will all make
it more difficult to spot an ambush.'

'Noise and smoke, yes, I understand. But scents – why that?
Surely they can't know there are Space Wolves on board.'

'Can't they? Why make that assumption? You are assuming
that whoever did it thinks and senses like a human; that may not
be the case. Many alien races have made their homes on hulks.'

'You're not a particularly reassuring man to talk to in a situation like this, Ragnar.'

'This is not a particularly reassuring situation.'

'Aye, you are right there.'

Suddenly the stink that hit his nostrils suggested something
that was not even remotely human. The figure emerging from
the smoke reinforced this impression.

It was larger than a man and it moved much, much faster.
Four huge arms, tipped with monstrous rending claws,

swivelled from its shoulders. Row upon row of hideous fangs gleamed in its mouth. A horny shell of armour encased its body. It loped along on clawed and padded feet. Its manner suggested the scuttling of some enormous insect. The memories placed in his brain by the teaching engines told him what it was instantly.

'Genestealer!' Ragnar yelled, taking a bead on the thing with his bolt pistol and squeezing the trigger. Quick as he was, the thing was quicker. It jinked to one side and his shells passed over its head. Ragnar had never seen anything move so swiftly. Its reflexes made his own seem slow by comparison. The fear he had felt earlier returned like a wave of ice running through him and, for one horrible vital moment, he froze. The thing came straight at him and it was on him before he could react. Its weight crashed into him, bowling him over with irresistible force.

In an instant its face was in his, snarling and snapping. He could smell its foetid breath, see the thick, mucus-like saliva dribbling from its mouth. He could feel those impossible strong talons grasp him, and heard his armour begin to crack under the pressure. He knew that his split-second of hesitation was going to cost him his life.

Blood and flesh splattered his face. The blade of a chainsword sheared through chitin an inch before his eyes and the beast stopped moving.

'Get up!' he heard Sven bellow. 'We're under attack.'

Ragnar shook his head and sprang to his feet, throwing the genestealer's corpse to one side with the force of his movement. He was appalled. In the moment of crisis he had frozen, as he feared he might. Only Sven's quick thinking had saved him. The fact that he had been surprised by the thing's speed and strength was no excuse. He was a Space Wolf. Nothing was supposed to be able to take him unprepared.

No sense in worrying about it now, he realised, hearing the padding of dozens of approaching feet, and seeing the monstrous forms of half a dozen genestealers emerge from the smoke. In his state of heightened awareness he noticed that their carapaces were all blotched and cracked. They had an odd, diseased look that differed from the images placed in his brain by the tutelary engines.

The beast within him snarled in fury. He knew that it, too, had been shocked by its near-death, and that its rage was all the stronger because of it. Gratefully Ragnar surrendered to it.

Laser bolts spat over his shoulder as the inquisitors' guards opened fire. He heard the thunder of bolters as Sergeant Hakon and Inquisitor Sternberg opened up too, and he could hear more bolter fire from the rear. It was Strybjorn and Nils, he realised. The things were attacking from behind them too, then. So these were no mere beasts. An inhuman intelligence was at work here, guiding the attack.

Ragnar raised his pistol and shot. This time his aim was true. The shell passed right through the head of one of the stealers. He howled with satisfied bloodlust and fired again. The stealers were too closely packed to miss, but this time the armour of his target's carapace partially deflected the shot so that instead of killing it cleanly, it merely removed one of its huge clawed arms. If the creature felt any pain it gave no sign, and it kept on coming.

The smell of burning flesh filled the air as the lasguns bit home. Ragnar could see armour sizzle and liquefy and run under the heat. Still the beasts came on. From behind him came the sound of battle cries and the screams of dying men. The smell of spilled entrails and human blood assaulted Ragnar's nostrils. He knew that behind him the battle had become close and deadly.

The terrible suspicion that at any moment one of the genestealers was going to break through and claw him in the back filled his mind. He dared not look back though, for doing so meant taking his eyes from those swiftly closing inhuman foes. They were so quick that any distraction might prove fatal, and he was not risking such a mistake a second time.

Half the stealers had fallen now but the rest were almost within striking distance. He could hear curses from the guards behind him and sense their fear, and he knew that they would not be much help when the melee came. They were but ordinary men, however well trained, and there was no way they could stand against the fury of the stealers' charge.

Ragnar did not wait for them to come to him. Filled with the beast's anger, he sprang forward, swinging his chainsword through a huge arc which ended with it buried in the insect-like skull of one of the stealers. With a reflex like the death strike of a scorpion it lashed out with its claws. Ragnar sprang back but not quickly enough. One of the dying stealer's talons connected glancingly and the force of the buffet sent him flying backward off-balance to land beside Karah.

Ragnar rolled over, brought his feet below him and regained his balance. He stood in a fighting crouch and had a perfect view of the struggle before him. Sergeant Hakon had joined the melee and Inquisitor Sternberg and Gul were at his side. Together with Sven they fought savagely with the surviving stealers. It was impossible to tell who fought with the greater fury, the humans or the aliens. Such was the savagery of the battle.

Even as he watched, Hakon clubbed one of the genestealers with the butt of his pistol. Bones and armour crunched with the force of the impact, and as the alien beast fell backwards the sergeant decapitated it with one sweep. Sternberg blasted another in the face point blank sending a huge gout of blood and brain and splintered skull everywhere. Gul wrestled with one of the creatures and in a show of near superhuman strength was holding his own.

From out of the corner of his eye, Ragnar saw that one of the stealers had flanked Sven and was about to spring in his back. The Blood Claw was busily engaged by two of the stealers' brood and could do nothing to stop it. Ragnar growled; it was time to repay his debt.

He leapt forward, landing on the genestealer's back, just as it had intended to land on his comrade's. The vile thing began to tumble forward. Ragnar clubbed it on the back of its head with his pistol, smashing through the skull. As it tumbled forward, to sprawl on the deck he brought his heel down on its neck, just as he had seen Gurg do to Lars. Vertebrae snapped as the neck broke. He snapped off a shot over Sven's shoulder, risking the chance that his battle-brother might move into its way, in order to remove the threat of one of the other monsters facing his friend, then as a last precaution he decapitated the stealer at his feet with his chainsword.

He looked up in time to see Sven finish his last monstrous opponent, and together they sprang to aid Hakon and the others. They chopped into the genestealers in a storm of chainsaw blades and bolter shells, and in moments the conflict was over. From behind him, the sounds of battle had also ceased. Ragnar glanced around.

He could see that Strybjorn and Nils still stood. Their armour was so covered in filth that their Blood Claw emblems were obscured and reeking gore steamed on their carapaces. Around them lay the corpses of dead genestealers – and half a dozen dead humans, all from the ranks of the guards.

'It seems we have repulsed the attack,' said Sternberg, panting hard.

'Yes, but how many more of these dire things lie between us and our target?' Sergeant Hakon asked.

CHAPTER TWELVE

RAGNAR STUDIED THE scene of carnage. The attack from the rear had been the stronger of the two and had inflicted greater casualties. That spoke of a swift, evil intelligence at work. It had struck where they were weakest, not strongest, and it had known enough about them to assault the precise spot. How could that be?

He dismissed the thought as irrelevant. It did not matter how. It just mattered that it had happened. More worrying still, looking back on it, was the fact that he had frozen when attacked. It could have cost him his life, he knew. Worse, it could have cost others theirs. If he was the weak link in the chain, it could have all sorts of consequences. If he had not been there Sven might have fallen, and perhaps the genestealers would have reached Karah. From there, who knew?

In this place, at this time, all of their lives were in each other's hands. He knew that they all relied on each other, and that the failure of one could easily lead to the doom of them all. He resolved that this was the first and last time he would ever let the others down.

He became aware of the fact that Sven was staring at him. The guilty sense that the other Blood Claw knew his thoughts flooded into Ragnar's mind.

'What?' he asked savagely.

'Nothing. I was just going to say thank you for saving my damn life, that's all.'

Ragnar let that sink in for a moment. Sven had not noticed his fear. He thought Ragnar had behaved well. 'No. Thank you for saving mine. It would have been the end for me if you had-n't cut down the genestealer when it was on top of me.'

Sven's crooked grin lit up his ugly face. 'Think nothing of it. I don't. Having you around makes the rest of us look good. That's why I did it.'

'Thanks anyway, oh gracious one.' Ragnar felt better already. He glanced around at the others. Sternberg and Karah looked fine, if a little shaken. Sergeant Hakon was spraying synthiflesh on his face to cover a gaping wound. Even as Ragnar watched the artificial skin closed over the gash, sealing and cleansing it. Ragnar knew it was quite a bad wound for the sergeant to need the arcane stuff at all, but if Hakon was in pain, he gave no sign of it. Looking at him, Ragnar wondered how often in his long career Hakon had been wounded. Had he ever felt the way Ragnar did, after taking damage? If so he had not let it affect him too deeply. Ragnar resolved that in future he would be like the sergeant. If Hakon could learn to endure, so could he.

The guards moved around, seeing to their own wounded. Watching them, Ragnar became aware of just how fragile a thing a human being was. The corpses looked pitiful. Some had been split open by the stealers' claws, reduced to slashed sacks of slimy organs and wet, bloody muscle. Compared to those, some of the others looked strangely rested; their wounds looked minor, so small that they should not have been able to kill a grown man – and yet they had.

The survivors looked tired and weary after a battle that had left him feeling mostly invigorated. He wondered if this was natural for some men, or yet another part of the reconstruction of his body as a Space Marine. He wished there were someone he could ask about these things.

Already Gul, Sternberg and their own corporals were starting to chivvy them into some sort of marching order. Warily Nils and Strybjorn came closer. Ragnar could see that like him they were constantly scanning their surroundings for new threats.

Strybjorn's face was gloomy as always. A bright intense light burned in Nils's face. He seemed exalted.

'That was a good fight,' he said. 'Must have killed about five of the four-armed bastards single-handed. They were all over us for a bit. We showed them back.'

Strybjorn shrugged and glared off into the distance. He seemed possessed by a strange melancholy. At the same time, his scent spoke of a furious excitement that was, if anything, stronger than Nils'.

'We killed a few down here as well,' said Sven. 'Would have killed more if bloody Ragnar hadn't decided to lie down on the floor and have a kip in the middle of the battle.'

'All right! Form up!' Gul yelled. 'We're moving on.'

'We're getting close now,' Karah said by way of encouragement, though her face gave the lie to her confidence.

'Bet we'll meet more of those bloody stealers before we get what we're looking for.'

'They're what I'm looking for,' Nils said, as he and Strybjorn hung back to cover the rear.

'Aye, easy for you to say,' muttered Sven. 'But it's Ragnar and me who are on bloody point.'

THE INSIDE OF the hulk became darker and gloomier. Here and there traces of flesh-like substance became visible on the walls. Ragnar smelled new scents in the air. Traces of something organic. The sort of smells you got when you opened a human body or gutted an animal. Musks, like exotic perfumes. Overlaying it all a strange alien aroma like the one the genestealers had possessed and yet subtly different, as if it belonged to something related to them, and yet not wholly like them.

'Smells like we're crawling around inside somebody's body, doesn't it?' said Sven. Ragnar nodded. It was not a pleasant sensation, and it was getting worse.

Along with the smell, there was an oppressive sense of presence in the air. It was like the one which surrounded the ork chieftain in some ways. It suggested a powerful psychic force. Ragnar knew that they were moving ever closer to the intelligence that had guided the stealers. He wondered whether they would discover it in possession of the fragment of the talisman they sought, and perhaps using it in the same way as Gurg had.

He would not be surprised if that was the case. He glanced back to see how Karah was taking it.

She seemed lost in heated discussion with Sternberg. Her face was drawn and a frown was painted on her brow. It looked as if she was in pain, and growing more so with every step. He guessed that if the presence that enveloped them was strong enough to be sensed by a non-psyker like him then it must be causing her considerable distress. He imagined that the psychic spoor must be as strong to her as the scent was to him. It was not a reassuring thought.

There was a definite change in the walls of the corridors now Here and there, traces of glistening slime were visible. Occasionally patches of a substance resembling flesh clung to the walls like a patch of mould. If he looked closely he could see the remains of a near translucent membrane. It was as if something had burst out of the metal and strode off. In his mind, he pictured obscene, man-sized monsters hatching from the walls. He shuddered as he tried to shake off the image.

As they pressed on, he noticed that massive vein-like pipes, made from the same organic substance, began to run between the patches on the walls. From within he could hear the obscene gurgling of fluids. What was this, he wondered? Now it really seemed as if they were deep within the innards of some massive living creature.

And yet, if he looked closely, he could tell that whatever it was, it was unwell. There was a sense of sickness about the thing. There was a smell of rot, of corruption, of festering pus, in the air. It made him think of Nurgle, the Dark God dedicated to disease and decay. Whatever vast beast surrounded him was sick; this was not its natural condition. Thinking back to the genestealers they had fought earlier, he remembered their blotched carapaces and the sores on their flesh. They too had been sick. It was as if some dreadful power was at work here, one that could warp even the genestealers and that had created them to its own purposes.

'This does not look bloody good,' he heard Sven murmur. The words drew him from his reverie and forced him to consider his surroundings in more than the automatic manner he had been doing so. He instantly saw what Sven meant. In the distance he could see a mass of organic material that in some way suggested the components of a huge living machine.

Overhead greenish lights burned above the organic machines. They reminded Ragnar of the phosphorescent algae that swam in the seas of Fenris, but much brighter and more concentrated.

He could see vast tubes inside which egg-shaped objects moved by peristaltic action. He could make out something that resembled a huge pulsing heart surmounted by what looked like an exposed brain. Enormous filaments stretched out in every direction, connecting to fleshy nodes that burrowed into the floor of the hulk. The whole thing glistened with fibrous green-white mucus. He knew at once that they had reached the centre of the corruption that he had sensed, that this was the heart of the darkness within this vessel.

In the centre of the thing's mass of brain tissue something glittered, and Ragnar knew immediately that he was looking on the third and final part of the crystal they had sought.

Even as he watched, a horde of living creatures emerged from the centre of the fleshy mass, moving with an inhuman precision, as if they were all cells in one mighty organism. He could see huge insect-limbed creatures that bore what looked like guns made from living flesh. There were smaller fleeter creatures, all legs and jaws and lashing tails. There were genestealers, chittering and snarling as they sprang. And something else – something massive and monstrous with enormous mandibles that looked as if they could chop a man in two by simply closing. He knew at once what they faced.

'Tyranids,' he heard Sergeant Hakon say, his voice full of both dread and wonder.

Ragnar shuddered. These were the feared warriors of the swarms which had menaced humanity on several occasions in the past and which he knew, from the Chapter records, had slain many Space Wolves in their passing. What were these? Some remnant of one of the great hive fleets that had swept through the human realm? Or were they secret infiltrators, harbingers of a new tyranid invasion to come?

And in the instant that they began their swarming charge, he could see that some sickness was at work here too. They looked flawed, ill made, as if the process that created them had not quite worked properly. They did not accord with any of the artificial memories. They looked like sick distorted parodies. Limbs hung loosely from their sides. Boils and warts erupted from their flesh. Thin yellow mucus wept from their mouths and breathing membranes. It was as if they had been infected by some terrible plague. Even their movements were sick and limping.

This was something new, he thought. In all the records, there were no references to diseased tyranids. They sometimes infected whole worlds with their biomechanical spores, but there was never any reference to them suffering illness. Not that it meant anything, Ragnar thought after a moment's reflection. There were many gaps in the old records, and who really knew much about these heretical aliens?

Perhaps there was a connection of some sort between the disease here and the plague on Aerius. Then the time for all wondering was past, as the tyranids attacked.

They swept forward in a huge wave. The giant hive warriors bellowed eerie alien challenges. The smaller things chittered and aimed small, organic looking guns. Their chitin gleamed greenly in the half-light.

'Watch out!' Sven bellowed. There was a grinding sound, and then the bizarre organic guns began to spit a hail of projectiles towards them. He threw himself flat, letting the shells pass overhead. Groans of agony from behind him told him that others had not been so swift or so lucky.

Drawing a bead with his bolter he opened fire himself, concentrating on the genestealers and the huge hive warriors. He knew that soon they would be upon him and that he was going to have to rise into a fighting crouch or be butchered where he lay, but right at this moment he wanted to thin out their numbers a little.

Shouted orders from behind told him that others had had the same idea. Las beams pulsed over his head as the remnants of the inquisitor's bodyguards returned fire. The thunder of bolt pistols told him that his battle-brothers were joining in the combat. He saw some small circular objects go whistling overhead, and a shockwave of death ripped through the onrushing tyranid line. Someone had enough sense to lob grenades into the tightly packed mass, he thought. Good idea! He thumbed his grenade dispenser. One of the small circular microgrenades dropped into his cupped hand. He squeezed twice to set the timer and then threw.

It arced away and landed among the tyranid attackers. The first few passed over it without harm, but an instant later the explosion smashed into a tall hive warrior and some of the smaller brood. Great chunks of the beast's carapace blasted outwards, then the huge creature toppled like a felled tree. Its smaller kin were shredded instantly. Cold satisfaction filled Ragnar as he reached for another grenade.

Some of the alien shells chewed into the ground near him. He could see them shatter and smelled an acrid acidic stink as greenish fluid bubbled forth. He knew it was a form of corrosive that would eat flesh as well as armour. The stench was appalling. He was glad none of it had splashed his flesh.

He rolled to one side so that the beasts could not get a bead on him, snatching his pistol as he went. Something sprayed on his hand, and he smelled a scent like burning from his gauntlet. Knowing there was nothing he could do about it right now, he sprang to his feet and unloaded shot after shot into the tyranid horde.

There were so many of them he could not miss. Each shell smashed into a victim. Heads flew apart, flesh tore, and alien body fluids oozed forth to splatter the deck. Any human force would have broken under the relentless fire the Marines and their allies spewed forth. The tyranids kept on coming, oblivious to any casualties. It was quite terrifying to see the way they maintained their advance and Ragnar could smell the barely suppressed fear of the men all around him. Only the Space Wolves, the two inquisitors and Gul seemed immune. He could hear Sternberg shouting encouragement to his men, and Gul bellowing orders for the troops to hold steady. He sensed Karah mustering her psychic powers.

It was as if a river of pure light passed all around him now. The guards' fire was steady despite their panic. They had obviously realised that their best hope of survival lay in obeying their commanders, and inflicting as many casualties as possible. The whole front rank of the tyranid onslaught was scythed down. For a moment, a brief moment, it appeared that their relentless advance might halt. They wavered, their ranks thinned by human fire and a torrent of grenades. The cohesion of the whole group seemed to fail, and it looked like they might actually turn tail and run. But then the wavering stopped, and they picked up momentum again, leaping over the corpses of their fallen, determined to get to grips with their enemies.

Ragnar steeled himself for the shock of impact, knowing that in the next few heartbeats he might die. This time he was determined that come what may, he would not freeze, and that, if he were to die, he was going to take some of these inhuman monsters to hell with him. Sven let out a long howl and charged forward. Ragnar watched him plough into the monstrous mass, cleaving about him as he went. The savage teeth of his chainsword ripped through chitin like it was paper and exposed pulpy innards. Weapons of flesh and bone were chopped in two. They fell to pieces, leaking blood and pus just like the monsters that carried them.

The Wolf watched for a moment, and then decided that Sven had the right idea. He leapt forward and felt the shock of impact as his chainsword smashed through organic armour. It was like being a swimmer diving into a sea of flesh. All around him monstrous things bellowed. Distorted alien faces, twisted in unreadable expressions that might have been hatred or hunger, surrounded him. Unnatural eyes glittered with hatred and malice. The stink of the tyranids was all but overwhelming, and goaded the beast within him to savage excess. He lashed out, clearing a path to Sven's side, and they stood back to back against the horde.

Lasguns flashed in the darkness. Grenade explosions strobed across his sight. He smelled burning and blood and the sour stench of disease. The deck flexed beneath his feet, resonating to the blasts of the bombs. The air in his chest vibrated with the sounds of battle. He pulled the trigger of his bolt pistol, and shells cleaved a path of destruction through the aliens. They were so tightly packed that they could not dodge. Bolter fire blasted clean through the body of one and exploded in the chest of the tyranid behind. He ducked the sweep of a huge claw, and sheared it off with his return stroke. Greenish slime pumped forth to spray him. The rotating blades of the chainsword sent droplets of it spraying across the room.

For the next few seconds he was too busy to think, let alone notice what was happening all around him. Duck and strike, parry and thrust, move and lash out, that was all he could do. It was fighting at a pace too fast for thought. Instinctively he knew he would live or die according to the speed of his reflexes. He existed only in the moment, feeling nothing except his own movements, noticing nothing save the flickering motion of his foes. It was terrifying and exhilarating, he felt as if he were being carried along on some great wave of excitement and action and fear. This was what it meant to be alive. He felt perfectly poised and balanced, every sense was stretched to the maximum, and every sinew was tautened by the need to deal death, and avoid swift retribution.

He hacked out with the chainsword and disembowelled a nearby beast. He sensed something huge moving through the horde pushing things aside like an orca moving through a shoal of fish. Suddenly he was face to face with one of the mighty hive warriors. It towered almost twice his height above him. In two of its four claws it held swords of razor-sharp chitin. In the other two it clutched one of the weird living guns. Its huge jaws opened and it bellowed a challenge even as the blades swept down from both sides.

Ragnar twisted, ducking to avoid the sweep of the right hand blade, raising his chainsword to block the swing of the left. The force of the impact almost tore the weapon from his hand, but he willed his fingers to stay closed and clench its hilt, and raised his pistol intending to put a shot through the creature's eye. It read his intention clearly and brought its blade round swiftly, smiting the barrel of the bolt pistol, smashing it to one side so that the shell flashed outward and upward, instead of into its own flesh.

Ragnar howled his own battle cry and leapt forward, bringing his feet down on the creature's huge legs and using them as a springboard to propel his leap to the level of the tyranid's head. Before it could react this time, his chainsword swept out and ripped right through the thing's neck, severing vertebrae and taking the head clean from its shoulders. Even as it began to tumble, he landed on its falling body and leapt once more, the force of his leap carrying him through into the mass of smaller creatures beyond.

He landed on top of one, flattening it to the ground, and kept moving, chopping and slashing, swinging and shooting, until he had left a ring of dead and dying monsters behind him. Two of the sick-looking genestealers moved in from each side. Their movements were far slower than the ones he had faced earlier and yet still much quicker than a normal man's. As they closed, he dropped to one knee, allowing their claws to pass over his head, then he sent his chainsword arcing out to open both their bellies. He sprang back to avoid their instinctive strike and barrelled into Sven who had been coming up behind him. For an instant pure reflex action almost caused him to lash out at his fellow Blood Claw, but at the last second he brought himself under control, and redirected his strike at the falling stealers. This time he cleaved one of their heads clean in two. Before he could move Sven had hacked the other one into pieces. Suddenly there was no movement around them. Ragnar realised that they were in a calm spot on the battlefield, and had an instant's respite from the fury of combat. He glanced around to see how the battle was going.

Looking back he could see the mass of tyranids had swept into the humans. The fighting had degenerated into a ruck in which all semblance of discipline and formation had been lost, and it was a battle which favoured the tyranid style of fighting more than that of the servants of the Imperium.

As he watched he could see guards lash out with the butts of their lasguns and be cut down in return by the claws of alien monsters. Here and there small pockets of humans still held together and cleared the area around them with fans of firepower, but these small islands were being overwhelmed by the relentless tides of battle. Off to the right he could see the inquisitors and Gul and Sergeant Hakon were still holding their own. And in the distance chilling wolf-like howls told him that Strybjorn and Nils still fought on.

Looking closely he could see an aura of light flickering around the talisman on Karah's breast. Searing beams of white-hot power lashed out from her hands to strike her foes. The glow underlit her face and blazed within her eye sockets, making her look positively daemonic. She was causing terrible casualties with her power, but even so, it was obvious to Ragnar that unless something were done, and quickly, the human forces would be overwhelmed and their quest would end in disaster and death. The tyranids still fought on as if they were all talons on one vast claw, exhibiting a co-ordination and a fury that was simply too much for the humans.

He glanced around to see if there was anything he could do. He saw that the way was clear to the vast organic machine and the talisman they had come to find. Perhaps he could make a grab for it, and the human force could make a fighting retreat. It seemed worth a try.

He raced forward over a carpet of living flesh towards the heart of a living engine made of flesh, and bone and gristle.

'I hope you know what you're bloody well doing,' he heard Sven shout, and immediately understood why. As if responding to a more pressing threat, the tyranids had wheeled away from the bulk of the human force, and were heading towards Ragnar and Sven in one unstoppable mass. Now why would they be doing that, he wondered? There had to be a reason.

Almost as quickly as he asked the question, the answer flashed into his head – they were protecting something important. They assumed that the two Blood Claws were threatening something vital to their own safety. The problem was that Ragnar had no idea what, and he did not have many seconds to find an answer to the riddle. There was only one thing he could think of, so he holstered his pistol and even as he moved lobbed a grenade into the mass of brain-like tissue. As one the tyranid horde let out a shriek of pain and near human horror. They milled around confused for a heartbeat before advancing once more.

Ragnar knew he was on to something. He kept moving forward and threw more and more grenades. The explosives threw up great gobbets of flesh where they tore through the mass of tissue. With every explosion the horde halted and howled. Ragnar knew this was not usual. Never in all the records had the creatures shown a weakness like this in the past. Was this some mutation brought on by their long stay in the hulk or was it a flaw created by the disease from which they so obviously suffered? He did not know; he was only grateful that it was so.

Sven had obviously understood what he was doing for he too was now sending grenade after grenade flying into the organic machine. From behind him, Ragnar could hear the human force, freed from the close assault, reform and begin to send a torrent of fire into their alien enemies. The distraction had bought them the time they so desperately needed. Now they were scything down the tyranid scum as if they were grass.

'Keep it up!' Ragnar yelled. He was running now down the corridors in the machine, tossing grenades left and right, feeling a sense of triumph every time the horde of creatures shrieked their alien agony. In the avenues around him the tyranids moved, but their actions seemed slower now and less co-ordinated.

Suddenly, he realised that he was before the great central pillar. High up on it glittered the fragment of the talisman they had come to reclaim. He knew instantly what he must do. Leaping up, he lashed out with his blade. The intricately scalloped flesh of the tyranid bio-machine parted. Fluids leaked forth like tears. The talisman came free and dropped into Ragnar's outstretched hand.

He grabbed it tight and landed beside Sven. Instantly there was silence, as if someone had thrown a switch and somehow turned the battle off. The horde stopped moving as if they had been animated only by the presence of the talisman in their midst. Somewhere in the distance, Ragnar sensed rather than heard a psychic shriek, as if something were in its death throes. Then as swiftly as they had stopped, the tyranids were in motion again – but this time there was little rhyme or reason to their actions. They moved in all directions, as if the guiding intelligence were gone. The smaller creatures seemed as insensate as beasts. The larger things appeared to struggle to control them. The relentless firing of their human opponents continued to take its toll, and this time, bereft of the unifying presence of whatever had dwelled within the machine, they turned and fled, scattering in all directions.

Ragnar risked a glance at Sven and returned his companion's wide grin with one of his own. He could hardly believe it. It was over and they had won. The inquisitors and Gul raced over. Karah reached out, indicating he should give the talisman to her. Seeing the zealous glow burning in her eyes, he felt oddly reluctant to do so for a moment – but nonetheless he gave it to her. She smiled, and there was little human in the smile.

'It is ours,' she said. 'Now we must get to Aerius and complete our quest.'

Somehow, the words sounded desperately ominous. Ragnar felt a shiver pass through him.

CHAPTER THIRTEEN

THE *LIGHT OF TRUTH* shimmered out of the Immaterium in the outer reaches of the Aerius system. Ragnar felt a surge of pride and hope. Soon their quest would be over. They had brought back the Talisman of Lykos as they had intended. During the voyage from the hulk, Inquisitor Isaan had managed to reassemble its three parts to create a unified whole.

Ragnar risked a glance across the command deck at her and was suddenly uneasy. Despite her tanned features, she looked pale and drawn, as if the glittering emerald amulet on her neck was draining her of her very life force. Her face was gaunt, and there were flecks of grey in her hair that had not been there short weeks before. The amulet, now a single stone of wondrous beauty, pulsed on its chain at her throat. There was something about its eerie alien loveliness that set the hairs on the back of his neck rising. He wondered if he was the only one who felt this way. His battle-brothers seemed to be showing no signs of sharing his unease, and he had not discussed it with any of them.

He wondered what would happen next. A strange silence had descended. The ship's astropaths had not been able to contact their counterparts on the planet. This was not a good sign. Only death could silence an astropath totally.

The others were watching expectantly the holo-pit set into the centre of the bridge. Now that they were within hailing distance of Aerius they would soon be able to speak directly with the surface of the planet, rather than communicate via astropath. Ragnar wondered what they would learn.

'My lord inquisitor, we are within hailing distance,' Chief Initiate Vosper announced finally, after what had seemed like hours of waiting.

'Emperor be praised,' Inquisitor Sternberg replied. 'See if you can make contact with the governor's palace.'

'It shall be so, my lord.' The man gestured to his minions, and the technical plainsong intensified as the crew moved sliders on their control altars. Ragnar saw Vosper pull two gargoyle-headed levers forward and suddenly there was a flickering light in the holo-pit.

Suddenly they were looking at the Imperial governor. It was a shocking sight. The man must once have been tall and powerful and impressive looking, that much was obvious. He leaned back on a throne carved to represent the double-headed Imperial eagle; its eyes were diamonds and it rested on a dais of marble. The man's armour looked as if it had been intended for a much larger warrior. His cheeks were sunken, the bones were evident on the hands which clutched the throne's armrests. A feverish light burned in the man's eyes.

'Inquisitor Sternberg!' he croaked. 'Is that you?'

'Secretary Karmiakal! Where is Governor Tal?'

'Tal… Tal is dead, my lord. Most of his cabinet are dead as well. They have all succumbed to the plague that ravages our world.'

Sternberg looked shocked and then overcome with grief. 'You are the acting governor then?'

'I have that honour. Was your quest… successful?' There was a note of desperation in the man's voice that was truly pathetic, Ragnar thought.

'Aye, we have the talisman with us.'

'Then you must bring it down to us. It is our last hope. This dreadful disease has infected over fifty per cent of the population. The death toll is enormous. Bodies choke our streets, too many for the mortuary wagons to take away.'

'We will do what we can,' said the inquisitor. 'I will bring my shuttle down at once. Please ask the Administratum to grant us immediate landing clearance.'

'It shall be so, inquisitor. Although I doubt that there are enough people left alive manning the aerial defences to cause you any trouble, even if you attempted to land without clearance.'

The figure in the globe flickered and vanished, leaving the folk on the bridge to glance at each other in appalled silence.

'We must go at once,' said Sternberg. 'It seems we have arrived not a moment too soon.'

As one the inquisitors, Gul and the Space Wolves left the bridge and made their way to the shuttle bay.

RAGNAR WATCHED AERIUS swell in the porthole of the shuttle. He was glad they had taken the spacecraft rather than the teleporter. Sternberg had not wished to risk a malfunction by that ancient and temperamental device at this late stage. Aerius was a smaller world than Fenris, that much was obvious, and the surface of its landmasses glittered darkly in the sun's light. As the shuttle drove downwards into the atmosphere he realised exactly why. The entire surface of the continent at which they were aimed was sheathed in metal. The whole surface was one huge industrial city. The black clouds that obscured the sky below them were not natural, but the products of enormous factories. Chimneys as large as mountains spewed chemical pollutants into the sky.

Here and there he could see monstrous burning pits that looked like lakes of molten lava. He guessed, from the knowledge placed in his brain by the tutelary engines, that these were the waste products of the titanic factories for which Aerius was famous. As they came lower, individual details became visible, and the scale of what he was witnessing became almost too much to comprehend. They were passing over buildings the size of islands back on Fenris. There were thousands of them, in all shapes and sizes, mountainous structures so large that they could surely not be the work of man. They seemed, rather, the products of the imagination of insane gods. A growing sense of wonder filled him. Intellectually Ragnar had known the Imperium was capable of building on this scale. But it was one thing to know something was possible; it was quite another to see it for yourself.

The shuttle began to buck as it hit turbulence in the atmosphere. Ignoring the lurching and rolling, Ragnar pressed his nose against the porthole and continued to watch. He realised that what he had thought were rivers were massive roadways, threading their way between the skyscrapers which rose to dizzying heights above the ground.

'How many people do you think live down there?' Ragnar asked Sven.

'Too bloody many!' replied the Blood Claw. 'But less than there were, because of the plague,' he added blackly.

'It is said that a million, million people lived on Aerius,' Inquisitor Sternberg said. He had obviously overheard Ragnar's question. 'No one knows for sure. The Ecclesiarchy have never been able to get more than a small percentage of them on the census rolls.'

'It must be a very bountiful world,' Ragnar said.

'Bountiful and terrible,' Sternberg replied. 'It is one of the most productive Hive Worlds in the Imperium. Its manufactories supply over half the worlds of this sector. If it were lost it would be a terrible blow to the Imperium.'

'You don't think that is even remotely a possibility though, do you?' Ragnar said.

'It is more than a possibility. With its defences so weakened, a determined invasion by orks or Chaos or any of the other blasphemous alien races could easily seize of destroy the great factory districts.'

'Then it's a good thing we got here in time to save it,' Nils said with a smile.

'We haven't saved it yet,' Karah Isaan cut in ominously.

THE BLACK PYRAMID was not quite as large as Ragnar had expected. True, by the standards of the villages he had grown up in it was huge, easily the size of a hill, but it was dwarfed by the towering structures that surrounded it. Even so, it was the most impressive building out of all those Ragnar could see. Its sides glittered like glass and the crystalline reflections of its dismal surroundings were visible in its shimmering sides. More impressive still was the palpable aura of power that surrounded it. You could tell simply by looking at it that here was a building which held or concealed something of tremendous importance.

Ragnar watched the shuttle's reflection grow in its side, and then stabilise as the craft first hovered, then began to descend. He felt relieved at the prospect of setting foot on solid ground after weeks cooped up aboard a starship. The shuttle shivered as its landing gear touched the metal-swathed ground.

'Well, we're here at last,' said Nils.

THE FIRST THING Ragnar noticed when he set foot upon the ground was the number of corpses. Bodies filled the whole vast plaza before the pyramid. They lay everywhere, in various states of decomposition. It was only after a few horrifying moments that he realised that some of the bodies were not dead and rotting, but were still alive, albeit barely, in the grip of the terrible plague.

The second thing he noticed was the pyramid itself. It seemed much larger now than it had from the air. It had a sense of presence, of majesty, that dwarfed all of the much larger buildings around it. Of all the buildings in the area, it alone drew the eye. And yet there was something about it that made Ragnar feel very uneasy indeed. For all its glittering beauty, there was a sense of menace about the pyramid that made his hackles rise. All the misgivings he had felt way back on the Fang and which had haunted him occasionally on their trip, seemed to return redoubled.

He tried to tell himself that it was simply the presence of all these sick people that made his flesh crawl, but he knew it was not so. There was something about the pyramid itself that filled him with dread and made him want to shout a warning to the others. All his instincts rebelled as he contemplated it. He was surprised that the others did not feel the same way. It seemed so obvious to him.

Perhaps this was just another symptom of the malaise that had affected his mind ever since he was wounded. Perhaps he was seeing a threat where none existed. Surely this must be the case. Surely the others could not be so blind.

'Look at that,' he heard Nils breathe.

He glanced skyward in the direction his comrade was pointing and saw thousands of glittering contrails moving through the upper atmosphere, descending through a gap in the clouds.

At first, he thought they were under some form of attack but then he realised that these were falling stars, so many of them that they were visible in daylight. The stars will fall, he thought. As the gap in the clouds widened, he caught sight of something else: a monstrous red comet, dragging a tail of greenish-yellow behind it lit up a fifth of the sky. Ragnar knew without having to be told that he looked upon the Balestar.

'What now?' he heard Hakon ask.

'We go in,' Sternberg replied sombrely. 'The oracle was quite clear on that. To end the plague the talisman must be brought to the hidden chambers within the pyramid.'

'And where is the entrance?'

'We will find it,' Sternberg said grimly.

THEY HAD TO step over the bodies of the dead as they approached the building. To Ragnar they looked almost like sacrificial victims offered up to some evil god. There was something deeply disturbing and offensive to his sense of rightness in the manner in which they simply lay there, sprawled out obscenely.

Even worse were the groaning half-dead who begged for water, or to be put out of their misery, as the newcomers approached. Ragnar tried to ignore their pleas, but they sank into his mind despite all his efforts.

He saw Gul bend and snap one's neck with a chop of his hand. Then the huge warrior looked at all of the folk that lay around him, and then shrugged pathetically, as if overwhelmed by the sheer scale of what they were witnessing.

'Bloody cheerful place,' Sven muttered, as if sensing Ragnar's mood and attempting to lighten it. He looked at Ragnar and smiled mockingly. 'Are you sweating, Ragnar? I hope you are not coming down with a fever.'

Ragnar could tell from his scent that he was joking, but even so he wondered whether Sven had spotted something that he had not. Was he really sweating? A hand to his brow told him he was not. He let out a deep breath and tried to ignore the deep and offensive stench of pestilence that filled his nostrils.

The pyramid loomed larger in his sight. How were they going to get inside, Ragnar wondered? The prophecy had not exactly been specific on that subject. To tell the truth, he suddenly realised that he had no real idea of what they were supposed to be doing at all. Until now, he had simply been following others who presumably knew better than he did. It was like being a character in one of the old sagas. You did not question the wisdom of what the soothsayers said, you simply did it. Now, he was starting to wonder. What relevance could finding some mystical talisman, however powerful, have to combating death on this scale. The plague was a force that was invisible and yet omnipresent, and it was bringing a whole mighty world to its knees.

Ragnar felt his lips twist into a smile that might have been a snarl. It was a little late to be having such thoughts now, he realised. He wondered what was wrong with him. Why had his thoughts become so defeatist over the past few weeks? Perhaps it was because of his wounds, or perhaps it was because of some other external reason. But what? And why was he thinking this way now? What influences were at work here?

They were alongside the pyramid now, walking under its vast shadow. Ragnar could see his reflection mirrored in the black marbling of its side. His image seemed subtly distorted – thinner, weaker, its eyes feverish, its skin blotched as if with plague. For a moment the thought struck him that this was an omen; that he was looking at a picture of his future doom. He pushed the idea aside with a shiver. He noticed his flesh had started to itch. He fought down the urge to scratch and kept marching.

They were at the exact centre of the pyramid's west wall now. He noticed that Karah's eyes were closed and that a nimbus of power played round her head. Tendrils of force ran from it to the amulet and then back again. Questing fingers of power reached out from her and flowed over the pyramid's side. As they did so, lines of eldritch fire sprang into being, revealing a complex pattern in the curious runic script of the eldar. For a moment the symbol blazed bright as the sun, and the sight of it burned its way into Ragnar's brain. There was something ominous about it that set his nerves on edge, as if it were shrieking a warning that he did not understand.

He wanted to go forward and tell the others to stop, that they were disturbing something best left well alone. He wanted to but he could not. He realised that like the others he was caught up by the simple momentum of their quest. He had no reason to stop them, and they had no reason to listen. All he had were his forebodings and what were they when weighed against the chance to save billions of lives?

Even as he watched the shimmering symbol vanished, and with it went part of the wall of the pyramid. It simply vanished like mist, leaving a gap in the stonework that revealed the maw of a great dark tunnel. Despite himself, Ragnar was impressed by the magic, and he felt a small surge of excitement. Whatever they were doing, they were making progress. They had pierced the wall of a structure that had proved invulnerable for millennia.

Inquisitor Sternberg produced a glowglobe from a deep pocket in his cloak and they advanced into the gloom. The walls of the pyramid's interior were not made from the same mystical substance as its outer walls. They appeared to be carved from pure granite, and seemed much older than the external walls. It appeared that they were within the remains of a much older site.

The walls were inlaid with frescoes and scrollwork bearing more eldar symbols, and for the first time Ragnar wished that he could read that arcane language. He felt that he might learn at least part of the great secret that was concealed within this structure. What was this place, he wondered? Was it some vast tomb built to protect the corpse of some ancient eldar king? Judging from what he had seen on the space hulk he decided that this was unlikely, but how could he know for sure? He had no idea how typical the eldar on that hulk were of their race in general. He doubted that they would have built anything as crude as this. And then again, didn't the eldar shun the surface of worlds, and hadn't they done so since mankind had first encountered them? Was this something from the distant past, from the time before the eldar had abandoned planetary surfaces? Now he truly wished he could understand the writings on the wall.

All around him he felt the swirl of mystical forces. Instinctively he rose on the balls of his feet, ready to meet any threat. Even as he did so, he knew it was a futile gesture. The builders of this complex would not resort to anything so crude as traps and deadfalls and guardians. The things that protected the pyramid would be far subtler. Spells, curses, pure psychic force was what they could expect here, and these were things he was not really equipped to deal with. These were matters for

Rune Priests, not simple warriors. For all his inexperience, poor Lars might have been better prepared for this than he. He had at least spent time with the Chapter's mystic masters.

Was that why he was dead, Ragnar suddenly wondered? Was there a huge pattern of events at work here of which he had caught only the faintest glimpse? Was this all part of some immense plot, on a scale which he could not begin to comprehend? Had the appearance of the falling stars, and their quest and the death of his comrade all been part of the web of some vast scheme? He shook his head. He was imagining things. This gloomy place was starting to get to him.

At the edge of his vision, he thought he saw a host of shadowy inhuman figures gathering. He had seen their likeness before. They looked like eldar.

'Be very still,' Karah said in a voice that carried eerily in the echoing corridor. 'Be very still if you value your lives.'

Ragnar could see no threat but her tone and her scent warned him that she was serious, so he froze on the spot. He stretched his senses to their limits and still could detect nothing. So he waited. Karah raised her hands and the amulet blazed bright once more. As she did so, more lines of fire became evident. They shimmered into being in the air before them, millions and millions of beams all criss-crossing in an intricate web of light. At her gesture they brazed brighter and brighter – and then suddenly faded.

'We... we can go on,' she stammered, in the tone of voice of one who had just seen and avoided a deadly threat by a matter of inches.

They pressed on into the heart of the pyramid. The aura of gloom deepened. Ragnar's sense of being surrounded by hidden powers intensifying as they worked their way deeper into the maze.

Scant moments later, the air ahead of them swirled. A figure materialised, seemingly coalescing out of thin air. Ragnar gazed at the apparition, his mind suddenly filled with stories of ghosts he had heard back on Fenris. It was not an inappropriate thought either. The figure before him might have been the spirit of a warrior returned to haunt the living.

It was an eldar, inhumanly tall and slender. and garbed in exotically beautiful curved armour. A huge crest rose from its gaunt helmet. Strange weapons dangled from its belt. It stood before them with its arms folded across its narrow chest. It wore an over-tunic decorated with diamond patterns, and the sleeves and leggings of its armour were decorated in gaudy checks. When it spoke its voice was thrilling and musical.

'Go back, humans,' it pealed. 'You should not have come here.'

The alien was not real, Ragnar realised. He could catch no scent, and it shimmered translucently. He knew that if he reached out he could put his hand through it. Still, what was the purpose of this projection. Was it simply a way of communicating with them, or was it a distraction, intended to keep them occupied while something else sneaked up to attack them?

'We go where we will,' Hakon responded. Ragnar glanced around, sniffing the air to make sure his suspicions were not correct. 'We are the Emperor's servants, in the Emperor's realm, and it is not for any alien to tell us where we may go.'

The eldar shook its head sadly. 'I mean you no harm, Space Wolves. I bring a warning. You meddle with things that are best left undisturbed. You seek to awake something that should not be awoken. If you persist along this path, it will lead only to catastrophe on a scale you cannot comprehend.'

There was an echoing quiet as the alien's words sank in. What was this talk about warnings and catastrophes? Was the eldar sincere or was this all some sort of trick? Sven stood slack jawed behind him, as well he might. Ragnar himself felt like he was confronting some mythical creature from one of the ancient sagas.

'What is this?' he heard Sternberg ask. 'What do you wish of us, ancient one?'

The eldar pointed to the talisman hanging at Karah's breast. 'Do not seek to remake that which was broken. Do not take it to the place of the curse. Do not set the imprisoned one free. You have been warned. Even now the forces that hold it are unravelling and the spell which has kept my brethren and I here to guard it is almost undone. Go back! Go back! Before it is too late, go back!'

Even as it spoke the figure shimmered and vanished. The inquisitors and the Space Wolves stared at each other. No one spoke. There was nothing to say. All of them knew they had come too far to turn back. All of them considered the ghostly eldar's words.

What was the thing that should not be awakened? Was this a sincere attempt to avert their doom on the part of the alien, or was it some unfathomable attempt to manipulate them for its own purposes.

He did not know. He only knew that if they did not bring the talisman back to Aerius in one piece the whole world would die? And that if they did, the plague would end, although he suspected at terrible cost. The Oracle had said this. The Space Wolves' own Rune Priests had confirmed it. Surely, even though the eldar possessed their own dark wisdom, and possibly an ability to see the pattern of the future, it could be no greater than that of the Imperium's own sages?

Ragnar's head swam from trying to understand the swirling complexities of the situation. He pushed all thoughts aside, glad for the moment that he was not the leader here, that he did not need to make decisions, that it was not his task to wrestle with the mysteries that surrounded him. All he needed to do, at this moment, was fight when called on to, and win if it were humanly possible.

He smiled as this knowledge lodged itself in his brain. It was good to reduce things to such elemental simplicity. It was even better to be able to find something to concentrate on that kept his mind from pondering on things of which he had no understanding.

As THEY VENTURED further into the heart of the pyramid, Ragnar realised that the corridors were laid out like a maze. They twisted and turned with neither rhyme nor reason, and did so in such a manner as to befuddle the head of any normal man.

'Why is the place like this?' he heard Nils ask.

'Russ take me!' Sven snapped back. 'Can't you see they were just trying to confuse any fools who came in. Fools like us actually.'

'No, Space Wolf. You are wrong,' Karah said. 'The maze is set out according to some kind of arcane geomantic principle. The runes in the wall and the layout of the corridors are all part of a pattern designed to funnel unseen energies. I can sense the flow all around us, being channelled and directed.'

'Why?' Ragnar asked.

'I don't know,' she responded. 'Maybe it is all part of the system that has kept the pyramid inviolate for all these centuries. Maybe it's something more. I sense that there is something powerful at the centre, though. I can feel that too.'

Not a tomb then, Ragnar thought. A temple? A nexus of mystical forces? A machine that focussed power? Who could guess why the aliens had built this place here.

Three more times they stopped, and waited anxiously while Karah dispelled the lines of fire. Then suddenly it was over. They had reached the end of the tunnel and the end of their journey.

In an open chamber which echoed hollowly with their footsteps, they came to stand before an immense stone door covered in runes. Ragnar wondered what lay beyond.

'How are we going to open this?' Sven asked, his voice too loud in the echoing chamber.

'Explosives,' Nils suggested.

'Don't have any,' Strybjorn sniffed.

'We've got our grenades.'

'Won't make a dent in this. Unless I miss my guess, it must be ten strides thick and weigh tons.'

Ragnar contemplated the immense weight of dressed stone standing before them. It seemed as massive and immobile as the pyramid itself had from the outside and just as unbreachable. Yet now they were here, in the centre of the vast, ancient monument. He knew that given time they would find a way into its secret heart.

Karah Isaan walked up to the vast stone door and placed her hands flat upon it. As she did so, lines of brilliant white light emerged from her hands and spread like a web of fire across the stone. This time the pattern did not fade away, but flashed and sparked for several long moments.

There was an earthquake-deep rumbling and a sudden swirling cloud of dust. In one motion, the stone descended into the floor, leaving the way clear into the chamber in the heart of the pyramid.

As it did so, Ragnar felt a sudden terrifying feeling of utter dread, and an overwhelming sense of evil.

Barely a heartbeat later, a deep rolling laughter, wicked and yet strangely jovial, boomed out around the chamber, and then a mighty voice spoke.

'Greetings, fools! In the name of beloved Uncle Nurgle, I, Botchulaz, favoured spawn of the most disgusting Lord of Disease, bid you welcome. I thank you from the bottom of my heart for freeing me.'

Along with his companions, Ragnar entered the chamber warily, weapons held ready, knowing that there was no way he could defend himself from what waited within.

The floor was caked in what looked like the hardened remains of a millennia of effusions of pus and snot and phlegm. In the middle of the floor, on an altar that looked as if it was carved from a mound of pure hardened mucus, lounged an obese and profoundly disturbing figure. It was truly huge. It was obscenely fat and its skin was a blotched and unhealthy green. It rippled to the ground in many leathery folds. The reek from it was worse than any sewer. Tiny horns emerged from its foul, bulbous head. Its eyes were tiny and sparkled with ancient malice. The thing gave a long, hacking cough that sent a great shower of snot spraying out onto the floor. Where the disgusting eruption landed, each drop formed into a tiny capering figure that resembled its creator. They danced across the floor for a moment and then sank into the carpet of filth, disappearing without trace.

'Emperor save us, an Unclean One...' he heard Sternberg mutter, and a shiver of horror passed up Ragnar's spine. The Unclean One was the ancient name for a type of terrible, terri-fyingly powerful daemon, devoted to the service of Nurgle, the Lord of Pestilence, and now it appeared he was in the presence of such a being. 'Now all is clear to me.'

As Ragnar watched, the greenish stuff of the altar writhed and reformed. Tiny gargoyle faces emerged, stuck out their tongues, hawked and spat and then vanished into the substance of the structure again like ripples disappearing from the surface of a pool.

'Excuse me for not rising,' said the daemonic thing. 'But I am not in the best of health.'

It laughed uproariously as if it had just made some astound-ingly funny jest, and its laughter only died out in another long and hacking cough.

'Daemonic scum! Prepare to die!' roared Hakon.

'Please be a little quieter. Can't you see I'm not well?' said the vile daemon, looking at the sergeant with watery eyes brimming with cynical humour. 'You humans can be so tiring. Almost as bad as those eldar pests who trapped me here. Well, it's been a boring few thousand years but oddly restful too, so I suppose I mustn't grumble. But now I have things to do. A plague daemon's work is never done, you know.'

Ragnar looked at the daemon in astonishment. He knew that its words were not actually being spoken aloud but somehow were appearing in his head as if by magic. And he knew also that despite the humorous tone of the daemon's remarks, its speech was simply a way of belittling and distracting them. There was a wicked intelligence at work here.

'You shall not leave this place!' shouted Sternberg. An appalled look flashed across the inquisitor's face. He looked like a man who has found out that his whole life's work had been a mockery. Ragnar felt a certain sympathy for him. The inquisitor had come here believing that he was about to save his home world from the plague – but he had just found out that he freed one of the deadliest daemons in existence. A malefic being, that he had sworn to oppose with his life if need be, had been unleashed upon the universe through his actions.

And mine, Ragnar realised.

The daemon's laughter gurgled forth. 'On the contrary, my little human friend. I shall. I am very keen to see the outside world once more. I tell you, you don't know the meaning of boredom until you've spent two thousand years animating statues made from your own filth, and then trying to teach them to dance. Still, every cloud has a silver lining. You know, I have devised some very interesting new disease spores.'

'You'll never have the chance to spread them,' Sergeant Hakon spat. He looked ready to strike, but Ragnar could tell from his posture and his scent that he was unsure of himself. The daemon's odd conversational manner and its obvious poise had thrown him. Ragnar could tell that his whole pack was struck by a similar unease. Possibly they were all dumbfounded by the thought they had been used as pawns by this vile gurgling monstrosity.

'Now, now, don't be like that,' Botchulaz simpered. 'I am entitled to my little bit of fun, you know. Have a little sympathy. You're not the one who had been stuck here for millennia with only your own secretions for company. I mean, those eldar were unnaturally cunning, if you ask me, almost too much for a poor bumbling creature such as myself. All those wards and gates, all that power bound up in that lovely talisman. All those ancient warrior ghosts to keep my followers away. One of those accursed intricate patterns which only reveals its flaw every three thousand years when stars are falling from the sky and the moons are in the right alignment. It was tricky arranging this, I don't mind telling you. Surely you don't grudge me a little amusement?'

'We shall slay you where you stand,' Nils dared to say.

'Foolish boy, you can't slay me. I am a daemon prince of Nurgle. You might, if you were very powerful and very lucky, be able to destroy this living vessel and return my essence to the warp, but you could not kill me. Not even your Emperor could do that. Believe me, I know, I met him once. A nice enough chap but very dour.'

Ragnar could not believe he was hearing this blasphemy. And yet, he realised, it was perfectly possible that the unholy fiend's words were true. According to holy writ the Emperor had fought against the plague daemons of Nurgle over ten thousand years ago. Was it really so unbelievable that this creature had been one of them? No more unbelievable than the fact that it had survived in the heart of this pyramid all this time, and schemed for its release, using them all as its pawns, directing them all from across the vastness of space.

Almost as if it sensed his thoughts, the daemon swivelled its blubbery head and looked over at him. Its face broke into a wide grin which revealed row upon row of thousands of blotched green and brown fangs. There was a ghastly stench of halitosis and gum disease. 'It wasn't easy, I can tell you. Only at certain times could I send my thoughts questing outwards, to make contact with my minions and get you people to do my will. Seemed like an age, believe me. Oh, what am I saying? It was an age since I first got stuck here. The eldar again – they never liked me, you know. I suspect the Farseers built this pyramid as a trap for my kind ages ago. You can never tell with them, they can predict the future in an odd sort of way, and they are subtle in a way you lot have never been.

'Anyway, I blundered right into it, I was only here to spread some new spores and a little good cheer among my worshippers and they dropped right out of the sky and began their rituals. Nobody was more surprised than I was when I got sucked into this prison. I might have been stuck here forever, too, if your people hadn't interfered and slaughtered the eldar.

'Broke the blasted amulet too, and carried it away and I thought: Well, that's that; I'm stuck, aren't I? The amulet was the key to the whole thing and then it was broken and gone. It was hard to maintain a positive attitude, what with my poor health and all. I was so depressed that it took me centuries to get in contact with the minions and find out even the location of one piece. And then, there was all the trouble of finding a reason for you to go and get it for me. It had me worried, I don't mind admitting.'

The daemon was mocking them, Ragnar realised. It was boasting about how it had used them, all the while speaking in tones of false sympathy and humour. Why were they standing here listening to it, Ragnar wondered? Were they all hypnotised? Memories of how he had almost been ensnared by the sorcery of Madok came back to him. That had been a close run thing, and surely this creature must be a hundred times more powerful than Madok?.

'Oh, that reminds me: dear Gul, it's time for your reward.'

'Thank you, master.'

Commander Gul stepped smartly from their ranks to come face to face with the daemon. Suddenly it seemed much larger, as if somehow it had changed its size without them ever noticing. It loomed over the massive figure of the inquisitors' bodyguard, then reached forward to lick his face with a long, slime-soaked tongue.

'No need to look so shocked,' the daemon said to them all. 'I needed to have somebody to keep you all on the right track. And Gul has been my servant for many years, haven't you, Gul?'

'Yes, master.'

'Man and boy, like his father before him, and his father before that, and so on. I won't bore you with a tedious repetition of all the sorceries that were needed to conceal his true nature from your tests. They were many and varied in nature and one so likes to preserve some of the mysteries. Anyway, it was my worshippers who did most of it, and I'm not one to hog all the credit. Suffice to say that they were difficult and costly in terms of energy and sacrifice.'

'Gul, you are a traitor to all of humanity,' Sternberg said. Frank disbelief showed in his face. He obviously had difficulty adjusting to the thought of his trusted henchman's betrayal.

'And you are a fool who believes he knows the truth,' Gul replied with a sneer.

Hatred twisted Ragnar's gut. Gul had accompanied them on their quest pretending to be their ally and all the time they had been serving his vile purposes. Lars and others had died so that this man, if man you could call him, could find his way here and abase himself before Botchulaz.

'Now, now,' said the plague-thing. 'There's no need for harsh language. All's well that ends well, and so on.'

Botchulaz's mocking tone fuelled Ragnar's righteous rage. He knew now that this unending torrent of cheerful clichés was nothing more than a wicked jest of the daemon's. In its heart it hated them all, and this was its way of showing contempt for their intelligence.

Ragnar managed to throw off the spell of the daemon's voice long enough to raise his bolt pistol and aim a shot at Gul. The shell flew straight and true and exploded within the cultist's heart.

'That wasn't very nice, Ragnar,' Botchulaz said as Gul collapsed at his feet. The former bodyguard gazed up at the plague daemon the way a hound might gaze at a beloved master. 'I had rather planned to reward Gul, too. His wasn't an easy task, you know. Pretending loyalty to your Emperor and his rather over-zealous Inquisition was a bit draining for a man of his background.'

Gul reached up and tugged at Botchulaz's leg. His fingers made a hideous sucking sound as they drew back. Ragnar noticed their tips were covered in slime. 'Yes, yes,' said the daemon soothingly. 'Don't worry. I'll see you right. Least I can do, really.'

Ragnar drew a bead on the daemon, which met his fierce gaze with one of its own. Yellowing teeth were revealed by its wide grin. 'You wouldn't...' it said cheerfully.

Ragnar pulled the trigger and sent shell after shell streaking towards the daemon. One went into its head; three more went into its stomach. Botchulaz's face crumpled inwards like a rolled up piece of paper. The shells sank without trace in the rippling folds of flab around his midriff. For a moment, Ragnar thought he might have done the thing some harm, but then the face sprang back into its normal shape – and then there was sound like a cork being pulled from a bottle, as the bolter shells were expelled from its flesh.

'That hurt, a little,' it said in a pained voice. A horrible coughing sound began deep in its throat and for a moment Ragnar thought that perhaps he had damaged the monster after all. It bent forward, clutching its midriff where the bullets had gone in. A spew of vile stuff vomited from its mouth. Ragnar watched as the foul stuff bubbled downwards, engulfing the dying Gul. Even as Ragnar watched in disgust and horror, it filled the dying man's wounds, closing them, and began to spread outwards over his flesh, leaving a blotched mouldy crust as it went.

Gul gasped and shook like a man in the terminal stage of a dreadful fever. Then the shaking stopped and his whole body seemed to swell. His muscles ballooned out and his skin took on a sick greenish yellow tinge. Weird lights blazed within his eyes and he rose to his feet, fingers flexed like the talons of a hawk.

'There we go,' said Botchulaz. 'One good turn deserves another, that sort of thing.'

Karah Isaan seemed to snap out of her trance. She yelled a fierce chant and raised her arms high above her head. A wave of white-hot psychic energy flowed out from her towards the daemon. A wall of searing fire enveloped Botchulaz and made his outline shimmer and dance. The daemon's skin seemed to bubble and pop and for a moment, Ragnar thought the inquisitor might actually succeed in banishing it. Then the plague daemon's outline congealed. It turned towards Karah and seemed to belch forth a tidal wave of energy of its own. Thousands of serpents of sickly green and yellow light entwined around her, encasing her form. She gave one long moan of agony, her skin suddenly blotched and discoloured and then she fell motionless onto the ground. Botchulaz stood there, steam rising from his skin as it knitted back together. He nodded amiably to himself, checked all his limbs to make sure they were intact, looked around and laughed pleasantly.

'Well, it's been fun, but I mustn't dawdle. I have some business to attend to. I'm sure Gul will see to your deaths.'

Ragnar watched in astonishment as a web of green and yellow light erupted from the plague daemon's body. The air was suddenly filled with a sense of vast energies unleashed. The walls of the pyramid began to change colour. Ragnar knew this did not bode well for anybody on the surface of Aerius, but he did not really see what he could do about it right now.

Gul was looking less and less healthy. His whole form slumped forward now, as if the flesh had partially melted. His fingers were extruding long talons. Massive boils were erupting through the crust around his body. There was a smell similar to putrefaction but even more sickly sweet in the air.

'I am immortal,' he said.

'We'll bloody well see about that,' Sven yelled, leaping forward. Ragnar moved to join him.

CHAPTER FOURTEEN

A DOZEN THINGS happened at once. The Blood Claws, Sergeant Hakon and the inquisitors all sprang into action. Writhing figures began to emerge from the vile carpet of muck caking the floor, whole bodies pulling themselves out, like swimmers emerging from the sea. They were vaguely humanoid, resembling smaller, less distinct versions of Botchulaz. Their heads were featureless blanks save where two sightless eyes had been poked in them. Their bodies had a fluid boneless quality. From their stink Ragnar could tell they had been created from snot, mucus and other daemonic excreta.

Something snared his ankle, and looking down he saw a smiling face looking up at him. It seemed to have been carved from the floor but Ragnar knew full well it had not been there moments before. It leered at him with a crazed daemonic mirth which echoed Botchulaz's.

He kicked out with his leg, tearing the arm free from the ground. The fingers remained glued to his ankle and the whole form continued to emerge from the sludge. Bolters sounded all around as more bolts tore into Gul and the vile things the daemon had summoned. Ragnar heard the strange sucking sound once more as the shells bit home. They seemed to have no effect on the creatures. Ragnar found this to be hardly surprising. They were boneless, had no internal organs, and were animated only by dark sorcery. They would not succumb to wounds that would have felled a normal man.

Gul laughed insanely, inspecting his altered flesh, capering with glee. 'Now, servants of the False Emperor,' he said. 'You will most assuredly die.'

Ragnar shifted his leg but the grip strengthened and the snot thing's arm lengthened. He felt the constriction increase, and to his horror saw that the ceramite was starting to give way in places. He lashed out with his chainsword and severed his captor's arm at the shoulder. The blades screamed and tore and then cut right through. The arm came away and he was able to move.

Looking around he saw that more and more of the eerie figures were pulling themselves from the floor. His battle-brothers blasted them with bolter fire but their flesh parted and knitted together again. He saw Sven lash out with a chainsword and chop off a head. It rolled free, was picked up by another shambling monstrosity of snot and mucus, which attached the head to its own chest. Gul stood in the centre of it all, encased in his blotched carapace, and howled with crazed mirth. Even as Ragnar watched one of the hideous figures reached out. Its arms stretched and a spray of its own disgusting slime smashed into Inquisitor Sternberg's face. Ragnar wondered what possible harm this would do, until he saw streams of pus emerge through the inquisitor's eyeballs. A moment later, under the extreme pressure of the vile fluid that had been forced into it, his head ripped apart.

For a brief moment, Ragnar imagined the inquisitor's last moments, worms of diseased plasma wriggling through the mush of his brain, and tendrils of foulness extruding down his throat into his stomach, choking off all air. Ragnar glanced over at Sergeant Hakon and knew from the veteran's gritted teeth expression that the old Space Wolf was thinking along the same lines.

It was time to get out of here. Ragnar picked up Karah's unconscious form and threw it over his shoulder. Carving a green path through the knee-deep slime, he made for the exit of the chamber. Seeing him go, Gul drew his pistol and aimed it. His movements were slow and his hand trembled like that of a man with the ague but Ragnar knew it would not matter. All it would take was one shot.

He dived forward, hoping that presenting a moving target might throw off the Nurgle worshipper's aim. A bolt pistol shell churned the floor behind him. Ragnar kept moving, offering up a prayer to Russ and the All-Father. He heard the other Blood Claws shouting war cries as they, too, began to retreat from the room.

Vile hands tugged his ankles, slowing him down. A terrible slurping sounded every time he raised his feet from the floor. It was like being trapped in a well-remembered nightmare, one in which deadly foes pursued him, and he was unable to make any headway in his escape.

He heard another shot ring out and half-expected to feel a sudden agonising blast of pain in his chest. None came. He turned his head and saw that Sergeant Hakon had blasted Gul aside, and was now trying to fight his way clear of the mucus beasts emerging from the walls and floors. Ragnar wanted to go to his aid but some instinct warned him that it was imperative that he get Karah to safety. Perhaps the psyker would have some idea as to how to contain the plague daemon and its minions. He was certain of one thing: he did not.

He breathed a sigh of relief as he saw Strybjorn and Sven move to the sergeant's aid. They lopped off inhuman limbs with their chainswords, and then pulled Hakon to safety through the door. Ragnar glanced around in panic, wondering what had become of Nils. Back in the heart of the room was a humanoid figure, completely encased in hardening goo. Even as he watched, more and more greenish figures threw themselves on it, and the struggling stopped.

In a moment, all that remained was Nils's outline, encased in hardened green stuff. Horror filled Ragnar. This was an abomination, and one against which there seemed to be no defence. Normal weapons appeared to have no effect against these creatures. Their soft, magically animated forms were impervious even to bolter shells, and simply knitted together again when struck with chainsword blades. It was like fighting with trolls, only worse; even trolls had not engendered this level of horror in him.

'Go! Go!' Sergeant Hakon ordered. 'There is nothing we can do for him now.'

Ragnar wanted to stay, to at least try, but he could see the sense of the sergeant's words. By staying they would only guarantee themselves a horrible death, one that was in no sense heroic. A sacrifice that would not help the teeming millions on the planet's surface who would soon fall victim to the daemon.

At least the things were slow moving. If they ran, he and his companions should be able to outpace them. He wondered what had happened to Gul. He had caught no sight of the traitor since Hakon had shot him. If there was any justice, Ragnar thought, he would be drowning in the mucus that covered the floor. Somehow he doubted they were going to be that lucky.

Making sure Karah's slight, lifeless form was secure on his shoulder, he began to trot back the way they had come, following the scent trail they had left on the way in. Behind him, echoing footsteps told him his remaining battle-brothers were on his trail.

THEY EMERGED from the pyramid into night and an ominous silence. Ragnar wondered what had happened. Surely everyone could not be dead already. The daemon's powers could not possibly be so virulent, could they? But how could he know what the thing was capable of? How could he measure the abilities of a being that had managed to stay alive in the heart of the Black Pyramid for millennia and which was capable of the dark magic he had just witnessed. Its powers far and away dwarfed those of Madok, the sorcerer-warrior of the Thousand Sons he had killed back on Fenris, and who was his only previous experience of the fell terrors of Chaos sorcery. Perhaps Botchulaz could indeed bring this world to its knees. Perhaps he had already done so. Ragnar had no way of knowing.

He glanced around, out into the mist and silence. The patterns of tiny lights on the starscrapers glowed in the distance. Overhead he could see the running lanterns of aircars and descending spaceships. Behind him a strange greenish yellow glow suffused the surface of the pyramid. It pulsed eerily, and even as he watched the shimmering light seemed to separate itself from the structure, coalesce into a cloud and drift off into the night air. Thousands upon thousands of misty tendrils extended themselves outwards, a manifestation of a dark sorcery he could not quite comprehend. He was sure it boded no good for the inhabitants of Aerius.

As he watched, the lights along the side of the Black Pyramid flickered and reassembled themselves into a new pattern. Ragnar could have sworn that for a brief instant he saw the leering face of the plague-thing looking down on them. Moments later, he was convinced that the face was itself made up of thousands upon thousands of smaller versions of Botchulaz, all capering and prancing and posturing. Even as he watched, liquid began to coalesce on the side of the pyramid. Droplets of green slimy sweat seemed to ooze from the very stone. It became apparent to Ragnar that whatever magic the eldar had used to imprison Botchulaz, it was no longer working.

He realised that he himself was not feeling too good. His head felt light and sweat was pouring from his brow. He stifled a sneeze and realised that he was rapidly becoming feverish, ill in a way he had not been since he first became a Space Marine. Not even his altered physique was immune to the vile contagion created by the daemon, Botchulaz. All he could do now was pray to Russ and the Emperor that he was strong enough to resist the illness.

It occurred to him then that if the disease was now strong enough to affect even Space Marines, it must be a terrible scourge indeed for ordinary mortals.

'Smell that,' he heard Sven say. Ragnar sniffed the air and realised what his battle-brother meant. There was an odd taint to the night air which had not been there before. His nostrils seemed to tingle.

'Vile sorcery,' Sergeant Hakon said. 'Of the worst sort.'

'What are we going to do about it?' Strybjorn asked.

Hakon looked at the unconscious figure of Karah. 'We need to find out what is going on. What the daemon has planned.'

'I think that is just about to become obvious,' Sven said, pointing at the crowd of sickly figures which lay around the square. Ragnar's foreboding increased as the eerie mystical reek intensified, swathing them in an almost tangible cloud. It was like the smell of sewage mingled with rotting flesh, only greatly intensified and a thousand times worse. The unhealthy mob had begun to moan and writhe. A few of them were starting to clamber unsteadily to their feet. They did not look as if they had recovered, though. If anything they looked worse. Their faces were pale. Pustules erupted all over their bodies. Their movements had a terrible slowness, like those of old men in the last stages of some terminal illness. Their flesh had an odd greenish yellow tint. Their sweat looked more like mucus than any normal body fluid, and gave their flesh a loathsome, nausea-inducing sheen. A strange greenish glow had entered their eyes, a sorcerous light that burned dimly beneath the rheum which crusted their eyeballs. Ragnar sensed the flow of alien energies around and through them. He knew now that they had passed beyond being human, and had fallen under the evil spell of the plague daemon.

As if to confirm this, the first of the newly arisen plague victims turned towards the Blood Claws. It opened its mouth and let out an eerie sound, half shriek, half gurgle; a noise that made Ragnar think of a man drowning in the mucus that filled his lungs and throat. Slowly the infected man shambled towards them, arms outstretched, mouth agape, eyes blazing.

Ragnar looked at his companions. He was not frightened. Compared to what they had just escaped in the pyramid these few corrupted souls were nothing. Then, in a moment, true realisation dawned, and what he was seeing became suddenly quietly terrifying. Across this world were millions of plague-infected mortals. If all of them, or even some, were turned into Nurgle's creatures by this disease then the Plague Lord would soon have an enormous army under his sway. Worse than that, if the pestilence were to spread off world, soon systems, even entire segmenta might fall to him. Was it possible that the monstrous being was really this powerful? Truly, if it were so, then this was a threat not merely to the world of Aerius but to the whole Imperium! Despite himself, his respect for the dark powers of Botchulaz increased.

'Perhaps we should return to the ship and get Inquisitor Isaan some treatment,' Sven suggested, looking at her recumbent form with concern.

'No!' Ragnar said suddenly. All eyes turned to him. 'If she is infected, if we are infected, all we will do is spread this contagion to the *Light of Truth*. Who knows where it might go from there?'

'Ragnar speaks the truth,' Hakon agreed. 'We must keep this place quarantined at all costs!'

The sergeant spoke into the comm-net, relaying details of their situation to the ship, telling them to broadcast an interdiction order to all vessels in the system, and informing them to request the presence of an Imperial battlefleet to contain the threat. Ragnar saw the sense of this, but wondered what good it would do. By the time a fleet could get here, the damage would be done.

Ragnar glanced back at the crowd. They were beginning to surround the Space Marines and their comrades. Ragnar was not sure what they hoped to accomplish, unarmed against armoured and well-equipped troops. As he watched, though, the crowd shambled forward, arms outstretched, fingers extended like talons. He was reluctant to open fire on these pitiful victims of Botchulaz's daemonic machinations. They were, after all, the people he was sworn to protect, who their mission had been intended to save.

'Fire at will!' Sergeant Hakon said. 'These people are beyond saving. They are no longer human, merely vessels of evil.'

He matched his action to his words and opened fire. Bolter shells blasted through the chest of the first unfortunate, sending him tumbling back into the crowd. It did not even slow his fellow plague victims down: they shambled forward mindlessly, intent on pulling down Ragnar and his comrades. Ragnar realised that they might just possibly manage it too, by sheer weight of numbers. He reached for a grenade and lobbed it into the mass of bodies. The explosion tore them apart, sending blood and body fluids and internal organs spraying everywhere.

Lasgun beams and bolter shells smashed into the walls beside him. Now he saw what was happening. There was no way through the press of bodies. There were too many of them, and some of them were armed. They could not fight their way clear. By sheer weight of numbers the plague victims were forcing them back into the pyramid.

Karah stirred. When she spoke, her voice was weak but her words were clear and distinct. 'Leaving here will do no good. The daemon is… tapping into the power of the pyramid itself, using the energies that once trapped him to fuel his sorcery. We must… stop him here and now, or we will not stop him at all. We must go back in there… and finish this…'

At least she's still alive, he thought and snapped off a shot into the oncoming crowd. It spoke with one voice, roaring and gurgling, and in that eerie cry, Ragnar thought he heard an obscene echo of the plague daemon's mirth.

'Let's move!' Hakon yelled; his keen senses had obviously picked up her words. He raced back into the pyramid. Within heartbeats, the Blood Claws had followed him. Behind them, the mob howled and gurgled sickly, leaving Ragnar wondering what sort of hell they had found themselves dropped into.

Around them the blackness of the ancient eldar pyramid closed in once more.

IT WAS QUIET. Ragnar placed his back against the cool stone of the wall and took a deep breath. His head swirled. He felt feverish. He knew it was the effects of the daemon's magic. His body was trying to throw off the symptoms of the plague, so far unsuccessfully. Looking at the others he could see that they did not look any better. Sweat beaded Sven's forehead and his skin had taken on a sickly, greenish-yellow hue.

'You look like an ork,' Ragnar said.

'You don't look so bloody handsome yourself,' Sven responded. 'I've seen corpses look healthier.'

'The power of Chaos is strong here,' said Strybjorn.

Sven let out a bitter bark of laughter. 'Thank you for pointing that out. Without your help I am sure we would never have noticed.'

Strybjorn glared at Sven and snarled. The air between them was suddenly tense with violence. Sergeant Hakon laid a restraining hand on Sven's shoulder and Ragnar stepped between them.

'We are all sick and tired and there is a daemon loose on this world. Now is not a time to be at each other's throats,' said Hakon. 'We must stand together or we will never find a way to stop this madness.'

Despair filled Ragnar at the sergeant's words. They had all witnessed the daemon's power. It seemed invincible and unstoppable. There was nothing they could do against such a being. Nothing. It had used them as pawns from the very start. It was too clever for them. Its ageless eternal evil was more than any mortal man could overcome.

What could four of them hope to do against such a creature and its minions? The monsters it had created were bad enough, but he knew now that, outside the pyramid, an army dedicated to Chaos was coming into being, an army made of the infected bodies of the plague's victims, reinforced no doubt by the members of the secret cult that had worked for so long to ensure Botchulaz's freedom. Who knew how many of them there were, and what positions of power they had attained. If Sternberg's own trusted lieutenant had been one of them, how many others might there be?

Right from the start, they had been caught up in a web of evil from which they had not been able to escape. Ragnar wondered if they had ever had a chance to break free, if any decision could have been made differently that would have allowed them to avoid freeing the plague daemon and saved the lives of his comrades?

Guilt swept through Ragnar. He had believed Sternberg and had become an unwitting pawn of the daemon, and so had all his companions. Unknowingly Lars and Nils had laid down their lives in the service of the foul powers of Chaos. It was a thought that made him ashamed to the core of his being.

It also made him angry. If he was if only partly responsible for the devastation they were watching, Botchulaz was all the more so. It had been the daemon's malign intelligence that had planned all of this, Ragnar did not blame Sternberg or his companions or himself half as much as he blamed that vile monster, and he swore that if it was the last thing he did, he would have revenge on the daemon.

With the anger came a sense of betrayal. They had all been let down. The prophecies that had led them here had proved false. He felt hopelessness returned when he realised that the daemon's powers had been great enough to reach out from this sealed pyramid halfway across the galaxy to sway the minds of even the Rune Priests of the Space Wolves. Or were they?

The prophecy had said only that the evil would end when the talisman was brought to the central chamber of the pyramid. It had not said anything about the cost in human lives. But had they not brought the talisman to the appointed place, and had they not failed even then?

Ragnar forced himself to think back. Was that what had in fact happened? Karah had been blasted unconscious before she had a chance to use its power. The daemon's minions had forced them to retreat. If they had stayed put, perhaps they might have been able to achieve something. But what?

The brief hope that had flickered in his mind died away. He was clutching at straws, deluding himself. There was no hope;

they had failed. There was nothing left but to lie down and die. He felt a touch on his forehead and looked down to see that Karah's eyes were open. She looked at him in understanding, as if reading his thoughts. She smiled wanly.

'I think you are right,' she said through cracked lips. ' Perhaps the talisman is the key – and used properly we might seal the daemon within its prison once more.'

'How can you know that?'

'I have had more chance to study the layout of this pyramid than anyone save its builders. I have communed with the forces at play here. I think I can see a way to activate them again and imprison that evil thing once more.'

'And what if you are wrong?'

'What do we have to lose?' she shrugged. 'We are already as good as dead.'

Ragnar heard the sharp intake of breath from his battle-brothers, and looked around to see that they were all nodding their agreement. The despair that had been written on every face was gone, to be replaced by looks of single-minded determination.

'She's bloody well right,' Sven said for all of them. 'We've nothing to lose, and everything to gain.'

'We have a chance to settle our score with the plague-thing. I, for one, welcome that.'

'Then let us go and face our doom!' said Ragnar. 'At least we may die as worthy sons of Russ!'

All of them nodded agreement save Sergeant Hakon. His thin lips were compressed into a snarl.

'Not yet,' he said. 'I would know more of what we should do. Our heroic deaths might redeem us in the eyes of Russ, but it will do nothing for the people we are sworn to protect. I would know more of what you plan, Karah Isaan.'

'Very well,' she said. 'Listen.'

And as Ragnar listened his heart sank once more.

THEY RACED ON, deep into the heart of the pyramid. Ragnar clutched his weapons in his white-knuckled fists. His chainsword was ready. His bolt pistol was held level. If any enemy came into his sight, they would die. All around he could catch the strange scents of the diseased ones. They had entered the great pyramid from the square and wandered about within.

Ragnar could smell the sickness in them, and there were other scents, more subtly tainted, that he assumed belonged to the cultists who worshipped Botchulaz. He bared his fangs in a snarl. He wanted to get to grips with those traitors to humanity. He wanted them to pay with their lives for their betrayal of the Imperium and their fellow men.

The corridors were shadowy. Strange witchfires burned in alcoves in the walls. Their yellowish-green light reminded him of the magical energies the plague daemon had unleashed. It had conjured this glow forth for its own fell purposes, probably to allow its worshippers to hunt down the Space Wolves. So far they had managed to avoid the foul creatures. The pyramid was huge, the corridors seemingly endless. Even the massive number of diseased ones could not be everywhere. They had managed to avoid them by taking different turnings, trusting to their sense of direction, that they would be able to return to the correct path at need. It was slowing down their progress though, and Ragnar could not help but feel that every second counted. With every heartbeat he sensed the daemon's power spreading. The plague was getting stronger, more and more people would fall under its foul sway, and succumb to the daemon's magic. Worse yet, he felt his own strength lessening, and his own brow becoming more feverish.

At the back of his mind, he could hear a strange whispering voice, full of mad gurgling mirth, urging him to lie down, to rest, just for a moment. By doing so, he would regain his strength. He knew this was the work of Botchulaz, the start of the plague daemon's spell. He knew that if he lay down, he would lie down forever and rise again as the daemon's minion. He determined that he would never do that, that he would rather put his own bolt pistol to his brow and pull the trigger than become a slave of such evil. He could tell by the way his battle-brothers snarled that they too had reached the same decision. A soft hand came to rest on his shoulder.

'And that, too, would be a victory for the spawn of Nurgle,' Karah said grimly. 'If all who are strong-willed enough to resist his power feel the same way, soon there will be none left to resist him. Be assured that this, too, is just another manifestation of the daemon's Chaos-spawned power. To give in to it will grant him victory as surely as falling to his plague spores.'

He saw the others look at her blankly, then slowly under-standing dawned in their eyes. They realised that their dark mood was also a product of the evil spell. Ragnar sensed their spines stiffen as they prepared to resist it. He realised that he, too, could do no less.

By Russ, how his joints ached, though. And now his nose had started to run. He heard Sven stifle a sneeze. Heard Strybjorn clear his throat of phlegm. Even Sergeant Hakon coughed. This was not good. How could four weakened Space Marines and one weary psyker overcome the power that has created such a potent disease? He tried to dismiss the thought, to tell himself that it was merely a product of Botchulaz's wicked spell, but he knew that it was not so, that the despair that gnawed at his heart was only too real.

Muttering a prayer to the Emperor he lengthened his stride, moving ever closer to the heart of the darkness that festered at the core of the pyramid.

FROM UP AHEAD he could hear chanting. It was an unclean sound, so unlike the pure plainsong that filled Imperial tem-ples. It was not like the guttural war cries of orks. It was something far worse. It was like the roaring of a sea of phlegm. It was the sound of hundreds of voices bubbling from froth-corrupted lungs. It was the pained murmuring of men lashing out in fever dreams. It was the sound of a throng which had given itself over wholly to the worship of Nurgle.

The stink was worse here. The walls were caked with filth. Huge gobs of greenish spittle stuck to his boots as he moved. Puddles of rank urine glittered in the greenish glow. A stench like that from festering wounds reached his nostrils. His skin felt obscenely warm and moist with his own fever sweat. He did not know if he could force himself to go on, and yet he knew he had to.

'Sounds like they're having a big bloody festival up there,' said Sven. 'Wonder what they're celebrating?'

He paused as if expecting some reply, and then glanced around. Ragnar knew without being told that he was waiting for some disparaging reply from Nils, a reply that would never come. He saw the pain in Sven's eyes when that realisation dawned, and he realised that it was a pain he himself shared. In the centre of his being a small bright spark of anger was

fanned. It lent him strength to resist the sickness. It gave him
the power to carry on.

'Let's go and interrupt them,' he snarled. 'Let's show them
they haven't won yet.'

'Good enough,' said Sven.

Sergeant Hakon nodded agreement. Ragnar sensed that
Karah and Strybjorn shared his renewed determination. Briefly
he permitted himself a smile, wondering whether they were all
mad. Not that it mattered much, he thought, mad or no, this
was a battle it was unlikely any of them would be returning
from.

The central chamber was full of sickening worshippers of the
Lord of Disease. They were wrapped in cowled cloaks of sickly
green, belted with yellow sashes; odd stains marked the coarse
fabric. A sickly sweet scent of corruption filled the air. Ragnar
saw that each of the worshippers bore a weapon, and he knew
that these were the secret masters of the plague cult come to
pay homage before their master. A strange buzzing filled the
air. Standing upright before an altar that looked as if it were
made of hardened snot was Gul, his face blotched, his bloated
arms raised as he guided the cultists in their worship. On the
altar sprawled Botchulaz. A web of sorcerous energy emerged
from his body and vanished into the altar and the walls of the
pyramid. Ragnar did not doubt that this energy was being used
to power the plague spell across the worldcity.

As Ragnar watched the plague daemon let out his long
tongue. It snaked up his face and entered his nostril, emerging
caked with a thick moist blob of mucus which it slurped back
into its mouth. As if sensing their presence, Botchulaz raised its
gaze to meet Ragnar's.

'Oh, there you are,' it sniffed. 'Jolly good. I was wondering
when you would be back. Nice of you to show up, actually.
Saves us the trouble of going looking for you.'

Sven took a step forward. 'I'm going to take this chainsword
and stick it up your bloody–'

'I think we get the idea of your intentions,' Botchulaz interrupted, with a fruity chuckle. 'Sad to see such hostility in one
who is soon to be such a trusted minion. Still, we'll have all
eternity for some pleasant little chats, you and I.'

There was something in the daemon's rich mellow voice that
suggested that any talks he and Sven had would be anything

but pleasant. Ragnar suddenly realised what the buzzing sound was. The whole chamber was filled with clouds of monstrous fat bluebottles. The flies crawled all over the worshippers. Only the area around the altar was clear of them. He realised that every fly in the city must have found its way here. Briefly he wondered why. Perhaps they were one of the vectors of the plague. Maybe somewhere in their tiny minds was a spark of the worship of the Lord of Decay. He did not know, and he realised that right at this moment he did not care. All he wanted to do was slaughter his foes, and get to grips with the daemon that had manipulated him and his comrades. As if unaware of their hostility and the fact that his worshippers were rising to snatch up weapons, Botchulaz burbled on mockingly.

'I'm sure you'll soon find out the error of your ways, and come to regret all this nastiness. It's so much easier when people can just get on and–'

The firing of a bolt pistol sounded shockingly loud in the confined space of the central chamber. A massive hole appeared in the plague daemon's chest, swiftly followed by several more as Sergeant Hakon blasted away. For a moment, Ragnar felt a surge of hope as he looked into the daemon's disgusting innards but then the wounds closed with a hideous sucking sound.

Botchulaz let out a strange tut-tutting sound and said; 'Really, there was no need for that.'

The scorn in his words was evident. His worshippers threw themselves forward, blades bared, pistols and lasguns in every fist. A tidal wave of diseased cultists flowed towards them. Ragnar bared his teeth in a snarl. This was the sort of fight he could understand.

'Just keep them busy,' he heard Karah mutter. 'Distract the daemon if you can. I will need some time to remake the spell on the pyramid. Be ready to go when I say the word.'

Knowing what she intended, part of Ragnar wanted to tell her not to do it. But another part of him, the part that was ever loyal to the Emperor and to humanity knew that there was no other choice, and that she would not listen to him, or to anybody else. A sadness filled him that was nothing to do with the loss of his comrades. It was something akin to what he had felt on the day he had watched Ana depart on the Grimskull ships, a sad sorry feeling that he would never see her again, never have a chance to talk to her or touch her...

Savagely he suppressed these feelings as unworthy of a Space Wolf. They were both warriors of the Emperor, and they both would perform their duties, and that was all there was to it. He needed no such distractions at this moment anyway, not with a seething sea of rage-filled plague cultists advancing on him with death in their hearts and weapons in their hands.

He could see too that ectoplasmic energy was emerging from Botchulaz and that the hideous mucoid figures were beginning to extrude from the floor, though the sheer mass of the cultists was stopping them from coming out fully. There was just not enough space for them to seep through. For the moment Ragnar was truly glad of this.

'Remember, when I give the word, get out of here,' he heard Karah say again. The depths of concern in her voice wrenched at his heart.

'I will not leave you,' he said.

'You must, you all must. Someone must bear tidings of what happened here to the Inquisition lest it happen again. The more of you who try, the greater the chance that one of you will win free,' she said grimly.

Ragnar could tell from the tone of her voice that she did not believe that there was much hope for any of them, but she was willing to give them a chance. At that moment he did not know how he would find the strength to depart from here, or the desire. She seemed to sense his thoughts.

'It is your duty, Ragnar,' she said. 'You were right about that. Don't forget.'

Sensing the power of the daemon and seeing the number of its followers, he wondered if it mattered. There was only the slimmest chance of their plan working. It relied on so many untested things. Could she really remake the spells that the eldar had woven? Could any human? He could not tell. It was not an area in which he could claim any knowledge.

He simply knew that she would have to try, and that they would have to distract the daemon and its minions while she did. There was only one way he knew that was possible and that was to fight on against the hopeless odds, and pray to Russ and the Emperor that they might succeed. All things considered though, it was not a bad death. At least he would send a few of these lost souls ahead of him to welcome him to Hell. Still, he thought wryly, he might have hoped for a more heroic set of final opponents than these disease ridden, pox-accursed heretics and their burbling master.

Pushing that thought from his mind, he sprang forward into the fray like a swimmer diving into waves. Ahead of him loomed cowled cultists. In their hands they carried rusty-looking and mucus-befouled blades. Their pistols and rifles were shoddy and appeared corroded. They moved listlessly, like men in the last throes of some terminal disease. He lashed out with his chainsword and sheared away an arm. Fingers clutched reflexively in their death spasm on the trigger of a laspistol and a beam of glittering light spurted upwards towards the ceiling. Ragnar howled and his long lonely call was answered by his battle-brothers as they prepared to sell their lives dearly. The mocking burbling laughter of Botchulaz echoed through the chamber. 'Gul, please welcome our new comrades appropriately. Unfortunately, I must return my attention to the great spell of uncleanness. Still, I am sure you can give our friends the reception they deserve...'

As the daemon spoke the web of energy swirling out from the altar intensified, the buzzing of the flies grew louder and each of the insects became surrounded by a halo of sickly light. Their eyes glittered like miniature gemstones and in a cloud they swirled through the air. Ragnar felt their soft tickling against his face, and hastily closed his mouth lest the buzzing creatures find their way inside. He could only guess what foul effect this might have, and he did not want to risk it.

Two more cultists threw themselves at him, bringing their blades down in a flashing arc. In his plague-weakened state Ragnar was too slow to entirely avoid them. One sword rang against his armour but did not penetrate. One clanged against his chainsword blade. Sparks flew where they met. He brought his bolt pistol round and pulled the trigger. One of the cultist's head exploded as a shot blasted through the bridge of his nose and emerged from the back of his head. Part of his cowl ripped away as the shell passed through, the remainder of it swelled like a sail catching a breeze as it filled with brain jelly.

Ragnar exerted his strength pushing the chainsword down against the sword. His foe resisted desperately but was no match for Ragnar's power. The Wolf pushed forward and his blade bit into the man's chest. There was a shriek as its blades scraped against a hidden chest plate. It slithered around in his grip like a living thing but by the application of all of his strength Ragnar pushed it ever inwards and the armour parted. Blood sprayed against the Wolf's face as he bisected his foe. Droplets of it hit the buzzing flies, turning them crimson.

The stench was sickening and the feel of the flies against his face was near unbearable. The air thrummed with sorcerous energy as the daemon threw more and more power into its plague spell. Insane visions streamed through Ragnar's brain. In his mind's eye, he saw the infirm rise from their sick beds to snatch up whatever came to hand, and turn on those who cared for them. He saw diseased solders open fire on their officers, and sick officers treacherously mow down their men. He saw the plague spread across the cities and the plains like wildfire, and knew that it was unstoppable, that it was pointless to resist, that it would be better to simply lie down and accept his fate.

In his mind the beast howled and gibbered. It did not accept defeat the way Ragnar's rational mind wanted to. It simply saw a challenge before it that had to be overcome in order to live. It did not care about odds, or evil sorcery, or the power of its daemonic foe. It wanted only to rend and tear its foes, and to fight its way out of this trap or die trying. Its unquenched spirit lent Ragnar strength, and suddenly he felt better. The disease-weakness drained from him, and moment by moment he felt himself becoming stronger and faster. He was reminded of a time, long before he had become a Space Marine, when he has fought against the horde of the Grimskulls with a strength that was near supernatural. He knew better than to fight against this fury; instead he just surrendered to it.

It seemed to him that his foes were slowing down. They moved like men underwater, as if the air itself was thickening around them, and slowing them down. Ragnar knew that this was an illusion caused by the fact that he himself was now moving and thinking faster. He raced forward chopping and cleaving, wanting to fight his way to the centre of the enemy force and confront Botchulaz himself. He had no thought of what would happen when he got there. He merely set his mind to the task and his body obeyed.

In the distance he could hear the thunder of bolter fire as his battle-brothers fought on. He could smell the scent of heated bone as the chainsword blade cut through it. The stink of death mingled with the corrupt scent of disease. He lashed out, hacking through two foes at once, throwing himself flat beneath a return blow, rolling over, and pumping a bolter shell into the groin of one of the cultists, and snarling with satisfaction at the man's high-pitched wail of agony. He flipped himself over and rose swiftly, sensing rather than seeing something that reached out for him from the throng.

He realised it was one of the odd conjured things, the mucoid creatures that had slain Nils. He rolled to one side evading its grasp, but even as he did so it followed, attempting to seize him once more. He could see its strange doughy face, the eyes that were like two holes poked in snow, an obscenely gaping mouth the expression of which reminded him of its foul daemonic master.

As he moved, he lashed out with his blade, taking away the legs of two cultists. They fell between him and the monster, but did not even slow it down. Its pliable body stretched around them, and its outstretched claws still reached for Ragnar. With the beast howling within his head, he felt no fear, but the part of his mind that was still rational was uneasy. He did not want to die the same way as Nils. It was a fate similar to drowning, a thing all Fenrisian warriors feared, only worse, for being caught by this sorcerous thing meant to be encased within the flesh of something daemonic. Who knew what might come afterwards?

He holstered his bolt pistol and tapped the grenade dispenser on his belt. A small explosive disk dropped into his hands. As the creature came for him he tossed it. The fuse was set for one second. It exploded in the middle of his pursuer, and blasted it to fragments. Cultists howled as pieces of its flesh scored their faces. Ragnar felt a brief flash of triumph that vanished almost as quickly as it came. Even as he watched the dismembered fragments of the thing began to writhe across the floor towards each other. In a short while the creature would reform, as strong as before and would pursue him once more.

Still, he had earned himself a brief respite. He ploughed on towards his goal, refusing to be distracted, refusing to simply wait for his foe to flow together once more. He had a brief interval in which to kill these Nurgle worshippers and perhaps confront their ultimate master. He had no idea what he would do then, but anything seemed better than waiting to be slaughtered like a lamb.

He raced onwards towards the monstrous altar on which the plague daemon lay like a giant slug. Clouds of glowing flies brushed his face. From nearby he heard a chanting that told him one of the cultists was working some sort of evil spell of its own. With a single fluid movement, Ragnar drew his bolt pistol, turned towards the source of the sound and unleashed a bolt shell with pinpoint accuracy. There was a hideous scream as the stricken cultist fell backwards. Tendrils of energy emerged from his body like maggots eating their way out of his flesh. Whatever strange forces he had intended to summon were running out of control, and consumed his flesh like a forest fire devouring dry tinder. A pungent stink filled Ragnar's nostrils. He chopped down another cultist, and suddenly, shockingly, found himself face to face with Gul. The Wolf's heart went cold as the deathless warrior reached out to seize him, insane eyes blazing.

'Good,' breathed the worshipper of darkness. 'I have hoped for this moment ever since you slew my agents on the *Light of Truth*.'

'Enjoy your last few breaths, traitor,' said Ragnar, and lashed out with the chainsword. Gul's parry was deceptively slow. Somehow his blade was just in time to intercept Ragnar. The Blood Claw leaned forward with all his weight, hoping to smash through Gul's guard as he had done with the earlier Nurgle worshipper, but Gul was strong, far stronger than he had expected. With a flex of his bloated arms, he cast Ragnar back into the crowd. The young Space Marine went flying, to land at the feet of Sergeant Hakon. The veteran Wolf howled a challenge and launched himself at Gul. Their blades flickered almost too fast for mortal eyes to follow as they met in single combat.

Sparks flickered before Ragnar's eyes as he tried to pull himself to his feet. He felt hands grasp at him, trying to restrain him while others brought weapons to bear. With a roar of fury, he threw them off, and prepared to launch himself into the fray once more. He would aid Sergeant Hakon to destroy Gul and then…

No, Ragnar, said a voice in his head that he recognised as Karah's. *Distract the daemon. Sergeant Hakon can look after himself.*

Ragnar sensed a change in the atmosphere around him. Currents of power flowed through the pyramid now and they were not all directed by Botchulaz and his revolting plague spell. It seemed that the inquisitor had been at least partially successful in using the talisman to tap into the pyramid's power. It looked like he was not the only one to sense it. Botchulaz's eyes snapped open, as if he had just become aware of this new threat. He looked down at Ragnar as if capable of reading his thoughts, and then those ancient evil eyes turned in the direction of the entrance to the central chamber. A slow smirk of understanding spread across his inhuman face. Understanding – and perhaps, at last, fear.

Hope filled Ragnar. He could see another light now in the floor of the chamber, a brilliant ruby and emerald glow that warred with the daemon's sickly luminescence. It seemed to be coming from out of the walls of the pyramid and swirling inwards to converge on a spot in the exact centre of the chamber, a mandala of light at the hub of which stood the daemonic altar.

Botchulaz let out a long moan, and muttered. 'That isn't very friendly, you know.'

He raised a bloated paw and prepared to send a bolt of energy lashing out at Karah. An aura of evil light played around his talons. Ragnar knew that if this foul dark energy found its target then the eldar spell would never be completed, and the daemon would be free to do its evil work. It became very clear to him what he must do. As the daemon brought its hand forward to cast the bolt, Ragnar leapt directly at Botchulaz. His heavy armoured form crashed into the daemon's slimy arm, knocking it to one side, causing the flash of energy to go marginally astray and strike its target only a glancing blow. Karah's screams were still terrible to hear but the flow of ancient eldar energies had not stopped. At least, their plan had a small chance of working.

'You have no idea, how very, very foolish that was, my little friend,' rumbled Botchulaz, looming over Ragnar. Suddenly all pretence of humour had dropped away from the daemon, and its massive putrid presence was fearsome indeed. Its shadow fell on Ragnar like the spectre of imminent death. Its eyes glowed with terrible power, and looking into their depths Ragnar felt his soul begun to be sucked from his body.

For a brief terrifying instant, he caught a glimpse of the pit from which the daemon had crawled. He saw it was only a small fragment of a greater corruption, of the awesome entity known to men as Nurgle, that it had been broken off from its parent and sent out into the universe to work its evil, but that it was still linked to its creator and all the other children it had spawned. For a moment, knowledge of a universe infested with dreadful dark things threatened to invade Ragnar's brain and crush his sanity. He saw the slow subtle working of decay in everything, even his own living flesh. He saw the way it relentlessly tore at everything, even the work of the other Lords of Chaos. He saw that disease lived in all things, the one invincible unstoppable foe, that could turn even its opponent's own bodies into weapons against them. He saw the certainty of inevitable triumph that all the fragments of the Lord of the Decay shared, and the horrid humour that spawned. He knew that even if they won this day, Nurgle would win in the end. His victory was inevitable.

Within him, the barely contained wolf-beast howled in denial. He offered up prayers to the Emperor and to Russ to preserve his sanity as Botchulaz prepared to crush his mind and feast on his soul. An ocean of filthy corrupt knowledge struggled to pour itself into his brain. He vaguely glimpsed the process by which plagues were birthed and the millions of different spores by which they were spread. He saw that they existed microscopic and silent on every world, in every place, even within his own altered frame. He saw himself consumed by a million different diseases, felt the symptoms of countless plagues, writhed in the grip of innumerable slow deaths. This was a torture of the most hellish sort, a spell unleashed by a foe who hated him and all he stood for.

He knew now that he had just moments to live, and that something worse than the mere extinction of life loomed before him. He knew that part of his immortal essence was about to be drawn into Botchulaz and that for all eternity he would suffer these torments along with the daemon's mockery. And he saw how much the daemon was looking forward to it.

Desperately he tried to cast the daemon forth, but he was not strong enough. He was but one mortal man pitting himself against a thing whose life span was measured in millennia and whose power was immeasurable in mortal terms. He sensed the triumph that filled Botchulaz, at this prospect obscuring all other desires for one brief moment – then he felt something else, a cold clean power that was part human and part something else scything into his brain and freeing him from the daemon's grasp. For a second he felt as if he were surrounded by others. He sensed the presence of Karah, and thousands upon thousands of other souls. These were alien presences, as undying as the daemon, eldar warriors who had been bound within the pyramid to prevent the daemon's escape. They moved forward to do battle with the daemon and briefly Ragnar felt himself hugged by Karah; her words of soft farewell passed into his mind.

Suddenly his eyes were open and he was falling free of the daemon's clutches. In one glance he took in the scene. Botchulaz writhed on the altar. His flesh was opening and reuniting again as if he were being cut with thousands of invisible blades. He seemed to fight against a shadowy host, and from the corner of his eye, Ragnar thought he could make out many invisible presences. The cultists shrieked in terror as the eldar ghosts moved among them. Many died without any physical hands being laid upon them at all.

The traitor Gul fell at the feet of Sergeant Hakon, his head separated from his body by one mighty blow from the sergeant's sword. He saw Strybjorn and Sven fighting back to back against a few cultists. He saw the walls were coruscating with green and red and gold, and the air itself seemed to shimmer as the eldar's ancient binding spells were reinstated. He looked around and saw Karah sprawled in the dirt, and he knew from her posture that she was already dead, her soul unbound from its body in the final effort to unleash the power of the talisman. He felt a great explosion of hatred and fury pass through him, and he wanted to dive into the mass of his enemies and slay them out of hand. Even as he landed and prepared to spring forward he felt a powerful hand grasp his shoulder, and he turned snarling to look into the burning eyes of Sergeant Hakon.

'Time to go, Ragnar,' he said. 'Time to do our duty, just as she did.'

In his hands the sergeant held the Talisman of Lykos. It looked dim and dormant now, drained of all energy, but nevertheless Ragnar knew it was best that it be taken away from this place. It would not do to leave the key to the prison within the daemon's grasp. Ragnar nodded and moved to join his battle-brothers.

Together the Blood Claws fought their way out into the night.

EPILOGUE

RAGNAR LOOKED OUT on the wastes of Hesperida and thought about the words of the Chaos-worshipping sorcerer he had killed earlier.

Botchulaz sends his greetings.

Had the daemon escaped? Ragnar doubted it. The ancient eldar spells still held it, he was sure. Perhaps its thoughts had simply trickled across the warp and allowed it to contact his worshippers, as it had once contacted Gul and his predecessors. Or perhaps it was all a trick. Who could tell with the worshippers of Chaos. Certainly, after the pyramid was sealed again, the plague had died back. The infected victims had simply keeled over and died. They had been buried in huge plague pits hastily bulldozed in the ground.

At least some things had ended happily. Brother Tethys had found his way back to Galt. Ragnar had met him again in better circumstances many years later. And the *Light of Truth* had taken the surviving Space Wolves and the Talisman of Lykos back to Fenris. As far as Ragnar knew, the thing was still there in the vaults of the Fang, just one more trophy among millions.

He heard the voices of the Blood Claws below him, and felt less envy now. Memory had taught him one thing this evening.

Even at their age life had not been so simple as he had wanted to believe it had. He felt more sympathy for them now, remembering his own losses, long-past: of Nils and Lars and Sternberg – and most of all of Karah, who had given her life to hold the daemon imprisoned and whose spirit was bound into the pyramid as surely as those of the eldar ghosts and Botchulaz himself.

He pushed the memories aside. Tomorrow was a new day, with new battles to be fought and new foes to be overcome. He knew he had better make ready.

COMING SOON

**More storming Warhammer
40,000 action in NECROPOLIS,
a brand new Gaunt's Ghosts
novel from Dan Abnett.**

**Here is a brief preview
of the action in store...**

From NECROPOLIS:

THE IMPERIAL WAY OF DEATH

'True to the Throne and hard to kill!'
— The battle-pledge of the Volpone Bluebloods

'ENOUGH!' GAUNT SNARLED.

The gunfire which had been shaking the martial court died away fitfully. The air reeked of laser-discharge, cartridge-powder and blood. VPHC corpses littered the floor and the shattered wooden seating ranks. One or two Bluebloods lay amongst them.

The half-dozen or so surviving VPHC officers, some wounded, had been forced into a corner, and Gilbear and his men, high on adrenalin, were about to execute them.

'Hold fire!' Gaunt snapped, moving in front of Gilbear, who glowered with anger-bright eyes and refused to put up his smoking hellgun. 'Hold fire, I said! We came down to break up an illegal tribunal. Let's not make another wrong by taking the law into our own hands!'

'You can dispense it! You're a commissar!' Gilbear growled and his men agreed loudly.

'When there's time... not here. You men, find shackles. Cuff these bastards and lock them in the cells.'

'Do as he says, Gilbear,' Sturm said, approaching and holstering his pistol. The Blueblood troopers began to herd the prisoners roughly out of the room.

Gaunt looked around the chamber. Pater sat against the far wall, with Bwelt fanning his pallid face with a scribe-slate. Daur was releasing the Narmenian defendants.

The room was a ruin. Sturm's elite troops had slaughtered more than two thirds of the VPHCers present in a brutal action that had lasted two minutes and had cost them three Bluebloods. Tarrian was dead, his rib-cage blasted open like a burned-out ship's hull.

Gaunt crossed to Kowle. The commissar was seated on one of the lower seating tiers, head bowed, clutching a hell-burn across his right bicep.

'It's the end for you, Kowle. You knew damn well what an abuse of the law this was. I'll personally oversee the avulsion of your career. A public disgrace… for the Peoples' Hero.'

Kowle slowly looked up into Gaunt's dark eyes. He said nothing, as there was nothing left to say.

Gaunt turned away from the disturbing beige eyes. He remembered Balhaut, in the early weeks of the campaign. Serving as part of Slaydo's command cadre, he had first encountered Kowle and his wretchedly vicious ways. Gaunt had thought he embodied the very worst aspects of the Commissariat. After one particularly unnecessary punishment detail, when Kowle had had a man flogged to death for wearing the wrong cap-badge, Gaunt had used his influence with the Warmaster to have Kowle transferred to duties on the south-west continent, away from the main front. That had been the start of Kowle's career decline, Gaunt realised now, a decline that had led him to the Vervunhive posting. Gaunt couldn't let it go. He turned back.

'You had a chance here, Pius. A chance to make good. You've the strength a commissar needs, you just have… no control. Too busy enjoying the power and prestige of being the chief Imperial Commissar to the armies of Verghast.'

'Don't,' whispered Kowle. 'Don't lecture me. Don't use my name like you're my friend. You're frightened of me because I have a strength you lack. It was the same on Balhaut, when you were Slaydo's lap-dog. You thought I would eclipse you, so you used your position to have me sidelined.'

Gaunt opened his mouth in astonishment. Words failed him for a moment. 'Is that what you think? That I reported you to advance my own career?'

'It's what I know.' Kowle got to his feet slowly, wiping flecks of blood from his cheek. 'Actually, I'm almost glad it's over for me. I can go to my damnation relishing the knowledge that you've lost here. Vervunhive won't survive now, not with the likes of you and Sturm in charge. You haven't got the balls.'

'Like you, you mean?' Gaunt laughed.

'I would have led this hive to victory. It's a matter of courage, of iron will, of making decisions that may be unpalatable but which serve the greater triumph!'

'I'm just glad that history will never get a chance to prove you wrong, Kowle. Surrender your weapon and rank pins.'

Kowle stood unmoving for a while, then tossed his pistol and insignia onto the floor. Gaunt looked down at them for a moment and then walked away.

'Appraise me of the situation upstairs,' Gaunt said to Sturm. 'When you arrived, you said the hive was under assault.'

'A storm on all fronts. It looked grim, Gaunt.' Sturm refused to make eye contact with the Tanith commissar. 'Marshal Croe was ordering a full deployment to repulse.'

'Sir?'

Gaunt and Sturm looked round. Captain Daur stood nearby, his face alarmingly pale. He held out a data-slate. 'I used the stockade's codifier link to access House Command. I thought you'd want an update and...'

His voice trailed off.

Gaunt took the slate and read it, thumbing the cursor rune to scroll the illuminated data. He could barely believe what he was seeing. The information was already a half-hour old. The Shield was down. Massive assaults and shelling had punished the hive. Zoican forces were already inside the Curtain Wall.

Gaunt looked across at Grizmund and his fellow Narmenians, flexing their freed limbs and sharing a flask of water. He'd come down here on a matter of individual justice, and when his back was turned, hell had overtaken Vervunhive.

He almost doubted there'd be now anything left to return to at the surface.

* * *

UNDER THE CO-ORDINATED command of Major Rawne and Colonel Corday, the Tanith and Volpone units holding Veyveyr Gate staunchly resisted the massive Zoican push for six hours, hammered by extraordinary levels of shelling. There was no ebb in the heedless advance of Zoican foot troops, and the waste ground immediately outside the gate was littered for acres around with the enemy dead. Along the ore work emplacements at the top of the Spoil, Mkoll's marksmen and Ormon's Spoilers held the slag slopes with relentless expertise.

Mkoll voxed Rawne when his ammunition supplies began to dwindle. Both had sent requests to House Command for immediate resupply but the link was dead, and neither liked the look of the great firestorms seething out of the hive heartland behind them.

Larkin, holding a chimney stack with MkVenner and Domor, had personally taken thirty-nine kills. It was his all-time best in any theatre, but he had neither time nor compunction enough to celebrate. The more he killed, the more the memory of the Zoican's corrupt face burned in his racing mind.

At the brunt-end of the Veyveyr position, Bragg ran out of rockets for his launcher and discarded it. It was overheating anyway. His autogun jammed after a few shots, so he moved down the trench, keeping his hefty frame lower than the parapet as las-fire hammered in, and took over a tripod-mounted stubber whose crew had been shot. As he began to squeeze the brass trigger-pull of the thumping heavy weapon, he saw Feygor spin back and drop nearby. A las-round had hit him in the neck.

Lesp, the field medic attending the trench, scrambled over to Feygor, leaving a gut-shot Volpone who was beyond his help.

'Is he okay?' Bragg yelled.

Lesp fought with the struggling Feygor, clamping wet dressings around the scorched and melted flesh of his neck and trying to clear an airway.

'His trachea is fused! Feth! Help me hold him!'

Bragg fired a last burst, then dropped from the stub-nest and ran to Feygor and the slender medic. It took all of his gargantuan strength to hold Feygor down as Lesp worked. The las-hit had cauterised the wound, so there was precious little blood, but the heat had melted the larynx and the windpipe into a gristly knot and Feygor was suffocating.

His eyes were white with pain and fear, and his mouth clacked as he screamed silent curses.

'Feth!' Lesp threw the small, plastic-handled scalpel away in disgust and pulled out his long, silver Tanith knife. He stuck it into Feygor's throat under the blackened mass of the scorched wound and opened a slot in the windpipe big enough to feed a chest-tube down.

Feygor began breathing again, rattling and gurgling through the tube.

Lesp yelled something up at Bragg that a nearby shell-fall drowned out.

'What?'

'We have to get him clear!'

Bragg hoisted Feygor up in his arms without question and began to run with him, back down the lines.

THEY CHOSE A window each, coughing in the dust that the bombardment was shaking up from the old floor boards.

Milo saw las-rounds punching through the fibre-board sidings of the broken building, and heard the grunt-gasp of flamers. The enemy was right outside.

From the windows, under Baffels's direction, they fired at will. It was difficult to see what they were hitting. Filain and Tokar both yowled out victory whoops as they guessed they brought Zoicans down.

Rhys, one window down from Milo, stopped firing and sagged, as if very tired.

Milo spun around and called out to him, stopping short when he saw the bloodless las-hole in Rhys's forehead.

A falling shell blew out a silo nearby and the building shook.

Colonel Corbec's voice came over the microbead link, calm and stern.

'This is the one, boys. Do it right or die here.'

Milo loaded a fresh cell and joined his platoon in blasting from the chewed window holes.

MORE THAN THREE hundred Tanith were still resting, off-guard, in their makeshift chem-plant billet when the Shield came down and the onslaught began. Sergeant Bray, the ranking officer, had them all battle-dress and arm at once, and voxed House Command for instructions.

House Command was dead. Bray found he couldn't reach Corbec, Rawne or Gaunt… or any military authorities. What vox-links were still live were awash with mindless panicked traffic or the insidious chatter broadcasts of the enemy.

Bray made a command decision, the biggest he'd ever made in his career. He pulled the Tanith under his charge back from the billets and had them dig in amongst the rubble wastelands behind, wastelands created in the first bombardment at the start of the war.

It was an informed, judicious command. Gaunt had taught tactics thoroughly and Bray had listened. A move forward, towards Sondar Gate and the Square of Marshals three kilometres south would have been foolhardy, given the lack of solid intelligence. Staying put would have left them in a wide, warehouse sector difficult to secure or defend. The rubble wastes played directly to the Ghosts' strengths. Here they could dig in, cover themselves and form a solid front.

As if to confirm Bray's decision, mortar fire levelled the chem-plant billets twenty minutes after the Tanith had withdrawn. Advance storm-units of Zoican infantry crossed into the wasteland thirty minutes later and were cut down by the well-defended Ghosts. In the following hours, Bray's men engaged and held off over two thousand ochre-clad troops, and began to form a line of resistance that stymied the Zoican push in from Sondar Gate.

Then Zoican tanks began to arrive, trundling up through the blasted arterial roads adjoining the Square of Marshals. They were light, fast machines, built for infantry support, ochre-drabbed and covered with netting, with turrets set back on the main hull, mounting pairs of small-calibre cannons. Bray had thoughtfully removed all the rocket grenades and launchers from the billet stockpile, and his men began to hunt tanks in the jagged piles of the wasteland, leaving their las-rifles in fox-holes so they could carry, aim and load the rocket tubes. In three hours of intense fighting, they destroyed twenty machines. The slipways of the arterials were ablaze with crackling tank hulls by the time heavier armour units, massive main battle-tanks and super-heavy self-propelled guns, began to roll and clank up into the chem-district.

Caffran braced against the kick of the rocket launcher and banged off a projectile grenade that he swore went directly down the fat barrel of an approaching siege tank, blowing the turret clean off. Dust and debris winnowed back over his position, and he scrambled around to reach another fox hole, Trooper Trygg running with him with the belt of rockets.

Caffran could hear Bray yelling commands nearby.

He slipped into a drain culvert and sloshed along through the ankle deep muck. Trygg was saying something behind him, but Caffran wasn't really listening.

It was beginning to rain. With the Shield down, the inner habs were exposed to the downpour. The wasteland became a quagmire of oily mud in under a quarter of an hour. Caffran reached the ruins of a habitat and searched for a good firing point. A hundred metres away, Tanith launchers barked and spat rockets at the rumbling Zoican advance. Every few moments there would be a plangent thump and another tank round would scream overhead.

Cafran was wet through. The rainfall was cutting visibility to thirty yards. He clambered up on the scorched wreck of an old armchair and hoisted himself up into an upper window space, from which he could get a good view of the rubble waste outside.

'Toss me a few live ones!' he called down to Trygg.

Trygg made a sound like a scalded cat and fell, severed at the waist. Ochre-armoured stormtroops flooded into the ruin below Caffran, firing wildly. Another shot hit Trygg's belt of grenades and the blast threw Caffran clear of the building shell onto the rubble outside.

He clawed his way upright as Zoicans rushed him from three sides. Pulling out his Tanith dagger he plunged it through the eyeslit of the nearest. He clubbed the next down with his rocket tube.

Another shot at him, but missed.

Caffran rolled away, firing his loaded rocket launcher. The rocket hit the Zoican in the gut, lifted him twenty metres into the air, and blew him apart.

There was a crack of las-fire and a Zoican that Caffran hadn't seen dropped behind him.

He glanced about him.

Holding the las-pistol he had given her as a gift, Tona Criid crept out of cover. She turned once, killing another Zoican with a double-shot.

Caffran grabbed her by the hand and they ran into the cover of a nearby hab as dozens more Zoican troopers advanced, firing as they came.

In the shadows of the hab ruin, Caffran looked at her, one soot-smeared face mirrored by the other.

'Caffran,' he said.

'Criid,' she replied.

The Zoicans were right outside, firing into the ruins.

'Good to know you,' he said.

THE CAGE ELEVATORS carried them up as far as level sub-6 before the power in the Low Spine failed and the cars ground to a screeching halt. Soot and dust trickled and fluttered down the echoing shaft from above.

They exited the lifts on their bellies, crawling out through grill-doors that had half-missed the next floor, and found themselves in a poorly-lit access corridor between water treatment plants.

Gaunt and Bwelt had to pull Pater bodily out of the lift car onto the floor. The old man was panting and refused to go on.

Gilbear and his troops had fanned down the hallway, guns ready. Daur had guard of Kowle, and Sturm was trying to light a shredded stub-end of cigar. Grizmund and his officers were taut and attentive, armed with shotguns they had taken from the VPHC dead.

'Where are we?' Gaunt asked Bwelt.

'Level sub-6. An underhive section, actually.'

Gaunt nodded. 'We need a staircase access.'

Down the damp hallway, one of Gilbear's men cried out that he had found a stepwell.

'Stay with him and move him on when he's able,' Gaunt told Bwelt, indicating the ailing Pater.

He crossed to Grizmund. 'As soon as we reach the surface, I need you to rejoin your units.'

Grizmund nodded. 'I'll do my best. Once I've got to them, what channel should we use?'

'Ten-ninety-gamma,' Gaunt replied. It was the old Hyrkan wavelength. 'I'm heading up-Spine to try and get the Shield back on.

'Now get out there and prove my belief in you,' snarled

Gaunt. 'I need the Narmenian armour at full strength if I'm going to hold this place.'

General Grizmund and his men pushed on past and hurried up the stairs.

'Sounds like you've taken command, Gaunt,' said Sturm snidely.

Gaunt turned to him. 'In the absence of other command voices…'

Sturm's face lost its smile and its colour.

'I'm still ranking Guard commander here, Ibram Gaunt. Or had you forgotten?'

'It's been so long since you issued an order, Noches Sturm, I probably have.'

The two men faced each other in the low, musty basement corridor. Gaunt wasn't backing down now.

'We have no choice, my dear colonel-commissar. A full tactical retreat. Vervunhive is lost. These things happen. You get used to it.'

'Maybe you do… maybe you've had more experience in running away than me.'

'You low-life swine!' Major Gilbear rasped, stomping forward.

Gaunt punched him in the face, dropping him to the floor.

'Get up and get used to me, Gilbear. We've got a fething heavy task ahead of us and I need the best the Volpone can muster.'

The Volpone troops were massing around them, and even Pater had got up onto his feet for a better view.

'The Shield must be turned back on. It's a priority. We've got to get up into the top of the hive and affect that. Don't fight me here. There'll be more than enough fighting to go around later.'

Gaunt reached down his hand to pull Gilbear up. The big Blueblood hesitated and then accepted the grip.

Gaunt pulled Gilbear right up to his face, nose to nose.

'Let's go see what kind of soldier you are, colonel,' he said.

**Necropolis (Gaunt's Ghosts #3)
– coming soon from
the Black Library**

Also from the Black Library

SPACE WOLF
A Warhammer 40,000 novel
by William King

RAGNAR LEAPT UP from his hiding place, bolt pistol spitting
death. The nightgangers could not help but notice where
he was, and with a mighty roar of frenzied rage they raced
towards him. Ragnar answered their war cry with a
wolfish howl of his own, and was reassured to hear it
echoed back from the throats of the surrounding Blood
Claws. He pulled the trigger again and again as the
frenzied mass of mutants approached, sending bolter
shell after bolter shell rocketing into his targets. Ragnar
laughed aloud, feeling the full battle rage come upon
him. The beast roared within his soul, demanding to be
unleashed.

IN THE GRIM *future of Warhammer 40,000, the Space
Marines of the Adeptus Astartes are humanity's last hope. On
the planet Fenris, young Ragnar is chosen to be inducted into
the noble yet savage Space Wolves chapter. But with his
ancient primal instincts unleashed by the implanting of the
sacred Canis Helix, Ragnar must learn to control the beast
within and fight for the greater good of the wolf pack.*

Also from the Black Library

TROLLSLAYER
A Gotrek & Felix novel
by William King

HIGH ON THE HILL the scorched walled castle stood, a stone spider clutching the hilltop with blasted stone feet. Before the gaping maw of its broken gate hanged men dangled on gibbets, flies caught in its single-strand web.

'Time for some bloodletting,' Gotrek said. He ran his left hand through the massive red crest of hair that rose above his shaven tattooed skull. His nose chain tinkled gently, a strange counterpoint to his mad rumbling laughter.

'I am a slayer, manling. Born to die in battle. Fear has no place in my life.'

TROLLSLAYER IS THE first part of the death saga of Gotrek Gurnisson, as retold by his travelling companion Felix Jaeger. Set in the darkly gothic world of Warhammer, Trollslayer is an episodic novel featuring some of the most extraordinary adventures of this deadly pair of heroes. Monsters, daemons, sorcerers, mutants, orcs, beastmen and worse are to be found as Gotrek strives to achieve a noble death in battle. Felix, of course, only has to survive to tell the tale.

Also from the Black Library

SKAVENSLAYER
A Gotrek & Felix novel
by William King

'BEWARE! SKAVEN!' Felix shouted and saw them all reach for their weapons. In moments, swords glittered in the half-light of the burning city. From inside the tavern a number of armoured figures spilled out into the gloom. Felix was relieved to see the massive squat figure of Gotrek among them. There was something enormously reassuring about the immense axe clutched in the dwarf's hands.

'I see you found our scuttling little friends, manling,' Gotrek said, running his thumb along the blade of his axe until a bright red bead of blood appeared.

'Yes, Felix gasped, struggling to get his breath back before the combat began.

'Good. Let's get killing then!'

SET IN THE MIGHTY city of Nuln, Gotrek and Felix are back in Skavenslayer, the second novel in this epic saga. Seeking to undermine the very fabric of the Empire with their arcane warp-sorcery, the skaven, twisted Chaos rat-men, are at large in the reeking sewers beneath the ancient city. Led by Grey Seer Thanquol, the servants of the Horned Rat are determined to overthrow this bastion of humanity. Against such forces, what possible threat can just two hard-bitten adventurers pose?

Also from the Black Library

DAEMONSLAYER
A Gotrek & Felix novel
by William King

THE ROAR WAS so loud and so terrifying that Felix almost dropped his blade. He looked up and fought the urge to soil his britches. The most frightening thing he had ever seen had entered the hall and behind it he could see the leering heads of beastmen.

As he gazed on the creature in wonder and terror, Felix thought: this is the incarnate nightmare which has bedevilled my people since time began.

'Just remember,' Gotrek said from beside him, 'the daemon is mine!'

FRESH FROM THEIR adventures battling the foul servants of the rat-god in Nuln, Gotrek and Felix are now ready to join an expedition northwards in search of the long-lost dwarf hall of Karag Dum. Setting forth for the hideous Realms of Chaos in an experimental dwarf zeppelin, Gotrek and Felix are sworn to succeed or die in the attempt. But greater and more sinister energies are coming into play, as a daemonic power is awoken to fulfil its ancient, deadly promise.

Also from the Black Library

EYE OF TERROR
A Warhammer 40,000 novel
by Barrington J. Bayley

Tell the truth only if a lie will not serve

'WHAT I HAVE to tell you,' Abaddas said, in slow measured tones, 'will be hard for you to accept or even comprehend. The rebellion led by Warmaster Horus succeeded. The Emperor is dead, killed by Horus himself in single combat, though Horus too died of his injuries.'

Magron groaned. He cursed himself for having gone into suspended animation. To be revived in a galaxy without the Emperor! Horrible! Unbelievable! Impossible to bear! Stricken, he looked into Abaddas's flinty grey eyes. 'Who is Emperor now?'

The first hint of an emotional reaction flickered on Abaddas's face. 'What need have we of an Emperor?' he roared. 'We have the Chaos gods!'

IN THE DARK and gothic future of Warhammer 40,000, mankind teeters on the brink of extinction. As the war-fleets of the Imperium prepare to launch themselves on a crusade into the very heart of Chaos, Rogue Trader Maynard Rugolo seeks power and riches on the fringe worlds of this insane and terrifying realm.

Also from the Black Library

FIRST & ONLY
A Gaunt's Ghosts novel
by Dan Abnett

'THE TANITH ARE strong fighters, general, so I have heard.' The
scar tissue of his cheek pinched and twitched slightly, as it
often did when he was tense. 'Gaunt is said to be a resourceful
leader.'

'You know him?' The general looked up, questioningly.

'I know *of* him, sir. In the main by reputation.'

GAUNT GOT TO his feet, wet with blood and Chaos pus. His
Ghosts were moving up the ramp to secure the position. Above
them, at the top of the elevator shaft, were over a million
Shriven, secure in their bunker batteries. Gaunt's expeditionary
force was inside, right at the heart of the enemy stronghold.
Commissar Ibram Gaunt smiled.

*IT IS THE nightmare future of Warhammer 40,000, and mankind
teeters on the brink of extinction. The galaxy-spanning Imperium is
riven with dangers, and in the Chaos-infested Sabbat system,
Imperial Commissar Gaunt must lead his men through as much in-
fighting amongst rival regiments as against the forces of Chaos.
First and Only is an epic saga of planetary conquest, grand
ambition, treachery and honour.*

Also from the Black Library

GHOSTMAKER
A Gaunt's Ghosts novel
by Dan Abnett

THEY WERE A good two hours into the dark, black-trunked forests, tracks churning the filthy ooze and the roar of their engines resonating from the sickly canopy of leaves above, when Colonel Ortiz saw death.

It wore red, and stood in the trees to the right of the track, in plain sight, unmoving, watching his column of Basilisks as they passed along the trackway. It was the lack of movement that chilled Ortiz.

Almost twice a man's height, frighteningly broad, armour the colour of rusty blood, crested by recurve brass antlers. The face was a graven death's head. Daemon. Chaos Warrior. *World Eater!*

IN THE NIGHTMARE future of Warhammer 40,000, mankind teeters on the brink of extinction. The Imperial Guard are humanity's first line of defence against the remorseless assaults of the enemy. For the men of the Tanith First-and-Only and their fearless commander, Commissar Ibram Gaunt, it is a war in which they must be prepared to lay down, not just their bodies, but their very souls.

ABOUT THE AUTHOR

William King was born in Stranraer, Scotland, in
1959. His short stories have appeared in *The Year's
Best SF, Zenith, White Dwarf* and *Interzone*. He is also
the author of the first Ragnar adventure, *Space Wolf*,
and three volumes chronicling the adventures of
Gotrek & Felix: *Trollslayer, Skavenslayer* and
Daemonslayer. He has travelled extensively
throughout Europe and Asia, but he currently lives
in Prague, in the Czech Republic, where he is
currently hard at work developing the fourth Gotrek
& Felix adventure, *Dragonslayer*!